# Celebrating the Jewish Holidays

# Celebrating the

## POEMS, STORIES, ESSAYS

## Edited by Steven J. Rubin

BRANDEIS UNIVERSITY PRESS

Published by the University Press of New England

Hanover & London

# Jewish Holidays

Brandeis University Press
Published by University Press of New England,
Hanover, NH 03755
This collection and introductory material ©
2003 by Brandeis University Press
Printed in the United States of America
5 4 3 2 1

Library of Congress Cataloging-in-Publication Data
Celebrating the Jewish holidays : stories, essays, poems / edited by Steven J. Rubin.
    p. cm.
ISBN 1–58465–184–9
1. Fasts and feasts—Judaism. I. Rubin, Steven J.
BM690 .C438 2003
296.4'3—dc21                                          2002151143

To the memory
of my Mother
Mollie K. Rubin
(1910–2002)

# ⚹ Contents

# Celebrating the Jewish Holidays

# 🌺 General Introduction

This is a book, as its title indicates, about "celebrating" the Jewish holidays. It is neither a scholarly inquiry into the history of holiday observance nor a volume delineating the specifics of Jewish practice and customs. While the reader will find in the introductions to individual sections a brief history of each holiday and an explanation of the various traditions associated with the festival in question, the heart of this volume is the more than one hundred selections by some of the world's greatest Jewish writers. *Celebrating the Jewish Holidays* commemorates holiday tradition and meaning from a purely personal and imaginative perspective, celebrating as it does the beauty and significance of the Sabbath and annual festivals through poetry, fiction, and memoir. The purpose of this volume is to provide readers with a different, more compelling way of understanding and appreciating the Jewish holidays, one that originates with the creative spirit.

The Jewish year is marked by weekly, monthly, and annual festivals that help define and weave together the rich fabric of Jewish life. Throughout the centuries and across many lands, these holidays have occupied a central position not only in Jewish culture and religion, but within the collective imagination of the Jewish people as well. From the very beginning, Jewish writers sought to give voice to the meaning and spirit of the Jewish holidays. Often this took the form of poems and songs composed for holiday observance, as in the case of the early poetry included in this collection. Later writers used the subject of holiday observance to probe other, more general themes, such as the nature of religious belief and identity. Many authors — understanding the importance of the holidays — have written moving personal essays, recalling family celebrations and articulating the significance of those occasions. For several of the twentieth- and twenty-first-century writers included here, the holidays have provided an opportunity either to question the meaning and purpose of holiday tradition or to affirm their connection to that tradition. As readers will discover, all the works included in this collection relate both to the Jewish holidays in particular and to the Jewish spirit in general.

Judaism is a diverse religion, with many differences in basic practices and beliefs. Throughout the centuries Jews have spoken various languages and inhabited many lands. Within this multicultural tapestry, however, is the common thread of holiday observance. And as many of the selections in this volume illustrate, the holidays themselves — with their accumulated rituals and traditions — are one of the principal forces that bind Jews of varied backgrounds together. In the words of the Hebrew essayist Ahad Ha Am, "More than Israel has kept the Sabbath, the Sabbath has kept Israel." And so it is with the other festivals as well. Throughout the turmoil of Jewish history and often under the most extreme circumstances, the holidays have enabled the Jewish people to remain connected to each other and to their collective past.

The roots of Jewish holidays vary. Some have their origins in ancient seasonal rituals or festivals, while others were established to commemorate important historical events. Several are a combination of the two. A number of holidays are also associated with agricultural or astronomical phenomena: the new moon, the Fall harvest, the planting of new trees, or the harvesting of the first fruits. Those holidays specifically mentioned in the Torah (The Five Books of Moses) are designated as "major" holidays; all others are considered "minor." In truth, however, these classifications hold little significance, and the six holidays included in this volume (Sabbath, Rosh Hashanah, Yom Kippur, Hanukkah, Purim, and Passover) are those I believe to be most relevant to contemporary Jewish life and culture.

Holiday observance, as readers will find, varies from country to country and from century to century. The Sabbath depicted by the medieval poets of Spain, for example, is very different from that which is rendered by the writers of the New World at the end of the twentieth century. The circumstances surrounding holiday observance described by nineteenth-century Yiddish writers differ greatly from those recounted by twentieth-century English-language authors. And while most writers associate the celebration of Rosh Hashanah and Yom Kippur (the "High Holidays") with fall, those from Central and South America describe a spring observance, lending a somewhat different atmosphere to those holidays.

Nevertheless, there is a surprising similarity in the mood and spirit evoked by each of the holidays included in this volume. Sabbath is restful and reflective; Rosh Hashanah and Yom Kippur are solemn and introspective; Hanukkah is joyous; Purim is frantic, often hilarious; Passover is respectful, honoring as it does freedom from bondage. Although every holiday involves some degree of synagogue observance, some — such as Rosh Hashanah and Yom Kippur — are mostly liturgical and filled with prescribed prayer and ritual. Others, such as Hanukkah and Passover, are traditionally celebrated in the home.

Although each holiday has its unique origins and rituals, readers will find that many of the works in this collection share common themes and motifs linking the holidays to each other and ultimately to all of Jewish tradition. Almost every holiday celebration, for example, pays tribute to Jewish history. "Our memory must be long," declares Adrienne Rich in her poem "At the New Year," and the concept of honoring and recalling a past that has often been traumatic but is nonetheless cherished is central to almost all Jewish holiday celebrations. This linking of individual identity with the collective experience of the group is one of the enduring tenets of Jewish culture and one that has defined Jewish identity throughout the ages. As many of the writers included in this collection observe, the celebration of the holidays is one of the foremost means by which one feels connected to one's ancestors.

There are other motifs that recur and enrich the many poems, stories, and essays reprinted here: the enduring and comforting aspects of family celebration, the sense of being part of tradition that comes with the holidays, the importance of food (both the consuming and preparing) as a cultural touchstone, the search for an authentic identity within increasingly pluralistic societies, and the sense of irony and humor that has sustained the Jewish people for so many generations. More than any other, however, the theme of connectedness, of belonging — as Ilan Stavans states in his Hanukkah "Reminiscence," to "an endless chain of generations" — is reinforced through the traditions and rituals of every holiday celebration and resonates throughout much of the literature included in this collection.

Many of the writers represented here are familiar figures: Sholom Aleichem, I. L. Peretz, Isaac Bashevis Singer, Emma Lazarus, Elie Wiesel, Chaim Potok, Adrienne Rich, Alfred Kazin, and Cynthia Ozick, to name only a few. One or two — such as Golda Meir and Theodor Herzl — are better known for their political than for their literary accomplishments. Several — such as Kadia Molodowsky, Ruth Brin, Israel Joseph Singer, Joseph Opatoshu, Irena Klepfisz, Chana Bloch, Meyer Levin, and Marcia Falk — are less well known but have nevertheless produced noteworthy works. Still others, writing in the late twentieth and early twenty-first centuries (Stavans, Richard Chess, Allegra Goodman, Marjorie Agosín, Nathan Englander, and Robin Becker, for instance), have only recently begun to receive attention and will surely continue to do so in the coming years. Many other talented authors who have written about the Jewish holidays in significant ways could have been included had space allowed, and readers are encouraged to discover on their own the rich variety of all manner of Jewish literature.

Judaism is a multilingual, multinational, surprisingly heterogeneous religion, and I have tried to capture this diversity (of thought, culture, background, and language) in this collection. Among the many authors represented, readers will find poets from medieval Spain (Ha-Levi Ben Labrat, Solomon Ibn Gabirol, and Yehuda Halevi), fiction writers from eastern Europe (the Singer brothers, Aleichem, Peretz, Sholom Asch, Abraham Reisen, and others), Latin American poets and essayists (Stavans, Agosín, and Sam Goldemberg), Hebrew-language authors from Europe and Israel, (Isaac Luria, Hayim Nahman Bialik, Yehuda Amichai, and Saul Tchernichovsky), early American authors (Lazarus and Penina Moise), and many talented twentieth-century British, American, Israeli, and Canadian authors too numerous to mention.

Although very different in terms of the time they lived, the language in which they wrote, and the country of their origin, the authors included in this collection have chosen to write about the holidays in ways that express their memories, thoughts, dreams, and beliefs about (and in some cases objections to) the holidays in question. All the works contained in this collection relate to the significance and tradition of the Jewish holidays and present those meanings in creative and personal fashion. What these holidays represent, the memories they hold, and the significance ascribed to each, are the true subjects of this volume.

*Celebrating the Jewish Holidays* is a book that can be read and enjoyed in its entirety. But it is also a collection that can provide occasional pleasures as well, one that can be visited and revisited as the spirit and season dictate. My hope is that readers of all faiths and Jews of varying degrees of observance will find in this collection a memorable and unique approach to the Jewish holidays. For those with little knowledge of Jewish traditions, this book will serve as an introduction to the many moods and motifs of the holidays. Those who are more familiar with the Jewish holidays and those who regularly celebrate the Sabbath and annual festivals will, I trust, discover much to augment their knowledge and love of Jewish traditions. It is my hope, too, that readers will be able to incorporate various poems, stories, and essays from this collection into their own "celebration" of the holidays. *Celebrating the Jewish Holidays* is, finally, a tribute not only to the imaginative spirit so essential to holiday observance, but to the spirit of survival and continuity that has characterized all of Jewish civilization.

# Sabbath

## Most Precious of Days

 Introduction

*Observe the sabbath day and keep it holy, as the LORD your God has commanded you. Six days you shall labor and do all your work, but the seventh day is a sabbath of the LORD your God; you shall not do any work . . .*
—Deuteronomy 5.12–14

Of all the Jewish holidays and festivals, the Sabbath is perhaps the most essential to Jewish observance. Its weekly occurrence has so permeated Jewish life and custom that one tends to overlook its significance. Throughout Jewish history, the Sabbath has been of primary importance as a holy day, as a means of transcending ordinary existence, and as a source of community and familial cohesion. Known as "Shabbat" in Hebrew and "Shabbos" in Yiddish, no holiday is more central to Jewish religion and culture.

While most Jewish festivals can be traced to seasonal and agricultural rituals, the origins of Sabbath observance remain obscure. Most historians agree that no such concept as a "day of rest" was ever articulated before it appeared in the Bible. Ancient societies often observed certain "unlucky" days, when activities were restricted as a precaution against evil spirits. The Hebrew word "shabbat" may have had its roots in the Babylonian "shabbatum," a word used to describe the day of the full moon—when it was believed that the moon stood still, a particularly bad omen. But there is no record of a civilization prior to the ancient Hebrews who had a fixed day every week of every month throughout the year where all work ceased, not out of fear, but out of respect for creation and reverence for God.

Reference to "Sabbath" appears in Genesis, in Exodus and Deuteronomy (as the fourth of the Ten Commandments), and in numerous other biblical passages, giving clear indication that the holiday was observed in one form or another from the very beginnings of recorded Jewish history. Genesis offers an early and basic religious explanation for the Sabbath observance: "And God blessed the seventh day and declared it holy, because on it God ceased from all the work of creation that He had done" (2.3). By linking the celebration of Sabbath with the act of creation, the

Biblical quotations throughout this book are from the *Tanakh: A New Translation of The Holy Scriptures According to the Traditional Hebrew Text*, The Jewish Publication Society, 1985.

ancient Hebrews were able to metaphorically re-create in human terms the divine pattern of six days of labor and a seventh day of rest. In emulating God's behavior, they lent dignity and "creativity" to their six days of work and spirituality to their day of rest.

While the concept of Sabbath is articulated in Genesis, the main precept of Sabbath observance (the formal forbidding of labor) is prescribed as the fourth of the Ten Commandments, and as such appears twice in the Bible with slight variations of wording and emphasis. In Exodus the reader is told: "Remember the sabbath day and keep it holy" (20.8). Exodus links the Sabbath with the creation and states that the holiday is proof of God's special covenant with the Jewish people: "It shall be a sign for all time between Me and the people of Israel" (31.17). Deuteronomy, on the other hand, instructs one to "observe the sabbath day and keep it holy" (5.12) and connects the Sabbath with the liberation of the Jews from slavery: "Remember that you were a slave in the land of Egypt and the LORD your God freed you from there with a mighty hand and an outstretched arm; therefore the LORD your God has commanded you to observe the sabbath day" (5.15).

The multiple and in many cases quite specific laws for keeping the Sabbath were codified by the ancient rabbis and scholars in the various books of the Talmud, the collection of rabbinic commentaries and interpretations of biblical law. Whereas the Bible gives few instructions other than the prohibition of labor, the Mishna (the body of Jewish law composed around 200 c.e.) delineates thirty-nine major categories (with further subdivisions) of such forbidden tasks as the lighting of fires, cooking, trade, business transactions of any sort, travel, and the carrying of objects. Later, other constraints and customs developed, but all seem to relate in one fashion or another to stipulations concerning forms of "getting and spending."

For those who observe the Sabbath, these restrictions, far from being onerous, help define the special qualities of the day: tranquillity, contemplation, freedom from the routine of the work week, and the giving of oneself over to spirituality. Physical comfort and pleasure (eating, drinking, reposing, inviting guests into the home, and wearing one's finest clothes, for example) are also an integral part of the Sabbath tradition. The numerous customs that have developed over the centuries to commemorate the Sabbath (special prayers, lighting candles, a Sabbath challah bread, eating a festive meal prepared the day before), are all associated with the unique and celebratory aspects of the holiday. The ancient rabbis even decreed it a special mitzvah (blessing) for husband and wife to make love on the Sabbath.

The delight that Jews traditionally take in the Sabbath is reflected in many of the literary selections included in this section. Isaac Luria's, "I Spread the Board This Sabbath Eve," Kadia Molodowsky's "Song of the Sabbath," Marcia Falk's "Will," and Richard Chess's "Bless Us with Peace, Angels of Peace" all express the positive, restful, and joyful qualities of the Sabbath. Luria's poem links the sensual pleasures of food, wine, music, and sumptuous surroundings with the Sabbath Eve celebration and with "the Glory of the Lord." Molodowsky's "Song of the Sabbath" speaks of the "pure, clean flame" of the Sabbath lights capable of dispelling the anxiety of weekdays filled with arguing, flighting, and slaughtering. Written several generations later, Chess's poem "Bless Us with Peace" expresses similar thoughts: while the Sabbath "cannot cure all ills" it can heal spirits damaged during the week.

So special and spiritually satisfying was the Sabbath that it was portrayed by ancient sages as a foreshadowing of the world to come, a taste of paradise here on earth, and a sign of the messianic age. This linking of Sabbath and heaven is lovingly developed in Isaac Bashevis Singer's mystical short story "Short Friday," included in this section, in which husband and wife actually transcend their physical world through the perfection of their precious, shared Sabbath.

The Sabbath is often identified with thoughts of one's mother and with motherhood in general. This is clearly the case in the excerpt included here from Alfred Kazin's memoir, A Walker in the City; in the fictional selections from Sholom Asch and Michelle Herman; and in the poems of Aaron Leyeles, Hayim Nahman Bialik, Alicia Suskin Ostriker, and Irena Klepfisz. Kazin's father figures prominently in his memories of Friday evenings, but it is clearly his mother who keeps the family "stitched together." The young protagonist of Asch's novel Salvation understands that he has two mothers: a "weekday mother" who "haggled with peasants, screamed, scolded, lied"; and a "Sabbath mother" whose "loveliness shone from her face, from her eyes, from her darkly glowing skin." In the excerpt from her novel Missing, Herman describes the various emotions and frustrations that invariably arise between generations and between mother and daughter, especially as Friday evening approaches and the traditional "Shabbos" dinner must be prepared.

The Sabbath has often been personified in legend and literature as a feminine entity: a beautiful "bride," a lovely "princess," or a gracious "queen." The ancient rabbis wrote of greeting the Sabbath as one would a noble lady or a beautiful woman. The sixteenth-century Kabbalists expanded this queenly image to include that of a bride, and thereby envisioned the Sabbath as a mystical union between God the King and his "bride," the Sabbath "Queen." Grace Paley, in her poem "The Five Day Week," calls forth the image of "Sabbath calm Queen of Days." For Ostriker, the Sabbath "bride . . . the lady we share with God" is beckoned by the woman of the household and becomes part of the family circle and of the "here and now."

Traditional female symbols — home, hearth, table, motherhood, and nature — are frequently associated with the Sabbath and are depicted as counterpoints to the archetypal male (weekday) concepts of labor, commerce, war, and violence. Molodowsky imagines the days of the week as "six kings" with whom she fights and argues, while the Sabbath represents the serenity and beauty of the natural world: "The Greenness of the mountains / is the greenness of the Sabbath. / The silver of the lake / is the silver of the Sabbath." In "Shabbat Moment," Marge Piercy describes the Sabbath as "the time for letting time go" and the moment to open one's inner self to the quiet loveliness of nature: "Tilt your neck and let / your face open to the sky / like a pond catching light / drinking the darkness."

The three personal essays included in this section express various psychological, religious, familial, and cultural associations evoked by Sabbath memories. The chapter included here from Kazin's *A Walker in the City* centers on Kazin's extended family and the importance of those connections. In contrast, the short excerpt from Margo Minco's holocaust memoir, *Bitter Herbs*, is dominated more by fear and anxiety than by tranquillity — lending even greater poignancy to the works expressing gratitude for a Sabbath celebrated peacefully and freely. Elizabeth Erlich, in a chapter reprinted here from her memoir *Miriam's Kitchen*, voices concern about the difficulties of observing Sabbath custom and practice in late-twentieth-century suburban America. Some traditions, however, are worth preserving — even within the hectic pace of the modern secular world.

Throughout Jewish history, Sabbath observance has remained a constant and compelling aspect of Jewish life. The other holidays and festivals that follow in this collection — Rosh Hashana, Yom Kippur, Hanukkah, Passover, and Purim — mark the seasons in important ways; in many cases they are also connected with significant historical events. But the rhythm of daily Jewish life revolves around the celebration of "Shabbat" every week of every month. For observant Jews, the Sabbath is a sacred time of spirituality, commemorating the creation of the universe and paying tribute to God's special covenant with the Jewish people. As many of the selections that follow illustrate, the Sabbath holds a special meaning for less observant and secular Jews as well: it is a time when one pauses to reflect, renew relationships with family and friends, enjoy the pleasures of this world, and find one's own inner peace.

# Poetry

# ❧ A Song for the Sabbath

## DUNASH HA-LEVI BEN LABRAT

He will proclaim freedom for all his sons,
And will keep you, as the apple of his eye.
Pleasant is your name, and will not be destroyed.
Repose, relax, on the Sabbath day.

Seek my sanctuary and my home.
Give me a sign of deliverance.
Plant a vine in my vineyard.
Look to my people, hear their laments.

Tread the wine-press in Bozrah,
And in Babylon, that city of might.
Crush my enemies in anger and fury.
On the day when I cry, hear my complaint.

Place, O God, in the mountain waste,
Fir and acacia, myrtle and elm.
Give those who teach, and those who obey,
Abundant peace, like the flow of a stream.

Repel my enemies, O zealous God.
Fill their hearts with fear and despair.
Then we shall open our mouths, and fill
Our tongues with praise for your power.

Know wisdom, that your soul may live,
And it shall be a diadem for your brow.
Keep the commandment of your Holy One.
Observe the Sabbath, your sacred day.

*Translated by David Goldstein*

## I Spread the Board This Sabbath Eve

ISAAC LURIA

I spread the board this sabbath eve,
    And now do I invite
The Ancient Sage, the Holy One.
    Now may His radiant light
Shine in our cups, and may His lore
    Illume our feast tonight!

May He His radiant beauty shed,
    And we His splendor see,
The while He whispers soft and low
    His hidden mystery.
And tells us, as we gather round,
    Of wonders yet to be—

Of sabbath feasts which in His courts
    For us shall yet be spread,
When we shall taste His holy meats
    And break His holy bread,
And all the wine of His great pow'r
    Shall rush into our head!

When in a living tether He
    Shall tie the souls of all,
And nevermore shall flower fade
    And never blossom fall,
And all in one great music break,
    All creatures great and small;

And they shall make sweet minstrelsy
    To crown the festive board,
And His great name be on their lips,
    Forevermore adored;
And they at last find words to tell
    The glory of the Lord.

*Translated by Theodor H. Gastor*

## ⁂ My Mother, Her Memory Be Blessed

HAYIM NAHMAN BIALIK


My mother, her memory be blessed, was a perfect saint
and in her widowhood was poor as dirt.
And Sabbath evening came, the sun in the tops of the trees
and in her house no candle stood nor feast.

She looked around and found yet, a miracle, two cents —
"Bread or the candles?" — she hesitates, hesitates
ran out and came back, and in her thin hand a sacrifice
two candles white, ready to be blessed.

Seven stars above, and my mother's Sabbath eve
has seven candles to it — eyes.
Will God rob his own Sabbath's holiness? And if he did how should
    she?
May his name be blessed in thanks for the two!

And let it be blessed on a tablecloth, clean, without crust of bread —
and she wears a Sabbath headdress on her pale head —
and changes her dress, and prepares for God
the holiness of the Sabbath.

And when she lit the candles she could not be still
for it galled her, for her heart boiled
and the righteous one wept, and a tear from the grooves of her
    cheek
fell — and one candle hissed and went out.

Sabbath stood shamed and blind in one eye —
the woman exploded:
"Do you scorn, Lord, a widow's gift? And has your handmaiden
    sinned? —
And what, tell me, was your Sabbath's crime?

"Why have you plucked out her eye?" And while she stood with
    her eyes shut
and covered with palms, all trembling,
her shoulders danced with her headdress, from choking back tears
and the heat of prayer.

Abysses in her soul cried out, mothers and cherubs
wept in her throat.
No heart above had heard, nor no one yet seen from the throne of
    God
a soul so wrapped in its sadness.

Then there fell from the cheek of the righteous one a single burning
    tear
one sliver of flame
and as it fell there lit in the house a double light to fire
the candle that went out.

My mother just opened her dimming eyes to see:
the light of creation there shining
for the Divine Presence had kissed them —
and may her saintliness shine for us and all of Israel.

*Translated by Atar Hadari*

# 🪶 Sabbath Hours

**A. LEYELES**

Spicy smell of tall shadowy eucalyptuses
With tender, tinder-red fans of blossoms
And flowers like delicately cut-up raw meat;
Lurking mountains, like camels resting on their knees
After a week-long dusty march;
Gardenful, flowering wide expanses
Of the golden, eternal Young-Summer—
Sabbath in California.

High mountains of sand and thought
Separate Los Angeles from Lodz.
Deep abysses of rushing brooks and turbulent moods
Lie between two quiet Sabbath-hours,
Shaking their hands over half a century.

The late Sabbath afternoon in Lodz comes lovely and leisurely,
With the modest green of fresh shtshav,
With rye bread, milk and farmer's cheese,
And with a boy's lurking, impudent blondness
Under Mama's and Papa's restful gazes.

How can dull shtshav
Compare with the vanity of eucalyptuses and palms,
With orange-blossoms which make you groggy with aromas
More fragrant than young honey?
What is the link that ties a boy's sated happiness
In the lap of Sabbath peace, running with milk and love,
To the soft peace of sun-steeped mountains—
Like a wide-open, over-ripe, giant yellow rose?

Over the bridge of half a century
Walks from Lodz my mother the Queen,
My father with his beard of dark gold.
Mother brings bread and an earthenware bowl of shtshav.

Shtshav — sorrel soup

Father's kindly greenish eyes are like blessings
In the boy's sheltered heart:
Sabbath, Sabbath,
Sabbath in the whole world.

Half a century is the blink of an eye.
Seven-thousand-miles — the smallest step,
When suddenly, unexpectedly,
Like the sound of a violin, flutters by
The golden wing of the craved-for, blessed
Holy peace
Of Sabbath.

Translated by Benjamin and Barbara Harshav

# 🐝 Song of the Sabbath

### KADIA MOLODOWSKY

I quarreled with kings till the Sabbath,
I fought with the six kings
of the six days of the week.

Sunday they took away my sleep.
Monday they scattered my salt.
And on the third day, my God,
they threw out my bread: whips flashed
across my face. The fourth day
they caught my dove, my flying dove,
and slaughtered it.
It was like that till Friday morning.
This is my whole week
the dove's flight dying.

At nightfall Friday
I lit four candles,
and the queen of the Sabbath came to me.
Her face lit up the whole world,
and made it all a Sabbath.
My scattered salt
shone in its little bowl,
and my dove, my flying dove,
clapped its wings together,
and licked its throat.
The Sabbath queen blessed my candles,
and they burned with a pure, clean flame.
The light put out the days of the week
and my quarreling with the six kings.

The greenness of the mountains
is the greenness of the Sabbath.
The silver of the lake
is the silver of the Sabbath.
The singing of the wind
is the singing of the Sabbath.

And my heart's song
is an eternal Sabbath.

*Translated by Jean Valentine*

# ❧ The Five Day Week

GRACE PALEY

The five-day week was set like a firecracker
The five-day week       ah       like a long bath in the
              first bathtub of God
The five-day week was sunny all year       (I remember)
The five-day week gave at last what she'd always longed for
              a cheerful noisy companion
              to Sabbath calm Queen of days

## 🐝 Shabbat Moment

MARGE PIERCY

A scarf trailing
over the lilac sunset,
fair weather clouds,
cirrus uncinus
silk chiffon.
Twilight softens the air,
whispering, come,
lie down with me.

Untie the knots of the will.
Loosen
your clenched grip
barren hills of bone.
Here, no edges to hone,
only the palm fallen
open as a rose about
to toss its petals.

What you have made,
what you have spoiled
let go.
Let twilight empty
the crowded rooms
quiet the jostling colors
to hues of swirling water
pearls of fog.

This is the time
for letting time go
like a released balloon
dwindling.
Tilt your neck and let
your face open to the sky
like a pond catching light
drinking the darkness.

# 🪴 Sabbath

from *A Meditation in Seven Days*

**ALICIA SUSKIN OSTRIKER**

Come, my friend, come, my friend
Let us go to meet the bride
— Sabbath Song
And in between she would work and clean and cook. But the food, the food. . . .
O the visits were filled with food.
— Melanie Kaye/Kantrowiz


Not speculation, nothing remote
No words addressed to an atomic father

Not the wisdom of the wise
Nor a promise, and not the trap of hereafter

Here, now, through the misted kitchen windows
Since dawn the dusk is falling

Everywhere in the neighborhood
Women have rushed to the butcher, the grocer

With a violet sky she prepares the bread, she plucks
And cooks the chicken, grates the stinging horseradish

These are her fingers, her sinewy back as she scrubs
The house, her hands slap the children and clean them

Dusk approaches, wind moans
Food ready, it is around her hands

The family faces gather, the homeless
She has gathered like sheep, it is her veiny hands

That light the candles, so that suddenly
Our human grief illuminated, we're a circle

Practical and magical, it's
Strong wine and food time coming, and from outside time

From the jewelled throne
Of a house behind history

She beckons the bride, the radiant
Sabbath, the lady we share with God

Our mother's palms like branches lifted in prayer
Lead our rejoicing voices, our small chorus

Our clapping hands in the here and now
In a world that is never over

And never enough

# Der Mames Shabosim/My Mother's Sabbath Days

IRENA KLEPFISZ

Inspired by Vella Grade in Chaim Grade's memoir

Bay undz iz es geven andersh.    I knew nothing
of the 613 mitsves   which did not bind me      nor
of the 3 which did    though I am sure my grandmother
Rikla Perczykow   knew them all   and I have a vague
image   of her covering her eyes      and swaying.

Shoshana   Rózka   Lodzia   Mamma Lo   and more recently
Rose   in short: my mother    in all her reincarnations
did not pass on       such things.
She'd given them up      even before she'd ever claimed them.
She was more modern       and besides       there were other matters
to teach       so by age 11    kh'bin shoyn geven a brenendike sotsyalistke
I was a passionate socialist   impatient   so impatient
to grow      into my knowledge   never guessing
there was no choice   for work   and rest   wrestled
in every human life      with work   inevitably
the unbeatable winner.

So for us it was different.    Erev shabes    was plain    fraytik
or more precisely: piontek.       I remember   summer evenings
I'd wait for her   at the Mosholu stop of the Lexington line.
Bright heat and light   at 6 o'clock.      She was full
of tales      of Miss Kant   the designer      a career woman
longing for home and family       in love with a handsome pilot
of Scottie   the model      who married smart      a wealthy buyer
and now sat brazenly chic   in a reform synagogue.
I listened      eager   to understand these widow tales   of romance
amid the rush      of each season's showing   and once   even

Bay undz iz es geven andersh (Yiddish) — At our house it was different.
mitsves (Yiddish) — obligatory good deeds required of Jewish men (613) and
women (3).
Erev shabes (Yiddish) — Friday night, Sabbath eve.
fraytik (Yiddish) — Friday.
piontek (Polish) — Friday.

saw    on a page of the *Times*    a mannequin    dressed in
the very gown    Mamma Lo had made.

All the way up Jerome Avenue    we'd walk    past the Jewish deli
where we never ate    (what was the point if you could make it at
    home?)
past the pizza place    where occasionally    while shopping    she'd
    buy me
a slice    past the outdoor groceries    fruit stands    fabric       shoes
lingerie    and stationery stores — till Gun Hill Road    and Jade
    Gardens.
Perhaps I knew it was *treyf*.       She certainly did
but was not concerned.       We'd order       the salty wonton soup
chow mein    or pepper steak    and though she mocked the food
she never resisted.
It was Friday. The shop was closed.    We'd eat dinner and like the
    rich
lean leisurely back in our booth.    I didn't know it was *erev shabes*.
Still — she rested.

treyf (Yiddish) — non-Kosher.

## ❧ Will

**MARCIA FALK**

Three generations back
my family had only

to light a candle
and the world parted.

Today, Friday afternoon,
I disconnect clocks and phones.

When night fills my house
with passages,

I begin saving
my life.

## 🪻 Bless Us with Peace, Angels of Peace

RICHARD CHESS

The window's curtain drawn back,
Six panes of nightfall
Reflect wan faces that recall
The week and what it sorely lacked:

Humor, cash, good health.
Candlelight cannot cure all ills,
Nor can wine, a few drops of which spill
From the uplifted cup like excessive wealth.

But by the prayer with which we unveil
The braided breads, risen
Like our pride in being chosen
To receive Shabbat, our spirits heal.

Stuffed on *hallot*, our double portion,
We ease into the next course of fortune.

# Memoir

## ❧ The Kitchen

from *A Walker in the City*

ALFRED KAZIN

The last time I saw our kitchen this clearly was one afternoon in London at the end of the war, when I waited out the rain in the entrance to a music store. A radio was playing into the street, and standing there I heard a broadcast of the first Sabbath service from Belsen Concentration Camp. When the liberated Jewish prisoners recited the *Hear O Israel, the Lord Our God, the Lord is One*, I felt myself carried back to the Friday evenings at home, when with the Sabbath at sundown a healing quietness would come over Brownsville.

It was the darkness and emptiness of the streets I liked most about Friday evening, as if in preparation for that day of rest and worship which the Jews greet "as a bride" — that day when the very touch of money is prohibited, all work, all travel, all household duties, even to the turning on and off of a light — Jewry had found its way past its tormented heart to some ancient still center of itself. I waited for the streets to go dark on Friday evening as other children waited for the Christmas lights. Even Friday morning after the tests were over glowed in anticipation. When I returned home after three, the warm odor of a coffee cake baking in the oven and the sight of my mother on her hands and knees scrubbing the linoleum on the dining room floor filled me with such tenderness that I could feel my senses reaching out to embrace every single object in our household. One Friday, after a morning in school spent on the voyages of Henry Hudson, I returned with the phrase *Among the discoverers of the New World* singing in my mind as the theme of my own new-found freedom on the Sabbath.

My great moment came at six, when my father returned from work, his overalls smelling faintly of turpentine and shellac, white drops of silver paint still gleaming on his chin. Hanging his overcoat in the long dark hall that led into our kitchen, he would leave in one pocket a loosely folded copy of the New York *World*; and then everything that beckoned to me from that other hemisphere of my brain beyond the East River would start up from the smell of fresh newsprint and the sight of the globe on the front page. It was a paper that carried special associations for me with Brooklyn Bridge. They published the *World* under the green dome on Park Row overlooking the bridge; the fresh salt air of New York harbor lingered for me in the smell of paint and damp newsprint in the hall. I felt that my father brought the outside straight into our house with each day's copy of the *World*. The bridge somehow stood for freedom; the *World* for that rangy kindness and fraternalism and ease we found in Heywood Broun. My father would read aloud from "It Seems To Me" with a delighted smile on his face. "A very clear and courageous man!" he would say. "Look how he stands up for our Sacco and Vanzetti! A real social conscience, that man! Practically a Socialist!" Then, taking off his overalls, he would wash up at the kitchen sink, peeling and gnawing the paint off his nails with Gold Dust Washing Powder as I poured it into his hands, smacking his lips and grunting with pleasure as he washed himself clean of the job at last, and making me feel that I was really helping him, that I, too, was contributing to the greatness of the evening and the coming day.

By sundown the streets were empty, the curtains had been drawn, the world put to rights. Even the kitchen walls had been scrubbed and now gleamed in the Sabbath candles. On the long white tablecloth were the "company" dishes, filled for some with *gefillte* fish on lettuce leaves, ringed by red horseradish, sour and half-sour pickles, tomato salad with a light vinegar dressing; for others, with chopped liver in a bed of lettuce leaves and white radishes; the long white *khalleh*, the Sabbath loaf; chicken soup with noodles *and* dumplings; chicken, meat loaf, prunes, and sweet potatoes that had been baked all day into an open pie; compote of prunes and quince, apricots and orange rind; applesauce; a great brown nutcake filled with almonds, the traditional *lekakh*; all surrounded by glasses of port wine, seltzer bottles with their nozzles staring down at us waiting to be pressed; a samovar of Russian tea, *svetouchnee* from the little red box, always served in tall glasses, with lemon slices floating on top. My father and mother sipped it in Russian fashion, through lumps of sugar held between the teeth.

Afterwards we went into the "dining room" and, since we were not particularly orthodox, allowed ourselves little pleasures outside the Sabbath rule — an occasional game of Casino at the dining-room table where we never dined; and listening to the victrola. The evening was particularly good for me whenever the unmarried cousin who boarded with us had her two closest friends in after supper.

They were all dressmakers, like my mother; had worked with my mother in the same East Side sweatshops; were all passionately loyal members of the International Ladies Garment Workers Union; and were all unmarried. We were their only family. Despite my mother's frenzied matchmaking, she had never succeeded in pinning a husband down for any of them. As she said, they were all too *particular* — what a calamity for a Jewish woman to remain unmarried! But my cousin and her friends accepted their fate calmly, and prided themselves on their culture and their strong *progressive* interests. They felt they belonged not to the "kitchen world," like my mother, but to the enlightened tradition of the old Russian intelligentsia. Whenever my mother sighed over them, they would smile out of their greater knowledge of the world, and looking at me with a pointed appeal for recognition, would speak of novels they had read in Yiddish and Russian, of *Winesburg, Ohio,* of some article in the *Nation.*

Our cousin and her two friends were of my parents' generation, but I could never believe it — they seemed to enjoy life with such outspokenness. They were the first grown-up people I had ever met who used the word *love* without embarrassment. "*Libbe! Libbe!*" my mother would explode whenever one of them protested that she could not, after all, marry a man she did not love. "What is this love you make such a stew about? You do not like the way he holds his cigarette? Marry him first and it will all come out right in the end!" It astonished me to realize there was a world in which even unmarried women no longer young were simply individual human beings with lives of their own. Our parents, whatever affection might offhandedly be expressed between them, always had the look of being committed to something deeper than *mere* love. Their marriages were neither happy nor unhappy; they were arrangements. However they had met — whether in Russia or in the steerage or, like my parents, in an East Side boarding house — whatever they still thought of each other, *love* was not a word they used easily. Marriage was an institution people entered into — for all I could ever tell — only from immigrant loneliness, a need to be with one's own kind that mechanically resulted in the family. The family was a whole greater than all the individuals who made it up, yet made sense only in their untiring solidarity. I was perfectly sure that in my parents' minds *libbe* was something exotic and not wholly legitimate, reserved for "educated" people like their children, who were the sole end of their existence. My father and mother worked in a rage to put us above their level; they had married to make *us* possible. We were the only conceivable end to all their striving; we were their America.

So far as I knew, love was not an element admissible in my parents' experience. Any open talk of it between themselves would have seemed ridiculous. It would have suggested a wicked self-indulgence, a preposterous attention to one's own feelings, possible only to those who were free enough to choose. They did not consider themselves free. They were awed by us, as they were awed by their own imagined unworthiness, and looked on themselves only as instruments toward the ideal "American" future that would be lived by their children. As poor immigrants who had remained in Brownsville, painfully conscious of the *alrightniks* on Eastern Parkway—oh, those successes of whom I was always hearing so much, and whom we admired despite all our socialism!—everything in their lives combined to make them look down on love as something *they* had no time for. Of course there was a deep resentment in this, and when on those Friday evenings our cousin or her two friends openly mentioned the unheard-of collapse of someone's marriage—

"Sórelle and Berke? I don't believe it."

"But it's true."

"You must be joking!"

"No, it's true!"

"You're joking! You're joking!"

"No, it's true!"

—I noticed that my parents' talk had an unnaturally hard edge to it, as if those who gave themselves up to love must inevitably come to grief. Love, they could have said, was not *serious*. Life was a battle to "make sure"; it had no place, as we had no time, for whims.

Love, in fact, was something for the movies, which my parents enjoyed, but a little ashamedly. They were the land of the impossible. On those few occasions when my mother closed her sewing machine in the evening and allowed herself a visit to the Supreme, or the Palace, or the Premier, she would return, her eyes gleaming with wonder and some distrust at the strangeness of it all, to report on erotic fanatics who were, thank God, like no one we knew. What heedlessness! What daring! What riches! To my mother riches alone were the gateway to romance, for only those who had money enough could afford the freedom, and the crazy boldness, to give themselves up to love.

Yet there they were in our own dining room, our cousin and her two friends—women, grown-up women—talking openly of the look on Garbo's face when John Gilbert took her in his arms, serenely disposing of each new *khayimyankel*, poor wretch, my mother had picked for them, and arguing my father down on small points of Socialist doctrine. As they sat around the cut-glass bowl on the table—cracking walnuts, expertly peeling the skin off an apple in long even strips, cozily sipping at a glass of tea—they crossed their legs in comfort and gave off a deliciously musky fragrance of face powder that instantly framed them for me in all their dark coloring, brilliantly white teeth, and the rosy Russian blouses that swelled and rippled in terraces of embroidery over their opulent breasts.

They had a great flavor for me, those three women: they were the positive center of that togetherness that always meant so much to me in our dining room on Friday evenings. It was a quality that seemed to start in the prickly thickness of the cut-glass bowl laden with nuts and fruits; in the light from the long black-shaded lamp hanging over the table as it shimmered against the thick surfaces of the bowl and softened that room where the lace curtains were drawn against the dark and empty streets — and then found its unexpectedly tender voice in the Yiddish folksongs and Socialist hymns they taught me — "Let's Now Forgive Each Other"; "Tsuzamen, Tsuzamen, All Together, Brothers!" Those Friday evenings, I suddenly found myself enveloped in some old, primary Socialist idea that men could go beyond every barrier of race and nation and language, even of class! into some potential loving union of the whole human race. I was suddenly glad to be a Jew, as these women were Jews — simply and naturally glad of those Jewish dressmakers who spoke with enthusiastic familiarity of Sholem Aleichem and Peretz, Gorky and Tolstoy, who glowed at every reminiscence of Nijinsky, of Nazimova in The Cherry Orchard, of Pavlova in "The Swan."

Often, those Friday evenings, they spoke of der heym, "Home," and then it was hard for me. Heym was a terrible word. I saw millions of Jews lying dead under the Polish eagle with knives in their throats. I was afraid with my mother's fears, thought I should weep when she wept, lived again through every pogrom whose terrors she chanted. I associated with that old European life only pain, mud, and hopelessness, but I was of it still, through her. Whenever she would call through the roll of her many brothers and sisters and their children, remembering at each name that this one was dead, that one dead, another starving and sure soon to die — who knew how they were living these days in that miserable Poland? — I felt there was some supernatural Polish eagle across the sea whose face I should never see, but which sent out dark electrical rays to hold me fast.

In many ways der heym was entirely dim and abstract, nothing to do with me at all, alien as the skullcap and beard and frock coat of my mother's father, whom I never saw, but whose calm orthodox dignity stared up at me from an old cracked photograph at the bottom of the bureau drawer. Yet I lived each of my mother's fears from Dugschitz to Hamburg to London to Hester Street to Brownsville through and through with such fidelity that there were times when I wished I had made that journey too, wished I could have seen Czarist Russia, since I had in any event to suffer it all over again. I often felt odd twinges of jealousy because my parents could talk about that more intense, somehow less experimental life than ours with so many private smiles between themselves. It was bewildering, it made me long constantly to get at some past nearer my own New York life, my having to live with all those running wounds of a world I had never seen.

Then, under cover of the talk those Friday evenings, I would take up *The Boy's Life of Theodore Roosevelt* again, and moodily call out to those strangers on the summer veranda in Oyster Bay until my father spoke his tale of arriving in America. That was hard, too, painful in another way — yet it always made him curiously lighthearted and left me swimming in space. For he had gone off painting box cars on the Union Pacific, had been as far west as Omaha, had actually seen Sidney Hillman toiling in Hart, Schaffner and Marx's Chicago factory, had heard his beloved Debs making fools of Bryant and Taft in the 1908 campaign, had been offered a homestead in Colorado! *Omaha* was the most beautiful word I had ever heard, *homestead* almost as beautiful; but I could never forgive him for not having accepted that homestead.

"What would I have done there? I'm no farmer."

"You should have taken it! Why do we always live here!"

"It would have been too lonely. Nobody I knew."

"What a chance!"

"Don't be childish. Nobody I knew."

"Why? Why?"

"Alfred, what do you want of us poor Jews?"

So it was: we had always to be together: believers and non-believers, we were a people; I was of that people. Unthinkable to go one's own way, to doubt or to escape the fact that I was a Jew. I had heard of Jews who pretended they were not, but could not understand them. We had all of us lived together so long that we would not have known how to separate even if we had wanted to. The most terrible word was *aleyn*, alone. I always had the same picture of a man desolately walking down a dark street, newspapers and cigarette butts contemptuously flying in his face as he tasted in the dusty grit the full measure of his strangeness. *Aleyn! Aleyn!* My father had been alone here in America as a boy. His father, whose name I bore, had died here at twenty-five of pneumonia caught on a garment workers' picket line, and his body flung in with thousands of other Jews who had perished those first years on the East Side. My father had never been able to find his father's grave. *Aleyn! Aleyn!* Did immigrant Jews, then, marry only out of loneliness? Was even Socialism just a happier way of keeping us together?

I trusted it to do that. Socialism would be one long Friday evening around the samovar and the cut-glass bowl laden with nuts and fruits, all of us singing *Tsuzamen, tsuzamen, alle tsuzamen!* Then the heroes of the Russian novel — our kind of people — would walk the world, and I — still wearing a circle-necked Russian blouse "*à la Tolstoy*" — would live forever with those I loved in that beautiful Russian country of the mind. Listening to our cousin and her two friends I, who had never seen it, who associated with it nothing but the names of great writers and my father's saying as we went through the Brooklyn Botanic Garden — "Nice! but you should have seen the Czar's summer palace at Tsarskoye-Selo!" — suddenly saw Russia as the grand antithesis to all bourgeois ideals, the spiritual home of all truly free people. I was perfectly sure that there was no literature in the world like the Russian; that the only warm hearts in the world were Russian, like our cousin and her two friends; that other people were always dully materialist, but that the Russian soul, like Nijinsky's dream of pure flight, would always leap outward, past all barriers, to a lyric world in which my ideal socialism and the fiery moodiness of Tchaikovsky's *Pathétique* would be entirely at home with each other. *Tsuzamen, alle tsuzamen!* How many millions would be with us! China was in our house those Friday evenings, Africa, the Indian masses. And it was those three unmarried dressmakers from the rank and file who fully wrapped me in that spell, with the worldly clang of their agate beads and the musky fragrance of their face powder and their embroidered Russian blouses, with the great names of Russian writers ringing against the cut-glass bowl under the black lamp. Never did the bowl look so laden, never did apples and tea smell so good, never did the samovar pour out with such steaming bounty, as on those Friday evenings when I tasted in the tea and the talk the evangelical heart of our cousin and her two friends, and realized that it was we — we! — who would someday put the world on its noblest course.

"Kinder, kinder," my mother would say. "Enough *discusye*. Maybe now a little music? Alfred, play *Scheherazade!*"

## ≈ Sabbath

from *Bitter Herbs*

MARGA MINCO

I looked down over my mother's book, over the finger with which she traced the lines to enable me to follow the prayers, down through the lattice-work of the screen to where I saw my father standing wearing his prayer shawl. I could not help thinking of the synagogue at Breda. There Father had had a roomy pew all to himself. It had been just like a coach without wheels. To get out of it, he had to open a little round door and descend a few steps. The door squeaked, and when I heard it squeak I would look down.

Father would go to the center of the building. I would follow with my eyes his shining top hat and his ample prayer shawl, which floated out behind him a little as he walked. He would ascend the stairs of the *almemmor*, the dais in the middle of the synagogue from which the scrolls of the Law are read, and whither he was "summoned" to distribute blessings. Suddenly I would hear our names, between the half-chanted Hebrew texts. The names sounded very beautiful in Hebrew. And they were longer, because Father's name was always added to them. Then my mother would also look down through the grille and smile at Father. The other women in the gallery would nod to my mother, to show that they had heard, and wait to see whether their husbands would give them a blessing, so that my mother would be able to nod to them in their turn. It was a custom in the Breda congregation.

But now I saw Father sitting somewhat toward the back, on a bench among other men. He was wearing an ordinary hat, and he remained where he was until the end of the service. It was a long service. Special prayers were said for the Jews in the camps. Some women wept. In front of me one woman was sitting who blew her nose repeatedly, huddled behind her prayer book. She had on a reddish-brown *bandeau*—the wig worn by our married women—which had sagged backward a little under her hat.

My mother had laid her prayer book beside her on the seat. She was staring fixedly into space. I put my hand on her arm.

"It's very cold in Poland now," she whispered.

"Yes, but she was able to take warm clothes with her, wasn't she?" I said softly. "She had a rucksack lying ready."

Mother nodded. The cantor raised his voice in another prayer and we all stood up. Down below, someone had taken a Scroll from the Ark. The Scroll was covered with purple velvet, and there was a silver crown on it from which little bells hung. The Scroll was carried round the building. The bells tinkled. As the Scroll went past them the men kissed the tip of the velvet.

After a while, the final hymn burst forth. It is a cheerful melody, and I never ceased to be surprised by the rather exuberant way in which the congregation plunged into it. Singing, the men folded up their prayer shawls, and the women put on their coats. I saw my father carefully stowing his shawl away in the special bag intended for the purpose.

In front of the synagogue people waited for each other. They shook hands and wished each other "Good Sabbath." Father was already there when we came out. I remembered how I had hated having to walk home with the rest after Sabbath service, when I was a child. I was always frightened of running into children from my school.

Most of the people quickly dispersed over the square. Some went in the direction of Weesperstraat; others made for Waterlooplein. An acquaintance of my father asked us whether we cared to walk part of the way home with him along Nieuwe Amstelstraat.

"I've sent my wife and children into the country," he said. "At the moment it's better for them to be there than here."

"Why haven't you gone with them?" my mother asked.

"Oh, well," he said, "that's not in my line. I'll manage all right."

"Are you on your own at home now?" Mother asked him.

"No," he answered, "I'm staying with my sister. She's not doing anything about it either, for the time being."

"What could you do, actually?" asked my father.

"Well," said his friend, "you can shut the door behind you and disappear. But then, what are you going to live on?"

"Exactly," said my father. "You've got to live. You've got to have something to live on."

We were standing on the corner near the Amstel River. An ice-cold wind was blowing in our faces. My father's acquaintance shook hands all round. "I've got to go that way, to my sister's," he said. He crossed the bridge to Amstelstraat, a small, hunched figure, with the collar of his black overcoat right up round his ears and his hand on his hat.

We walked along beside the Amstel, and came to the bridge where it is joined by the Nieuwe Herengracht canal. We crossed the bridge, under the yellow board. The board bearing in black letters the German word "Judenviertel."

A couple of children with woollen scarves round their necks were hanging over the parapet, throwing bread to the seagulls. The birds, skimming low over the water, nimbly caught the scraps. A Black Maria drove down the other side of the canal. A woman pushed a window up and shouted something. The children dropped the rest of the bread on the ground and ran inside.

"Let's take the shortest way home," said my mother. We went along the canal.

"We'll be there in no time," said my father.

"You hear of more and more people going underground," I said.

"Yes," said Father. "We'll have to see about finding something for you too."

"No," I said. "I'm not going alone."

"If we were still in Breda it'd be easier," my mother said. "There we should have had an address in a minute. Here we know nobody."

"There we might perhaps have been able to move in with the neighbors, just like that," I said.

"Oh, we could have gone anywhere we liked," said Mother. "We had friends everywhere."

"Here it costs a lot of money," said my father, "Where am I to get it from?"

"If only we knew more people. . . ." said Mother.

"Let's wait and see," said my father. "Perhaps it won't be necessary. And if it isn't necessary, there you sit, among strangers, and you're only a nuisance and a worry to them."

We were home once more. Father put the key in the lock. I glanced involuntarily up and down the street before I went inside.

In the living room the stove was burning and the table was set. Mother had done that before we left. Father went to wash his hands.

Then he came and stood with us at the table, took the embroidered cloth from the Sabbath bread, broke the crust off it, and divided it into three pieces while praying. He dipped the bread in salt. I muttered grace, and ate the salted crust.

"That's right," said my father, and sat down.

*Translated by Roy Edwards*

# ⚘ Sabbath

from *Miriam's Kitchen*

ELIZABETH EHRLICH

The flier has come in the mail. Summer is over. Today, it rains. school is starting. The air is cool. As the flier proclaims, it is time to register for soccer.

It is a good sport, soccer. My son is ready. He runs down the street with a black-and-white ball, pivots, and kicks it back to the stop sign. It's a nice team sport. I know, because we were registered once. My daughter, older than her brother, has a little gilt trophy on her shelf, and there are shin-guards deep in her closet. I think she would like to play soccer again.

In this town, soccer, like softball and hockey, is a Saturday morning sport. Everyone subscribes. Sport is beneficial. Sport is social. Sportsmanship is a value to be learned, a value tied in with a larger American way to be. Teamwork, competition, doing your best, losing well: The playing field is a training ground for citizenship. And the kids have good clean fun.

But Saturday, Sabbath: a day of sacred time, of human equality, a day for the spirit. A few years ago we joined the team, and then we tried for Sabbath. On soccer Saturdays, we could not find what we were looking for.

We dropped soccer for Sabbath then, an interim strategy rather than decisive play. Sabbath, eclectic and inconsistent as we keep it, has become the necessary high point, the organizing principle, the raison d'être of our week. Still, we don't know quite what to do about it, how far to go, whether to codify and settle into routine. The place where we live, dynamic equilibrium, is inherently unstable. Without consciousness, effort, restraint, everything tends toward chaos. But I can't bear routine.

God rested, that's what the telling is. Fact or metaphor, I have come to respect the mysterious internal logic that made the once-a-week day of rest, that indeed created the concept of "week," a miraculous gift when humankind had no such concepts. If you are tilling the soil or driving a wagon or baking bread or slaughtering meat for six days, how strange and good to stop for a day and face yourself in the mirror of yourself. How much more crucial in our confusing time, when that mirror within seems more elusive. Our gaze is distracted by so much noise.

Even turn off the noise, though: something fundamental has changed since Sabbath arrived on the scene. People still live, weep, love, whelp, and die. But the human condition is no longer the age-old stark dichotomy of work or rest. *Le weekend* has evolved, bastard descendent of Sabbath, and with it, arriviste ideas — leisure, recreation, fun. I have nothing against such notions. I sacrificed my ankle to the ice-skating rink, without regret. I pore through guidebooks for things to do, from apple-picking to rummage sales, wishing to do them all.

However, is recreation work or rest, and is it a mode for Sabbath?

I live in a town where Saturday is for errands, and Saturday is for sport. When I set off for synagogue, *shul*, in blouse and skirt, my neighbors are lacing sneakers and stretching kinks out of middle-aged backs. I face the Ark as the Torah reading begins. Symbolically present for the revelation at Sinai, I miss the chance to wave at a friend at the gym. I pass up the sidewalk sale. I lose out on the impromptu cup of coffee that stimulates community life. Here are my children, in their dresses and *kippot*, skullcaps, learning to pray in the synagogue with a handful of other kids. This is good for them, I think, but so would soccer be.

Why not let them play soccer, their eager cleats piercing the muddy grass? Why not join other good folks to cheer and carpool, to pour juice and keep track of error, free shot, goal? This isn't work, and it isn't routine. It's not washing the car or investing in mutual funds or filling in woodpecker holes in the siding. It is social, it is even uplifting. It is a compelling Saturday ritual of its own. And while it is pagan to worship sport, this I know: If there is a God, God gave beauty to bodies at play on the field.

The high holidays are upon me, calling for renewal of effort and faith. Team registration is upon me as well. There is only one Saturday morning to have at nine o'clock each week.

Is Sabbath objective reality?

If I drive my car to the shopping mall on Saturday and buy a pair of shoes, is it still the day of rest? Maybe Sabbath is the tree falling in the forest. If I choose to go shopping, though, I have willingly ignored its fall. That is not the same, quite, as just not hearing the distant tree.

When I see the house into order and provide grape juice and wine; when I gather in the children and bathe them; when I wash my hands and adorn myself and light candles of a Friday night, do I observe the Sabbath or actually bring it into being? Does observance of the Sabbath create a reality, or — as with a mathematical formula — does it express and symbolize something already out there in the universe? The scientist, the mathematician "discovers" a law, rather than inventing it. Relativity, gravity, calculus, they say, were out there all along to be named and claimed.

Or is Sabbath more kin to the artist's paradox? The laws of perspective are representational, but the painting is its own reality. Spirituality, like vision, is flawed and emotional, shaped by experience. That *Shabbas* feeling cannot be attained from a color-by-number kit.

So what happens to Sabbath, unmarked and unobserved? Does it curl up its toes and vanish? Does it become the property of those who seek it? Is it always there, waiting for consciousness, recognition, choice? Does it matter if we miss a few?

Sabbath, seventh day of creation: God rested. We are to close out the workaday world for a little while. But how? In the traditional mode, women provide the means. In practice, there are dishes to wash and beds to make and babies to change and children to run after at synagogue and meals to set out after the Friday sun slips behind the rising earth and during that rotation of earth and glimpse of moon that we know as Saturday. Only a man, and a rare man today, would say that this is not "work" next to driving a car or flipping a light switch — actions proscribed in the strictest readings.

The vernacular has it both ways. When you light your candles and say *kiddush*, you "welcome" the Sabbath. The Sabbath arrives, and you celebrate. When you wash your floor, dust, cook, and set the table on Friday, however, you "make" Sabbath. So, what exactly is it that women do?

Are women God?

Does the Sabbath exist independently from the preparation, from the tradition? Can you meet your family for a pizza dinner on Friday, relax together for the first time all week, drive home after dark, snuggle up to a video tape, feel happy to be alive, and call it *Shabbas*? Can you go to the beach with your family on Saturday, enjoying the creation on a beautiful day, and fulfill the observance? The rabbis rather firmly say no. A tired man and woman might prefer yes.

Here's a puzzle: If you race home from the office, snap off the cartoons, shake your roast chicken out of a box, and light the candles exactly by sundown; if you bound out of bed next day though you desperately need your sleep, and then head out to services in the rain on foot when driving would be more restful; if you stand and sit in the chapel, your concentration constantly interrupted by children, and then you return home in the rain, exhausted: this might pass for *Shabbas*, and the rabbis would probably confer their blessing.

Possibly religion is not appropriate for parents of young children.

At my house, we are sitting on a metaphoric fence. We go to synagogue sometimes, stay home sometimes, and occasionally, go out and do. We walk to shul and drive to shul. We have had pleasant Sabbath mornings, at home in pajamas with no TV. We catch up with each other, rest and drift, play Scrabble and read and ignore the phone. We try not to drive, we avoid errands and yard work. Once in a while, though, we get in the car, and head for museum or nature preserve. We have taken a prayer book to water's edge and started our hike with Hebrew words of thanksgiving and praise. So far, we feel, we are getting the spirit of the thing.

Can it hold, however? In the rabbinical wisdom, you must set a standard, or risk a slippery slope. The beach today becomes the amusement park tomorrow, and then the video arcade. If you're in your car anyway, heading back from the museum, you may as well pick up milk, mail a letter, buy shoes. Home on Saturday morning, I sometimes begin to putter about. Why not pull a few weeds, straighten a closet, or—sit kids at the computer and tackle a pile of bills? Soccer season fades to hockey, and then to softball; a year of Saturdays rolls by.

The subjective mental construct collapses, and Sabbath slips from the hand.

One winter morning in the middle of a week I got on a train in Yonkers going north, and I didn't step down until Buffalo. The train rumbled over the frozen bank of the Hudson River. I stared out into the gray river unwinding from its source: St. Lawrence, Great Lakes, Niagara. Here was the watery locus of a hundred years of family history in the Americas, more or less—Toronto, Detroit, New York, with a few scattered outposts, such as Buffalo, along the way. My immigrants followed industry or hunches or others of their tradition to these places, where their names now appear on headstones, chiseled cold.

At Buffalo station a tall sixty-year-old second cousin and his brother-in-law and his father, Sol, waited to meet me. My mother's cousin Sol was almost ninety then, nearly blind. I wanted to see him, I just wanted to see him, and to see his wife, Rita, by then practically deaf.

I hung up my coat. I saw Rita traversing the kitchen in her wheelchair. Once a tall cool walker in tailored skirts, she moved slowly now, pushing back at linoleum floor with heavy feet. Tightly, her hands gripped armrests. On Rita's lap balanced a plate, fused to a yellow stick of butter. This was one of many laborious trips she had made back and forth to get bagels and jam and butter from icebox to table in honor of me.

I saw she had put on lipstick.

"Are you here? Are you really here?" Rita shouted in my ear as I leaned to embrace. Her voice rang loud, gay, moist. Two years had made such a difference.

We brewed tea, toasted bagels. At the table we remained, Rita watching, unable to follow, Sol talking. The son and the son-in-law listened with me, for Sol remembered and still remembers everything, and he told it all in his eerily fresh voice, that of a much younger man.

"We used to spend *Shabbas* with our cousins. We would walk home after dinner, Saturday nights." Sol was remembering boyhood, the 1910s, as the youngest of nine children of immigrants. "It was a good mile and a half, a good walk for little kids. You'd get seven or eight blocks from home, and ask to take the streetcar.

"'Did you see the third star?' Mother would say."

"No, you didn't. Well, that's it. You couldn't do anything until you saw the third star. It could be pouring down rain."

Sabbath, in the rabbis' view, wasn't over for sure until three stars had appeared in the evening sky. Sol's mother was a devout woman. She insisted that her husband wear a beard, and she herself had a *sheytl*, a marriage wig, although "she didn't wear it that often," Sol said with a little smile. She was superstitious too, and regularly consulted gypsies.

"You just had to walk in the rain," said Sol.

"Cream cheese! Just getting a little cream cheese!" This announcement from Rita, suddenly setting wheelchair in motion again. "Yes, indeed! This is how the other half lives!" she called.

"Three stars," Sol mused. "But it didn't do you any harm."

For years of my life Sabbath didn't exist. I was unaware of it from week to week. Friday night was another going-out night, a night for political meetings or German Expressionist films. Saturday was all worldly purpose — errands and chores, laundry, haircuts, a jog in the park — topped off by an evening of special plans. I belonged to the universal Sunday, sleeping late, then waking for newspaper supplements, pleasure excursions, pancake restaurants, or that Jewish twist on Sunday, the bagel-and-lox brunch.

There came a day, though, a Saturday morning years ago. I was already, or so I thought, confirmed in my views and ways. I handed my husband a To Do list. Forget it, he said, "It's *Shabbas*."

This startled me, and it made me laugh, and I let him alone with his coffee and magazines. Saturday rest was a reference point, something that never had left him. His father walked to synagogue every Saturday, and his mother waited at home with a meal prepared the day before. He owned a separate time grid, the ancient lunar calendar, with its periodic soundings and pauses, and this he kept beneath and between his awareness of standard time.

I chortled and let him alone: I shared the reference in a pale, fuzzy way. I did not yet know my husband's parents well, and could not possibly conceive then of an every-Saturday synagogue rhythm like theirs. Indeed, I never thought of it. My Saturdays rarely took me into Jewish precincts. If I happened to see someone walking to shul, I registered it as local color. This had nothing to do with me.

Still, I shared something. When my husband refused to take my errand list that Saturday, I laughed but I liked it, and this stayed with me.

We moved slowly forward, shadowed by the past. We sent our daughter to school to learn what there was to learn. She sang her daily prayers upon rising and "Hear O Israel" before bed, when she was scared of dark things in the night. We lit our Friday night candles; she opened her book and made kiddush, telling of creation and Sabbath, and blessing the wine in an archaic tongue. She sealed and sanctified our dinner with Birkhat ha-Mazon, the after-meal grace, which she knew by heart at seven years old.

And then she asked questions. "If God created the world in six days, when were the dinosaurs?" she asked. And soon, "Does Grandpa keep kosher?" We wanted the questions and even dissent. We tested ritual, made accommodations, accepted inconsistency. We wanted form and content too. We wanted Sabbath, a reference point.

We had a year of candlelit Friday nights at home, and then a second, and then a third. My Fridays grew shorter and shorter, as getting ready for Friday night squeezed work from the day, week after week. One hectic Friday we couldn't go on, so we went out. We went out to dinner on Friday night.

The restaurant, perfectly nice, felt strange. We felt strange in it. We ordered our chow fun noodles, our vegetarian spring rolls, our broccoli, bean curd, and rice. It was relaxing, at the end of a long busy week, to just order, sit back, sip ginger ale and Chinese beer. It was relaxing and strange, and we seemed subdued, watching night fall outside and wondering if it was Shabbas.

I saw people I knew. Acquaintances, friends I don't see much, also were dining out. Fringed paper lanterns trembled above, fish flickered in a tropical tank. It was festive. It was a relief. I won't have to do dishes, I said, justifying. But we were all aware of Friday night. We were here, not home, self-conscious.

Then we heard singing, the next booth over, a young, deep voice. "What?" said my daughter, ginger ale in midair, shy and dying to look. "Can't be." But it was: Birkhat ha-Mazon, the after-meal grace. Two youngish men and their father had set down their chopsticks. One sang, and sang it all, every rich bit of that long blessing, words of appreciation and joy. And why not? Why not live and bring Sabbath with you?

It was dark when we left. We walked home in the dark, under the winter sky. A good eight blocks, and my daughter was singing — Birkhat ha-Mazon. She did not know that the words remind us there is a universe out there, beyond one's own sated contentment. She recited by rote, thanking God for the good Chinese dinner, calling on us to feed the poor, praying for the dawn of peace.

She is still young, but someday — soon — she will understand the words she sang.

The form is hers, and form holds content.

# Fiction

## ⚜ The Weekday Mother and the Sabbath Mother

from *Salvation*

SHOLOM ASCH

When Yechiel was reaching his tenth year even his mother Rivke had to admit what everybody else was already convinced of: her boy was growing up into "a savage." First of all, he had no pleasure in learning things. It was not merely that he was a "dunderhead," and that one had a hard job to make him understand the doctrines of the Talmud and their interpretations; he himself had no wish to learn. Very often he played truant from school, and helped his mother at the market or spent the day in the fields and woods. In general he displayed very early an inclination to plunge into everybody's business but his own.

His brother Issachar, who was three years older, was very different; the "seal of God" was imprinted on his brow, as was but right in a Jewish boy. His face seemed to consist of nothing but eyes and side curls. His lathelike little body was lost in a rep caftan which seemed three times too wide for him. Though only thirteen, he already observed fast days of his own will, and even stuck his nose now and then in Cabbalistic books. The younger brother was considerably taller and broader although he was only ten. His arms and legs were as strong as those of a peasant boy. His face was burned by the sun, roughened and sprinkled with freckles. His walk was a rush. The long tails of his caftan, which was always open, fluttered in the wind, his side curls and his fringes flew out in all directions.

On market days Yechiel would hastily seize the poles and planks that made up his mother's stand and be away with them before she could stop him. In a twinkling he had the stand set up by his own efforts, loaded whole piles of cloth on his back and bore it off to the market place. He not only helped his mother but the other market women too, the clothes dealers and hatmakers. When his father heard of it he rushed out of the House of Study and drove like a whirlwind into the confusion of peasants' wagons. Among the stamping horses and screeching fowls suddenly two fluttering side curls and a disheveled beard bobbed up and a lean body violently drove a way for itself through the crowd.

"This is bad, Rivke! You'll end in Hell if you go on like this, keeping your son from his studies!"

With these words Boruch-Moishe snatched his son away from the stand and with a sudden jerk lifted him on his angular shoulders. Two naked legs and two disheveled curls dangled above his father's shoulders, and Yechiel was borne at quick march to school.

But the mother remained beside her market stand with a bleeding heart. Was not her Boruch-Moishe right? She was keeping her son from the right way by involving him in her profane work!

During the last years Rivke had fallen away sadly. Bearing children had exhausted all her powers, and she was only a shadow of herself. Her skin was lined and seamed, and although she was not yet thirty she looked like an old woman. Her body was nothing but skin and bone, and under her dark headcloth, which sat always askew, a wasted face looked out. Only her figure remained youthful; she was still slender and straight as a tree, with limbs light and graceful as the branches of a water willow.

Of the children that she had borne since Yechiel, three, to her great grief, had not survived. They had had to leave this world prematurely because of sins committed by others. All this grief for her dead children and trouble with her living ones had undermined her health. On top of that there was the worry of her profane traffic in the market. Yet that had to be, she had been created for it; she was a woman and such was her lot. But that was no reason why she should draw her own child into her unhappy fate. Her Yechiel was born for something different; he was a man.

Rivke already saw herself in Hell among serpents and salamanders, damned for eternity. Her Boruch-Moishe sat in Paradise and studied the holy Law, but the footstool at his feet which she strove to deserve by her efforts to earn bread for the family must remain empty. She would not be allowed to set foot in Paradise, for she kept her own child from his studies. So it seemed to Rivke that she had lost both worlds, this world and the next.

When she came home in the evening and with her feeble breath blew to a flame the smoldering fire under the tripod on the hearth, so that she might cook the meager supper, her husband strewed salt on her wounds.

Boruch-Moishe sat at his own table beside the only lamp in the room. Rivke busied herself at the hearth by the light of a burning pine torch. Because of her work at the market the boiled potatoes and cabbage soup were later than usual in coming to table. As Boruch-Moishe had already said the evening prayer, though the supper was not yet served, he was unwilling to begin his evening studies. So as not to sit in idleness he glanced through a little moral book (in which his eldest son immediately followed his example) and employed the opportunity to read his wife a lecture for keeping Yechiel from his lessons. While doing so he rocked in his chair and slowly stroked his thick black beard until every hair was in place. He brought out his rebukes in the Talmud singsong without raising his eyes from the book lying before him, for otherwise his glance might have rested on a woman.

"Our wise men say that there is no more grievous sin than that of keeping children from studying the Law. Any one who keeps children from their studies is to be classed with a man who has committed every sin, or a man who does a murder on Yom Kippur, the Day of Expiation, when it falls on a Sabbath. For it is written: 'It is the voices of children who study the Law that keep the world in existence. So in holding your child from his lessons you are bringing the world to destruction. . . . ' "

Rivke stood at the hearth bending over the pot of potatoes, into which fell tears from her red-lidded eyes inflamed with sun and wind. She softly repeated, "I am bringing the world to destruction — woe is me!"

Yechiel was sitting on the floor going through his Talmud lesson by the light of the torch that burned on his mother's hearth. He had no place reserved for him at the table like his elder brother: that was intended to show the savage that he was not worthy to sit with other people at the table, which served both for study and for eating and in that resembled God's altar.

In spite of his childishness of mind the boy could not reconcile his idea of the divine with evil, punishment, and hellish torments. As he saw it, evil, punishment, and hellish torments had nothing to do with God, but rather with diabolical powers, devils, and all that was bad. What such things were like, his childish imagination could not clearly grasp, but in any case they did not come from God. And whenever he heard something evil ascribed to God he rebelled against the thought in his very soul, as if a personal wrong were being done to him; and he considered it his duty to stick up for God. Without taking time to shut or cover with a cloth the great folio which he held in his hands, he cried across to the table from his place on the floor, "Mother, you won't have to roast in hell! God is a kind Father; he won't let my mother be tortured in Hell!"

"Oh, you're at it next, are you? You dare to disobey me, you dare to contradict me and sin against the commandment to honor your father!"

Boruch-Moishe rose, loosened the leather belt round his waist, seized the savage, and laid him across his knee, "This is what a son gets who doesn't honor his father!"

And Boruch-Moishe laid on with all his might.

But instead of sobbing the savage shouted, "And God won't let my mother roast in Hell!"

"Oh, dear, dear, that I should hear such words! Yechiel, you mustn't set yourself against your father!" The mother burst into tears.

"Don't you be afraid, mother! Don't cry! God is good!"

"You see now!" Boruch-Moishe pushed the savage back to his place on the floor and flung a glance at his wife as if to say that she was to blame for everything.

Although a child, Yechiel had already his own ideas of God. Though he could not picture to himself how God looked, he was firmly convinced of one thing: that God was everywhere and whoever wished could find Him at any time. One had only to ask Him, had only to shut one's eyes, pray humbly and earnestly, and tell oneself: Now I am standing before God. Then one actually stood before Him as before, say, a king. One was afraid of a king; one was not only afraid of God, but loved Him too.

Yechiel knew also that God was to be found always with the Jews in the House of Study, but only once a week in his parents' home. He came on Friday evening at sunset, when the Sabbath candles were lit. But in Yechiel's heart God dwelt always; there He had his dwelling place, and He knew everything that happened in Yechiel, all that Yechiel thought and wished. The boy spoke with Him as with a friend about all that moved him, "Forgive me for having eaten this apple without saying the blessing. The evil one had me in his clutches and I forgot. To make up for it I'll say the blessing twice before I eat this pear; once for the apple I have eaten, and once for the pear."

But Yechiel felt the presence of God most clearly of all during divine service in the little synagogue, when the Jews drew their prayer shawls over their heads and intoned the eighteen petitions, and particularly when the priest pronounced the benediction. During the benediction one was not allowed to look up. But just because it was forbidden, one wished to do it, and let oneself be persuaded by one's evil thoughts: then one could see God hovering over the priest's hands. . . .

The synagogue was stiflingly hot. It was Sabbath, the final prayer was being said. Densely packed, the worshipers stood side by side, their heads enveloped in their prayer shawls, and intoned softly the eighteen petitions. All were sunk in breathless devotion, sighs broke from their lips, and on their faces was a look of ecstasy. Yechiel stood behind his father, with his prayer book in his hand. His heart was full, but he was not praying. This set prayer did not delight him; he wanted to do something for God that nobody else had ever done. God would see that it was different. If God were only to ask him to do something! How gladly he would obey, even if it were to leap into fire!

While he was considering what he could do in God's honor he thought of the tumblers who came every year to the fair. He could not turn a somersault as he had seen them doing; it was the one feat of theirs that he had admired most. But he had learned another trick; he could stand on his hands and remain there until you counted ten. That was the longest he could manage. But for God he could hold out until you counted a hundred, more, two hundred! And he would do it, "Now, dear God, I will show you what I can do for you."

And at the very moment when the whole congregation was waiting with bated breath for the Rabbi to take two steps backward, which was the signal that the prayer was at an end, the savage made a run and stood on his hands behind his father's back.

He stood so, his legs in the air, and murmured, "Count, dear God, count. . . . One, two, three. . . ."

One can imagine what shame Yechiel brought on his father by such and similar exploits. Blows and punishments were of no avail. The savage went on with his tricks. In the middle of the divine service, when the congregation were breathless with devotion, he would stand on his hands or turn a cartwheel; once he actually whistled through his fingers.

When Rivke heard of this she thought she would sink through the floor with shame, and despairingly wrung her hands. Her face streaming with tears, she went over to her son, bowed over him, and sobbed bitterly, "My poor child, why do you bring such shame on me?"

But Yechiel could not tell his mother that he did all this solely for God. Patiently he endured his father's blows, and bravely he swallowed his pain when Boruch-Moishe's thin bony fingers seized his arm like pincers and bored into his flesh until all his limbs trembled. Yechiel did not mind that; the only thing that troubled him was that his mother was so deeply hurt. But he could not spare her that; what he did was for the love of God. And God stood nearer to him than any one else, even his parents; for God, too, knew what Yechiel knew; that he did these strange things not because he himself wished to, but because the evil one goaded him on to do them. He did not want to offend his mother, but to be an obedient son to her; he desired nothing more ardently than to learn diligently and sit perpetually over books like his brother Issachar and be praised by everybody; he did not wish to run off to the market place to help his mother, but he could not look on while she dragged the heavy planks from the shop into the street, he could not endure that she should stand in the market quite by herself.

The father — and the boy knew that — was destined for other things. He had to sit and study in the House of Study. The other life was for his mother; she was a woman and it was her lot. Only a few days before Yechiel had seen his mother compelled to wrestle with a gigantic peasant for a few yards of cloth. Her neck grew tense, her face was dreadful to see, her red-rimmed bloodshot eyes started out of their sockets. With supernatural strength she shouted for help, "Good people! He's robbing me in broad daylight!" Yechiel could never forget the moment when the peasant gave his mother a blow on the chest, so that she rolled into the middle of the street. Everybody saw it. Yechiel had stood by crying.

Since then his respect for his mother had sunk greatly; it seemed to him as if she had been cast out. She was exempt from most of the precepts of religion. She did not need to study the Word. It sufficed for her to follow a very few commandments; with that all her religious obligations were absolved. But in return she had to stand in the market place, haggle and fight with peasants, and earn the family's bread so that the father, Issachar, and Yechiel might go to the school or the House of Study and devote themselves to learning.

But one day in the week his mother stood so high that no one else approached her, not even his father with all his study of the Law and his treasures laid up in the next world. In a clap Yechiel had a quite different mother, and she was the most important and respectworthy figure in the whole house. All week she was an ordinary, everyday mother. But for a few short hours on Friday evening, from the time when the men went to God's house until the moment when, after the prayer in salutation of the Sabbath, they returned again: in that brief span she was completely changed. No, she was not changed; she was transformed into another mother.

To Yechiel it seemed as though he had two mothers: a weekday and a Sabbath mother. The weekday mother was the one with the shabby old wig, whose black satin band, showing at her brow, was turned green with the sun. His weekday mother stood in the market place, haggled with peasants, screamed, scolded, lied. But when Yechiel returned with his father from the House of Study another mother rose to meet him, his Sabbath mother with a silken shawl on her head and wearing a velvet jacket. Her Sabbath wig was like a crown above her festively gleaming brow. Infinite maternal loveliness shone from her face, from her eyes, from her darkly glowing skin. Her neck looked different; it was soft as down, supple and very very smooth, so that it was a pleasure to gaze at, and he felt a longing to bury his face in it. But the Sabbath shone most gloriously of all on his mother's high and noble brow, which gleamed like a sun.

Yet everything else was altered too, the shelves, the table, the whole room. To Yechiel it was as if, while the men were away, some mysterious change had happened to his mother of which the others knew nothing and were permitted to know nothing. While she was reciting the prayer over the Sabbath candles a holy angel must have visited the house and cast the glory of God over her face, over the table and all the room.

He learned to see his mother with different eyes, because she was connected with the divine beauty of the Sabbath. And now he found the explanation for which hitherto he had sought in vain; in reality his mother was a Sabbath mother; it was only during the worldly turmoil of the week, and because the Jewish people were in exile, that she had to endure being transformed into a weekday mother. But when the Messiah came, then there would only be a Sabbath mother forever and ever. . . .

*Translated by Willa and Edwin Muir*

# ◌ Short Friday

ISAAC BASHEVIS SINGER

In the village of Lapschitz lived a tailor named Shmul-Leibele with his wife, Shoshe. Shmul-Leibele was half tailor, half furrier, and a complete pauper. He had never mastered his trade. When filling an order for a jacket or a gaberdine, he inevitably made the garment either too short or too tight. The belt in the back would hang either too high or too low, the lapels never matched, the vent was off center. It was said that he had once sewn a pair of trousers with the fly off to one side. Shmul-Leibele could not count the wealthy citizens among his customers. Common people brought him their shabby garments to have patched and turned, and the peasants gave him their old pelts to reverse. As is usual with bunglers, he was also slow. He would dawdle over a garment for weeks at a time. Yet despite his shortcomings, it must be said that Shmul-Leibele was an honorable man. He used only strong thread and none of his seams ever gave. If one ordered a lining from Shmul-Leibele, even one of common sack-cloth or cotton, he bought only the very best material, and thus lost most of his profit. Unlike other tailors who hoarded every last bit of remaining cloth, he returned all scraps to his customers.

Had it not been for his competent wife, Shmul-Leibele would certainly have starved to death. Shoshe helped him in whatever way she could. On Thursdays she hired herself out to wealthy families to knead dough, and on summer days went off to the forest to gather berries and mushrooms, as well as pinecones and twigs for the stove. In winter she plucked down for brides' featherbeds. She was also a better tailor than her husband, and when he began to sigh, or dally and mumble to himself, an indication that he could no longer muddle through, she would take the chalk from his hand and show him how to continue. Shoshe had no children, but it was common knowledge that it wasn't she who was barren, but rather her husband who was sterile, since all of her sisters had borne children, while his only brother was likewise childless. The townswomen repeatedly urged Shoshe to divorce him, but she turned a deaf ear, for the couple loved one another with a great love.

Shmul-Leibele was small and clumsy. His hands and feet were too large for his body, and his forehead bulged on either side as is common in simpletons. His cheeks, red as apples, were bare of whiskers, and but a few hairs sprouted from his chin. He had scarcely any neck at all; his head sat upon his shoulders like a snowman's. When he walked, he scraped his shoes along the ground so that every step could be heard far away. He hummed continuously and there was always an amiable smile on his face. Both winter and summer he wore the same caftan and sheepskin cap with earlaps. Whenever there was any need for a messenger, it was always Shmul-Leibele who was pressed into service, and however far away he was sent, he always went willingly. The wags saddled him with a variety of nicknames and made him the butt of all sorts of pranks, but he never took offense. When others scolded his tormentors, he would merely observe: "What do I care? Let them have their fun. They're only children, after all. . . ."

Sometimes he would present one or another of the mischief makers with a piece of candy or a nut. This he did without any ulterior motive, but simply out of good-heartedness.

Shoshe towered over him by a head. In her younger days she had been considered a beauty, and in the households where she worked as a servant they spoke highly of her honesty and diligence. Many young men had vied for her hand, but she had selected Shmul-Leibele because he was quiet and because he never joined the other town boys who gathered on the Lublin road at noon Saturdays to flirt with the girls. His piety and retiring nature pleased her. Even as a girl Shoshe had taken pleasure in studying the Pentateuch, in nursing the infirm at the almshouse, in listening to the tales of the old women who sat before their houses darning stockings. She would fast on the last day of each month, the Minor Day of Atonement, and often attended the services at the Women's synagogue. The other servant girls mocked her and thought her old fashioned. Immediately following her wedding she shaved her head and fastened a kerchief firmly over her ears, never permitting a stray strand of hair from her matron's wig to show as did some of the other young women. The bath attendant praised her because she never frolicked at the ritual bath, but performed her ablutions according to the laws. She purchased only indisputably kosher meat, though it was a half cent more per pound, and when she was in doubt about the dietary laws she sought out the rabbi's advice. More than once she had not hesitated to throw out all the food and even to smash the earthen crockery. In short, she was a capable, God-fearing woman, and more than one man envied Shmul-Leibele his jewel of a wife.

Above all of life's blessings the couple revered the Sabbath. Every Friday noon Shmul-Leibele would lay aside his tools and cease all work. He was always among the first at the ritual bath, and he immersed himself in the water four times for the four letters of the Holy Name. He also helped the beadle set the candles in the chandeliers and the candelabra. Shoshe scrimped throughout the week, but on the Sabbath she was lavish. Into the heated oven went cakes, cookies and the Sabbath loaf. In winter, she prepared puddings made of chicken's neck stuffed with dough and rendered fat. In summer she made puddings with rice or noodles, greased with chicken fat and sprinkled with sugar or cinnamon. The main dish consisted of potatoes and buckwheat, or pearl barley with beans, in the midst of which she never failed to set a marrowbone. To insure that the dish would be well cooked, she sealed the oven with loose dough. Shmul-Leibele treasured every mouthful, and at every Sabbath meal he would remark: "Ah, Shoshe love, it's food fit for a king! Nothing less than a taste of Paradise!" to which Shoshe replied, "Eat hearty. May it bring you good health."

Although Shmul-Leibele was a poor scholar, unable to memorize a chapter of the Mishnah, he was well versed in all the laws. He and his wife frequently studied The Good Heart in Yiddish. On half-holidays, holidays, and on each free day, he studied the Bible in Yiddish. He never missed a sermon, and though a pauper, he bought from peddlers all sorts of books of moral instructions and religious tales, which he then read together with his wife. He never wearied of reciting sacred phrases. As soon as he arose in the morning he washed his hands and began to mouth the preamble to the prayers. Then he would walk over to the study house and worship as one of the quorum. Every day he recited a few chapters of the Psalms, as well as those prayers which the less serious tended to skip over. From his father he had inherited a thick prayer book with wooden covers, which contained the rites and laws pertaining to each day of the year. Shmul-Leibele and his wife heeded each and every one of these. Often he would observe to his wife: "I shall surely end up in Gehenna, since there'll be no one on earth to say Kaddish over me." "Bite your tongue, Shmul-Leibele," she would counter, "For one, everything is possible under God. Secondly, you'll live until the Messiah comes. Thirdly, it's just possible that I will die before you and you will marry a young woman who'll bear you a dozen children." When Shoshe said this, Shmul-Leibele would shout: "God forbid! You must remain in good health. I'd rather rot in Gehenna!"

Although Shmul-Leibele and Shoshe relished every Sabbath, their greatest satisfaction came from the Sabbaths in wintertime. Since the day before the Sabbath evening was a short one, and since Shoshe was busy until late Thursday at her work, the couple usually stayed up all of Thursday night. Shoshe kneaded dough in the trough, covering it with cloth and a pillow so that it might ferment. She heated the oven with kindling-wood and dry twigs. The shutters in the room were kept closed, the door shut. The bed and bench-bed remained unmade, for at daybreak the couple would take a nap. As long as it was dark Shoshe prepared the Sabbath meal by the light of a candle. She plucked a chicken or a goose (if she had managed to come by one cheaply), soaked it, salted it and scraped the fat from it. She roasted a liver for Shmul-Leibele over the glowing coals and baked a small Sabbath loaf for him. Occasionally she would inscribe her name upon the loaf with letters of dough, and then Shmul-Leibele would tease her: "Shoshe, I am eating you up. Shoshe, I have already swallowed you." Shmul-Leibele loved warmth, and he would climb up on the oven and from there look down as his spouse cooked, baked, washed, rinsed, pounded and carved. The Sabbath loaf would turn out round and brown. Shoshe braided the loaf so swiftly that it seemed to dance before Shmul-Leibele's eyes. She bustled about efficiently with spatulas, pokers, ladles and goosewing dusters, and at times even snatched up a live coal with her bare fingers. The pots perked and bubbled. Occasionally a drop of soup would spill and the hot tile would hiss and squeal. And all the while the cricket continued its chirping. Although Shmul-Leibele had finished his supper by this time, his appetite would be whetted afresh, and Shoshe would throw him a knish, a chicken gizzard, a cookie, a plum from the plum stew or a chunk of the pot-roast. At the same time she would chide him, saying that he was a glutton. When he attempted to defend himself she would cry: "Oh, the sin is upon me, I have allowed you to starve. . . ."

At dawn they would both lie down in utter exhaustion. But because of their efforts Shoshe would not have to run herself ragged the following day, and she could make the benediction over the candles a quarter of an hour before sunset.

The Friday on which this story took place was the shortest Friday of the year. Outside, the snow had been falling all night and had blanketed the house up to the windows and barricaded the door. As usual, the couple had stayed up until morning, then had lain down to sleep. They had arisen later than usual, for they hadn't heard the rooster's crow, and since the windows were covered with snow and frost, the day seemed as dark as night. After whispering, "I thank Thee," Shmul-Leibele went outside with a broom and shovel to clear a path, after which he took a bucket and fetched water from the well. Then, as he had no pressing work, he decided to lay off for the whole day. He went to the study house for the morning prayers, and after breakfast wended his way to the bathhouse. Because of the cold outside, the patrons kept up an eternal plaint: "A bucket! A bucket!" and the bath attendant poured more and more water over the glowing stones so that the steam grew constantly denser. Shmul-Leibele located a scraggly willow-broom, mounted to the highest bench and whipped himself until his skin glowed red. From the bathhouse, he hurried over to the study house where the beadle had already swept and sprinkled the floor with sand. Shmul-Leibele set the candles and helped spread the tablecloths over the tables. Then he went home again and changed into his Sabbath clothes. His boots, resoled but a few days before, no longer let the wet through. Shoshe had done her washing for the week, and had given him a fresh shirt, underdrawers, a fringed garment, even a clean pair of stockings. She had already performed the benediction over the candles, and the spirit of the Sabbath emanated from every corner of the room. She was wearing her silk kerchief with the silver spangles, a yellow and gray dress, and shoes with gleaming, pointed tips. On her throat hung the chain that Shmul-Leibele's mother, peace be with her, had given her to celebrate the signing of the wedding contract. The marriage band sparkled on her index finger. The candlelight reflected in the window panes, and Shmul-Leibele fancied that there was a duplicate of this room outside and that another Shoshe was out there lighting the Sabbath candles. He yearned to tell his wife how full of grace she was, but there was no time for it, since it is specifically stated in the prayer book that it is fitting and proper to be amongst the first ten worshipers at the synagogue; as it so happened, going off to prayers he was the tenth man to arrive. After the congregation had intoned the Song of Songs, the cantor sang, "Give thanks," and "O come, let us exult." Shmul-Leibele prayed with fervor. The words were sweet upon his tongue, they seemed to fall from his lips with a life of their own, and he felt that they soared to the eastern wall, rose above the embroidered curtain of the Holy Ark, the gilded lions, and the tablets, and floated up to the ceiling with its painting of the twelve constellations. From there, the prayers surely ascended to the Throne of Glory.

The cantor chanted, "Come, my beloved," and Shmul-Leibele trumpeted along in accompaniment. Then came the prayers, and the men recited, "It is our duty to praise . . ." to which Shmul-Leibele added a "Lord of the Universe." Afterwards, he wished everyone a good Sabbath: the rabbi, the ritual slaughterer, the head of the community, the assistant rabbi, everyone present. The cheder lads shouted, "Good Sabbath, Shmul-Leibele," while they mocked him with gestures and grimaces, but Shmul-Leibele answered them all with a smile, even occasionally pinched a boy's cheek affectionately. Then he was off for home. The snow was piled high so that one could barely make out the contours of the roofs, as if the entire settlement had been immersed in white. The sky, which had hung low and overcast all day, now grew clear. From among white clouds a full moon peered down, casting a day-like brilliance over the snow. In the west, the edge of a cloud still held the glint of sunset. The stars on this Friday seemed larger and sharper, and through some miracle Lapschitz seemed to have blended with the sky. Shmul-Leibele's hut, which was situated not far from the synagogue, now hung suspended in space, as it is written: "He suspendeth the earth on nothingness." Shmul-Leibele walked slowly since, according to law, one must not hurry when coming from a holy place. Yet he longed to be home. "Who knows?" he thought. "Perhaps Shoshe has become ill? Maybe she's gone to fetch water and, God forbid, has fallen into the well? Heaven save us, what a lot of troubles can befall a man."

On the threshold he stamped his feet to shake off the snow, then opened the door and saw Shoshe. The room made him think of Paradise. The oven had been freshly whitewashed, the candles in the brass candelabras cast a Sabbath glow. The aromas coming from the sealed oven blended with the scents of the Sabbath supper. Shoshe sat on the bench-bed apparently awaiting him, her cheeks shining with the freshness of a young girl's. Shmul-Leibele wished her a happy Sabbath and she in turn wished him a good year. He began to hum, "Peace upon ye ministering angels . . ." and after he had said his farewells to the invisible angels that accompany each Jew leaving the synagogue, he recited: "The worthy woman." How well he understood the meaning of these words, for he had read them often in Yiddish, and each time refected anew on how aptly they seemed to fit Shoshe.

Shoshe was aware that these holy sentences were being said in her honor, and thought to herself, "Here am I, a simple woman, an orphan, and yet God has chosen to bless me with a devoted husband who praises me in the holy tongue."

Both of them had eaten sparingly during the day so that they would have an appetite for the Sabbath meal. Shmul-Leibele said the benediction over the raisin wine and gave Shoshe the cup so that she might drink. Afterwards, he rinsed his fingers from a tin dipper, then she washed hers, and they both dried their hands with a single towel, each at either end. Shmul-Leibele lifted the Sabbath loaf and cut it with the bread knife, a slice for himself and one for his wife.

He immediately informed her that the loaf was just right, and she countered: "Go on, you say that every Sabbath."

"But it happens to be the truth," he replied.

Although it was hard to obtain fish during the cold weather, Shoshe had purchased three-fourths of a pound of pike from the fishmonger. She had chopped it with onions, added an egg, salt and pepper, and cooked it with carrots and parsley. It took Shmul-Leibele's breath away, and after it he had to drink a tumbler of whiskey. When he began the table chants, Shoshe accompanied him quietly. Then came the chicken soup with noodles and tiny circlets of fat which glowed on the surface like golden ducats. Between the soup and the main course, Shmul-Leibele again sang Sabbath hymns. Since goose was cheap at this time of year, Shoshe gave Shmul-Leibele an extra leg for good measure. After the dessert, Shmul-Leibele washed for the last time and made a benediction. When he came to the words: "Let us not be in need either of the gifts of flesh and blood nor of their loans," he rolled his eyes upward and brandished his fists. He never stopped praying that he be allowed to continue to earn his own livelihood and not, God forbid, become an object of charity.

After grace, he said yet another chapter of the Mishnah, and all sorts of other prayers which were found in his large prayer book. Then he sat down to read the weekly portion of the Pentateuch twice in Hebrew and once in Aramaic.

He enunciated every word and took care to make no mistake in the difficult Aramaic paragraphs of the Onkelos. When he reached the last section, he began to yawn and tears gathered in his eyes. Utter exhaustion overcame him. He could barely keep his eyes open and between one passage and the next he dozed off for a second or two. When Shoshe noticed this, she made up the bench-bed for him and prepared her own featherbed with clean sheets. Shmul-Leibele barely managed to say the retiring prayers and began to undress. When he was already lying on his bench-bed he said: "A good Sabbath, my pious wife. I am very tired . . ." and turning to the wall, he promptly began to snore.

Shoshe sat a while longer gazing at the Sabbath candles which had already begun to smoke and fliicker. Before getting into bed, she placed a pitcher of water and a basin at Shmul-Leibele's bedstead so that he would not rise the following morning without water to wash with. Then she, too, lay down and fell asleep.

They had slept an hour or two or possibly three — what does it matter, actually? — when suddenly Shoshe heard Shmul-Leibele's voice. He waked her and whispered her name. She opened one eye and asked, "What is it?"

"Are you clean?" he mumbled.

She thought for a moment and replied, "Yes."

He rose and came to her. Presently he was in bed with her. A desire for her flesh had roused him. His heart pounded rapidly, the blood coursed in his veins. He felt a pressure in his loins. His urge was to mate with her immediately, but he remembered the law which admonished a man not to copulate with a woman until he had first spoken affectionately to her, and he now began to speak of his love for her and how this mating could possibly result in a male-child.

"And a girl you wouldn't accept?" Shoshe chided him, and he replied, "Whatever God deigns to bestow would be welcome."

"I fear this privilege isn't mine anymore," she said with a sigh.

"Why not?" he demanded. "Our mother Sarah was far older than you."

"How can one compare oneself to Sarah? Far better you divorce me and marry another."

He interrupted her, stopping her mouth with his hand. "Were I sure that I could sire the twelve tribes of Israel with another, I still would not leave you. I cannot even imagine myself with another woman. You are the jewel of my crown."

"And what if I were to die?" she asked.

"God forbid! I would simply perish from sorrow. They would bury us both on the same day."

"Don't speak blasphemy. May you outlive my bones. You are a man. You would find somebody else. But what would I do without you?"

He wanted to answer her, but she sealed his lips with a kiss. He went to her then. He loved her body. Each time she gave herself to him, the wonder of it astonished him anew. How was it possible, he would think, that he, Shmul-Leibele, should have such a treasure all to himself? He knew the law, one dared not surrender to lust for pleasure. But somewhere in a sacred book he had read that it was permissible to kiss and embrace a wife to whom one had been wed according to the laws of Moses and Israel, and he now caressed her face, her throat and her breasts. She warned him that this was frivolity. He replied, "So I'll lie on the torture rack. The great saints also loved their wives." Nevertheless, he promised himself to attend the ritual bath the following morning, to intone psalms and to pledge a sum to charity. Since she loved him also and enjoyed his caresses, she let him do his will.

After he had satiated his desire, he wanted to return to his own bed, but a heavy sleepiness came over him. He felt a pain in his temples.

Shoshe's head ached as well. She suddenly said, "I'm afraid something is burning in the oven. Maybe I should open the flue?"

"Go on, you're imagining it," he replied. "It'll become too cold in here."

And so complete was his weariness that he fell asleep, as did she.

That night Shmul-Leibele suffered an eerie dream. He imagined that he had passed away. The Burial-Society brethren came by, picked him up, lit candles by his head, opened the windows, intoned the prayer to justify God's ordainment. Afterwards, they washed him on the ablution board, carried him on a stretcher to the cemetery. There they buried him as the gravedigger said Kaddish over his body.

"That's odd," he thought, "I hear nothing of Shoshe lamenting or begging forgiveness. Is it possible that she would so quickly grow unfaithful? Or has she, God forbid, been overcome by grief?"

He wanted to call her name, but he was unable to. He tried to tear free of the grave, but his limbs were powerless. All of a sudden he awoke.

"What a horrible nightmare!" he thought. "I hope I come out of it all right."

At that moment Shoshe also awoke. When he related his dream to her, she did not speak for a while. Then she said, "Woe is me. I had the very same dream."

"Really? You too?" asked Shmul-Leibele, now frightened. "This I don't like."

He tried to sit up, but he could not. It was as if he had been shorn of all his strength. He looked towards the window to see if it were day already, but there was no window visible, nor any windowpane. Darkness loomed everywhere. He cocked his ears. Usually he would be able to hear the chirping of a cricket, the scurrying of a mouse, but this time only a dead silence prevailed. He wanted to reach out to Shoshe, but his hand seemed lifeless.

"Shoshe," he said quietly, "I've grown paralyzed."

"Woe is me, so have I," she said. "I cannot move a limb."

They lay there for a long while, silently, feeling their numbness. Then Shoshe spoke: "I fear that we are already in our graves for good."

"I'm afraid you're right," Shmul-Leibele replied in a voice that was not of the living.

"Pity me, when did it happen? How?" Shoshe asked. "After all, we went to sleep hale and hearty."

"We must have been asphyxiated by the fumes from the stove," Shmul-Leibele said.

"But I said I wanted to open the flue."

"Well, it's too late for that now."

"God have mercy upon us, what do we do now? We were still young people . . ."

"It's no use. Apparently it was fated."

"Why? We arranged a proper Sabbath. I prepared such a tasty meal. An entire chicken neck and tripe."

"We have no further need of food."

Shoshe did not immediately reply. She was trying to sense her own entrails. No, she felt no appetite. Not even for a chicken neck and tripe. She wanted to weep, but she could not.

"Shmul-Leibele, they've buried us already. It's all over."

"Yes, Shoshe, praised be the true Judge! We are in God's hands."

"Will you be able to recite the passage attributed to your name before the Angel Dumah?"

"Yes."

"It's good that we are lying side by side," she muttered.

"Yes, Shoshe," he said, recalling a verse: *Lovely and pleasant in their lives, and in their death they were not divided.*

"And what will become of our hut? You did not even leave a will."

"It will undoubtedly go to your sister."

Shoshe wished to ask something else, but she was ashamed. She was curious about the Sabbath meal. Had it been removed from the oven? Who had eaten it? But she felt that such a query would not be fitting of a corpse. She was no longer Shoshe the dough-kneader, but a pure, shrouded corpse with shards covering her eyes, a cowl over her head, and myrtle twigs between her fingers. The Angel Dumah would appear at any moment with his fiery staff, and she would have to be ready to give an account of herself.

Yes, the brief years of turmoil and temptation had come to an end. Shmul-Leibele and Shoshe had reached the true world. Man and wife grew silent. In the stillness they heard the flapping of wings, a quiet singing. An angel of God had come to guide Shmul-Leibele the tailor and his wife, Shoshe, into Paradise.

*Translated by Joseph Singer and Roger Klein*

# ❧ from Missing

MICHELLE HERMAN

"Myraleh, tell me please, what day is today?"

"Today is Friday, Mama."

"Friday." This was a surprise. "And how is it Friday already?"

"*How* is it Friday, Mama? Like always."

"But so fast," Rivke said. "I don't know where the week goes. The days run away."

"Time flies," Myra agreed.

"But if it's Friday already" — Rivke spoke mainly to herself, muttering — "I have to then make *shabes*. This it's hard to believe I forgot."

"Oh, Ma," Myra said, "why don't you just skip it for once?"

"Skip *shabes*?" Rivke chuckled. "I don't think this is possible. Once a week comes *shabes*. About this a person doesn't have a choice."

"What I *mean*" — Myra's impatience was plain — "is skip the preparation. It's too much for you, it tires you out."

"*Ach*," Rivke said. "Too much for me it isn't." This wasn't true. For some time she had felt that it really was too much for her. It was only for *shabes* that she cooked; the rest of the week she ate cold cereal, fruit, pot cheese, crackers. For supper she might boil an egg or heat canned soup; for lunch she nibbled lettuce leaves, or salted and ate a good tomato if she happened to have one — it was enough for her. But on Fridays she had to gather all her strength to cook a chicken, steam a potful of rice, make a *tsimes* if someone had remembered during the week to bring her sweet potatoes and carrots — a box of prunes she always had — and peel and chop vegetables for soup. "*Shabes* is *shabes*," she told Myra. "For this I have no choice but to prepare."

"But if just once you *didn't* make *shabes*, would it be the end of the world?"

"The end of the world, no. But if somebody comes, there has to be to eat."

"If someone *comes*," Myra said — oh, she was irritated, Rivke could tell by the way she stretched out "comes" into two parts, as if she were singing: *cah-ums* — "somebody can go down" — *dow-un*, more singing — "and on Brighton Beach Avenue pick up a take-out chicken from Fechter's."

"Myra," Rivke said, "please. For what do I need a take-out chicken?

I can take out of the freezer right now my own chicken to cook and you know yourself it will taste better than from Fechter's."

She expected to hear, "You're right, Mama," but Myra said, "First of all, a chicken's not going to defrost in time for you to cook it before *shabes* — you should have taken it out last night. And *second* of all, who are you expecting to come, anyway? Last week you were angry, you said a whole chicken and a pot of cabbage soup went to waste because no one came. 'I can't eat so much,' you told me. 'How can I eat so much?' If you don't cook so much, you won't waste so much."

"But tomorrow someone might come."

"*Who?*"

"Who? I don't know who. I have five children."

"I know, Ma, but . . ." But she stopped, and after a pause long enough to make Rivke wonder what she had planned to say, all that finally emerged was, "I just hate to see you tire yourself with cooking."

"Oh, tire, shmire," Rivke said and hoped for a laugh.

Myra instead sighed. "I'll tell you what, Ma. Why don't you do whatever you want to do."

"Ah, what I want to do! This would be nice, if I could do what I want to do. I'd go dancing, I'd take a trip someplace." Still no laugh. "I'm joking, *mamaleh*," she said gently. "This was a joke, you understand. Where would I go for a trip?" Myra kept silent. Rivke, with a sigh of her own, said, "*Tokhter?*, will you tell me something? If today is Friday, then what is the number — the date?"

"The fifteenth," Myra said, and added after a second, "of March."

"Of March I know," Rivke said. "By you, I don't know what month is this?" She was startled herself by how angry she sounded.

"Well, I'm sorry, Mama, but —"

"When comes the day that I can't tell you what is the month, this is when you'll know it's finished with me. All right?"

"Oh, Ma, listen —"

"It wouldn't hurt you, Myra — would it hurt you? — to say, 'All right, Mama'?"

"All right, Mama," said Myra.

Rivke took a moment to collect herself — she didn't like this, for such a feeling to come to her so quickly — and only when she was once again able to speak pleasantly did she say what she wanted to say. "So if it's already the fifteenth of March, then I'm thinking that *peysekh* is coming soon, yes?"

"Yes, that's right — in three weeks — and it's a good thing you reminded me because I needed to talk to you about that. Last night Rachel called to ask me what we're doing this year for the holiday."

"Yes? And what did you say?"

"That's what I wanted to talk about. She asked me if I'd make a seder — well, not really a seder, but a big dinner, like a turkey dinner maybe, you know, like you used to do when she and Mark were too little to sit still for a seder? But I don't know, it seems like such a lot of work for just the four of us — because it would be only you and me and Harry and Rachel; Mark I think is planning to go to the first-night seder at his in-laws'. So I just don't know. What do you think?"

"It's Papa's birthday, *peysekh*."

"I know that, Ma. Rachel knows too, that's why she was concerned. Naturally we don't want you to be alone for this. That's the reason I'm asking you what you want to do. We'll do something, this much I promise. I'm just not sure what, exactly. But I don't want you to worry about it."

"Worried I'm not," Rivke said. "What happens will happen. To tell you the truth, where I was last year for *peysekh* I don't even remember."

"Last year you were with Amos and Frances. You don't remember? You spent the whole week with them."

"Oh, yes, I remember now." In fact she didn't — she had no memory of this at all — but she could see that today was not a good day to tell Myra something like this; she would leap on it right away as evidence of her feebleness. Besides, Rivke told herself, it was likely that if she thought about it later, when she could concentrate, the memory would come to her. In the meantime, before Myra could ask her any questions, she said, "You know, Myraleh, for a seder I don't have so much strength any-more —"

"Oh, Ma," Myra interrupted, "no one expects you to make a seder, for God's sake. You haven't made a seder for — for I don't know how long."

"I wasn't thinking I was going to make a seder," Rivke said mildly. "Old I am, crazy I'm not. I was only going to say that while a seder is one thing, Papa's birthday is something else."

"Ma — I told you. You won't be alone."

"Oh, alone." She pronounced the word with distaste. "I'm always alone."

"You're not always alone."

"Visits are visits," Rivke said, "and alone is alone. I feel alone."

To this Myra seemed to have nothing to say, and Rivke after a moment went on, "Do you know what I sometimes think? I sometimes think that if Papa had known what was in store for me, he wouldn't have left me."

"Oh, Ma. To have these kinds of—"

"Listen, Myraleh, I'm telling you something. Papa must have thought: She'll be all right; I can go. He left me so fast I didn't have time to tell him he was wrong. If there had been time to talk, I would have said, 'Sol, you're making a mistake.' But he should have known himself that this was a mistake."

"Mama," Myra said, "be reasonable."

"Reasonable." Rivke considered this. "What's reasonable? Is it to you reasonable that we're talking now about making a celebration of Papa's birthday without Papa?"

"Oh, no, Ma, this is up to you. If you'd rather not celebrate Papa's birthday, all you have to do is tell me."

"This is not the point," Rivke said.

"Tell me what's the point, then, Mama."

Rivke was silent, thinking. Why should it be, she wondered, that what was obvious to her was never obvious to her children? There were some things that could not be said: things for which words were not enough— would never be enough, no matter how many words one strung together. One had to know.

For a little while she remained silent, listening to Myra's silence—an aggravated, quick-breathing silence—at the other end of the line. Finally she said, "Do you remember, Myra, the song, a yidisheh song, *Vos Geven iz Geven un Nishto?*"

"I don't think I ever knew it."

"*Vos geven iz geven un nishto,*" Rivke sang—not well; she had some difficulty remembering the melody. "What was, was, and isn't anymore," she translated. "This is what the song says."

"A sad song," Myra said. But it seemed to Rivke that she spoke reluctantly.

"That's right, it's a sad song. *Vos geven iz geven*: everything that once was is now gone."

"Ma—not everything is gone."

"Ah, this is true," Rivke said. "It's true: I'm still here. Old, but here. Right?" She coughed out a short laugh and didn't wait for a response. "But I'll tell you what, *mamaleh.* I'm here, and I'm also not here. Most of me is already gone, most of what I was. This is what happens. You'll see it yourself. The years go by; time takes away. Time takes away, and what does it give back?" Rivke paused; she laughed—but as she laughed it dawned on her suddenly that she was exhausted; she was so thoroughly tired she wasn't sure she could continue the conversation for even a minute longer. "It gives back nothing," she said. And then: "Myraleh, I think I need now to go lie down. We'll talk tomorrow in the morning."

"Mama, are you okay?"

"Okay, yes. Don't get scared. I just got tired all of a sudden. Now I'm going to take a nap, I think. Or maybe I'll go in the bath."

"A bath is a good idea, Ma, a bath is very restful. But promise me that if you take a bath you'll be careful getting in and out."

"Careful I am always."

Yes, a bath *was* a good idea, she thought as she hung up the phone. It was just what she needed; for she was not only tired, she also had a bad feeling in her that she could not explain and wanted to be rid of, and a nap couldn't be relied on for that — a nap might even sink the feeling deeper into her — while a good hot bath might float it away.

She had always liked a bath. She would take a bath every day — twice a day, even — if it were only not so difficult for her to get out of the tub when she was through. Even so she managed it three, sometimes four times a week. She had devised, over the years, a method for getting herself out of the bath which — though it took forever — was safe and had never yet failed her. First she would grasp with her left hand the soap dish that was cemented into the wall over the tub, at the same time pushing with her right hand on the edge of the tub itself. Then, proceeding slowly and resting often, she would bring herself up into a crouch (much patience was required for this, for sometimes the process took twenty minutes or more: she would reach the necessary position and her ankles would tremble so that she would have to drop forward in the tub to her knees, remain there for a moment to collect her strength, then try again, pushing backwards until she was on her feet once more — and then her ankles would again give way and she would return to her knees, pause again for a rest, rock back to her feet, and so on — over and over again). When finally she was planted firmly on the balls of her feet, the next step was to turn herself around (as she did this she imagined that she looked like a great pink frog) to face, squatting, the back of the tub. Then came the hardest part. With first her left hand and then her right she had to reach for the towel bar above the toilet, which stood just beside the tub. To manage this took at least a dozen attempts. But once she had grabbed hold of it, she could use the towel bar to pull herself up until she was half-standing; and from there it wasn't so difficult — one hand pulling on the towel bar, the other pushing on the toilet — to stand up altogether. All that was needed now was to keep hold of the towel bar and concentrate on balancing on one leg as she raised the other over the side of the tub—then she was finished.

It was a pity, she thought, that no one would ever see how well she could accomplish such a trick at her age. The only person who had ever seen her do this, of course, was Sol. For a long time he had hoisted her up and out of the tub when she was through with her bath, but when he began to grow too weak and unsteady himself, she had had to work out her own system. He used to come in to watch—he came running when he heard the water gurgling as it started to drain from the tub—and though she wouldn't let him help (that would be the end of both of them, she thought, if he fell down while tugging on her), she didn't mind if he watched from the doorway. He kept quiet, watching with his arms folded and his expression serious—he knew enough not to distract her with talk until she was safely out of the tub—and when she was out, and stood dripping in the center of the bathroom trying to catch her breath and waiting for her heart to slow down, he would shake his head and murmur, "Acrobat."

She was already in the bathroom and had begun to draw her bath when she remembered the chicken she had meant to thaw. Returning to the kitchen, she told herself—repeating it out loud several times—that she mustn't forget the water running in the bathtub. One afternoon not long ago she had started a bath and when the telephone rang forgot about it; the Russian lady downstairs had come up screaming in her Cossack language—Rivke had been badly frightened by her—and it was not until the woman, still scolding and carrying on, had pushed past her and run into the bathroom to shut off the water herself that Rivke understood that she had flooded the bathroom below hers.

In the kitchen she stuck her head in the freezer and surveyed what was there: two chickens left of the four that Myra had bought the last time she'd shopped for her. She looked from one to the other and finally took the smaller one from the freezer and set it on the countertop to thaw. Maybe it would, she thought, and maybe it wouldn't. If it didn't, she could always hold it under hot water to finish the job. She calculated how much time it would take to cut it in pieces and boil it; then she opened the broom closet and looked behind the door at the calendar she kept tacked up there—she had to look for a long time before she could read the small print to see what time she was supposed to bentsh candles tonight. Another rapid calculation, and she determined that if the chicken was still icy at four o'clock she would try, with a little hot water, to help it along.

Oh, but what a difference from how preparing for shabes used to be.

She would be cooking from six o'clock in the morning—not just a boiled chicken and a soup with carrots and onions and celery, plain rice, the simplest *tsimes*; but roast chicken and soup with *kneydlekh*, an elaborate *tsimes* like no one else could make, *kishke* and stuffed cabbage, chopped liver, noodle *kugl*, *gefilte* fish and the hot homemade mustard Sol liked with it, plus horseradish with beets mixed in for the children . . . and also sponge cake, pound cake, or honey cake, and the little chocolate cookies Myra loved, which she, Myra, had herself invented and each week helped Rivke to make: cookies made from plain sugared dough mixed with U-Bet syrup. And, in between the cooking, cleaning, so that everything should be nice for *shabes*. By the time the sun had set she would be ready to collapse—all day she had worked without pause. This was how preparing for *shabes* used to be.

*Used to be, used to be,* she mocked herself, looking at the frozen chicken already dripping pinkish water from the seams of its cellophane wrapping. *Still knocking on the same pot, Rivke. Used to be!* How many years, after all, had it been since this "used to be"? Many years—so many it was a miracle she could remember so well what had been, when she couldn't count on herself to remember for half an hour that she had left the water running in the bathtub. *Shabes* even before she had lost Sol had for many years not been *shabes* anymore, not what it was when she still had the children. When had she last worked a whole day *makhn shabes*? Twenty-five years ago at least—when Rachel was small and she was the one to help with the chocolate cookies, and Mark was only a baby: when Myra and her family were still living in Brighton, only two blocks away in a building facing the ocean, before they found a bigger apartment to move to on Homecrest Avenue, the one they lived in for—how long?—four years? five years?—before they moved away from Brooklyn altogether. When they moved to the new apartment that was farther away, Rivke understood. She knew that it was necessary for them to move—they were too crowded in the three rooms they had here; they were living as Rivke and Sol had lived: Myra and her husband sleeping on a Castro in the living room, the two children together in the bedroom. In the new apartment the children would have their own room, Myra and Harry theirs. This was as it should be, and Rivke told her daughter she was glad in her heart that she would have what Rivke had not—a room of her own to share with her husband, privacy, a door to close for a moment to have some quiet. Still, once the move was made, Rivke suffered. In her apartment it was too quiet without Myra coming in and out all day long, dropping off the children for an hour or for the afternoon; and she didn't know what to do with the days she used to spend with the children at Myra's, now that Harry no longer called to say, "Ma, can you come over this morning?" — or this evening or this afternoon — or to ask her to pick Rachel up from school or come by to give her lunch. After they moved to Homecrest Avenue, she told him again and again that she would take the bus to their new apartment, she didn't mind; she would still come and stay with the children anytime. But her son-in-law said, "We appreciate it, Ma, it's good to know, but it isn't necessary."

How was it not necessary? What was the difference? It was so much trouble to ride a bus? She told Harry, "It's no trouble for me to come to you by bus." But no, he said, it wasn't "necessary." And before they had moved, Rivke had spent entire days in their apartment, looking after the children; and for whole days the children were with *her* — often they stayed overnight. She was used to the children, and especially she was used to Rachel; from the first day that Myra had brought her home from the hospital Rivke had spent hours with the child — it was possible that she had spent more time with her in those years before the move than Myra had! She was so used to Rachel trailing around after her, hanging on to her nightgown, her housedress, her apron, asking questions, telling her long stories without taking a breath, demanding that she guess the answer to riddles, that after the child had moved with her parents and brother to the new apartment Rivke felt that a piece of her own self had been torn away. It was terrible to be separated from the child — it was worse than she had guessed. She missed her so badly sometimes that — hiding it from Sol, who did not approve of her mourning the move — she wept over it. She spent whole days remembering things Rachel had said or done; she sat for hours at a time daydreaming about the child's infancy, when she had been left with Rivke sometimes from morning till night: Rivke could see herself as she had been then, standing at the stove stirring soup with the tiny Rachel slung over her shoulder asleep.

Even when Myra came with the children on the bus to visit, it wasn't the same. And even though for a long time she came nearly every Friday night for dinner, these *shabes* meals weren't what they had been. These were visits, something different from before. Even the children knew that something had changed, and behaved differently themselves; they were polite, they sat on the couch with their ankles crossed instead of running around as they used to. Oh, little by little things changed. The years passed — and then more years passed — and suddenly she and Sol were alone more often than not, for *shabes* and otherwise. *This is life*, Rivke would tell herself on those Friday nights that she and Sol sat down to eat their *shabes* dinner alone. *Di tsayt ken alts ibermakhn* — with time everything changes. One doesn't stay busy with children forever.

And now look — look how busy: running to go lie in the bathtub. This was her preparation for *shabes*. Nothing to do but sit in the bath — and the only food in sight the yellow rock of a chicken making puddles on the counter. She gazed at it with displeasure. An ugly thing. With longing she remembered the chickens of earlier days: it used to be she could buy a fresh-killed chicken around the corner and take it home to pluck its feathers herself — and, while it was in the oven, boil the feet for Myra, who loved them, and the *pupik* for Reuben, the neck for Amos; the liver she would put under the broiler for a few minutes for Lazar; and the little pack of yolks that hadn't yet become eggs, which she had removed from inside the hen before roasting it, this was for Sammy. Everyone was happy then. And the chicken itself, when it came out of the oven, was delicious. But these chickens — today's chickens, which Myra bought for her from one of the few kosher butchers left in the neighborhood (did the Russians care about kosher? — ha) and brought home to wrap in plastic and put in the freezer — these chickens had no flavor. Not to mention no feet, no sack of eggs hidden within (Myra as a child had called them "baby eggs"), and a pathetic long-dead look and feel to them that sickened her. This chicken on the counter didn't even look to her like food. This was a rock, not a chicken. And — she realized this suddenly as she stood looking at it — this rock would never thaw out in time to be cooked before *shabes*. Hot water or no, it wouldn't be ready in time. It couldn't possibly be. She was surprised at herself for not realizing this before. Where was her head? she wondered. Then she realized something else, which surprised her even more. She didn't care one way or the other if it *didn't* thaw out in time. What if she couldn't cook the chicken today? If someone came, child or grandchild, tonight or tomorrow, he could go down to Fechter's and buy an already cooked chicken.

"So, is this such a problem?" she said, speaking directly to the frozen chicken. She shrugged. "Not such a problem, no." And, after a minute, added in a whisper that was almost a growl, "So — then . . . the hell with it."

This was the biggest surprise of all, hearing what had come out of her mouth. She stood, blinking, in the kitchen, completely astonished at herself.

# Rosh Hashanah

## The Honey of Promises

# 🌺 Introduction

*The LORD spoke to Moses, saying: Speak to the Israelite people thus: In the seventh month, on the first day of the month, you shall observe complete rest, a sacred occasion commemorated with loud blasts. You shall not work at your occupations; and you shall bring an offering of fire to the LORD.*
—Leviticus 23.23–25

Rosh Hashanah, literally the "head of the year," is the Jewish New Year. It occurs on the first day of the month of *Tishri* and begins a ten-day period of prayer and introspection culminating with Yom Kippur, the Day of Atonement. Although distinct holidays, the two are generally referred to as the "High Holidays," and the ten-day period that includes both is known as *Yamim Nora'im*, the Days of Awe, or *Aseret Yemei Teshuvah*, Ten Days of Repentance.

Rosh Hashanah and Yom Kippur differ in several significant ways from most other annual Jewish holidays. Neither has its origin in an agricultural festival; neither marks a major event in Jewish history. Rather than home celebrations, both are primarily synagogue-based holidays. For the great majority of Jews, observing Rosh Hashanah and Yom Kippur means attending worship services. And while other holidays are joyful, often exuberant, Rosh Hashanah and Yom Kippur are more somber and contemplative, characterized by reflection, prayer, and penitence.

The origins of Rosh Hashanah can be traced to the Torah (the Five Books of Moses), the source for all "major" Jewish holidays. Although there is no specific mention of a "New Year" celebration, the Torah does proclaim — as the passage above indicates — that the first day of the seventh month is to be a special day, "a sacred occasion commemorated by loud blasts." As there is no reference to the "head of the year," many scholars believe this passage indicates that the first of *Tishri*, at the time the Torah was written, was nothing more than an especially notable new moon festival. (The shofar, or ram's horn, was traditionally blown on the occasion of the new moon.) Nevertheless, in time, the first of *Tishri* was designated as the festival of the New Year. Some historians believe this came about as a result of the significance the number seven held in ancient times. Most agree that other major holidays were also designated at various times as the New Year, and it may be that *Tishri* 1 was eventually chosen as the "head of the year" precisely because it had no other historical association. It is clear, however, that, by the time of the Second Temple (c. 350 B.C.E.), the official Jewish New Year was celebrated on *Tishri* 1 and that most of the religious and cultural features that characterize the holiday today were in place.

According to tradition, Rosh Hashanah not only celebrates the arrival of the New Year, but commemorates the creation of the universe as well. Yet Judaism teaches that creation is an ongoing process, with God continually renewing his work. This concept of re-creation, central to the spirit and practice of Rosh Hashanah, takes place not only within nature, but also within each individual. Rosh Hashanah, therefore, affords an opportunity for personal reflection, as well as for self-improvement and self-renewal. This process of repentance — called *teshuvah*, literally "turning" — is central to the ethical and moral theme of both Rosh Hashanah and Yom Kippur. It is every person's annual opportunity for "re-creation," the Jewish method of transformation and purification, of rejecting past transgressions, and for "turning" toward God and one's better self.

An important aspect of the holiday observance, one that is commensurate with the mood and purpose of Rosh Hashanah, is the ceremony of *tashlich*, the subject of several of the literary selections included in this section. According to custom, members of the congregation leave the synagogue on the afternoon of the holiday in order to "cast off" (*ve-tashlich*) their sins by throwing bread crumbs (in some cases, sticks or stones) into a nearby body of water. This ritual, which has been traced back as far as the tenth century, derives from the prophet Micah: "And You will hurl all our sins / Into the depths of the sea" (7.19), and symbolically represents the discarding of the sins of the past year.

The practice of *tashlich* is recalled in detail and with fondness by Bella Chagall in the excerpt reprinted here from her memoir, *Burning Lights*. It also forms the imaginative background for Isaac Bashevis Singer's short story and the point of departure for other, less obvious themes in the poems by Gerald Stern and Marge Piercy, included in this section. For Singer, the occasion of *tashlich* provides his young protagonist with the promise of new romance. For both Stern and Piercy, *tashlich* is an opportunity for self-reflection and for reviewing past (often difficult) memories. "This was a painful year," Stern recalls, "a painful / two years." But Rosh Hashanah, Stern understands, is not a time to obsess over past events, but to give thanks for the present. "It is a joy to be here," his poem concludes, "not just living / in terror, sleeping again, and breathing." Similarly, Piercy's poem relates personal events and emotions, private envies and betrayals. Although old resentments linger, the narrator must — as her grandmother instructed her — "carry crumbs to the water / and cast them out" in order to begin the new year refreshed and cleansed.

Introspection, a sense of gratitude, the importance of Rosh Hashanah rituals and traditions, are all themes the reader will discover in the selections reprinted here. Like Chagall, Chaim Grade, in the excerpt from his autobiography, *My Mother's Sabbath Days*, describes holiday observance in eastern Europe at the beginning of the twentieth century, while the Chilean writer Marjorie Agosín (*The Alphabet in My Hands*) recalls a Rosh Hashanah celebrated in spring rather than fall. Very different in tone and subject is Elie Wiesel's haunting memoir of life in Auschwitz. In the selection included here from *Night*, Wiesel recounts his fellow inmates' desperate efforts ("their faces stricken") to observe the holiday under the most extreme circumstances. The contrast between the idyllic memories of Grade and Chagall and those of Wiesel could not be more dramatic and only serves to emphasize the horror of the Holocaust and the enormity of all that was destroyed.

Although he was not a witness to Nazi atrocities, Harvey Shapiro, in his poem "For Paul Celan and Primo Levi," invokes the memory of two Holocaust survivors — both writers, both victims of suicide. Here, as in the passage reprinted from *Night*, Rosh Hashanah ironically becomes the occasion not for hope but for doubt and denial. The implication for both Wiesel and Shapiro is clear: in the face of the Holocaust, how can there be forgiveness, hope, or the possibility of *teshuvah*, knowing what one knows of history?

Most of the poems in this section, however — from Solomon Ibn Gabirol's eleventh-century "For New Year's Day" to those of several late-twentieth-century American poets — express reverence for God and optimism for the New Year. Those of Gabirol, Penina Moise, and Emma Lazarus, for example, are replete with praise for — in Moise's words — "the God of right," and acknowledge the traditional Rosh Hashanah motifs of hope and renewal. Lazarus also makes a logical case for the observance of Rosh Hashanah in autumn "when orchards burn their lamps of fiery gold." Far less attractive is the other New Year celebration that occurs "while the snow-shroud round dead earth is rolled."

Like much of the literature in this volume, many of the selections here express the idea of connectedness — the inevitable bond experienced by a people who have shared a long and cherished history. In the case of Shapiro, there is an identification with the victims of the Holocaust; for

Lazarus it is a connection to all Jews who have survived in spite of their "supreme suffering"; for Adrienne Rich, John Hollander, and Richard Chess it is an attachment to and an embracing of all Jewish history. "Our memory must be long," declares Rich in her poem "At the Jewish New Year," and for five thousand years the New Year has signaled a time for Jews to recall their collective past. Chess too, in his poem "The Eve of Rosh Hashanah, 500 Years After the Inquisition," sees a connection to the past and value in keeping that link alive. Hollander expresses similar thoughts of remembrance and attachment in his poem "At the New Year." For him, teshuvah is a continuous, existential process ("every single instance begins another year"), one that is essential to his humanity. And like Stern, Rich, Chess, and the medieval poet Gabirol, Hollander concludes his poem with an expression of gratitude for the gift of life and the ability to begin anew: ". . . as we go / Quietly on with what we shall be doing, and sing / Thanks for being enabled, again, to begin this instant."

The stories of both Joseph Opatoshu and Meyer Levin offer variations on the Rosh Hashana themes of renewal and return. Both share as background and setting for the world of Hasidism — the religious movement begun in eastern Europe in the eighteenth century. Opatoshu's nineteenth-century tale tells the story of a disciple of the famed Rabbi Nachman of Bratslav, the great-grandson of the founder of the Hasidic movement; whereas Levin's twentieth-century retelling of another Hasidic story has as its focus the founder himself, Rabbi Israel, the Baal Shem Tov. Serious in tone, both demonstrate the importance of spiritual transcendence, especially at the New Year. Abraham Reisen's "The Poor Community," on the other hand, reveals a different side of the spirit of Rosh Hashanah, one that is not without its humourous aspects. Set in the shtetl of nineteenth-century Europe, the story chronicles the tribulations of a community lacking sufficient funds or resources to conduct a proper New Year service. Among other problems (the town is without both its traditional shofar blower and its Torah reader), the village's shofar is deteriorating and will surely not withstand the rigorous blowing required on the holiday. The debate among the congregation is both comical and revealing, and the solution — while not ideal — satisfies the basic tenets of the Jewish community, namely that a service will take place and no one will be obliged to pray alone.

This basic concept of togetherness, each individual's connection to and responsibility for every other individual, is echoed in one form or another in all the selections in this section. Rosh Hashanah, as the reader will discover, is ultimately about how to make things better: not only for oneself, but also for one's community and one's world. Ten days after Rosh Hashanah, the focus shifts to repentance and atonement (another collective process), so that all can truly, as Hollander states, "begin anew."

# Poetry

# 🦌 For New Year's Day

SOLOMON IBN GABIROL

The breath of the remnant of Jacob shall praise Thee,
For with testimony confirmed Thou hast made him Thy witness
And keepest Thy covenant with him and Thy kindness;
Therefore shall he thank Thee on the day Thou hast appointed
    judgment.

The breath of the company of Israel shall ravish Thy heart,
    Daily proclaiming Thy Unity.
To be judged of Thee and by Thy hand inscribed
    In the book of life,
They stand this day according to Thy ordinance,
    For all things are Thy servants.

The breath of the nation set apart from the seventy
And weighing true in the scales of righteousness,
    Shall hail Thee as King,
A monarch of justice and righteousness,
Who sits on the Throne of righteousness,
    A righteous judge.

The breath of the congregations chosen of Thee shall thank Thee,
    And their bannered tribes,

O Thou who stretchest Thy hand to receive the transgressors of Thy
    judgments,
That Thou mayest be justified when Thou speakest
And be in the right when Thou judgest.

The breath of those conserved in Israel, Thy servants who fear Thee,
    Shall hail Thee as mighty.
Thou art near to all that call upon Thee, Righteousness and justice
    are the foundation of Thy throne.

The breath of the holy ones hallowing Thee, Responding in all their
 passion of desire,
  Acclaims Thee as holy.
Holy God, King living forever, they cry, And would that our mouths
 were as full as the sea
  With song!

Translated by Israel Zangwill

# 🌿 Rosh Hashanah

PENINA MOISE

Into the tomb of ages past
Another year hath now been cast;
Shall time unheeded take its flight,
Nor leave one ray of higher light,
That on man's pilgrimage may shine
And lead his soul to spheres divine?

Ah! which of us, if self-reviewed,
Can boast unfailing rectitude?
Who can declare his wayward will
More prone to righteous deed than ill?
Or, in his retrospect of life,
No traces find of passion's strife?

With firm resolve your bosom nerve
The God of right alone to serve;
Speech, thought, and act to regulate,
By what His perfect laws dictate;
Nor from His holy precepts stray,
By worldly idols lured away.

Peace to the house of Israel!
May joy within it ever dwell!
May sorrow on the opening year,
Forgetting its accustomed tear,
With smiles again fond kindred meet.
With hopes revived the festal greet!

# ❧ Rosh-Hashanah, 5643 (1882)

EMMA LAZARUS

Not while the snow-shroud round dead earth is rolled,
   And naked branches point to frozen skies, —
When orchards burn their lamps of fiery gold,
   The grape glows like a jewel, and the corn
A sea of beauty and abundance lies,
         Then the new year is born.

Look where the mother of the months uplifts
   In the green clearness of the unsunned West,
Her ivory horn of plenty, dropping gifts,
   Cool, harvest-feeding dews, fine-winnowed light;
Tired labor with fruition, joy and rest
         Profusely to requite.

Blow, Israel, the sacred cornet! Call
   Back to thy courts whatever faint heart throb
With thine ancestral blood, thy need craves all.
   The red, dark year is dead, the year just born
Leads on from anguish wrought by priest and mob,
         To what undreamed-of morn?

For never yet, since on the holy height,
   The Temple's marble walls of white and green
Carved like the sea-waves, fell, and the world's light
   Went out in darkness, — never was the year
Greater with portent and with promise seen,
         Than this eve now and here.

Even as the Prophet promised, so your tent
   Hath been enlarged unto earth's farthest rim.
To snow-capped Sierras from vast steppes ye went,
   Through fire and blood and tempest-tossing wave,
For freedom to proclaim and worship Him,
         Mighty to slay and save.

High above flood and fire ye held the scroll,
    Out of the depths ye published still the Word.
No bodily pang had power to swerve your soul:
    Ye, in a cynic age of crumbing faiths,
Lived to bear witness to the living Lord,
            Or died a thousand deaths.

In two divided streams the exiles part,
    One rolling homeward to its ancient source,
One rushing sunward with fresh will, new heart.
    By each the truth is spread, the law unfurled,
Each separate soul contains the nation's force,
            And both embrace the world.

Kindle the silver candle's seven rays,
    Offer the first fruits of the clustered bowers,
The garnered spoil of bees. With prayer and praise
    Rejoice that once more tried, once more we prove
How strength of supreme suffering still is ours
            For Truth and Law and Love.

# ❧ The Eve of Rosh Hashanah

YEHUDA AMICHAI


The eve of Rosh Hashanah. At the house that's being built,
a man makes a vow: not to do anything wrong in it,
only to love.
Sins that were green last spring
dried out over the summer. Now they're whispering.

So I washed my body and clipped my fingernails,
the last good deed a man can do for himself
while he's still alive.

What is man? In the daytime he untangles into words
what night turns into a heavy coil.
What do we do to one another —
a son to his father, a father to his son?

And between him and death there's nothing
but a wall of words
like a battery of agitated lawyers.

And whoever uses people as handles or as rungs of a ladder
will soon find himself hugging a stick of wood
and holding a severed hand and wiping his tears
with a potsherd.

*Translated by Chana Bloch and Stephen Mitchell*

## For Paul Celan and Primo Levi

HARVEY SHAPIRO

Because the smoke
still drifted through your lives,
because it had not settled —
what would that settling be?
A coming to terms with man's savagery?
God's savagery? The victim
digging deeper into his wound
for the ultimate face?
That would be like saying
we morn you, when you
have taken all the mourning words
and left us a gesture
of despair. To understand despair
and be comfortable with it —
something you could not do —
is how we live. Sun
drifting through smoke
as I sit on my roof in Brooklyn
with words for the Days of Awe.

## 🦎 Tashlikh

GERALD STERN

This one shows me standing by the Delaware
for the last time. There is a book in one hand
and I am making cunning motions with the other,
chopping and weaving motions to illustrate
what I am reading, or I am just enlarging
the text with my hand the way a good Jew did
before the 1930s. I am wearing
a Russian cap and a black overcoat
I bought in Pittsburgh in 1978,
a *Cavalier*, from Kaufmann's, a gabardine
with bluish buttons. Behind me in the locusts
and up and down the banks are ten or twelve others
in coats and hats, with books in their hands. We sing
a song for the year and throw our sticks in the water.
We empty our pockets of paper and lint. I know
that there are fish there in the Delaware
so we are linked to the silver chain, and I know
that the fire is wet and sputtering, a fire
to rest your boots on, perfect for the smoke
to rise just a little and move an inch at a time
across the water. I throw another stick —
this one a maple — onto the greasy rocks
and climb the hill; the rubber steps and the saplings.
I make a kissing sound with my hand — I guess
we all do. This was a painful year, a painful
two years. It is a joy to be here, sailing
back and forth across the highway, smelling
one thing or another, not just living
in terror, sleeping again, and breathing.

## ੭੩ At the New Year

JOHN HOLLANDER

Every single instant begins another new year;
    Sunlight flashing on water, or plunging into a clearing
In quiet woods announces; the hovering gull proclaims
    Even in wide midsummer a point of turning: and fading
Late winter daylight close behind the huddled backs
    Of houses close to the edge of town flares up and shatters
As well as any screeching ram's horn can, wheel
    Unbroken, uncomprehended continuity,
Making a starting point of a moment along the way,
    Spinning the year about one day's pivot of change.
But if there is to be a high moment of turning
    When a great, autumnal page, say, takes up its curved
Flight in memory's spaces, and with a final sigh,
    As of every door in the world shutting at once, subsides
Into the bed of its fellows; if there is to be
    A time of tallying, recounting and rereading
Illuminated annals, crowded with black and white
    And here and there a capital flaring with silver and bright
Blue, then let it come at a time like this, not at winter's
    Night, when a few dead leaves crusted with frost lie shivering
On our doorsteps to be counted, or when our moments of coldness
    Rise up to chill us again. But let us say at a golden
Moment just on the edge of harvesting, "Yes. Now."
    Times of counting are times of remembering; here amidst showers
Of shiny fruits, both the sweet and the bitter-tasting results,
    The honey of promises gleams on apples that turn to mud
In our innermost of mouths, we can sit facing westward
    Toward imminent rich tents, telling and remembering.
Not like merchants with pursed hearts, counting in dearth and
        darkness,
    But as when from a shining eminence, someone walking starts
At the sudden view of imperturbable blue on one hand
    And wide green fields on the other. Not at the reddening sands
Behind, nor yet at the blind gleam, ahead, of something
    Golden, looking at such a distance and in such sunlight,

Like something given — so, at this time, our counting begins,
    Whirling all its syllables into the circling wind
That plays about our faces with a force between a blow's
    And a caress', Like the strength of a blessing, as we go
Quietly on with what we shall be doing, and sing
    Thanks for being enabled, again, to begin this instant.

# ✿ At the Jewish New Year

ADRIENNE RICH

For more than five thousand years
This calm September day
With yellow in the leaf
Has lain in the kernel of Time
While the world outside the walls
Has had its turbulent say
And history like a long
Snake has crawled on its way
And is crawling onward still.
And we have little to tell
On this or any feast
Except of the terrible past.
Five thousand years are cast
Down before the wondering child
Who must expiate them all.

Some of us have replied
In the bitterness of youth
Or the qualms of middle-age:
"If Time is unsatisfied,
And all our fathers have suffered
Can never be enough,
Why, then, we choose to forget.
Let our forgetting begin
With those age-old arguments
In which their minds were wound
Like musty phylacteries;
And we choose to forget as well
Those cherished historics
That made our old men fond.
And already are strange to us.

"Or let us, being today
Too rational to cry out,
Or trample underfoot
What after all preserves

a certain savor yet —
Though torn up by the roots —
Let us make our compromise
With the terror and the guilt
And view as curious relics
Once found in daily use
The mythology, the names
That, however Time has corrupted
Their ancient purity
Still burn like yellow flames,
But their fire is not for us."

And yet, however we choose
To deny or to remember,
Though on the calendars
We wake and suffer by,
This day is merely one
Of thirty in September —
In the kernel of the mind
The new year must renew
This day, as for our kind
Over five thousand years,
The task of being ourselves.
Whatever we strain to forget,
Our memory must be long.

May the taste of honey linger
Under the bitterest tongue.

# A Three-Course Meal for the New Year

MYRA SKLAREW

This stalk of day-old bread
cannot move my soul
into the new year.
I am left behind again
in the synagogue
where the rabbi quotes
divorce statistics and heals
loneliness with transcendental
Jewish meditation.

I am left behind
holding the yellow ticket
which provides me
one unreserved seat
on the hard bench
of the sanctuary. I wave it
like a bee on a string,
afraid it will sting me,
afraid to let go.

Come to the synagogue,
the rabbi says,
but leave, he cautions,
with deliberate speed.
Four services going on
at the same time —
a little god spread thin
on next year's sandwich.

His fingers parted
in the cabalistic blessing,
I slip through the spaces
and come home, the new year
already at table before me.
The small husks of the days
of the old year hover in my room.

Later on I will take them out
to the river. And later
I will visit the grave
of my mother and offer praise
without knocking on wood
and take my first taste
of the sweet year.

# 🪸 Tashlich

MARGE PIERCY

Go to the ocean and throw the crumbs in,
all that remains of seven years.
When you wept, didn't I taste your tears
on my cheek, give you bread for salt?

Here where I sing at full pitch
and volume uncensored, I was attacked.
The pale sister nibbled like a mouse
in the closets with sharp pointy teeth.

She let herself in with her own key.
My trust garlanded her round. Indeed
it was convenient to trust her
while she wasted paper thin with envy.

Here she coveted. Here she crept.
Here her cold fluttering hands lingered
on secrets and dipped into the honey.
Her shadow fell on the contents of every drawer.

Alone in the house she made love
to herself in the mirror wearing
stolen gowns; then she carried them home
for the magic to color her life.

Little losses spread like tooth decay.
Furtive betrayals festered, cysts
hidden in flesh. Her greed swelled
in the dark, its hunger always roaring.

No number of gifts could silence
those cries of resentful hunger,
not for the baubles, the scarves,
the blouses she stole, but to be twenty

and pretty again, not to have to work
to live but merely to be blond and thin
and let men happen like rain in the night
and never to wake alone.

On the new year my grandmother Hannah
told me to carry crumbs to the water
and cast them out. We are tossing
away the trust that was too convenient

and we are throwing evil from the house
the rancid taint of envy spoiling the food
the pricing fingers of envy rumpling the cloth
the secret ill-wisher chewing from inside

the heart's red apple to rot it out.
I cast away my anger like spoiled milk.
Let the salty wind air the house and cleanse
the stain of betrayal from the new year.

## The Eve of Rosh Hashanah,
## 500 Years after the Inquisition

RICHARD CHESS

My headache is a house
Of old newspapers, torn
Envelopes, threads, buttons
Gnawed dolls strewn
Everywhere, and on the stove
One burner lit. Why did I kiss
The road that led here?

My heartache is in the yard,
A red spruce, just another
Summer flourish.
But when the grass slows
And the glory of maple
And oak fades, the spruce alone
Retains its green poise
Like the penitential poem
That has survived cold
Centuries and every fall
Ignites the fuse that burns
From my pew to medieval Spain.

My return is up the path of books.
I read about ladling
And bandaging and bathing,
Kind acts and conversions
Until my head aches and my heart
Aches, the lamp
Outside my window turned low,
Another book to read tomorrow.

Will we be visited this year
By sweetness, this year by sorrow?
Once we and the Torah

And Cordoba were one.
My prayer before sleep
Dissolves like honey in the cup of night,
And the dog, overfed,
Snores among its beheaded joys.

# Memoir

# 🦋 Rosh ha-Shanah

## from *Burning Lights*

### BELLA CHAGALL

The Fearful Days have come, and our whole house is in an uproar. Each holiday brings with it its own savor, each is steeped in its own atmosphere. A clear, joyful, purified air, as after a rain — this is the air of Rosh ha-Shanah.

After the black nights of the Selichot prayers a bright, sunny day dawns for the New Year. The week of Selichot is the most restless week. Father wakes up in the middle of the night, rouses my brothers, and all of them dress quietly and go off like thieves slinking through the door.

What are they looking for in the cold, in the dark streets? It is so warm in bed! And what if they don't come back at all — how mother and I would weep and weep! I am almost beginning to cry even now, and I wrap myself closer in my blankets.

In the morning when father drinks his tea his face is pale and fagged. But the bustle of the holiday eve dispels everyone's weariness.

The shop is closed at an early hour. Everybody makes ready to go to shul. There are more preparations than ever before, as if it were the first time they were going there. Each one puts on something new — one a fresh, light-colored hat, another a new necktie, still another a new garment.

Mother dons a white silken blouse; she seems refurbished, she has a new soul, and she is eager to go to shul.

One of my elder brothers opens the thick prayer book for her and creases down the pages from which she must pray. They are marked with notations made by grandfather's hand many years ago: "Say this."

Mother recognizes the lines over which she wept last year. A trembling comes over her and her eyes dim with tears. She is in a hurry to go to shul to weep over the words, as if she were reading them for the first time.

A stack of books has been prepared for her. She wraps them in a large kerchief and takes them all with her. Must she not pray for a good year for the whole family?

As for father's books and talis, the shames came to fetch them to the shul during the day.

I remain behind, alone. The house is empty, and I too feel emptied. The old year, like a thing forlorn, drags itself away somewhere outside.

The coming year must be a clear one, a bright one. I want to sleep through the night as quickly as possible.

On the following day in the morning I too go to shul. I too wear new garments from tip to toe. The sun is shining, the air is clear and alive. My new shoes give a dry tap. I walk faster. The New Year must be already arrived in shul. The shofar must be sounding there; even now it echoes in my ears. I fancy that the sky itself has come down lower and hurries to shul together with me. I run to the women's section, I push open the door. A whiff of heat comes from in there, as from an oven. The heavy air stifles my breath. The shul is packed full. The high lecterns are piled with books. Old women sit bent, sunk in their chairs. Girls stand almost on the heads of the grandmothers. Children tumble underfoot.

I want to elbow my way to mother. But she is sitting so far off, all the way up at the front, next to the window that opens into the men's section. As soon as I try to move, a woman turns around to me, a weeping face gives me an angry look.

"Oh! Oh!" She breathes wrath at me.

I am pushed from behind; I am suddenly freed, and thrown to the handrail.

My mother signals to me with her eyes. She is glad that I am near her. But where is the shofar? Where is the New Year?

I look at the walls of the men's section. The ark of the Torah is closed, its curtain drawn. Silently and calmly the two embroidered lions guard it. The congregation is in a tumult, as though busy with something else. Have I come too early or too late?

Suddenly from under a talis a hand holding a shofar stretches out and remains suspended in the air. The shofar blares out; everyone is awakened. They are very still. They wait. The shofar gives another blast. The sound is chopped off, as though the horn were out of breath.

People exchange glances. The shofar trumpets hoarsely. A murmur ripples through the shul.

What manner of shofar blowing is that? He lacks strength. Perhaps another man should be called up.

And then suddenly, as though the trumpet blower had pushed out the evil spirit that was clogging the shofar, there comes a pure, long sound. Like a summons it runs through the whole shul, sounding into every corner. The congregation is relieved: one gives a sigh, another nods his head. The sound rises upward. The walls are touched by it. It reaches me and my handrail. It throbs up to the ceiling, pushes the thick air, fills every empty space. It booms into my ears, my mouth, I even feel an ache in my stomach. When will the shofar finish trumpeting? What does the New Year want of us?

I recall my sins. God knows what will happen to me: so much has accumulated during the year!

I can hardly wait for afternoon. I am eager to go with mother to the rite of tashlich, to shake off all my sins, cast them into our big river. Other women and men are on their way. All of them walk down the little street that leads to the river bank. All of them are dressed in black; they might be going, God forbid, to a funeral. The air is sharp. From the high river bank, from the big city park, a wind is blowing; leaves are falling, yellow, red-yellow, like butterflies; they whirl in the air, turn over, scatter on the ground. Do our sins fly in the same way? The leaves rustle, stick to my shoes. I drag them along. Having them, it is less fearsome to go through the tashlich.

"Why do you stop all the time?" Mother pulls me by the hand. "Let the leaves alone!"

Soon everyone stops. The street seems suddenly to end; the deep, cool waters seem to be flowing up to our feet.

On the river bank dark clusters of people have gathered. The men, with their heads thrust out and their beards swaying, bend down to the water as though they wanted to see the very bottom. Suddenly they turn their pockets inside out; little crumbs, scraps, detach themselves from the linings. They recite a prayer aloud and throw their crumbs together with the sins, into the water. But how shall I shake off my sins? I have no crumbs in my pockets—I do not even have pockets.

I stand next to mother, shivering from the cold wind that lifts our skirts. Mother tells me the ritual words that I have to say, and the prayers together with the sins fall from my mouth straight into the water. I fancy that the river is swollen with all our sins, and it rolls along with its waters suddenly turned black.

My burden eased away, I return home. Mother at once sits down to read psalms. She wants still to make use of the day to obtain something more from God. A humming fills the dark room. The air becomes clouded, like mother's spectacles. Mother is weeping, silently shaking her head.

What shall I do?

I fancy that from the closely printed lines of the psalms our grandfathers and grandmothers come gently out to us. Their shadows sway, they draw themselves out like threads, encircle me. I am afraid to turn around.

Perhaps someone is standing at my back and wants to seize me in his arms?

"Mother!" I cannot contain myself, I shake her by the sleeve.

She raises her head, blows her nose, and ceases weeping. She kisses the psalter and closes it.

"Bashke," she says, "I'm going to shul. We'll be back soon, all of us. Will you set the table, my child?"

"Mother, is it for the shehecheyanu?"

As she goes out I open the cupboards. I drag out the tall paper bags filled with fruit and spread all of it out on the table. As in a great garden, thick green melons roll on the table. Beside them lie clusters of grapes, white and red. Big, juicy pears have turned over on their little heads. There are sweet apples that have a golden gleam — they look as if they had been dipped in honey. Plums, dark red, scatter all over the table.

Over what shall we offer the benediction of first fruits? Haven't we eaten of all these things all year long?

I notice that from another bag there protrudes, like a fir tree, a pineapple, a new, unfamiliar fruit.

"Sasha, do you know where pineapples grow?"

"Who knows?" She spreads her hands. "I've got other things to think about!"

No one knows whence the pineapple comes. With its scaly skin it looks like a strange fish. But its tail stands up at the top like an opened fan. I touch its stuffed belly, and it trembles from top to bottom. It is not a casual matter to touch the pineapple; it behaves somewhat like an emperor. I reserve the center of the table for it.

Sasha slices it pitilessly. The pineapple groans under her sharp knife like a live fish. Its juice, like white blood, trickles onto my fingers. I lick them. It is a tart-sweet taste.

Is this the taste of the New Year?

"Dear God," I whisper hurriedly, "before they all come back from shul, give a thought to us! Father and mother pray Thee all day long in shul to grant them a good year. And father always thinks of Thee. And mother remembers thy Name at every step! Thou knowest how toilworn they are, how care-ridden. Dear God, Thou canst do everything! Make it so that we have a sweet, good year!"

I quickly sprinkle powdered sugar on the pineapple.

"Gut yom-tov! Gut yom-tov!" My brothers run in, trying to outshout one another.

They are followed immediately by father and mother, who look pale and tired.

"May you be inscribed for a happy year!"

My heart leaps up. I imagine that God himself is speaking through their mouths.

Translated by Norbert Guterman

## from My Mother's Sabbath Days

CHAIM GRADE

For other women, the coming of the High Holidays is marked by the wearing of fur collars, velvet dresses, brooches set with seed pearls, golden bracelets — heirlooms from their grandmothers. Mother, for her part, has a black shawl and a jacket with mother-of-pearl buttons. But for her the most important sign of the festival is her white kerchief. It is in this that she wraps her Roedelheimer mahzor with its glossy brown binding. The gleaming kerchief is to her like the white curtain hung before the Holy Ark during the Days of Awe — a reminder that on the Day of Judgment, God is a pardoner of sins.

For my mother the very essence of the holiday lies in that white kerchief, whereas I find my joy of the season in a small bunch of grapes, like a cluster of frozen dewdrops, and a slice of red, juicy watermelon studded with black seeds. Mother buys these delicacies in honor of the New Year, so that I might recite the Sheheyonu, the blessing for new occasions. She herself also eats a little of these costly fruits. In the course of the two days of Rosh Hashanah, she also eats a plum and a pear — fruits she has not tasted earlier in the season. As a child I always marveled: where did she find the strength and patience to keep herself all summer long from sampling the fresh fruits in her own baskets, so as to be eligible to recite the Sheheyonu over them on the New Year?

On Rosh Hashanah, sitting in the women's section of the synagogue, she looked more joyous and radiant than any of the rich matrons with their fur collars. She is not a zogerke, a "spokeswoman" — no one has engaged her to pray for a good year for All-Israel — but the poor, unlearned women crowd around her to listen as she translates aloud into Yiddish the story that is being read from the Torah scroll:

"Sarah, the mistress, drove out the maidservant Hagar, with her child, into the desert. And Hagar wandered aimlessly until all the water in her goatskin bottle was gone. Then she placed the child under one of the trees and she herself sat down at a distance, as far as an arrow could fly, so that she would not see the death agony of the child. And she lifted her voice and wept. Then an angel of the Lord called out to Hagar and said to her that her son would become the father of a mighty nation. And God opened the eyes of Hagar, and she saw a well of water, and gave her child to drink."

Even the women who cannot read are familiar with this tale, and they sigh: Life has always been bitter for the lowly. In their hearts they feel resentment against Sarah for her ill-treatment of the servant-girl. Yet the poor women also realize that God is a merciful Father Who can help them as He helped the maidservant Hagar. The moral of the tale is sweet, sweet as the hallah dipped in honey that is eaten at the evening meal on Rosh Hashanah. But they cannot take much time to ponder this, for they are anxious to listen as my mother continues reading.

She reads how the ministering angels came before God and spoke to Him: "Lord of the Universe, do not take pity on Hagar's son, Ishmael. When the Children of Israel will be driven from their land, the children of Ishmael will meet them in the desert and give the exhausted Jews salty fish to eat and, instead of water, they will give the exiles skin-bottles filled with wind. It were better that Ishmael die of thirst now, while he is yet a child, than that such evildoers, the Arabs of the desert, should be his descendants." But God, blessed be He, answered the angels and said that each person may only be judged for that which he has already done, not for what he, or his children, may do in the future.

The women, peddlers and stall-keepers in the marketplace, have never heard this story before, and they are greatly moved and comforted by it. For who nowadays can vouch for his children, especially someone who is poor? One must indeed give thanks and praise unto Him Whose Name one may not utter unwashed, that He does not make a reckoning now for what will happen later.

The wealthy matrons hold mahzorim whose covers have corners edged in silver. But they cannot keep up with the cantor and frequently lose the place. From time to time a broad-beamed matron makes her way from the East Wall corner to the fruit-peddler sitting in the westernmost nook, almost at the outer door:

"Vellenka, a good year to you. What are they up to?"

Quickly and familiarly, Mother turns the gilt-edged pages of the rich woman's mahzor as she thinks to herself: "If only I knew how I stood with the Lord of the Universe as well as I know where the cantor and the congregation are up to in the prayers . . ."

Lisa the goose-dealer's wife stands at her place and stares in confusion into her prayerbook; she has lost the place and has no idea what is being said. But she refuses to ask Mother's help — she will not give the fruitseller that satisfaction. For ever-present to her mind is the recent occasion when she, Lisa, had openly combed and washed her hair on the Sabbath and Mother, so as not to have to witness such a desecration, had fled the courtyard with her Bible and gone back indoors.

When the cantor reaches the climactic U'nessa'neh Tokef prayer, there is such a crush of rich matrons and their prayerbooks about my mother that, if only she had as many customers pressing about her baskets, she herself would become a wealthy woman. Her hollow cheeks are aglow with a subdued yet sweet excitement. Till now she has been ashamed to weep aloud, lest she seem to be lamenting more than others her bitter lot of widowhood. Only when the cantor reaches the phrase "Who shall live and who shall die," at which everyone weeps, will she too permit the wellspring of tears to flow freely from her eyes. Just then, however, she begins to look about uneasily, and the women near her, who have today crowned her with honor and respect, ask with much concern:

"Vellenka, what are you looking for?"

"For my kerchief."

Mother, just about to weep, suddenly notices that her white kerchief is missing. She feels a throb in her heart: such a loss — may it not turn out to be an evil omen for the New Year! Lisa, noticing that Mother is looking in her direction, also begins to search, and finds a white kerchief on the window-sill near her. Overjoyed, she picks it up and hurries over to my mother, carrying it like a white flag of peace:

"Is this what you're looking for?"

"Yes, Lisa. Early this morning, before the other women came, I sat near your window to say the first part of the prayers. Here, near the wall, it's dark, and my eyesight is already weak."

"Vellenka," says Lisa, trembling on this Day of Judgment, "may you have great joy from your son. What are they up to now? You are learned in the 'black vowel signs' — and on a day such as this no other learning is worthwhile."

Lisa is here hinting at her own knowledge of Russian.

Mother quickly turns the pages of Lisa's prayerbook, reflecting as she does so that to observe the Sabbath is more important for true repentance. One cannot, with mere pious babbling on Rosh Hashanah, buy absolution for the sins of an entire year . . .

The women's section has become still, like a cooing dovecote where silence falls just before a storm. A cloud of long-pent-up bitterness seems to hang in the air; a sobbing arises from heavy-laden hearts. A clap of thunder resounds through the synagogue. The cantor begins to chant "U'nessa'neh tokef kedushas ha-yom . . . ," and before he has reached the words "who shall live and who shall die," the women's section is already drowning in a flood of tears.

*Translated by Channa Kleinerman Goldstein and Inna Hecker Grade*

# ⛣ from Night

ELIE WIESEL

The summer was coming to an end. The Jewish year was nearly over.

On the eve of Rosh Hashanah, the last day of that accursed year, the whole camp was electric with the tension which was in all our hearts. In spite of everything, this day was different from any other. The last day of the year. The word "last" rang very strangely! What if it were indeed the last day?

They gave us our evening meal, a very thick soup, but no one touched it. We wanted to wait until after prayers. At the place of assembly, surrounded by the electrified barbed wire, thousands of silent Jews gathered, their faces stricken.

Night was falling. Other prisoners continued to crowd in, from every block, able suddenly to conquer time and space and submit both to their will.

"What are You, my God," I thought angrily, "compared to this afflicted crowd, proclaiming to You their faith, their anger, their revolt? What does Your greatness mean, Lord of the Universe, in the face of all this weakness, this decomposition, and this decay? Why do You still trouble their sick minds, their crippled bodies?"

Ten thousand men had come to attend the solemn service, heads of the blocks, Kapos, functionaries of death.

"Bless the Eternal. . . ."

The voice of the officiant had just made itself heard. I thought at first it was the wind.

"Blessed be the Name of the Eternal!"

Thousands of voices repeated the benediction; thousands of men prostrated themselves like trees before a tempest.

"Blessed be the Name of the Eternal!"

Why, but why should I bless Him? In every fiber I rebelled. Because He had had thousands of children burned in His pits? Because He kept six crematories working night and day, on Sundays and feast days? Because in His great might He had created Auschwitz, Birkenau, Buna, and so many factories of death? How could I say to Him: "Blessed art Thou, Eternal, Master of the Universe, Who chose us from among the races to be tortured day and night, to see our fathers, our mothers, our brothers, end in the crematory? Praised be Thy Holy Name, Thou Who hast chosen us to be butchered on Thine altar?"

I heard the voice of the officiant rising up, powerful yet at the same time broken, amid the tears, the sobs, the sighs of the whole congregation:

"All the earth and the Universe are God's!"

He kept stopping every moment, as though he did not have the strength to find the meaning beneath the words. The melody choked in his throat.

And I, mystic that I had been, I thought:

"Yes, man is very strong, greater than God. When You were deceived by Adam and Eve, You drove them out of Paradise. When Noah's generation displeased You, You brought down the Flood. When Sodom no longer found favor in Your eyes, You made the sky rain down fire and sulphur. But these men here, whom You have betrayed, whom You have allowed to be tortured, butchered, gassed, burned, what do they do? They pray before You! They praise Your name!"

"All creation bears witness to the Greatness of God!

Once, New Year's Day had dominated my life. I knew that my sins grieved the Eternal; I implored his forgiveness. Once, I had believed profoundly that upon one solitary deed of mine, one solitary prayer, depended the salvation of the world.

This day I had ceased to plead. I was no longer capable of lamentation. On the contrary, I felt very strong. I was the accuser, God the accused. My eyes were open and I was alone — terribly alone in a world without God and without man. Without love or mercy. I had ceased to be anything but ashes, yet I felt myself to be stronger than the Almighty, to whom my life had been tied for so long. I stood amid that praying congregation, observing it like a stranger.

The service ended with the Kaddish. Everyone recited the Kaddish over his parents, over his children, over his brothers, and over himself.

We stayed for a long time at the assembly place. No one dared to drag himself away from this mirage. Then it was time to go to bed and slowly the prisoners made their way over to their blocks. I heard people wishing one another a Happy New Year!

I ran off to look for my father. And at the same time I was afraid of having to wish him a Happy New Year when I no longer believed in it.

He was standing near the wall, bowed down, his shoulders sagging as though beneath a heavy burden. I went up to him, took his hand and kissed it. A tear fell upon it. Whose was that tear? Mine? His? I said nothing. Nor did he. We had never understood one another so clearly.

The sound of the bell jolted us back to reality. We must go to bed. We came back from far away. I raised my eyes to look at my father's face leaning over mine, to try to discover a smile or something resembling one upon the aged, dried-up countenance. Nothing. Not the shadow of an expression. Beaten.

*Translated by Stella Rodway*

## ❧ Rosh Hashanah

from *The Alphabet in my Hands*

MARJORIE AGOSÍN

October in Chile is warm. The inhabitants take off their endless layers of scarves and excite to the explosion of greens and yellows. It is the season of aromas. Life is pursued. Retired people return to the spots that have been held for them. After a dark winter, balloons appear, morning glories, violets, caresses in the park. Cemeteries fill with flowers that always accompany the dead.

October in Chile, and it is the Jewish New Year, even though few people know it, and at times people in the street simply say that the Jews have closed their shops. My mother and I look at one another with delight, we laugh with such passion because we don't know what to say. We were bending over with laughter and also with humility and we were getting ready to celebrate this new year which, more than a fresh start on a calendar, marks a different way of viewing the world and becoming accustomed to it. Perhaps the Jewish New Year is a way of accepting time. Entangled and enormous, time is like a stellar shawl, like a time beyond our grasp, a useless time, and as such, a time submerged in otherness. My mother tells me to collect stones so that we can throw them in the river and ask for forgiveness. I tell her that there aren't many sins I can recall. Perhaps when I pulled my sister's hair, but most of all I just remember bits of scenes, intermittent and forgotten memory.

The Jewish New Year, and the ten days that surround it, is a time of not only introspection but of gratitude beyond alphabets and calendars, beyond thresholds and uncertain times. My grandfather would take me to the Sephardic synagogue because he felt at home there. It was, in truth, a great theater with reddish, dragon-like rugs leased by Jews from the capital and the provinces. They got together on these holy days. We walked unveiled in the smell of hyacinths, the light of spring glowing on our faces full of yearning. At last we had a holiday! Since I was little, strolling arm in arm with my grandfather, we spoke about how hardheaded God was with regard to the poor, about how the Andes looked like an enormous Chantilly cream pie. More than anything, I remember the Sephardic community gathering in the streets near the synagogue, smiling, singing with whistles and drums Old Castillian and gypsy melodies, and we, the *Kulturmenschen*, would walk austerely, germanically, to pray to a silent uncaring God who let millions die in the chambers of blue gas. My Omama Helena sent me a disapproving glance because she saw the questions in my eyes. She taught me to remain quiet in the face of the incomprehensible, the inexpressible. From that Jewish New Year on, I entered into an eternal conflict with God, and it was not just a passing phase of adolescence. I understood that religious knowledge goes beyond history, beyond books of fiction. It is a way to contemplate the sky, to approach the time of breezes, to embrace the beggars, and to go wherever our hearts may lead us.

*Translated by Nancy Abraham Hall*

# Fiction

# 🔖 The Poor Community

ABRAHAM REISEN

The little town of Voinovke, which consists of forty houses and thirty-five householders, since five of the houses stand empty, rocked and rumbled and boiled like a stream on the eve of Passover, when the snow begins to melt. But it wasn't the eve of Passover. It was a week before Rosh Hashonoh, and the community had no prayer leader.

In the nearby town of Yachnovke, which is several times larger than Voinovke, one could not only get a prayer leader, but quite a good one — with a neck, a double chin, and in general a cantor's bearing, only he would want to be well paid, and that was the trouble! The town of Voinovke had already disposed of its few public rubles on a cantor whom, through ill luck, the past summer had brought; he had prayed a full Sabbath service with a choir of six. In a way, it had been worth it: since Voinovke had been Voinovke, it had not heard such beautiful singing. The synagogue, which is over two hundred years old, as the older folks tell it, barely survived the cantor and his choir. The windows trembled, the walls shook, and from the ceiling big chunks of plaster fell. In great wonderment the community gave this cantor and his choir all of its public money, and now, a week before Rosh Hashonoh, it suddenly realized that it didn't have a single penny with which to hire a prayer leader. So the townspeople gathered in the synagogue to discuss the problem.

"That was certainly one of the most foolish things in the world!" exclaimed Ariah Leib the tailor, who looks upon himself as a Jew of some standing, since he has a long beard and a little boy who studies in the Yachnovke yeshiva.

"What a thing to do! It could happen only with us," said Chaim the glazier in support of his friend. "In the middle of the year to give a cantor all of our money!"

"Foolishness! Sheer foolishness!" added Chanon the teacher, shrugging his shoulders.

"You know what my decision would be?" said Zorach the shoemaker, stroking his beard in the manner of a rabbi. "I would have those who hired the cantor pay for a prayer leader with their own money. That's my advice," he said gravely, as if everything depended on his advice.

"But go find out who hired him! All of us hired him," said Zalmon the Smith. "All of us wanted at least once in our lives to hear some religious singing. It's hardly an unworthy desire. But when? When the town is rich!

A Yachnovke can afford to spend a few rubles for a cantor in the middle of the year, but not we paupers."

"Well, what shall we do?" asked several voices in the synagogue.

"It's very serious," answered one.

"Chaikel Sheps, you will pray with the Sabbath tune," said Zorach the shoemaker to the leader of the Sabbath prayers.

Chaikel Sheps does have a bit of a voice but doesn't know any prayer tunes other than those of the Sabbath.

"Try, Chaikel, try!" said several of the householders. "Make up your mind!"

Chaikel Sheps got red in the face and weakly replied, "I am afraid."

"Try, try! *Ha-me-lech!*" — Zalmon the smith showed him how.

"Aye, you can do it all by yourself," chimed in Chanon the teacher and went on, "*Yo-shev-el-chi-seh ram-veh-noh-soh-oh-oh! Ai-ai-ai-ai-ai-aai!*"

The whole gathering joined in, and for a few minutes the synagogue rang with the tunes of the High Holidays.

"Now everybody knows it, but when Rosh Hashonoh comes nobody will remember," one householder remarked.

Everybody took this idea seriously, and the gathering settled into deep thought.

"You know, we have no one to blow the *shofar* either," announced the *shammes*, in the middle of everything, from the Torah-reading platform.

The group was startled.

"How come? Where is Nachman?"

It seems that Nachman, a pale thin young man of about twenty, who has "eating days" and is studying by himself, had for two years blown the ram's horn for nothing.

"This year I will blow in the village of Sosnovtchine. They're giving me three rubles — three rubles . . ." he managed to stammer, fearing for his very skin, which had been clothed by the community.

"You're a cheapskate!" someone called out.

"A ruffian!" another shouted.

"One who always eats with paying," a third said, sneering.

A torrent of words poured down on poor Nachman. He felt as if he were being pricked with needles. "I have to earn something for a winter coat. I cannot—" he pleaded. "Forgive me, but the winter is cold."

"What do people want from him really?" they asked, retreating.

"He needs a winter coat. He is going around with nothing on, na-ked . . ."

"It really is so," everybody agreed.

"That means we have neither a prayer leader nor a *shofar* blower."

"It seems we have no Torah reader either," admitted the *shammes* from the platform.

"What do you mean?" They were startled. "Where is Old Peshes? Where is he? Where is he?"

"Old Peshes will also read in Sosnovtchine," confessed Nachman, as if he were somehow guilty. "He is getting two rubles."

The group was stricken. Some lowered their heads, as if looking for advice, while others lifted their heads toward the ceiling and stood deep in thought for a few minutes.

"What's there to think about?" asked one. "These High Holidays we'll pray individually. No more congregation."

"A pretty story, and a short one!" said another, laughing bitterly.

"This has to be written down in the permanent record."

"No more Voinovke!"

"Let's all chip in and hire someone with our own money," suggested Chanon the teacher, and was immediately taken aback by his own words.

"All right. Give me a ruble," said Zalmon the smith, extending his hand.

"I have none," said Chanon, shamefaced, "but there are householders who do have."

"Who has?"

"Nobody has!"

"The holidays that are coming — they're no trifle!"

The synagogue was in a turmoil. Everybody offered advice, but none of it was good.

Suddenly the old *shammes* banged the table on the platform, and everyone became quiet.

"I have a solution. Keep quiet awhile."

"Really? Really?" they all exclaimed impatiently.

The *shammes* inhaled deeply, took a powerful smell of snuff, wiped his nose, and finally spoke.

"This is the story. During the summer our community did something very foolish. We wasted our few rubles on a triviality. We forgot our poverty, our station, and we yearned to hear a cantor. Who knows really who he is! A cantor who rides from town to town can hardly well be such a pious man. A worthy cantor sits home. But the story is — well, it is a thing of the past. The conclusion is: we are left without a prayer leader for the High Holidays, without a *shofar* blower, without a Torah reader — absolutely without a thing. And if you want to know something else, the *shofar* itself is not as it should be. Now it will still blow, one way or another; but when Rosh Hashonoh comes, there will have to be so much blowing —a *trooeh*, a *shvorim*, a *tekieh gdoleh*—it will surely falter. Even last year it hesitated, if you will recall—I recall very well—and Nachman is a good blower."

Everybody looked at Nachman, and he blushed.

"Therefore my advice is that this year we should become partners with the Sosnovtchine *minyan*; that is, we should all pray there this year. Walking is permitted, and altogether it is three and a half *versts*; it will be a pleasant walk. We shall all save ourselves headaches: where shall we get a prayer leader, a Torah reader, a horn blower and also a horn? Because the horn, I repeat, the horn will give up on Rosh Hashonoh. Surely it won't be able to manage a *trooeh shvorim*—it is too old and already had a few faults. All that remains for us is Sosnovtchine."

After the *shammes's* talk they all began to grumble.

"From the town to the village, and on Rosh Hashonoh—no!"

"Let those yeshiva students come here!"

"What sort of high-and-mightys have they become?"

"In the past the yeshiva students used to come to us to pray."

"Now that they have learned Hebrew they make a *minyan* at home."

"Never mind the Hebrew, I'm sure they can count money."

"What do they lack? They have the best: bins filled with potatoes, with kraut, with chicken, with eggs—"

"Sour cream, butter and cheese—"

"May all troubles fall on their heads!"

"Sh-sh, don't curse them. It is the month of the High Holidays."

"Who is cursing? Who? Who?"

"Nobody, nobody . . ."

"Who has any complaint against them?"

"Berke of Sosnovtchine is a fine Jew; it will be a pleasure to pray in his home—a house as big as a field, three times the size of our synagogue."

"A fine Jew!"

"And what's wrong with the other yeshiva students? They're nice people!"

"Of course!"

"So it is settled that this year we'll pray in Sosnovtchine?"

"There is no other solution."

"A fine thing! As I'm a Jew, a mountain has lifted from my back!"

"What a mountain!"

"We must send someone to find out if he'll let us."

"What a question! It will be an honor to him!"

"It's no small thing! Townspeople coming to pray in a village!"

And the meeting ended in peace.

On the morning of the first day of Rosh Hashonoh, when the townspeople, on their way to Sosnovtchine, passed their old, dilapidated synagogue, standing there with cloudy eyes, woebegone and orphaned, their hearts felt sore and tight, and silently, without words, only with their eyes, they begged its forgiveness.

*Translated by Charles Angoff*

# 🦋 A Bratslaver Hasid

JOSEPH OPATOSHU

At midnight the Warsaw-Kiev train began to approach the Polish border. The third-class cars, which had left Warsaw packed, were almost empty now. There were only three passengers in the last car. Two of them lay on the lower benches, heads thrown to the side, arms outspread, as though dead. The third passenger, a deep-chested individual with a sparse, blond beard, looked like a Russian peasant. Lightly, he jumped down from an upper bench, dragging a bag after him, out of which rolled a loaf of black bread and a tin of honey. The two sleeping passengers awoke, looked at one another and asked the third man:

"What, are we at the border already?"

The third man did not answer; he did not seem to have heard or understood the question. Absorbed in what he was doing, he repacked the bread and honey and retied the bag. His fellow passengers agreed out loud that their companion was deaf and dumb. Turning their heads to the wall, they fell asleep again. Not until then did the deaf-mute open the car window; he put out his head for a moment, then pulled it back in. It was raining. The rain drummed on the roof, splattering against the panes.

The deaf-mute picked up the bag by its straps and threw it over his shoulder. Quietly, he left the car. He stood on the steps of the running board. The rain and wind blowing through the fields assailed him, but he stood motionless for a while. When his eyes had penetrated the darkness and his body had caught the vibrations of the chugging locomotive, the wheels biting into the rails, and the pounding rain, the deaf-mute climbed up the iron ladder to the wagon roof. For a moment he considered whether to remain on this car or to move on to another. A door scraped; the deaf-mute stretched out on his stomach and lay flat against the roof. The rain beat harder, the darkness thickened. The wind blew away every sound, the rain drenched every view. The deaf-mute had not expected the night to be so bad. He saw it as an act of God.

Going uphill, the train slowed. In the darkness, tongues of flame appeared, indicating the Polish border. The locomotive whistle shrilled, and the train screeched to a halt.

The deaf-mute's ears were so wide open and alert that he could distinguish in the rain and wind the merest scraping of a door, and lightest footstep. Nor was this to be wondered at. This was Wolf's twentieth illegal crossing of the border in the guise of a deaf-mute. Every Rosh Hashanah the Hasid made the trip to Uman to the grave of his former master, Rabbi Nachman of Bratslav. He traveled with neither passport nor visa. Together with bread and honey, the bag over his shoulder contained a volume of Rabbi Nachman's famous folk tales. He was certain in his heart that his rabbi had not really died—he was riding in the train with him. It was as though the rabbi had merely changed cars; one had only to call out—and he would hear. The journey from Warsaw to Uman was a difficult one—as difficult as "the throes of the grave." Moving from car to car in mid-journey, always fighting, always taking chances, Wolf's life was constantly in danger—both on the Polish and the Soviet sides of the border. Nevertheless, not once in the nineteen years since Rabbi Nachman's death had Wolf failed to visit his master's grave in Uman. This was the twentieth trip. Up to this point the journey had been fairly easy. God Himself was on his side. What a rain, what a wind, what darkness! Is the passport check over?

The locomotive shrieked. The cars lurched sideways. The rain lashed at Wolf's wet feet and drenched shoulders; the roof was too slippery for him to sit down. Wolf crept over to the iron ladder and stood under the roof, holding tight to the wet railing. Shutting his eyes, he pressed his lips, and wordlessly, soundlessly, recited some of Rabbi Nachman's sayings. The urgency to reach Uman and to be received by the rabbi at his grave—this was sufficient motive to keep Wolf warm. He no longer felt his feet soaking up water like a blotter, no longer feared to be pulled off the moving train at any moment. Joy rose in his breast, as though he were making a pilgrimage to Jerusalem. It was not as if he were undergoing a complete spiritual reformation—that was not the cause of this joy. Rather, he was happy because it was a sufficient achievement for a human being to lift up one shoulder toward heaven—and the rain, the darkness, the danger disappeared. Because man, after all, was created to raise up heaven. Otherwise, it would have been impossible for Rabbi Nachman to be sitting inside the car while his disciple, Wolf, stood on the roof. The Soviet border already?

Wolf fell prone. But this time he did not stay on the roof of the last car. Pushing his bag ahead of him to wipe a path through the wetness, he crept forward over the car roofs.

At the fourth car from the locomotive, Wolf stopped. There was no iron ladder on this car; no one would take the trouble to crawl up to the roof to check. The wind, blowing from the field and forest, angrily flung sheets of rain at him.

Wolf heard the passengers leave the cars and move toward customs. There, after their baggage and passports had been checked, they would transfer to a Russian train for Kharkov.

Not he. Wolf would remain lying on the roof of the Polish train, until the station lamps were extinguished and the railroad attendants left. Then he would descend and set forth through the wood to Shepetovka.

The locomotive began chugging again; smoke issuing from the chimneys sprayed the wet air with sparks. The train switched rails, moved on into the fields, and there stopped. It grew silent after a while. The only sound was the beating of the rain, the groaning and whistling wind. Then the Russian train departed.

Wolf had reached the roof of the last car. Light on his feet as a cat, the forty-year-old Hasid dropped down from the roof and lay under the car. He considered a moment the alternative of taking the highway toward Shepetovka, then thought better of it and decided on the fields. He crawled some two hundred feet on hands and knees, then straightened up. His arms and legs creaked as he began to walk. Yet, soaked through and through though he was, a warm glow entered his heart: he was to spend Rosh Hashanah with Rabbi Nachman's followers in Uman for the twentieth time.

Wolf passed through a field where the potatoes were dug up. There were small holes in the ground, mounds of dirt and puddles of water everywhere he put his feet. The night was full of rain and din; it was hard to tell where the noise was coming from. Suddenly, a dog started to bark. Wolf stood stock still. When the barking stopped, he moved on, to trudge, out of breath, toward the smithy that stood at the entry to Shepetovka.

Wolf knocked at the smithy window, then at the door. He heard steps, a voice:

"Who is it"?

"It is me, Wolf."

"From Warsaw?"

"Yes, Mendel."

A lock creaked open. The door opened; Wolf was struck by the warmth of the hearth. The two men greeted one another in the darkness, embracing. Thus standing, words were exchanged.

"Was it a hard journey?"

"This was an easy one. When do we go to Uman to visit the rabbi?"

"Tomorrow, if you wish."

The two men had a short drink in the darkness. Hastily, news was exchanged, tidings of the rabbi's Hasidim in Warsaw, Berdishev, and Uman. When the smith's wife went into the kitchen to sleep, both men got into the warm bed and immediately fell asleep.

*Translated by Jacob Sloan*

# 🎋 Tashlich

ISAAC BASHEVIS SINGER

Aaron the watchmaker did not live on our street, but when I climbed to the highest branch of the lime tree that grew in our garden, I could see his house clearly; it was the only one in the village that had a small lawn in front of it. The shutters of Aaron's house were painted green; flower pots stood in the windows; there were sunflowers in the garden. Aaron and his family lived on the ground floor, that is with the exception of his daughter Feigele; she had a room in the attic. At night a lamp burned in Feigele's window long after the lights downstairs had been extinguished. Occasionally I caught a glimpse of her shadow passing across the curtain. Mottel, Feigele's younger brother, had built a dovecote on the roof and often stood on the top of the building chasing pigeons with a long stick. Leon, the older boy, was studying at the polytechnic in Cracow, rode around the village on a horse when he came home on vacation. There was nothing that that emancipated family did not possess: they had a parrot, canaries, a dog. Aaron played the zither; his wife owned a piano—she came from Lublin and didn't wear a wig. Aaron the watchmaker, who was also both goldsmith and jeweller, was the only man in the village with a telephone in his house; he could speak directly to Zamosc.

I was not a native of that hamlet. I had been brought up in Warsaw but when the war came, my parents left the city and went to live with my grandfather the rabbi. There we were stuck in a village which was on no railroad and was surrounded by pine forests. My father was appointed assistant rabbi. I never stopped longing for Warsaw, its streets, its trolley cars, its illuminated show windows and its tall balconied residences. Aaron the watchmaker and his family represented for me a fragment of the metropolis. Aaron had a library containing books written in several languages. In his store one could put on earphones and listen to the radio. He subscribed to two Warsaw newspapers, one in Polish and one in Yiddish, and was always hunting for a chess partner. Feigele had attended the gymnasium in Lublin, boarding with an aunt while she was away from home, but now having received her diploma, had returned to her parents.

Aaron the watchmaker had been a student of my grandfather and had been considered a religious prodigy until he had been caught reading the bible in German translation, a sure sign of heresy. Like Mendelssohn, Aaron was a hunchback. Although he had not been officially excommunicated, it was almost as if he had been. He had a high forehead, a mangy-looking goatee and large black eyes. There was something ancient and half-forgotten in his gaze for which I knew no name and which made me think of Spinoza and Uriel Acosta. When he sat at the window of his store studying some mechanism through a watch glass, he seemed to be reading the wheels like a fortune teller does his crystal. All day his sad smile enunciated over and over again, "Vanity of vanities." Feigele had inherited her father's eyes. She kept to herself, was always to be seen strolling alone, a tall, thin girl with a long, pale face and thin nose and lips. She always carried two books under her arm, one thick and one thin. A strange gentleness emanated from her. By this time the fashionable girls cut their hair au garçon, but Feigele wore hers in a bun. She always took the road to the Russian cemetery. Once I saw her reading the inscriptions in the graveyard.

I was too shy to talk to her, wasn't even sure she knew who I was since she had a way of looking over people's heads. But I knew that, like me, she was living in exile. She didn't seem to ever stop meditating, would pause to examine trees and would reflectively stare down well shafts. I kept trying to meet her but couldn't think of a plan. Moreover, I was ashamed of my appearance, decked out as I was in a velvet cap, a long gabardine and red earlocks. I knew that I must seem to her just another chassidic boy. How could she guess that I was reading Knut Hamsun and Strindberg on the sly and studying Spinoza's Ethics in a Hebrew translation? In addition, I owned a work of Flammarion and was dabbling in the cabbala. In the evening, when I perched on the highest branch of the lime tree, I gazed up at the moon and the stars like an astronomer. Feigele's window was also visible to me and just as inaccessible as the sky. I had already been matched with the daughter of a rabbi. Every day my father read me a lesson from the Shulchan Aruch on how to become a rabbi. The villagers watched me constantly to make sure that I committed no transgressions. My father complained that my frivolity jeopardised this livelihood. All I needed was to be caught talking to a girl, particularly Aaron the watchmaker's daughter.

But when I sat in my tree at night watching Feigele's window I knew indubitably that my longing for her must someday bring a response. I already believed in telepathy, clairvoyance, mesmerism. I would narrow my eyes until the light from Feigele's lamp became thin, fiery filaments. My psychic messages would speed across the blackness to her, for I was seeking to emulate Joseph de la Reina, who by using the powers of Holy Names had brought the Grand Vizier's daughter in a trance to his bed. I called out to Feigele, trying to invade both her waking thoughts and dreams. I wrapped a phantom net around her like some sorcerer from the "Thousand and One Nights." My incantations must inevitably kindle love in her heart and make her desire me passionately. In return I would give her caresses such as no woman had ever received before.

I would adorn her with jewels dug from the moon. We would fly together to other planets and she would dwell a queen in supernal palaces. For reasons which I was unable to explain I became convinced that the beginning of our friendship would date from the reading of the Tashlich prayer on Rosh Hashana afternoon. This premonition was totally illogical. Probably an enlightened girl like Feigele would not even attend the ceremony. But the idea had entered into me like a dybbuk. I kept counting the days and hours until the holiday, formulated plans, conceived of the words I would say to her. Two or three times, perching among the leaves and branches, I noticed Feigele standing at the window looking out. I could not see her eyes but knew that she had heard my call and was searching for me in the darkness. It was the month of Ellul and every day the ram's horn was blown in the study house to drive away Satan. Spider webs drifted through the air; cold winds blew from the Arctic ice cap. So bright was the moon that night and day were nearly indistinguishable. Crows, awakened by the light, croaked. The grasshoppers were singing their final songs; shadows scampered across the fields surrounding the village. The river wound through the meadows like a silver snake.

It was Rosh Hashana and I put on the new gaberdine and new shoes I had been given and brushed my sidelocks behind my ears. What more could a young Chassid do to look modern? In the late afternoon I started to loiter on Bridge Street, watching the townspeople file by on their way to the Tashlich ceremony. The day was sunny, the sky as blue and transparent as it is in mid-summer. Cool breezes mingled with the warmth exuded by the earth. First came the Chassidim, marching together as a group, all dressed in fur hats and satin coats. They hurried along as if they were rushing from their womenfolk and temptation. I had been raised among these people, but now I found their disheveled beards, their ill-fitting clothes and their insistent clannishness odd. They ran from the Evil One like sheep from a wolf.

After the Chassidim came the ordinary Jews, and after them the women and girls. Most of the older women wore capes and gowns which dated from the time of King Sobieski; they had tiaras and bonnets with ribbons on their heads. Their jewelery consisted of heavy gold chains, long earrings so weighty they almost tore the lobes of their ears, and brooches inherited from grandmothers and great-grandmothers that vibrated as the women walked. My mother had on a gold silk dress and a pelerine decorated with rhinestones. But the younger women had studied the fashion magazines (which always showed up in the village a year or two after they had been issued) and were dressed in what they considered to be the latest style. Some of them wore narrow skirts that scarcely covered their knees and even bobbed their hair. The ladies' tailors stood to one side commenting on the dress of the women. They contrasted their handiwork with that of their competitors, and not only ridiculed each other's designs but the clients who wore them. I kept looking in vain for Feigele. My sorcery had failed and I walked with downcast eyes among the stragglers. Some of the townspeople stood on the wooden bridge reciting the Tashlich; other lined the river's banks. Young women took out their handkerchiefs and shook out their sins. Boys playfully emptied their pockets to be sure that no transgression remained. The village wits made the traditional Tashlich jokes. "Girls, shake as hard as you want, but a few sins will remain." "The fish will get fat feeding on so many errors."

I made no attempt to say the prayer but stood under a willow watching a huge red sun which was split in half by a wisp of cloud sink in the west. Flocks of birds dipped toward the water, their wings one instant silver, the next leaden black. The colour of the river turned from green to rose. I had lost everything that mattered here on earth, but still found comfort in the sky. Several of the smaller clouds seemed to be on fire and sailed across the heavens like ships with burning sails. I gaped at the sun as if I were seeing it for the first time. I had learned from Flammarion that this star was a million and a half times as large as the earth and had a temperature of six thousand degrees centigrade on its surface and hundreds of thousands in its interior. Everything came from it—light, warmth, the wood for the oven and the food in the pot. Even life and suffering were impossible without it. But what was the sun? Where did it come from? Whence did it travel, moving in the Milky Way and also with the Galaxy?

Suddenly I understood why the pagans had worshiped it as a god. I had a desire to kneel and bow down myself. Well, and could one be certain that it lacked consciousness? "The Guide to the Perplexed" said that the heavenly bodies possess souls, and were driven in their orbits by Ideas emitting a divine music as they circled. The music of the spheres now seemed to mingle with the twittering of the birds, the sound of the coursing river, and the murmur of the praying multitude. Then a greenish blue shimmer appeared on the horizon, the first star, a brilliant miniature sun. I knew that it had taken years for the rays from this fixed star to reach my eyes. But what were rays? I was seized by a sort of cosmic yearning. I wanted to cease existing and return to my sources, be once again a part of the universe. I muttered a prayer to the sun. "Gather me to you. I am weary of being myself."

Suddenly I felt a tug at my sleeve. I turned and trembled. Fiegele stood next to me. So great was my amazement that I forgot to marvel. She wore a black suit, a black beret, and a white lace collar. Her face lit by the setting sun shone with a Rosh Hashana purity. "Excuse me," she said. "Can you locate the Tashlich for me? I can't seem to find the place." Her smile seemed to be saying. "Well, this was the best pretext available." In her gaze there were both pride and humility. I, like Joseph de la Reina, had summoned my beloved from the Grand Vizier's palace.

She held in her hand a prayer book which had covers stamped in gold. I took one cover of the book and she grasped the other. I started to turn the pages. On one side of the page was Hebrew and on the other Polish· I kept turning the leaves but couldn't find the prayer either. The crowd had already begun to disperse, and heads kept turning in our direction. I started to thumb through the book more quickly. The Tashlich prayer just could not have been omitted. But where was it? Feigele glanced at me in wonder and her eyes seemed to be saying. "Don't get yourself so wrought up. It's nothing but a stratagem." The letters tumbled before my eyes; the prayer book trembled as through it were living. Inadvertently Feigele's elbow and mine touched and we begged each other's pardon. The prayer seemed to have flown from the book. But I knew that it was there and that my eyes had been bewitched. I was just about to give up looking when I saw the word "Tashlich" printed in big bold letters. "Here it is," I cried out, and my heart seemed to stop.

"What? Thank you."

"I haven't recited the Tashlich myself," I said.

"Well, suppose we say it together."

"Can you read Hebrew script?"

"Of course."

"This prayer symbolizes the casting of one's sins into the ocean."

"Naturally."

We stood muttering the prayer together as the crowd slowly moved off. Boys threw mocking glances at us; women scowled; girls winked. I knew that this encounter was going to get me in a great deal of trouble at home. But for the moment I revelled in my triumph, a sorcerer whose charms and incantations had worked. The look of religious devotion on Feigele's face made her appear even gentler. The sun had already disappeared behind the trees and in the distance the forest looked blue and like mountains. Suddenly I felt that I had experienced this moment before. Had it been in a dream or in a former life? The air was alive with sound: the croaking of birds, the buzzing of insects, a ringing as if from bells. The frogs began their evening conversation. A herd of cows passed near by, their hooves pounding the ground. It was a miracle that the animals did not drive us into the river. No longer did the book tremble in our hands. I heard Feigele murmur:

"The Lord looketh from Heaven, He beholdeth all the sons of men. . . . He fashioneth all their hearts alike. He considereth all their works . . ."

*Translated by Isaac Bashevis Singer and Cecil Hemley*

# ॐ The Prophecy of the New Year

MEYER LEVIN

*How Rabbi Israel Sought to Bring Heaven Down Upon Earth*

Little by little Rabbi Israel had given Power out of himself, that the weaker might be sustained. The well of his Force was deep, and might never become dry, yet the Power was not in him now as in earlier years. His soul went no more into Heaven, and yet he yearned for Heaven.

Then he desired to bring down Heaven on earth.

Though he knew the time had not yet come, he could not restrain his desire, and all of the strength that remained in him gathered and mounted for that attempt.

The pale first sun of the new year hung far in the midst of grey heaven, and the air was filled with the sound of the ram's horn blown in trumpet call. Some thought they could even see the sounds of the trumpet spreading in a faint glowing orbit through the greyness of the autumn day, as the call went forward.

The students sat about the long ancient table in the house of the Baal Shem Tov. Today it seemed to root its gnarled feet into the very ground, and take a new hold on life. Some of the students looked out into the halo of spreading light, and some sat staring at the blackened walls, as though the next instant the walls must draw aside and reveal the Empire of Mystery.

The prayer was ended. The Master began to speak the sermon of the New Year.

The students had not the strength to look into his glowing face; but when they closed their eyes each of his words came before them, and each word had a form; some were ablaze in light, some shadow dark, and some were pure and stainless as God's love on earth. With their eyes closed they sat, young and aged, and listened, and saw.

The voice of Rabbi Israel was ever as a gently sounded bell, though when he uttered fullest prayer his voice became as a cry of the lark's throat. But on the day of the New Year his voice was fresh and nimble. The ram's horn breathed through him and became a human call. The song of the *Tekia* knocked on the door of the soul, calling "come away"! The wavering notes of the *Scherwarim* wakened the freed souls like the freshness of day, and filled them with the tremblement of eternal longing. The high joyous cry of the *Terua* carried them up to Redemption.

And the Word upon which the Baal Shem spoke was the Word of the New Year:

"Sound on the mighty trumpet the sound of our Release!"

"Sound on the mighty trumpet!" he cried to the Almighty. "When the sphere of the year is rounded, and the souls of all things reach through the darkness toward a new birth, sound! See, Your children are become bitten under the assault of the storm. See, the fire of the wilderness has left her mark on them. But now the circle of Your year closes. The awful darkness on the other side has sent out her chill waves before her, already we feel their approach. Sound on the mighty Trumpet, O Lord, for the new Birth!

"Your punishment has bitten into our hand and eaten out the strength of life. Your banishment has hounded our feet until they tottered on solid earth. You sent the worm into our hearts, and they are gnawed like withered leaves. We have felt the icy hand of Your Will upon our foreheads, and our thoughts are stiffened and glazed. Sound on the mighty trumpet, O Lord, for our Release!

"The Angel of the Lord took hold of me during the night and led me outward, and I stood in nothingness, and the night lay upon my shoulders like a great burden, and the night rolled from below my prisoned feet. Then the Angel said, See! and the darkness faded, and I stood in a whited nothingness, and I saw.

"There between two chasms stood a narrow circular ridge. And within the ridge was enclosed a red depth like a sea of blood, and outside of it was a black depth like a sea of Night. And I saw, there walked a man upon the ridge, he walked like a blind man, with trembling feet, and his two weak arms wavered feeling against the darkness on one side of him and on the other; and his breast was all of glass, and I saw his heart flutter like a sick leaf in the wind, and on his brow was the mark of the icy Hand. The man went further and further around the ridge, without seeing to right or to left, and he was nearly come to the end of the circle, where his beginning had been. And I wanted to call to him, but that which I saw stopped my tongue, and I could not move it, as though it were stone. For suddenly the man had raised his eyes and seen what was on the right and on the left of him, then he staggered, and from each chasm arms reached upward to seize him.

"Then the Angel touched my lips, and my tongue was free, and I called and I shouted to him, "Lift up your wings and fly!" Then behold, the man lifted up wings! there was no more weakness or fear in him; then the ridge faded from beneath his feet, and the chasm of blood was dissolved in God's spring-water, and the chasm of night melted in God's light, and the City of the Lord lay before me, open everyways.

"Behold the year is a circle. We go on a narrow circular ridge between two chasms, and we do not see their depth. But when we come to the end of the way that is also its beginning, then the trembling of fear falls upon us as before the thunder from on high, and the lightning of the Lord flashes over the chasm, and we see the chasm, and we quiver.

"Then the trumpet sounds over us, and takes hold of our souls and carries them, each call of the trumpet carries myriads of souls upon its wings! And the sounds of the trumpet leap up to Heaven, and the Heavens listen, and fear and trembling comes over the Heavens as before the thunder of the Lord; and the trumpet resounds! And the Trumpet of the World carries on its wings that soul that shall be born out of all our souls, and is the soul of Messiah. And he climbs up to the Kingdom of Mysteries, and he beats with his wings on the Door, and the Door falls open, and behold, there is neither door nor wall remaining, but the City of God lies there, open everyways.

"Sound on the mighty trumpet, O Lord, for the birth of the soul!"

The voice of the Baal Shem Tov was like the trumpet, until it ceased. Then he arose from the table, and went into his chamber, and locked himself there. And there he remained, motionless in striving. For his utmost power was gone forward in his demand, and his soul awaited surely the coming of Messiah.

And the students also arose from about the table, and went out. As sleepwalkers they went through the streets, unseeing, and filled with yearning. At the borders of the city there was a hut where they would come together that they might undisturbed occupy themselves with thoughts of the Eternal. There they now went. And the Wings of the Voice were still over them.

But at that time there lived in the house of the Baal Shem Tov a young boy whose name was Joseph, and who was called Yohseleh. When the Master had gone into his chamber, and the students had all gone to their cottage outside the city, the boy remained alone at the long table, for he was too young to go with the others to their meditations. Yohseleh remained sitting there, within the darkening walls, and he felt the wings of the Voice upon his shoulders.

And when the first shadow of the twilight trembled goldenbrown over the white table-cloth, Yohseleh laid his head on his hands, he was in terror before the Will of the Voice, and he sank under the heaviness of the wings of the Voice that were on his shoulders. His closed fingers, pressed before his eyes, set him into deepest darkness; but in that darkness there wakened a Light that sang with the same Voice whose will he so feared. The Voice pressed upon Yohseleh with an irresistible force, and like tears long held back it suddenly burst forth, and Yohseleh cried, "Now and at once Messiah must come!"

Then the room became as far away, and the walls disappeared, and before him was a Light that gave out rings of illumination, as a night-time sun. And Yoseleh ran toward the Light. But here was the door, like a piercing, wakening pain. The boy stood for a second, as one on a narrow ridge between two chasms, who suddenly sees his danger. The Lightning of the Lord went out of him, and he was afraid, shuddering. But then the Power seized him as with the strength of the Cherubim, and the Voice cried, and Light fell once more into his heart and burned there. And Yohseleh opened the door and ran out, he ran through the streets of the city, and he ran in terrible haste until he came to the cottage of the students. Here his feet stopped. And his throat split open, and he cried, "Messiah!"

But there was no loud voice about him; only his own voice sounded and resounded slowly, and lived, and was like the Voice whose Wings he had felt upon his shoulders.

He forced his eyes to open, and made himself see.

There the aged ones sat on the threshold of the house, in a long, curved row, and every mouth was hard closed, and every look was far into the horizon, and not a limb moved.

Then Yohseleh heard his own voice crying, "Now and at once Messiah comes!" and he heard his own voice resounding in the midst of the staring silence. Then the soul of the boy flew upon the Wings of the Voice, and lay within the breast of the first of the students, and Yohseleh said, "Nachum, do you still remember how you fasted from one Sabbath to the other, that Messiah might come? Do you still remember how I came to you when you lay on the ground on the last day, and beat your forehead against the floor, how we cried and prayed together then? Now see, Messiah comes!" But the other was silent.

Then the soul rose and flew to the second student, and crept into his sleep, and Yohseleh said, "Elimelech, I saw you once bowed over a fire until your hairs fell into the flames, and your lips uttered the name, Messiah! Elimelech, he comes!" But the other was silent.

And again the soul went out, and flew to the third, and nestled in his hand, and Yohseleh said, "Yehuda, I heard you once when you spoke magic over the waters, and uttered dim words in the way of the wind. Your magic ran with the waters, and your enchantments flew with the wind. But now, Yehuda, hear me, now he comes, do you not hear him coming? Yehuda, let us go and greet him!" But he also was silent.

Yohseleh looked upon these aged ones, and his soul looked on them, and he saw them listening to a distant step. So they sat in a long, bent row, and listened to a distant step, and looked into infinity. Then loneliness came over Yohseleh and laid her cold hard hand upon the nape of his neck, and the nails of the fingers sank deep into his flesh, and the hand lay on his neck like a live, in-crawling mark. And Yohseleh saw how the Light went out of his own heart and faded from before his eyes. And Yohseleh felt how the wings upon his shoulders shrank, and fell away. And Yohseleh wanted to speak, but no voice came out of his throat. And Yohseleh wanted to go from there, but he could not lift his feet. And Yohseleh sat in the row with the others, and looked into the distance, and listened for a distant step.

So they sat together, until the stars came. And in his chamber the Baal Shem Tov struggled to force down the presence of Messiah. And as long as he continued the struggle, the sound of a distant step was in their ears. But when the sun was gone, the Baal Shem was empty of strength. And he knew that the heavens would not yield before his urge.

Then the binding power was loosed from the students. They arose, and returned to the city.

And Yohseleh stood in his house like a blind man, with unsteady feet, and his two hands wavered reaching out against the nothingness to left and to right of him, and his heart trembled like a sick leaf in the wind, and the mark of the icy hand was on his brow.

# Yom Kippur

## Day of Atonement

# ❧ Introduction

*And this shall be to you a law of all time: In the seventh month, on the tenth day of the month, you shall practice self-denial; and you shall do no manner of work. . . . For on this day atonement shall be made for you to cleanse you of all your sins; you shall be clean before the LORD.*
—Leviticus 16.29–30

"Yom Kippur," as Golda Meir states in her autobiography, "is a day unlike any other." And for many Jews, both observant and secular, it is the most solemn day of the year. Occurring on the tenth day of the Hebrew month of Tishri, Yom Kippur concludes the ten days of penitence, the "Days of Awe," which begin with Rosh Hashanah. Often, it is the only time of the year when synagogues are filled to capacity. The reason for the importance of Yom Kippur is partly historical, partly psychological, and partly theological.

The concept of expiating the sins of the past year so as to begin the new year cleansed and purified dates back to at least biblical times. The Torah (Leviticus 16) describes a series of rituals by which the ancients were to purge themselves of their transgressions of the past year, culminating in the transference of human sins to a goat which was then banished into the desert (Leviticus 16.20–22). This ritual and its attendant belief in the ability to consign the trespasses of humans to animals seem to have persisted for many centuries. Known in Hebrew as *kapparot*, it was later practiced with a fowl rather than a goat. The ceremony was also transformed by some into one in which coins were twirled in a sack while enumerating one's transgressions. The coins were then given to the poor. Today, it is customary to contribute to charity on Yom Kippur, a practice some trace to the ceremony of *kapparot*.

What has clearly survived for centuries is the mood and spirit of atonement, confession, and forgiveness that mark Yom Kippur observance. The holiday is a time for personal reflection—a final, year-end retrospective on the wrongs one may have committed ("knowingly or unknowingly") against friends, neighbors, and family. There is also something distinctly communal in the observance of the holiday. Traditional prayers are recited in the plural ("The sin we have committed against You by our arrogance; The sin we have committed against You by our insolence"), so that restitution is attempted collectively, as a community of like-minded (and equally culpable) individuals.

Like Rosh Hashanah, Yom Kippur is a mostly synagogue-based holiday, with prescribed prayers and rituals throughout the evening before and the day itself. The major themes of the holiday — repentance, renewal, introspection — are reflected in the prayers composed specifically for the holiday. As Yom Kippur is a day of remembrance, a special memorial service (or *yizkor*) is held during the day. The holiday, often referred to as "The Sabbath of Sabbaths" (*Shabbat Shabbaton*), is also a day of fasting. Self-denial has always been a part of the Yom Kippur observance: one is told to abstain from sex, cosmetics, bathing for pleasure, and from wearing leather shoes. A complete fast (no food or drink from sunset to sunset), however, is the principal mode of abstinence and one that serves several purposes. For some, fasting is a religious obligation. For others, it is a form of self-discipline as well. In a day that emphasizes the spiritual over the physical and the expiation of sins, fasting is a visible demonstration of the ability to control one's desires and urges. Fasting is also a means of awakening compassion, a reminder of those who are hungry and in need. For whatever reason, fasting is an integral part of Yom Kippur observance and — as several of the selections in this section make obvious — it is undoubtedly one of the most important aspects of the holiday.

The poetry here, which begins with the work of medieval poets Solomon Ibn Gabirol and Yehuda Halevi and concludes with a poem by the late-twentieth-century American writer Robin Becker, ranges from the devotional to the irreverent. Ibn Gabirol's "Confession," for example, intended for the Yom Kippur service, is liturgical and worshipful, as is Halevi's "Hear." Both poems acknowledge their speakers' frailties, while emphasizing God's power and grandeur. Several centuries later, however, such poets as Cynthia Ozick, Chana Bloch, and Robert Pinsky — all of whose work is included in this section — express more doubt than belief, more indignation than faith. The speaker in Ozick's poem "Yom Kippur, 5726," for instance, challenges the meaningfulness and purpose of Yom Kippur ritual. Rather than praise God or plead for forgiveness, she would prefer that God apologize to her, both for the state of the world and for her own self-doubt: "Let God renounce what's done/ And for his absence and my doubt/ Atone." Pinsky, too, questions the relevance of Yom Kippur observance in his poem "Avenue," whose narrator, drunk and "dead to the world," inhabits a universe where penitence is neither sought nor granted. In a different tone but similar spirit, Chana Bloch finds little meaning in the traditional Yom Kippur fast, in her poem "The Converts." Counting the hours until sunset, the poem's speaker can think only of food: "fish/ and little steaming potatoes." Only "the converts," those who have chosen Judaism deliberately and consciously, "sing every syllable," savor every word. And the narrator, recognizing their passion, can only covet "what they think we've got."

Not all the twentieth-century poems included in this section, of course, are characterized by a mood of cynicism or doubt. The poems of both Marcia Falk and Sam Goldemberg, for example, call forth the intended spirit of the holiday, as does Yehuda Amichai's memory poem, "On the Day of Atonement." In this poem, Amichai's speaker pauses in front of an Arab button and thread shop in the Old City of Jerusalem, and recalls that his father had a similar store in another place, another time. The narrator's concluding thoughts coincide with the end of the Yom Kippur service. The shopkeeper, the speaker observes, "lowered the shutter and locked the door," a gesture that replicates the "closing of the gates" referred to in the concluding prayers of the Yom Kippur service and one that reinforces the poem's theme of unspoken but not unrecognized brotherhood.

Memories of Yom Kippur come in various forms, and the notion of repentance and teshuvah seems to fit naturally with the concept of autobiography. The excerpt from Chaim Grade's memoir, a continuation of the selection reprinted in the Rosh Hashanah section, focuses on the author's mother and her self-sacrificing nature. Grade, however, in the spirit of the holiday, offers apologies for not being the devout son he believes his mother would have liked him to be. Marjorie Agosín recalls her early days of Yom Kippur observance in Chile in the two short pieces included here from her memoir, The Alphabet in My Hands. Golda Meir's memoir, My Life, records among other things her recollections of Israel's 1973 Yom Kippur war. The excerpt reprinted here is a personal glimpse into history from the perspective of one who was intimately involved with its making. For the careful reader, it is also Meir's public declaration of atonement, an exercise in the ritual of self-examination and repentance so essential to the meaning and purpose of Yom Kippur.

In the passage included here from Legends of Our Time, one of several memoirs of his years in the concentration camps, Elie Wiesel recounts the strange story of Pinhas, a fellow prisoner, who—with his own twisted logic—manages to defy his God on Yom Kippur. With this selection, ironically titled "The Day Without Forgiveness," one begins to understand the rationale for the objections raised by such poets as Ozick, Pinsky, and Bloch. Yom Kippur is a time for forgiveness and understanding, but the Holocaust brings a new perspective to one's view of the world and God's role in it.

Forgiveness in one form or another is the dominant theme of Yom Kippur, and every story in this section, like the personal essays, expresses some aspect of this motif. The short stories of Sholom Aleichem, I. L. Peretz, and Israel Joseph Singer — all written in Yiddish and set in the old-world culture of eastern Europe — share a somewhat ironic vision of repentance and what that might imply, given the absurdities of the human condition. Aleichem understands all too well that fasting on Yom Kippur is serious business, yet he manages to poke fun at the whole enterprise and the seriousness with which the pious approach this tradition in his story "A Yom Kippur Scandal." Peretz's "Yom Kippur in Hell" is equally sardonic, yet with a final note of existential futility. Israel Joseph Singer, older brother to the more famous Isaac Bashevis, in his short story "Repentance," gives another rather unconventional interpretation of teshuvah, which — for his Hasidic protagonist — involves more indulgence than abstinence, more celebration than observance. Like Aleichem, Singer and Peretz manage to mock tradition gently, and by so doing bring into question the larger concept of moral transgression and the possibility of forgiveness.

For the almost twenty authors represented in this section, Yom Kippur presents diverse and at times conflicting themes: abstinence and self-denial, yet joy and gratitude as well; self-reflection and repentance, but also doubts and questions; forgiveness and understanding for some, remembrance of those things that can never be comprehended for others. For many, this most serious of Jewish holidays represents the opportunity (as always in Jewish tradition) for inquiry, self-doubt, irony, humor, and a continual discussion as to the meaning and purpose of religious belief and practice.

Yom Kippur, with all its solemnity and synagogue-based observance, is followed by the colorful and joyous festival of Sukkoth, the fall harvest celebration that follows only a few days later. Sukkoth, in turn, is succeeded by Hanukkah, a winter holiday of warmth, light, and home celebration — and the subject of the subsequent section of this volume.

# Poetry

# ❧ Confession

SOLOMON IBN GABIROL

Shame-stricken, bending low,
My God, I come before Thee, for I know
That even as Thou on high
Exalted art in power and majesty,
So weak and frail am I,
That perfect as Thou art,
So I deficient am in every part.

Thou art all-wise, all-good, all-great, divine
Yea, Thou art God: eternity is Thine,
While I, a thing of clay,
The creature of a day,
Pass shadowlike, a breath, that comes and flees away. . . .

My God, I know my sins are numberless,
More than I can recall to memory
Or tell their tale: yet some will I confess,
Even a few, though as a drop it be
    In all the sea.

I will declare my trespasses and sin
And peradventure silence then may fall
Upon their waves and billows' raging din,
And Thou wilt hear from heaven, when I call,
    And pardon all. . . .

My God, if mine iniquity
Too great for all endurance be,
Yet for Thy Name's sake pardon me.
For if in Thee I may not dare
To hope, who else will hear my prayer?
Therefore, although Thou slay me, yet
In Thee my faith and trust is set:
And though Thou seekest out my sin,
From Thee to Thee I fly to win
A place of refuge, and within

Thy shadow from Thy anger hide,
Until Thy wrath be turned aside.
Unto Thy mercy I will cling,
Until Thou hearken pitying:
Nor will I quit my hold of Thee
Until Thy blessing light on me.

Remember, O my God, I pray,
How Thou hast formed me out of clay,
What troubles set upon my way.
Do Thou not, then, my deeds requite
According to my sins aright,
But with Thy mercy infinite.
For well I know, through good and ill
That Thou in love has chastened still,
Afflicting me in faithfulness,
That Thou my latter end may'st bless.

*Translated by Alice Lucas*

# 🌿 Hear

YEHUDA HALEVI

Hear, those who dare
To prostrate themselves before you.
Father, will you close your ear
To the deed of Your children?

Yes from the depths they called,
They fled from many hardships.
Oh do not let them leave empty-handed
Today from your paths.

A wave of guilt wanted to stifle
The hotly upwelling heart,
Don't do it for their sake,
Do it for Your sake, oh my rock.

And today erase their errors.
Accept their simple prayers as
An offering. Turn their heart to you,
And lend them your ear.

Refresh those who are weary with tears,
Gather in the lost lamb,
Let their shepherd arise,
And attend to his herd tenderly.

Those who walk upright,
Show them forgiveness today!
When late in the day they beseech you,
May your blessing find them.

*Translated by Thomas Kovach, Eva Jospe, and Gilya Gerder Schmidt*

# ❧ On the Day of Atonement

YEHUDA AMICHAI

On the Day of Atonement in the year 5728, I put on
dark holiday clothes and went to the Old City in Jerusalem.
For a long time I stood in the niche of an Arab's shop,
not far from the Nablus Gate, a store
for belts and zippers and spools of thread
in every shade and snaps and buckles.
A rare light and many colors, like a Holy Ark opened.

I said without speaking that my father
had a store like this for buttons and thread.
I told him without words about the decades,
the causes, events, that now I am here,
and my father's store was burned there and he's buried here.

When I finished it was time for the closing prayer.
He too lowered the shutter and locked the door,
and with all those who prayed, I went home.

Translated by Shirley Kaufman

# 🪰 Yom Kippur, 5726

CYNTHIA OZICK

i

Abstaining from the congregation
Torah is a meal I do not take
Synagogue a stomach of allegation
God the fast I will not break.

ii

From feeding on too much Jew
History reels with cramp:
The century a pew
For those who sigh and stamp.

iii

Beat on the door of the rib!
(As much go cup the dead.)
Kiss the Law's spangled bib!
(On Yom Kippur peddle bread.)

iv

The world will not down,
Digestion is shallow.
What God will not disown,
Who can swallow?

v

Sooner will the proton halt
Then he revoke:
Wherefore this feast of salt
And smoke.

vi

The hour is singled out:
Let God renounce what's done
And for his absence and my doubt
Atone.

vii
Let each man sup
On seasoned blows,
On armament and whip.
Then let the banquet close.

viii
(Jerusalem the city
Lasts deeper than our days
But a famine of pity
Gluts always.)

## 🏵 The Converts

CHANA BLOCH

On the holiest day, we fast till sundown.
I watch the sun stand still
as the horizon edges towards it. Four hours to go.
The rabbi's mouth opens and closes and opens.
I think: fish
and little steaming potatoes,
parsley clinging to them like an ancient script.

Only the converts, six of them in the corner,
in their prayer shawls and feathery beards,
sing every syllable.
What word
are they savoring now?
If they go on loving that way, we'll be here all night,

Why did they follow us here, did they think
we were happier?
Did someone tell them we knew
the lost words
to open God's mouth?

The converts sway in white silk,
their necks bent forward in yearning
like swans,
and I covet
what they think we've got.

# Avenue

ROBERT PINSKY

They stack bright pyramids of goods and gather
Mop-helves in sidewalk barrels. They keen, they boogie.
Paints, fruits, clean bolts of cottons and synthetics,
Clarity and plumage of October skies.

Way of the costermonger's wooden barrow
And also the secular marble cinquefoil and lancet
Of the great store. They persist. The jobber tells
The teller in the bank and she retells

Whatever it is to the shopper and the shopper
Mentions it to the retailer by the way.
They mutter and stumble, derelict. They write
These theys I write. Scant storefront pushbroom Jesus

Of Haitian hardware — they travel in shadows, they flog
Sephardic softgoods. They strain. Mid-hustle they faint
And shrivel. Or Snoring on grates they rise to thrive.
Bonemen and pumpkins of All Saints. Kol Nidre,

Blunt shovel of atonement, a blade of song
From the terra-cotta temple: Lord, forgive us
Our promises, we chant. Or we churn our wino
Syllables and stares on the Avenue. We, they —

Jack. Mrs. Whisenant from the bakery. Sam Lee.
This is the way, its pavement crackwork burnished
With plantain. In strollers they bawl and claw. They flourish.
Furniture, Florist, Pets. My mongrel tongue

Of nudnik and criminentlies, the tarnished flute
And brogue of quidnuncs in the bars, in Casey's
Black amber air of spent Hiram Walker, attuned.
Sweet ash of White Owl. Ten High. They touch. Eyes blurred

Stricken with passion as in a Persian lyric
They flower and stroke. They couple. From the Korean,
Staples and greens. From the Christian Lebanese,
Home electronics. Why is that Friday "Good"?

Why "Day of Atonement" for release from vows?
Because we tried us, to be at one, because
We say as one we traffic, we dice, we stare.
Some they remember that won't remember them —

Their headlights found me stoned, like a bundled sack
Lying in the Avenue, late. They didn't speak
My language. For them, a small adventure. They hefted
Me over the curb and bore me to an entry

Out of the way. Illuminated footwear
On both sides. How I stank. Dead drunk. They left me
Breathing in my bower between the Halloween
Brogans and pumps on crystal pedestals.

But I was dead to the world. The midnight city
In autumn. Day of attainment, tall saints
Who saved me. My taints, day of anointment. Oil
Of rose and almond in the haircutting parlor,

Motor oil swirling rainbows in gutter water.
Ritually unattainted, the congregation
File from the place of worship and resume
The rumbling drum and hautbois of conversation,

Speech of the granary, of the cloven lanes
Of traffic, of salvaged silver. Not shriven and yet
Not rent, they stride the Avenue, banter, barter.
Capering, on fire, they cleave to the riven hub.

# 🎋 Yom Kippur (Chacra Colorada, 1955)

ISAAC GOLDEMBERG

The synagogue is bursting
with ladies dressed up in antique jewelry
showing off furs collected in exile
the men in velvet skullcaps
— heads infested with letters and numbers —
buzz like flies
around the bimah
All the while down the Lima streets
old grey-bearded Jews
cautiously move along
with empty stomachs
knowing that on this day
God records in his Account Book
in His own handwriting
which souls to save and which to damn
They arrive punctually at the temple steps
(their memory escapes them over bridge
and desert)
The rabbi blows the shofar
The old men grab each other's hands
lowering their heads
they walk in like ghosts.

*Translated by Isaac Goldemberg and David Unger*

## ❧ Open Gate

MARCIA FALK

The arc of evening
slowly turning,

the sun's blue shadows
washed away,

the gate still open
as three stars wait

to pierce the sky —
In the corridor

where night
bares its maze

you begin
to begin again.

## 🪶 Yom Kippur, Taos, New Mexico

ROBIN BECKER

I've expanded like the swollen door in summer
    to fit my own dimensions. Your loneliness

is a letter I read and put away, a daily reminder
    in the cry of the magpie that I am

still capable of inflicting pain
    at this distance.

Like a painting, our talk is dense with description,
    half-truths, landscapes, phrases layered

with a patina over time. When she came into my life
    I didn't hesitate.

Or is that only how it seems now, looking back?
    Or is that only how you accuse me, looking back?

Long ago, this desert was an inland sea. In the mountains
    you can still find shells.

It's these strange divagations I've come to love: midday sun
    on pink escarpments; dusk on gray sandstone;

toe-and-finger holes along the three hundred and fifty-seven foot
    climb to Acoma Pueblo, where the spirit

of the dead hovers about its earthly home
    four days, before the prayer sticks drive it away.

Today all good Jews collect their crimes like old clothes
    to be washed and given to the poor.

I remember how my father held his father around the shoulders
    as they walked to the old synagogue in Philadelphia.

"We're almost there, Pop," he said. "A few more blocks."
I want to tell you that we, too, are almost there,

for someone has mapped this autumn field with meaning, and any
October, brooding in me, will open to reveal

our names — inscribed or absent —
among the dry thistles and spent weeds.

# Memoir

## ⅔ The Yom Kippur War

from *My Life*

GOLDA MEIR

Of all the events upon which I have touched in this book, none is so hard for me to write about as the war of October, 1973, the Yom Kippur War. But it happened, and so it belongs here—not as a military account, because that I leave to others, but as a near disaster, a nightmare that I myself experienced and which will always be with me.

Even as a personal story, there is still a great deal that cannot be told, and what I write is far from being definitive. But it is the truth as I felt and knew it in the course of that war, which was the fifth to be forced on Israel in the twenty-seven years that have passed since the state was founded.

There are two points I should like to make at once. The first is that we won the Yom Kippur War, and I am convinced that in their heart of hearts the political and military leaders of both Syria and Egypt know that they were defeated again, despite their initial gains. The other is that the world in general and Israel's enemies in particular should know that the circumstances which took the lives of the more than 2,500 Israelis who were killed in the Yom Kippur War will never ever recur.

The war began on October 6, but when I think about it now, my mind goes back to May, when we received information about the reinforcement of Syrian and Egyptian troops on the borders. Our intelligence people thought that it was most unlikely that war would break out; nonetheless, we decided to treat the matter seriously. At that time I went to general headquarters myself. Both the minister of defense and the chief of staff, David Elazar (who is known throughout the country by his nickname, Dado) briefed me thoroughly on the armed forces' state of preparedness, and I was convinced that the army was ready for any contingency—for full-scale war. Also, my mind was put at rest about the notion of a sufficiently early warning. Then, for whatever reason the tension relaxed.

In September we started to receive information about a buildup of Syrian troops on the Golan Heights, and on the thirteenth of that month an air battle took place with the Syrians, which ended in the downing of thirteen Syrian MIGs. Despite this, our intelligence people were very reassuring: It was most unlikely they said, that there would be any major Syrian reaction. But this time the tension remained, and what's more, it had spread to the Egyptians. Still our intelligence assessment remained the same, the continued Syrian reinforcement of troops was, they explained, caused by the Syrians' fear that *we* would attack, and throughout the month, including on the eve of my departure to Europe, this explanation for the Syrian move was repeated again and again.

On Monday, October 1, Yisrael Galili called me in Strasbourg. Among other things, he told me that he had talked to Dayan and that they both felt that as soon as I got back, we should have a serious discussion about the situation in the Golan Heights. I told him that I would definitely return the next day and that we should meet the day after.

Late on Wednesday morning I met with Dayan, Allon, Galili, the commander of the air force, the chief of staff and, because the head of intelligence was sick that day, the head of military intelligence research. Dayan opened the meeting, and the chief of staff and the head of intelligence research described the situation on both fronts in great detail. There were things that disturbed them, but the military evaluation was still that we were in no danger of facing a joint Syrian-Egyptian attack and, what's more, that it was very unlikely that Syria would attack us alone. The building and movement of Egyptian forces in the south was probably due to the maneuvers that were always held around this time of year, and in the north the bolstering and new deployment of forces were still explained as they had been before. The fact that several Syrian army units had been transferred only a week before from the Syrian-Jordanian border was interpreted as part of a recent détente between the two countries and as a Syrian gesture of goodwill toward Jordan. Nobody at the meeting thought that it was necessary to call up the reserves, and nobody thought that war was imminent. But it was decided to put a further discussion of the situation on the agenda for Sunday's cabinet meeting.

On Thursday, as usual, I went to Tel Aviv. For years I had been spending Thursdays and Fridays in my Tel Aviv office, Saturdays at my house in Ramat Aviv and returning to Jerusalem either late Saturday evening or early Sunday morning, and there seemed to be no reason for changing the pattern that week. In fact, it was a short week in any case, because Yom Kippur (the Day of Atonement) was to begin on Friday evening, and most people in Israel were taking a long weekend.

I suppose that by now, thanks in part to the war, even non-Jews who had never heard of Yom Kippur before know that this is the most solemn and the most sacred of all the days in the Jewish calendar. It is the one day in the year that Jews throughout the world — even if they are not very pious — unite in some sort of observance. Believing Jews, totally abstaining from food, drink and work, spend Yom Kippur (which, like all Jewish holidays and the Sabbath itself, begins in the evening of one day and ends in the evening of the next) in the synagogue, praying and atoning for sins that they may have committed in the course of the past year. Other Jews, including those who do not actually fast, usually find their own individual way of marking Yom Kippur, by not going to work, by not eating in public and by going to the synagogue, even if for only an hour or two, to hear the great opening prayer, Kol Nidrei, on the eve of Yom Kippur or to listen to the ritual blowing of the shofar, the ram's horn, that closes the fast. But for most Jews everywhere, regardless of how they observe it, Yom Kippur is a day unlike any other.

In Israel it is a day on which the country comes to a virtual standstill. For Jews, there are no newspapers, no television or radio broadcasts, no public transportation, and all schools, shops, restaurants, cafés and offices are closed for twenty-four hours. Since nothing, however, not even Yom Kippur, is as important to Jews as life itself, danger to life overrides everything, and all essential public services function, though many make do for those twenty-four hours with skeleton staffs. The most essential public service for all in Israel, unfortunately, is the army, but as many soldiers as possible are always given leave so that they can be at home with their families on this day.

On Friday, October 5, we received a report that worried me. The families of the Russian advisers in Syria were packing up and leaving in a hurry. It reminded me of what had happened prior to the Six-Day War, and I didn't like it at all. Why the haste? What did those Russian families know that we didn't know? Was it possible that they were being evacuated? In all the welter of information pouring into my office that one little detail had taken root in my mind, and I couldn't shake myself free of it. But since no one around me seemed very perturbed about it, I tried not to become obsessive. Besides, intuition is a very tricky thing; sometimes it must be acted upon at once, but sometimes it is merely a symptom of anxiety and then it can be very misleading indeed.

I asked the minister of defense, the chief of staff and the head of intelligence whether they thought this piece of information was very important. No, it hadn't in any way changed their assessment of the situation. I was assured that we would get adequate warning of any real trouble, and anyway, sufficient reinforcements were being sent to the fronts to carry out any holding operation that might be required. Everything that was necessary had been done, and the army was placed on high alert, particularly the air force and the armored corps. When he left me, the head of intelligence met Lou Kaddar in the corridor. Later she told me that he had patted her shoulder, smiled and said, "Don't worry. There won't be a war." But I was worried; furthermore, I couldn't understand his certainty that all was well. What if he were wrong? If there was even the slightest chance of war, we should at least call up the reserves. At any rate, I wanted a meeting at least of the cabinet ministers who would be spending the Yom Kippur weekend in Tel Aviv. It turned out that very few of them were around. I was reluctant to ask the two National Religious Party ministers who lived in Jerusalem to come to a meeting in Tel Aviv on the eve of Yom Kippur, and several other ministers had already left for their kibbutzim, which were all fairly far away. Still, nine ministers were in town, and I told my military secretary to schedule an emergency meeting for Friday noon.

We gathered in my Tel Aviv office. In addition to the cabinet members, the meeting was attended by the chief of staff and the head of intelligence. We heard all the reports again, including the one that concerned the rushed — and to me still inexplicable — departure of the Russian families from Syria, but again, no one seemed very alarmed. Nevertheless, I decided to speak my mind. "Look," I said, "I have a terrible feeling that this has all happened before. It reminds me of 1967, when we were accused of massing troops against Syria, which is exactly what the Arab press is saying now. And I think that it all means something." As a result, although as a rule a cabinet decision is required for a full scale call-up, that Friday we passed a resolution, suggested by Galili, that if necessary, the minister of defense and I could do so by ourselves. I also said that we should get in touch with the Americans so that they could get in touch with the Russians and tell them in no uncertain terms that the United States was not in the mood for trouble. The meeting broke up, but I stayed on at the office for a while, thinking.

How could it be that I was still so terrified of war breaking out when the present chief of staff, two former chiefs of staff (Dayan and Chaim Bar-Lev, who was my minister of commerce and industry) and the head of intelligence were far from sure that it would? After all, they weren't just ordinary soldiers. They were all highly experienced generals, men who had fought and led other men in spectacularly victorious battles. Each one of them had an outstanding military record, and as for our intelligence services, they were known to be among the best in the world. Not only that, but foreign sources with whom we were in constant touch agreed absolutely with the assessment of our experts. So why was it that I was still so ill at ease? Was I perhaps talking myself into something? I couldn't answer my own questions.

Today I know what I should have done. I should have overcome my hesitations. I knew as well as anyone else what full-scale mobilization meant and how much money it would cost, and I also knew that only a few months before, in May, we had had an alert and the reserves had been called up; but nothing had happened. But I also understood that perhaps there had been no war in May exactly because the reserves had been called up. That Friday morning I should have listened to the warnings of my own heart and ordered a call-up. For me, that fact cannot and never will be erased, and there can be no consolation in anything that anyone else has to say or in all of the commonsense rationalizations with which my colleagues have tried to comfort me.

It doesn't matter what logic dictated. It matters only that I, who was so accustomed to making decisions — and who did make them throughout the war — failed to make that one decision. It isn't a question of feeling guilty. I, too, can rationalize and tell myself that in the face of such total certainty on the part of our military intelligence — and the almost equally total acceptance of its evaluations on the part of our foremost military men — it would have been unreasonable of me to have insisted on a call-up. But I know that I should have done so, and I shall live with that terrible knowledge for the rest of my life. I will never again be the person I was before the Yom Kippur War.

Then, however, I sat in the office, thinking and agonizing until I just couldn't sit there anymore and I went home. Menachem and Aya had invited a few friends to drop in after dinner. Jews eat dinner early on the eve of Yom Kippur because traditionally it is their last meal for twenty-four hours, and by the time the stars are out the fast has begun. We sat down to eat; but I was very restless and had no appetite at all, and although they wanted me to stay on with their friends, I excused myself and went to bed. But I couldn't sleep.

It was a still, hot night, and through the open window I could hear the voices of Menachem and Aya's friends talking quietly in the garden below. Once or twice the children's dog barked, but otherwise it was a typically silent Yom Kippur night. I lay awake for hours, unable to sleep. Eventually I must have dozed off. Then, at about 4 A.M. the phone next to my bed rang. It was my military secretary. Information had been received that the Egyptians and the Syrians would launch a joint attack on Israel "late in the afternoon." There was no doubt anymore. The intelligence source was authoritative. I told Lior to ask Dayan, Dado, Allon and

Galili to be in my office before 7 A.M. On the way there, I caught sight of an old man going to synagogue, his prayer shawl over his shoulders holding the hand of a small child. They looked like symbols of Judaism itself, and I remember thinking sorrowfully that all over Israel, young men were fasting in synagogues today and that it was from their prayers that they would soon be called to arms.

## ⅋ from *My Mother's Sabbath Days*

CHAIM GRADE

On Yom Kippur, before the Afternoon Service begins, the beadle pounds on the cantor's table: there is to be a half-hour intermission.

The younger women, who have their little ones to feed, rush out from behind the partition of the women's section. The older matrons stay in their seats, resting or chatting about daughters-in-law and grandchildren. Also remaining in the synagogue are the poor market-women: all year long they are too harried and preoccupied to enter the beth midrash, at least, then, this one full day, the Day of Atonement, they wish to spend wholly within the sacred walls. Thus it is with astonishment that they see Vella the fruit-seller wrap up her books in her white kerchief, place the bundle on her "pew," and leave the synagogue.

Mother is going home to feed our cat: animals are not obligated to fast.

As soon as she reaches the wicket of the main gate, she can already hear the cat's cry. The animal senses her mistress's steps from afar and is scratching at the locked door. At this, Mother smiles — her only smile on this Day of Atonement. It warms her heart to know that at least one living creature is so closely tied to her. Lonely as she is, in whom else can she confide? Her only son has lately become increasingly moody, and sunk in melancholy. He sits in the smithy all day, reading, always reading. She has long understood that he would never be overly pious; now she pleads with him: "Why do you bury yourself in this hole-in-the-wall? At least go out for a walk sometimes. Other young fellows find joy in living." His only response is to grow still moodier.

She opens the door and the cat jumps up at her. From the cupboard, Mother takes the saucer filled with bread soaked in milk which she had prepared the day before, places it before the cat, and speaks to her:

"Lazybones, why do you always stay in this hole-in-the-wall? Go on out for a walk."

She realizes with a start that she is speaking to the cat exactly as she has often (not to compare the two) spoken to her son. "I must be growing senile," she thinks. But just then she hears another cat mewing. Lisa has locked her cat up in the house, and he is wailing with hunger.

Wasting no time, Mother hurries back to the synagogue. Lisa is chatting with her "fine ladies" about clothes, and about all the work she will have, on the eve of the festival of Sukkoth, preparing the geese for her customers. When she sees my mother, stern-faced, heading toward her, she becomes uneasy — this time, for the life of her, she cannot think of any offense she might have committed against tradition. On the Sabbath of Penitence, between the New Year and the Day of Atonement, she had not gone out walking with her umbrella, and even her husband had taken his prayer shawl and gone to the synagogue. . . . Mother called her aside:

"Lisa, you locked up your cat. Go, give him some food — he's not obligated to fast."

"But I'll miss the Afternoon Service," objects Lisa, fearful of losing her chance to plead for and win a favorable decree for the coming year.

"That doesn't matter." Mother renders judgment with the assurance of a rebbetzin: "The Almighty will wait for you. Your prayers will ascend to Heaven together with all the others."

Lisa obeys and goes to feed the cat. She walks with her head held so straight and stiff that, had a lamp filled with kerosene been placed upon it, not a drop would have spilled.

The congregation prepares to begin the Afternoon Service. But my mother, instead of reading in her Tehinah, as she usually does before the start of the congregational prayers, peers through the curtain into the men's section of the synagogue. The older men, wrapped in white linen kittels, are leaning against their oaken lecterns and resting. Others are making use of the intermission to study a paragraph or two of Mishnah. The young fellows stand in a huddle and talk. Only her son stands alone, in back of the cantor's pulpit, and speaks to no one. He looks pale, lost in his thoughts, and unkempt. She is saddened, and with a heavy heart, she murmurs:

"Lord of the Universe! All the world says that a mother's heart feels her child's pain. I, however, do not know what it is that weighs so heavily upon my son. Is your Torah so difficult that it robs a young man of all joy? I know I am not worthy of having a son who is a great scholar. Then let him at least be an honest Jew, a craftsman like Reb Boruhel, may he rest in peace."

Of all the voices raised in either the men's or the women's section, I hear only my mother's plaintive cry. The fine threads of her weeping stretch toward me, entwine themselves about me, as spider-webs in autumn entwine themselves about the gnarled branches of trees. I stand behind the bima, unable to pray. Why is she so meek and humble toward everyone? Why does she always feel that she has sinned before God? Why can't I rescue her from her exhausting toil, so that she will not waste away in the heat of summer and in the frosts of winter, sitting beside her baskets. She feeds me and believes in my piety, and here I am deceiving her. . . .

When, at nightfall, Yom Kippur ends and everyone leaves the synagogue, sons stand waiting for their fast-weakened mothers, to take them by the arm and lead them home. Only my mother always rushes home alone, to prepare sweetened tea — so that I may have something over which to pronounce the Havdalah blessings — as well as to warm my food for breaking the fast. She never thinks of herself.

This time, however, as she leaves the women's section, she abruptly stops, confused and surprised: I am waiting for her. I take from her the mahzor wrapped in the white kerchief, give her my arm and lead her home. The narrow synagogue street is filled with Jews reciting the blessing for the crescent of the New Moon. I do not stop. Mother utters a weak frightened laugh:

"Honoring your mother is an important commandment, but it would be better at the beginning of a new year, if you too recited the blessing for the New Moon."

"I am not that great rabbi of the Talmud whose mother washed his feet then drank the water. I can't forgive myself for letting you sacrifice yourself as you have so that I might study the Torah."

Mother is silent. She feels a wetness in her eyes, as though the dried up fountain of her tears is about to flow again. She has a premonition of some impending ill. On Rosh Hashanah she had lost her white kerchief and Lisa had found it and returned it to her. That was a rebuke from Heaven, for she had chastised Lisa, while her own son . . . She is afraid to think further, and takes the prayerbook from my hand, as though fearing that I might lose her last comfort — the white kerchief.

*Translated by Channa Kleinerman Goldstein and Inna Hecker Grade*

## 🪶 The Day Without Forgiveness

from *Legends of Our Time*

ELIE WIESEL

With a lifeless look, a painful smile on his face, while digging a hole in the ground, Pinhas moved his lips in silence. He appeared to be arguing with someone within himself and, judging from his expression, seemed close to admitting defeat.

I had never seen him so downhearted. I knew that his body would not hold out much longer. His strength was already abandoning him, his movements were becoming more heavy, more chaotic. No doubt he knew it too. But death figured only rarely in our conversations. We preferred to deny its presence, to reduce it, as in the past, to a simple allusion, something abstract, inoffensive, a word like any other.

"What are you thinking about? What's wrong?"

Pinhas lowered his head, as if to conceal his embarrassment, or his sadness, or both, and let a long time go by before he answered, in a voice scarcely audible: "Tomorrow is Yom Kippur."

Then I too felt depressed. My first Yom Kippur in the camp. Perhaps my last. The day of judgment, of atonement. Tomorrow the heavenly tribunal would sit and pass sentence: "And like unto a flock, the creatures of this world shall pass before Thee." Once upon a time — last year — the approach of this day of tears, of penitence and fear, had made me tremble. Tomorrow we would present ourselves before God, who sees everything and who knows everything, and we would say: "Father, have pity on your children." Would I be capable of praying with fervor again? Pinhas shook himself abruptly. His glance plunged into mine.

"Tomorrow is the Day of Atonement and I have just made a decision: I am not going to fast. Do you hear? I am not going to fast."

I asked for no explanation. I knew he was going to die and suddenly I was afraid that by way of justification he might declare: "It is simple, I have decided not to comply with the Law anymore and not to fast because in the eyes of man and of God I am already dead, and the dead can disobey the commandments of the Torah." I lowered my head and made believe I was not thinking about anything but the earth I was digging up under the sky more dark than the earth itself.

We belonged to the same *Kommando*. We always managed to work side by side. Our age difference did not stop him from treating me like a friend. He must have been past forty. I was fifteen. Before the war, he had been rosh yeshivah, director of a rabbinical school somewhere in Galicia. Often, to outwit our hunger or to forget our reasons for despair, we would study a page of the Talmud from memory. I relived my childhood by forcing myself not to think about those who were gone. If one of my arguments pleased Pinhas, if I quoted a commentary without distorting its meaning, he would smile at me and say: "I should have liked to have you among my disciples."

And I would answer: "But I am your disciple; where we are matters little."

That was false, the place was of capital importance. According to the law of the camp I was his equal; I used the familiar form when I addressed him. Any other form of address was inconceivable.

"Do you hear?" Pinhas shouted defiantly. "I will not fast."

"I understand. You are right. One must not fast. Not at Auschwitz. Here we live outside time, outside sin. Yom Kippur does not apply to Auschwitz."

Ever since Rosh Hashanah, the New Year, the question had been bitterly debated all over camp. Fasting meant a quicker death. Here everybody fasted all year round. Every day was Yom Kippur. And the book of life and death was no longer in God's hands, but in the hands of the executioner. The words Mi yihye u-mi yamut, who shall live and who shall die, had a terrible real meaning here, an immediate bearing. And all the prayers in the world could not alter the gezar din, the inexorable movement of fate. Here, in order to live, one had to eat, not pray.

"You are right, Pinhas," I said forcing myself to withstand his gaze. "You must eat tomorrow. You've been here longer than I have, longer than many of us. You need your strength. You have to save your strength, watch over it, protect it. You should not go beyond your limits. Or tempt misfortune. That would be a sin."

Me, his disciple? I gave him lessons, I gave him advice, as if I were his elder, his guide.

"That is not it," said Pinhas, getting irritated. "I could hold out for one day without food. It would not be the first time."

"Then what is it?"

"A decision. Until now, I've accepted everything. Without bitterness without reservation. I have told myself: 'God knows what He is doing!' I have submitted to His will. Now I have had enough, I have reached my limit. If He knows what He is doing, then it is serious; and it is not any less serious if He does not. Therefore, I have decided to tell Him: 'It is enough.'"

I said nothing. How could I argue with him? I was going through the same crisis. Every day I was moving a little further away from the God of my childhood. He had become a stranger to me; sometimes, I even thought He was my enemy.

The appearance of Edek put an end to our conversation. He was our master, our king. The *kapo*. This young Pole with rosy cheeks, with the movements of a wild animal, enjoyed catching his slaves by surprise and making them shout with fear. Still all adolescent, he enjoyed possessing such power over so many adults. We dreaded his changeable moods, his sudden fits of anger: without unclenching his teeth, his eyes half closed, he would beat his victims long after they had lost consciousness and had ceased to moan.

"Well?" he said, planting himself in front of us, his arms folded. "Taking a little nap? Talking over old times? You think you are at a resort? Or in the synagogue?"

A cruel flame lit his blue eyes, but it went out just as quickly. An aborted rage. We began to shovel furiously, not thinking about anything but the ground which opened up menacingly before us. Edek insulted us a few more times and then walked off.

Pinhas did not feel like talking anymore, neither did I. For him the die had been cast. The break with God appeared complete.

Meanwhile, the pit under our legs was becoming wider and deeper. Soon our heads would hardly be visible above the ground. I had the weird sensation that I was digging a grave. For whom? For Pinhas? For myself? Perhaps for our memories.

On my return to camp, I found it plunged into feverish anticipation. They were preparing to welcome the holiest and longest day of the year. My barracks neighbors, a father and son, were talking in low voices. One was saying: "Let us hope the roll call does not last too long." The other added "Let us hope that the soup is distributed before the sun sets, otherwise we will not have the right to touch it."

Their prayers were answered. The roll call unfolded without incident, without delay, without public hanging. The section chief hurriedly distributed the soup; I hurriedly gulped it down. I ran to wash, to purify myself. By the time the day was drawing to a close, I was ready.

Some day before, on the eve of Rosh Hashanah, all the Jews in camp —*kapos* included— had congregated at the square where roll was taken, and we had implored the God of Abraham, Isaac, and Jacob to end our humiliation, to change sides, to break his pact with the enemy. In unison we had said *Kaddish* for the dead and for the living as well. Officers and soldiers, machine guns in hand, had stood by, amused spectators, on the other side of the barbed wire.

Now, we did not go back there for *Kol Nidre*. We were afraid of a selection: in preceding years, the Day of Atonement had been turned into a day of mourning. Yom Kippur had become Tishah be-Av, the day the Temple was destroyed.

Thus, each barracks housed its own synagogue. It was more prudent. I was sorry, because Pinhas was in another block.

A Hungarian rabbi officiated as our cantor. His voice stirred my memories and evoked that legend according to which, on the night of Yom Kippur, the dead rise from their graves and come to pray with the living. I thought: "Then it is true; that is what really happens. The legend is confirmed at Auschwitz."

For weeks, several learned Jews had gathered every night in our block to transcribe from memory — by hand, on toilet paper — the prayers for the High Holy Days. Each cantor received a copy. Ours read in a loud voice and we repeated each verse after him. The *Kol Nidre*, which releases us from all vows made under constraint, now seemed to me anachronistic, absurd, even though it had been composed in similar circumstances, in Spain, right near the Inquisition stakes. Once a year the converts would assemble and cry out to God: "Know this, all that we said is unsaid, all that we have done is undone." *Kol Nidre?* A sad joke. Here and now we no longer had any secret vows to make or to deny: everything was clear, irrevocable.

Then came the *Viddui*, the great Confession. There again, everything rang false, none of it concerned us anymore. *Ashamnu*, we have sinned. *Bagadnu*, we have betrayed. *Gazalnu*, we have stolen. What? Us? We have sinned? Against whom? By doing what? We have betrayed? Whom? Undoubtedly this was the first time since God judged His creation that victims beat their breast accusing themselves of the crimes of their executioners.

Why did we take responsibility for sins and offenses which not one of us could ever have had the desire or the possibility of committing? Perhaps we felt guilty despite everything. Things were simpler that way. It was better to believe our punishments had meaning, that we had deserved them; to believe in a cruel but just God was better than not to believe at all. It was in order not to provoke an open war between God and His people that we had chosen to spare Him, and we cried out: "You are our God, blessed be Your name. You smite us without pity, You shed our blood, we give thanks to You for it, O Eternal One, for You are determined to show us that You are just and that Your name is justice!"

I admit having joined my voice to the others and implored the heavens to grant me mercy and forgiveness. At variance with everything my lips were saying, I indicted myself only to turn everything into derision, into farce. At any moment I expected the Master of the Universe to strike me dumb and to say: "That is enough—you have gone too far." And I like to think I would have replied: "You, also, blessed be Your name, You also."

Our services were dispersed by the camp bell. The section chiefs began to yell: "Okay, go to sleep! If God hasn't heard you, it's because He is incapable of hearing."

The next day, at work, Pinhas joined another group. I thought: "He wants to eat without being embarrassed by my presence." A day later, he returned. His face even more pale, even more gaunt than before. Death was gnawing at him. I caught myself thinking: "He will die because he did not observe Yom Kippur."

We dug for several hours without looking at each other. From far off, the shouting of the *kapo* reached us. He walked around hitting people relentlessly.

Toward the end of the afternoon, Pinhas spoke to me: "I have a confession to make."

I shuddered, but went on digging. A strange, almost childlike smile appeared on his lips when he spoke again: "You know, I fasted."

I remained motionless. My stupor amused him.

"Yes, I fasted. Like the others. But not for the same reason. Not out of obedience, but out of defiance. Before the war, you see, some Jews rebelled against the divine will by going to restaurants on the Day of Atonement; here, it is by observing the fast that we can make our indignation heard. Yes, my disciple and teacher, know that I fasted. Not for love of God, but against God."

He left me a few weeks later, victim of the first selection.

He shook my hand: "I would have liked to die some other way and elsewhere. I had always hoped to make of my death, as of my life, an act of faith. It is a pity. God prevents me from realizing my dream. He no longer likes dreams."

Nonetheless, he asked me to say *Kaddish* for him after his death, which, according to his calculations, would take place three days after his departure from camp.

"But why?" I asked. "Since you are no longer a believer?"

He took the tone he always used when he explained a passage in the Talmud to me: "You do not see the heart of the matter. Here and now, the only way to accuse Him is by praising Him."

And he went, laughing, to his death.

## 🦃 from *The Alphabet in My Hands*

MARJORIE AGOSÍN

### Kol Nidre

It was the most wondrous night of nights. The moon above the sky's open labyrinth lit the path of silence on this night of wonders, on this night when grown men repent, beat their breasts, and repeat words as if praying or moaning, "Mea culpa, mea culpa."

A woman seated beside us searches for her dead sisters in the melodies of Kol Nidre. She also looks for herself, bewitched by the horror, and she sings like an angel, her throat full of mist. Her voice is unrepentant, yet it murmurs: I seek the water of the living in the grottos of the dead.

My mother winks at me and says she is not sorry about anything. She has not sinned, she says. She has only played with the afternoon, with the leaves, and has marveled at the lavishness of leisure. She has stored her shoes with the somnolent autumn leaves and has visited the sick without offering false hope. I see her as if she were floating, green from head to toe, in a spiral of smoke, far from those men who beat their breasts and then yell over money or unrequited love.

In the distance I hear a woman sobbing, her voice a dry violin in all the deserts of the world. This is the night of Kol Nidre, the most wondrous night, the most wary night, the night of those who repent.

### Day of Atonement

We liked the Day of Atonement because we felt closer to the girls in our neighborhood who, every Sunday, disguised as starch, went to speak to the parish priest in those marvelous velvet rooms where one knelt to tell secrets about touching one's body in the resplendent solitude of night and yelling obscene words for the sheer pleasure of how it feels to stroke one's belly at the sound of them. But to whom could we confess about how bad we had been or how many dirty words we had said? Our family had few prohibitions. The Day of Atonement drew us closer to the Christian girls we so wanted to be like, girls with holy cards, First Communion girls. My mother didn't like to go to God's house where men beat their breasts then put their hands in their pockets to count money. None of that, my mother would say. So we would go to the river, dressed in white and carrying lilies. We washed our hair and looked for fresh stones. We threw the stones into the river with love, stones like prayers. The stones were for our sins, for the times we had disobeyed, been stubborn, wished for bad things to happen. We threw a lot of stones. We liked the sound they made, and we liked knowing that the turbulent, crystalline river, slippery as bubbles, swept away our sins and evil deeds. Later that afternoon we felt happy and light. God's house was everywhere, especially in my mother's hands that gently caressed us. That's how we celebrated the Day of Atonement.

*Translated by Nancy Abraham Hall*

# Fiction

# ᕾ Yom Kippur in Hell

### I. L. PERETZ

Once, on a perfectly ordinary day without a fair or even an auction, a clatter of wheels and a spatter of mud aroused the merchants in the marketplace. Who, they wondered, could it be? It was a horse-drawn carriage. As soon as they saw it, though, they turned away in fear and revulsion. Both horse and carriage were well known. They belonged to a police informer from the neighboring town who was on his way to the provincial capital. God only knew who would be the victim of his tale-bearing this time.

All of a sudden, the noise stopped. Involuntarily, the merchants turned to look. The carriage had come to a halt, the horse had lowered its head to drink from a puddle, and the informant was sprawled senseless on his seat.

Say what you will, the man was a human being. People ran to help — but he already looked quite dead. An expert stepped up and confirmed the diagnosis. The members of the Burial Society rolled up their sleeves and went to work.

The horse and carriage were sold to pay the burial expenses, the informer was laid to rest, and the little devils who sprout where they are sown spirited the dead man's soul off to hell and delivered it to the gate-keepers.

The informer was brought for interrogation to the gatehouse, where the chief clerk plied him with wearisome questions and yawned as he wrote down the answers.

Taken down a peg by his surroundings, the informer answered every-thing: place and date of birth, age when married, length of time supported by father-in-law, number of children, year of desertion of wife, nature of profession and how acquired, and whatever other vital information per-tained to his life on earth, which ended as he was driving his horse and carriage through the marketplace of Lahadam.

The clerk, who was in the middle of another yawn, sat up.

"Say that again Laha-what?"

"Lahadam," repeated the informer.

A gleam of interest flared in the clerk's eyes. "Did you ever hear of such a place?" he asked his assistants.

The assistant clerks shrugged and shook their heads, their mouths slightly open. "Never," they said.

"Would you check to see where it is?"

In hell every town has its registry, arranged in alphabetical order. Each letter has its file cabinet. The devils went through the whole L file: Leipzig, Lemberg, Lublin, every L on the map—Lahadam was not to be found.

"But it exists," insisted the informer. "It's a small town in Poland."

"Since when?"

"Since the local count gave it a charter twenty years ago. It has two fairs a year, a synagogue, a study house, a public bathhouse, two taverns for Gentiles . . ."

"Has anyone from there ever been here?" inquired the clerk.

"Not a soul," answered his assistants.

"Do you mean to tell us no one dies there?" the informer was asked.

"Why should no one die there?" he replied like a Jew, answering a question with a question. "They live packed together in squalor, the public bath can make you gag, the whole place is one big sty." The informer was beginning to feel in his element. "As a matter of fact, they have their own cemetery. And a burial society that charges an arm and a leg. Why, they even had an epidemic of plague there."

The informer received the sentence that was called for and an inquiry was called for too. Something was not right. How could a twenty-year-old town, and with an epidemic of plague no less, not have sent a single soul to hell?

Devils were sent out to investigate. Soon they flew back with their report:

"It's true, every word of it!"

There was indeed such a place, the devils explained, a town like any other, with here and there a good deed and a considerable lot of bad ones. The local economy? People managed, if not by hook, then by crook. So what was different about it? The cantor of the synagogue, that's what. Not that he himself was anyone special. But his voice! It was pure music, so tender and feeling that it could melt a heart of stone like wax. As soon as he started to pray, the whole congregation repented of their sins with such fervor that all was forgiven and forgotten in heaven above, whose gates stood open for every one of the townspeople. Just say you were from Lahadam and no more questions were asked!

Needless to say, it was a state of affairs that hell could not put up with. And it was a job for the director himself; no one else could be trusted to handle it.

What did Satan do?

He ordered fetched from the world of men a Calcutta cock with a comb as red as flame and had it placed before him on a table. Bewildered to find itself there, the rooster was too frightened to move. The archfiend crouched before it and crowed, fixing his evil eye on it until his black magic was done in a trice and the red comb was as white as chalk. Hearing a distant rumble of heavenly wrath he quickly finished his spell with the curse:

"Begone, O voice, until he dies!"

There's no need to tell you whom he had in mind. Before the Calcutta cock's comb could turn red again, the cantor of Lahadam had lost his voice. He could barely utter a word; no sound came forth from his throat.

It was no secret who was to blame. That is, it was no secret to those Jews from whom there are no secrets, although perhaps not to all of them. After all, it wasn't something that you talked about even if you knew. But there it was and nothing could be done. Had the cantor been a man of more spiritual substance, there were measures that might have been taken, but he was a no-account, a lightweight. And so, though he went from one wonder-worker to another, none was able to help him.

In the end, he turned to the saintly rabbi of Apt. Indeed, he all but went down on his knees and refused to leave the rabbi's room without an answer. You never saw such a pitiful sight.

The rabbi sought to comfort him. "I can tell you" he said, "that your hoarseness will last only until you die. Your deathbed confession will be said in a voice that will reach to the far ends of heaven."

"And until then?"

"It's hopeless."

"But why, Rabbi?" implored the cantor. "Why me?"

He pestered the rabbi of Apt for so long that the rabbi finally gave in and told him the whole story.

"In that case," croaked the cantor as he ran out of the rabbi's room, "I'll make sure that I get my revenge."

"How?" called the rabbi after him. "On whom?"

But the cantor was already gone.

This happened on a Tuesday, or perhaps it was a Wednesday. Thursday evening, when the fishermen of Apt went down to the river to haul in their catch for the Sabbath, their nets seemed heavier than usual. They pulled them out of the water: in them lay the drowned cantor!

He had jumped off the bridge. And just as the rabbi of Apt promised, his voice was restored in time for his last confession, since Satan's curse lasted only until his death. Yet since the confession could not be said underwater, his voice remained trapped with him — which is, as you will see, exactly what he had counted on.

The cantor was buried behind the graveyard fence, as is the custom with suicides, and the devils whisked his soul off to hell. When asked by the clerk at the gate for his life story, however, he refused to answer. He was prodded with sharp lances, with burning coals — not a word.

"Then take him away!"

As if they didn't know all about him anyway! In fact, they had been eagerly awaiting him. But as he was led on to a cauldron of boiling water that was being stoked just for him, he tapped his throat with his thumb and burst out:

"*Yisgada-al!* . . ."

The Kaddish — and in the special melody of Yom Kippur!

He sang — and his voice sounded far and wide, as good as ever, no, even better, sweeter and so much more tender. The cauldrons, which had reverberated with howls and groans, grew suddenly silent; then from within them, voices took up the prayer. The cauldron lids lifted, heads peered out for a look, scorched mouths began to sing along.

The devils attending the kettles did not join in, of course, but rather stood there dumbstruck, mouths agape, tongues hanging out, faces contorted, eyes red as coals, some still holding a log to stoke the fire with, others gripping an iron poker or trident. A few even threw themselves epileptically to the ground while the cantor went on singing. Beneath the cauldrons the fires died down. Here and there a dead man began climbing out.

The cantor sang on and hell's inmates sang with him, fervently, with all their hearts, their bodies made whole again, the flesh healed on their bones, their souls cleansed of all sin. When he reached the prayer in the Shimenesre that praises God the Resurrector, the dead came back to life and answered "Amen" in one voice. And when he sang the words "May His great name be blessed," they echoed back such a chorus of voices that the heavens opened on high, and the repentance of the damned reached the seventh heaven, where God's own mercy seat stands, and the moment of grace was so great that the sinners, now converted into saints, sprouted wings and flew out of the jaws of hell and through the open doors of paradise.

No one was left behind but the devils, writhing on the ground, and the cantor, who never budged from his place.

As in his lifetime, all repented through him but he himself could not repent. A suicide!

After a while hell filled up again. New quarters were added, but still the crowding was great.

*Translated by Hillel Halkin*

# 🌿 A Yom Kippur Scandal

### SHOLOM ALEICHEM

"That's nothing!" called out the man with round eyes, like an ox, who had been sitting all this time in a corner by the window, smoking and listening to our stories of thefts, robberies and expropriations. "I'll tell you a story of a theft that took place in our town, in the synagogue itself, and on Yom Kippur at that! It is worth listening to.

"Our town, Kasrilevka—that's where I'm from, you know—is a small town, and a poor one. There is no thievery there. No one steals anything for the simple reason that there is nobody to steal from and nothing worth stealing. And besides, a Jew is not a thief by nature. That is, he may be a thief, but not the sort who will climb through a window or attack you with a knife. He will divert, pervert, subvert and contravert as a matter of course; but he won't pull anything out of your pocket. He won't be caught like a common thief and led through the streets with a yellow placard on his back. Imagine, then, a theft taking place in Kasrilevka, and such a theft at that. Eighteen hundred *rubles* at one crack.

"Here is how it happened. One Yom Kippur eve, just before the evening services, a stranger arrived in our town, a salesman of some sort from Lithuania. He left his bag at an inn, and went forth immediately to look for a place of worship, and he came upon the old synagogue. Coming in just before the service began, he found the trustees around the collection plates. 'Sholom aleichem,' said he. 'Aleichem sholom,' they answered. 'Where does our guest hail from?' 'From Lithuania.' 'And your name?' 'Even your grandmother wouldn't know if I told her.' 'But you have come to our synagogue!' 'Where else should I go?' 'Then you want to pray here?' 'Can I help myself? What else can I do?' 'Then put something into the plate.' 'What did you think? That I was not going to pay?'

"To make a long story short, our guest took out three silver *rubles* and put them in the plate. Then he put a *ruble* into the cantor's plate, one into the rabbi's, gave one for the *cheder*, threw a half into the charity box, and then began to divide money among the poor who flocked to the door. And in our town we have so many poor people that if you really wanted to start giving, you could divide Rothschild's fortune among them.

"Impressed by his generosity, the men quickly found a place for him along the east wall. Where did they find room for him when all the places along the wall are occupied? Don't ask. Have you ever been at a celebration

—a wedding or circumcision—when all the guests are already seated at the table, and suddenly there is a commotion outside—the rich uncle has arrived? What do you do? You push and shove and squeeze until a place is made for the rich relative. Squeezing is a Jewish custom. If no one squeezes us, we squeeze each other."

The man with the eyes that bulged like an ox's paused, looked at the crowd to see what effect his wit had on us, and went on.

"So our guest went up to his place of honor and called to the *shammes* to bring him a praying stand. He put on his *tallis* and started to pray. He prayed and he prayed, standing on his feet all the time. He never sat down or left his place all evening long or all the next day. To fast all day standing on one's feet, without ever sitting down—that only a Litvak can do!

"But when it was all over, when the final blast of the *shofar* had died down, the Day of Atonement had ended, and Chaim the *melamed*, who had led the evening prayers after Yom Kippur from time immemorial, had cleared his throat, and in his tremulous voice had already begun—'Ma-a-riv a-ro-vim . . .' suddenly screams were heard. 'Help! Help! Help!' We looked around: the stranger was stretched out on the floor in a dead faint. We poured water on him, revived him, but he fainted again. What was the trouble? Plenty! This Litvak tells us that he had brought with him to Kasrilevka eighteen hundred *rubles*. To leave that much at the inn—think of it, eighteen hundred *rubles*—he had been afraid. Whom could he trust with such a sum of money in a strange town? And yet, to keep it in his pocket on Yom Kippur was not exactly proper either. So at last this plan had occurred to him: he had taken the money to the synagogue and slipped it into the praying stand. Only a Litvak could do a thing like that! . . . Now do you see why he had not stepped away from the praying stand for a single minute? And yet during one of the many prayers when we all turn our face to the wall, someone must have stolen the money . . .

"Well, the poor man wept, tore his hair, wrung his hands. What would he do with the money gone? It was not his own money, he said. He was only a clerk. The money was his employer's. He himself was a poor man, with a houseful of children. There was nothing for him to do now but go out and drown himself, or hang himself right here in front of everybody.

"Hearing these words, the crowd stood petrified, forgetting that they had all been fasting since the night before and it was time to go home and eat. It was a disgrace before a stranger, a shame and a scandal in our own eyes. A theft like that—eighteen hundred *rubles*! And where? In the

Holy of Holies, in the old synagogue of Kasrilevka. And on what day? On the holiest day of the year, on *Yom Kippur!* Such a thing had never been heard of before.

"'*Shammes*, lock the door!' ordered our Rabbi. We have our own Rabbi in Kasrilevka, Reb Yozifel, a true man of God, a holy man. Not too sharp witted, perhaps, but a good man, a man with no bitterness in him. Sometimes he gets ideas that you would not hit upon if you had eighteen heads on your shoulders . . . When the door was locked, Reb Yozifel turned to the congregation, his face pale as death and his hands trembling, his eyes burning with a strange fire.

"He said, 'Listen to me, my friends, this is an ugly thing, a thing unheard of since the world was created—that here in Kasrilevka there should be a sinner, a renegade to his people, who would have the audacity to take from a stranger, a poor man with a family, a fortune like this. And on what day? On the holiest day of the year, on *Yom Kippur*, and perhaps at the last, most solemn moment—just before the *shofar* was blown! Such a thing has never happened anywhere. I cannot believe it is possible. It simply cannot be. But perhaps—who knows? Man is greedy, and the temptation—especially with a sum like this, eighteen hundred *rubles*, God forbid—is great enough. So if one of us was tempted, if he were fated to commit this evil on a day like this, we must probe the matter thoroughly, strike at the root of this whole affair. Heaven and earth have sworn that the truth must always rise as one upon the waters. Therefore, my friends, let us search each other now, go through each other's garments, shake out our pockets—all of us from the oldest householder to the *shammes*, not leaving anyone out. Start with me. Search my pockets first.'"

"Thus spoke Reb Yozifel, and he was the first to unbind his gabardine and turn his pockets inside out. And following his example all the men loosened their girdles and showed the linings of their pockets, too. They searched each other, they felt and shook one another, until they came to Lazer Yossel, who turned all colors and began to argue that, in the first place, the stranger was a swindler; that his story was the pure fabrication of a Litvak. No one had stolen any money from him. Couldn't they see that it was all a falsehood and a lie?

"The congregation began to clamor and shout. What did he mean by this? All the important men had allowed themselves to be searched, so why should Lazer Yossel escape? There are no privileged characters here. 'Search him! Search him!' the crowd roared.

"Lazer Yossel saw that it was hopeless, and began to plead for mercy with tears in his eyes. He begged them not to search him. He swore by all that was holy that he was as innocent in this as he would want to be of any wrongdoing as long as he lived. Then why didn't he want to be searched? It was a disgrace to him, he said. He begged them to have pity on his youth, not to bring this disgrace down on him. 'Do anything you wish with me,' he said, 'but don't touch my pockets.' How do you like that? Do you suppose we listened to him?

"But wait . . . I forgot to tell you who this Lazer Yossel was. He was not a Kasrilevkite himself. He came from the Devil knows where, at the time of his marriage, to live with his wife's parents. The rich man of our town had dug him up somewhere for his daughter, boasted that he had found a rare nugget, a fitting match for a daughter like his. He knew a thousand pages of *Talmud* by heart, and all of the Bible. He was a master of Hebrew, arithmetic, bookkeeping, algebra, penmanship—in short, everything you could think of. When he arrived in Kasrilevka—this jewel of a young man—everyone came out to gaze at him. What sort of bargain had the rich man picked out? Well, to look at him you could tell nothing. He was a young man, something in trousers. Not bad looking, but with a nose a trifle too long, eyes that burned like two coals, and a sharp tongue. Our leading citizens began to work on him: tried him out on a page of *Gamorah*, a chapter from the Scriptures, a bit of *Rambam*, this, that and the other. He was perfect in everything, the dog! Whenever you went after him, he was at home. Reb Yozifel himself said that he could have been a rabbi in any Jewish congregation. As for world affairs, there is nothing to talk about. We have an authority on such things in our town, Zaidel Reb Shaye's, but he could not hold a candle to Lazer Yossel. And when it came to chess—there was no one like him in all the world! Talk about versatile people . . . Naturally the whole town envied the rich man his find, but some of them felt he was a little too good to be true. He was too clever (and too much of anything is bad!). For a man of his station he was too free and easy, a hail-fellow-well-met, too familiar with all the young folk —boys, girls, and maybe even loose women. There were rumors . . . At the same time he went around alone too much, deep in thought. At the synagogue he came in last, put on his *tallis*, and with his skullcap on askew, thumbed aimlessly through his prayerbook without ever following the services. No one ever saw him doing anything exactly wrong, and yet people murmured that he was not a God-fearing man. Apparently a man cannot be perfect . . .

"And so, when his turn came to be searched and he refused to let them do it, that was all the proof most of the men needed that he was the one who had taken the money. He begged them to let him swear any oath they wished, begged them to chop him, roast him, cut him up—do anything but shake his pockets out. At this point even our Rabbi, Reb Yozifel, although he was a man we had never seen angry, lost his temper and started to shout.

"'You!' he cried. 'You thus and thus! Do you know what you deserve? You see what all these men have endured. They were able to forget the disgrace and allowed themselves to be searched; but you want to be the only exception! God in heaven! Either confess and hand over the money, or let us see for ourselves what is in your pockets. You are trifling now with the entire Jewish community. Do you know what they can do to you?'

"To make a long story short, the men took hold of this young upstart, threw him down on the floor with force, and began to search him all over, shake out every one of his pockets. And finally they shook out . . . Well, guess what! A couple of well-gnawed chicken bones and a few dozen plum pits still moist from chewing. You can imagine what an impression this made—to discover food in the pockets of our prodigy on this holiest of fast days. Can you imagine the look on the young man's face, and on his father-in-law's? And on that of our poor Rabbi?

"Poor Reb Yozifel! He turned away in shame. He could look no one in the face. On *Yom Kippur*, and in his synagogue . . . As for the rest of us, hungry as we were, we could not stop talking about it all the way home. We rolled with laughter in the streets. Only Reb Yozifel walked home alone, his head bowed, full of grief, unable to look anyone in the eyes, as though the bones had been shaken out of his own pockets."

The story was apparently over. Unconcerned, the man with the round eyes of an ox turned back to the window and resumed smoking.

"Well," we all asked in one voice, "and what about the money?"

"What money?" asked the man innocently, watching the smoke he had exhaled.

"What do you mean—what money? The eighteen hundred *rubles!*"

"Oh," he drawled. "The eighteen hundred. They were gone."

"Gone?"

"Gone forever."

*Translated by Julius and Frances Butwin*

# ?️ Repentance

ISRAEL JOSEPH SINGER

Rabbi Ezekiel of Kozmir and his followers were great believers in the divine principle of joyousness.

Reb Ezekiel himself was a giant of a man, standing a full head above his Hasidic followers, and broader in the shoulders than any two of them placed side by side. On Holy Days the court of Reb Ezekiel was crowded with visiting Hasidim, and in the synagogue the mighty head of Reb Ezekiel, swathed in the silver-worked headpiece of his prayer shawl, swam above all others, a banner and a crown, an adornment to the gathering and the symbol of its glory.

Reb Ezekiel is no more than a memory today, but there are still extant two of his possessions: an ivory walking stick and a white satin gaberdine, which fastens at the front not with buttons but with silver hooks and eyes. The grip of the stick is so high that no man is able to use it for walking. A certain grandson of Reb Ezekiel, inheritor of the dynastic rights of this rabbinic line, puts on Reb Ezekiel's gaberdine once a year, on the New Year, when the ram's horn is to be blown for the opening of the heavenly gates; but if he tries to take a step in this mantle of his grandfather, he stumbles over the ends, which trail along the floor. To protect him not less than the illustrious garment, the followers of the grandson put down a carpet of straw on the floor of the synagogue for the two days of the New Year.

Rabbi Ezekiel and his followers believed not only in joyousness but in the virtue of good food.

Of the fast days that are sprinkled throughout the sacred calendar Reb Ezekiel and his followers observed only the Day of Atonement. Even on Tishe b'Av, the Black Fast that commemorates the tremendous calamity of the storming of the Temple, Reb Ezekiel and his followers ate. If it came to pass that a fool of a Hasid, having had a bad dream, insisted on fasting, he had to leave the court and go across the Vistula to the village opposite Kozmir.

At the court of Rabbi Ezekiel there were always dancing and singing; there was perpetual drinking of wine and mead. It was a common saying with the rabbi, his children, the Hasidic followers, and visitors: "It is not the study of the Law that matters, but the melody that goes with the studying; it is not the praying that matters, but the sweet chanting of the prayer."

One day a strange thing happened. Rabbi Naphthali Aphter, the greatest opponent and critic of Reb Ezekiel, actually came on a visit to the town of Kozmir, for the Sabbath of Repentance.

Rabbi Naphthali Aphter was the exact opposite of Reb Ezekiel of Kozmir. He was a weakling, a pygmy of a Jew, skin and bones, something a moderate wind could carry away. He fasted every day of the week—from Sabbath to Sabbath, that is. He broke his fast evenings with a plate of soup, nothing more; and lest he should derive from the soup anything more than the barest sustenance, lest he should take pleasure in the taste of food, he would throw into the plate of soup a fistful of salt. On Saturdays he permitted himself meat and fish, in honor of the sanctity of the Sabbath; he ate the eye of a fish and a sinew of flesh. When he ate, every swallow of food could be traced in its passage down his slender, stringy throat. Further to mortify his body, Rabbi Naphthali slept no more than two hours a night; the rest of the time he sat before the sacred books. And when he studied he did not follow the traditional custom, which bids the student set his repetitions to a sweet chant; this he considered a sinful concession to the lust of his ears. He muttered the words dryly under his breath. In the night he held the candle in his right hand, to be certain that he did not doze. His hand trembled, and the drops of grease fell on the yellow pages of the pious books, which he turned with his left hand. The tears ran down his withered, parchment-like cheeks and fell side by side with the drops of grease on the ancient pages, which smelled of wax, tears, hair, and mildew.

He repeated for the thousandth time, in the harsh mutter of his study: "*Shivoh medurei gehinom*—there are seven chambers in the courts of hell. The fire of the first chamber is sixty times as hot as the fire we know on earth; the fire of the second chamber is sixty times as hot as the fire of the first chamber; the fire of the third chamber is sixty times as hot . . . and thus it follows that the fire of the seventh chamber is hotter by sixty times sixty to the seventh time than the fire which we know on earth."

He continued: "Therefore happy are those who are only transformed into fish and animals, into trees and grasses. And there are also human souls that wander in the wildness of space, and there are others that are flung about as with slings, and their plight is bitterest of all."

Rabbi Naphthali had sundered himself completely from the things of this world. He had even separated himself from his wife and knew her no more. But wicked thoughts, evil visitations, tormented him, especially in the nights, and gave him no peace.

And this was not only when he lay down for the two hours of slumber which he permitted himself. Even while he sat at his sacred books shapes and phantoms in the likeness of females surrounded him. It was useless to close his eyes to them, for with closed eyes he only saw them better. They penetrated his ears too. They shook down great masses of black hair, they sang with voices of piercing sweetness, they danced immodestly and they flung their arms around him. They caressed his sparse liltle beard, they played with his stiff, flat earlocks, twining them around their fingers.

He fled from these visions and voices to the ritual bath, which lay in a corner of the yard of his house. He tore off his clothes, stumbled down the cold, slippery, stone steps, and flung his weak body into the black, icy water. But even then it seemed to him that he struck his head not against the harsh water but against silky cushions; and his body lay on soft down, tempting and exciting.

A naked woman, irresistibly beautiful, held him close in the hot bands of her arms. . . . He fled from the water and took vows to be harsher with his rebellious and pampered body. He halved his allowance of soup at the end of the day and doubled the salt with which he spoiled its taste. He wept day and night, and his eyes were never dry.

But the Evil Inclination, the Wicked One, whispered mockingly in his ear, "Fool that you are! You have separated yourself from your wife, who is a pure and good woman, to sin in secret with abominations of the night. You have left your simple couch of straw and feathers to loll on divans of silk and down . . ."

Rabbi Naphthali wept so long and so hard that at last the well of his tears dried up and his eyes gave out only a thin rheum. He longed to become blind, so that he might look no more on the sinful world.

But the Evil One read his thoughts and continued to whisper mockery into his ear. "Fool that you are! Why do you seek to rid yourself of the eyes of the flesh? Is it not because you know that with the eyes of the spirit and the imagination you can see sweet visions a thousand times more sinful?"

In the end Rabbi Naphthali decided to visit the rabbinic court of Kozmir. If fasting and mortification of the flesh will not help, perhaps Reb Ezekiel has better counsel, he thought.

He slung a sack over his shoulders, took his prayer shawl and phylacteries under his arm, and set out for Kozmir, planning to arrive there for the Sabbath of Repentance.

When they learned in the court of the Kozmir rabbi that Naphthali himself, the bitterest opponent and critic of Rabbi Ezekiel, had arrived on a visit, there was great rejoicing. Reb Mottye Godel, the chief beadle and grand vizier of the Kozmir rabbi, stroked his beard proudly and said to all the Hasidim, "This is a great victory. If Reb Naphthali himself comes here, the others will follow, and soon all the Jews will acknowledge our rabbi. I tell you, we will live to see that day."

Rabbi Naphthali arrived, of course, not on the Sabbath itself, but on the preceding day; and he asked at once to be admitted to the presence of Reb Ezekiel. But the Kozmir rabbi could not receive him. He was going, he declared, to the baths, to purify himself for the Sabbath. He remained in the baths longer than was his wont. In the steam room he climbed up to the highest and hottest level of the stairs and shouted joyously to the attendant to pour more water on the heated stones and to fill the room with more steam. His followers, who usually accompanied him to the highest steps, fled from him this time, unable to endure the heat.

The rabbi laughed loudly at them. "Fools," he cried, "how will you learn to endure the flames of hell?"

When he returned from the baths Reb Ezekiel lay down on the well-stuffed, leather-covered couch on which he rested in the daytime, and he seemed to have forgotten entirely about Reb Naphthali. After he had taken a nap he commanded that the Sabbath fish be brought in to him to taste, and then he remembered Reb Naphthali.

"Mottye," he said, "bring in the fish prepared for the Sabbath — and Reb Naphthali too."

It was a custom with Reb Ezekiel to taste the Sabbath fish the evening before. He said, "They that taste thereof have merited life, as the Holy Word says."

It was also his custom to sharpen the pearl-handled bread knife himself, and to slice the onions that were served with the fish on the Sabbath.

When Rabbi Naphthali entered, conducted by the chief beadle, Reb Ezekiel greeted him joyously. "Welcome, and blessed be thy coming," he exclaimed in a thundering voice, which sent tremors through Reb Naphthali. He put out his hand, seized Reb Naphthali's, and squeezed it so hard that Reb Naphthali doubled up.

"What good tidings have you for me, Reb Naphthali?" he asked happily.

"I have come to ask you for counsel on the matter of repentance," answered Reb Naphthali, trembling.

"Repentance?" shouted Reb Ezekiel, and his voice was as gay as if he had heard the sweetest tidings. "Repentance? Assuredly! Take a glass of brandy. What is the meaning of the word 'repentance'? It is: to turn! And when a Jew takes a glass of brandy he turns it upside down, which is to say, he performs an act of repentance."

And without waiting Reb Ezekiel filled two silver beakers with brandy in which floated spices and little leaves. "Good health and life, Reb Naphthali," he said and pushed one beaker forward.

Reb Ezekiel emptied his beaker at a gulp. Reb Naphthali broke into a stuttering cough at the mere smell of the drink, but Reb Ezekiel would not let him put it down. "Reb Naphthali, you have come for my counsel. The first thing then, which I will teach you, will be the mystery of eating and drinking."

He forced Reb Naphthali to swallow the brandy and then pushed toward him a huge piece of stuffed carp, highly seasoned. "This," he said with a smile, "comes from the hand of my wife. She is a valiant woman, a pearl of price, and her stuffed fish have in them not less than one-sixtieth of the virtue and taste of Leviathan himself."

The first piece Reb Naphthali tried to swallow stuck in his throat. But Reb Ezekiel would not be put off, and he compelled Reb Naphthali to eat. "Rabbi Naphthali, the road of repentance is not an easy one, as you see. But there is no turning back on it."

When it was impossible to make Rabbi Naphthali eat another bite, Reb Ezekiel took him by the hand, led him into the other room, and bade him stretch himself out on the well-stuffed leather-covered couch. Rabbi Naphthali refused to lie down. "What?" he said. "Lie down and sleep in the middle of the day? And with the Sabbath approaching?"

"It is better to sleep two days than to entertain one thought," said Reb Ezekiel and closed the door on him.

During the Ten Penitential Days between the New Year and the Day of Atonement, Reb Ezekiel taught Reb Naphthali the mystery of food and the inner significance of joyousness. Every day there was another banquet in the rabbinic court, and wine and mead were consumed in barrelfuls. The singing in the court was heard throughout Kozmir; it echoed in the surrounding hills and carried across the Vistula.

"Well, Reb Naphthali, are you visited by thoughts, by fantasies?" Reb Ezekiel asked him every day.

"Less now," answered Reb Naphthali.

"In that case, here's another glass of mead," said Reb Ezekiel, and he saw to it that Reb Naphthali drank it all down.

And every day, when the banquet was over, he led his guest into his own room and made him sleep on his leather-covered couch. "Sleep!" he said. "Ordinary, unlearned Jews are permitted to sleep in the daytime only on Sabbaths. But good and pious Jews who are followers of a Hasidic rabbi are enjoined to sleep by daylight every day in the week."

When they all sat at the dinner which precedes the eve of the Day Of Atonement, Reb Ezekiel kept closer watch than ever on the visitor. Not a minute passed but what he pressed on him another tidbit. "Reb Naphthali, eat, I say. Every mouthful you swallow is written down in your heavenly account as a meritorious deed. Eat heartily and swell the account."

In the court of Kozmir the Day of Atonement was the merriest day of the year. The rabbi himself stood at the pulpit and conducted the prayers. He did not let anyone replace him, but led the congregation from morning till evening, through all the divisions of devotion. He did not sit down for a minute, and his voice never ceased from singing.

All prayers were set to a happy chant in Kozmir, even the most doleful, even the martyrologies. The House of Prayer was jammed with Jews in prayer shawls and white robes. Above them all towered the rabbi, his head adorned with a skullcap wrought with gold embroidery, the crown and glory of the congregation. His voice rang as loudly in the closing prayer of the Day of Atonement as it had done in the opening prayer the evening before, though he had not tasted food or drink for twenty-four hours. Around him stood his dynasty, his sons and grandsons, all in silk and white satin, and their voices sustained him throughout the whole service. The melodious tumult of this choir was heard in town, in the hills, and in the village across the river; the congregation helped to swell it, and the day was observed with dancing as well as singing.

Around the door of the House of Prayer stood the feminine half of the dynasty, the rabbi's wife, his daughters, his daughters-in-law, his granddaughters. They too were dressed in silk and satin; on their bosoms shone gold-embroidered coverings; on their heads wimples glittered with precious stones; and their lips moved piously in whispered prayer.

Reb Naphthali bent down to the earth in the fervor of his devotions. He longed to squeeze at least one tear from his sinful eyes, but all his efforts availed him nothing. The riot of song all about him deafened him, and he could not concentrate on one miserable thought.

When the Day of Atonement was over, the congregants took the stubs of the burning candles from the boxes of sand and went out into the synagogue yard for the Benediction of the Moon. The moon swam luminously in a clear sky, and the congregants rejoiced in her light. "Welcome," they cried to her, dancing joyously. "Be thou a good sign and a bringer of good luck."

Reb Ezekiel stood in the midst of his Hasidim, radiant as the moon in the midst of the stars. "Welcome!" he cried thunderously to Reb Naphthali and took him by the hand as if he were about to draw him into a dance.

But in that instant Reb Naphthali was seized with a violent trembling, and before anyone could take hold of him he had slipped to the ground.

The Hasidim dropped to the ground beside him, but when they felt his hands and face, these were as cold as the damp grass on which he lay. There was no sign of breath in the frail body.

Panic seized the assembly. Hundreds of congregants tried to touch the body where it lay wrapped in prayer shawl and white robe. But those that were at the center lifted up the body of Reb Naphthali, carried it into the House of Prayer, and laid it down on the pulpit, where the Scroll is laid for the reading of the Law. Those that could not get into the House did not go to their homes but remained standing, petrified, and some of them began to weep audibly.

The panic lasted only a minute or two.

The door of the rabbi's room opened, and the rabbi, his face as radiant as when he had stretched out his hand to Reb Naphthali and the latter had fallen to the ground, looked out above the congregation. He had withdrawn for a moment, and now he was back with the congregation.

His voice rang out. "If anyone wants to weep, let him take a rowboat and pass to the other side of the Vistula. There is no weeping in Kozmir."

Amazed, silent, the Hasidim followed the gesture of the rabbi and filed into his room.

The table sparkled with gold and silver in the light of a hundred candles. Ranged along its center were dusty bottles of wine and mead, each surrounded by a heap of grapes and pears and pomegranates.

The Hasidim seated themselves. The rabbi drank, sang happily, and distributed morsels to his favorites. This night he was more generous than ever before. Children and grandchildren sat at the head of the table, snatched his gifts, and followed him in song.

The feasting lasted through the night, and only when the morning star was peeping in through the window did Mottye, the chief beadle, give the signal that the rabbi was now prepared to speak. The Hasidim crowded close to him, their hands on one another's shoulders.

Many minutes passed before the rabbi came to his pronouncement. He sat playing with the silver watch that lay in front of him on the table. He picked up a heavy bunch of grapes and moved it up and down as if he were estimating its weight. And throughout all this he chanted a Hasidic melody to himself.

When he had finished the melody and had let all the echoes die down about him, he opened his mouth and spoke. "I wanted to teach him the great mystery of joyousness, but he was unable to grasp it."

He looked out of the window toward the House of Prayer, where the little body of Reb Naphthali, wrapped in prayer shawl and white robe, lay on the pulpit, and he ended his pronouncement:

"He had sunk too far into habits of gloom, and there was no saving him."

*Translated by Maurice Samuel*

# Hanukkah

## The Power of Light

# 🌿 Introduction

*Therefore, they bore branches, and fair boughs, and palms also, and sang psalms unto Him that had given them good success in cleansing His place. They ordained also by a common statute and decree, that every year those days should be kept of the whole nation of the Jews.*
—II Maccabees 10. 7–8

As with several other holidays in the Jewish calendar, the origins of the Hanukkah festival derive from a combination of ancient seasonal ritual and the commemoration of historical events. Occurring close to the winter solstice and associated with symbols of warmth and light, Hanukkah may have begun as an early attempt to brighten the gloom and darkness of the long winter. Like Passover, however, Hanukkah also pays tribute to a documented historical occurrence. And like the Passover celebration, customs that may once have been part of a primitive, seasonal festival were gradually transformed and imbued with deeper historical and cultural significance. The rituals remained, but took on greater meaning and were in time explained in accordance with the specifics of the historical event. Today, Hanukkah celebrates the victory of a small group of Jewish warriors over their Syrian oppressors in the second century B.C.E. The holiday also commemorates the so-called "miracle" of Hanukkah: how a one-day supply of sacred oil remained lit for eight days in the Temple of Jerusalem that had been newly liberated and cleansed.

The earliest recording of the events surrounding the observance of Hanukkah can be found in the Books of Maccabees, part of the Apocrypha, a collection of ancient literature not deemed sacred enough to be included in the Bible. During the second century B.C.E., Antiochus Epiphanes, the Syrian ruler of the land of Israel, began a process of forced assimilation of the Jews into the Greco-Syrian culture and religion of the time. When the campaign of Hellenization did not progress as quickly or as smoothly as anticipated, Antiochus began persecuting and killing those Jews who did not willingly comply. The Temple in Jerusalem was seized and desecrated. A small band of Jewish rebels, led by Mattathias and his five sons — known as the Maccabees (literally the "hammers") — took to the hills, resisted, and eventually defeated the more powerful and numerous Syrian forces. With their victory in 165 B.C.E., they cleansed and rededicated the Temple and established an annual celebration to commemorate the event.

The Books of Maccabees, however, which recount all this in great detail, make no mention of what came to be considered the true "miracle" of Hanukkah. According to an account in the Talmud, written several hundreds years after the version recorded in the Books of Maccabees, the priests who cleansed the Temple found only enough consecrated oil to light the Temple menorah (the symbol of ancient Judaism) for one day. Yet the flame remained lit for eight days, enough time to allow for the procurement of a new supply. The Talmudic rabbis and scholars who codified Jewish law and practice, perhaps concerned about the appropriateness of a celebration commemorating a military victory, chose to deemphasize the significance of the Maccabees' triumph and to focus instead on the legend of the little cruse of oil as the embodiment of the true spirit of Hanukkah. In time, the miracle of the sacred lamp came to replace the victory of the Maccabees as the predominant occurrence of Hanukkah, and the menorah became the central symbol of the holiday. Nevertheless, the romantic and heroic legend of the Maccabees never really disappeared from Jewish consciousness. With the rise of Zionism in the nineteenth century and Israeli statehood in the twentieth, it came to represent for Jews throughout the world the true spirit of independence and resistance.

Today Hanukkah, which means "dedication" and occurs on the 25th day of the Hebrew month of *Kislev* (usually in December), is primarily a home-celebrated holiday, with the lighting of an eight-branched Hanukkah menorah (*Hanukiyah*) as its principal ceremonial event. Although some criticize the increasing commercialization of the holiday, especially in countries where it must compete with the celebration of Christmas, many of the traditions associated with Hanukkah originated in eighteenth and nineteenth-century eastern Europe. The most common of these includes the eating of potato pancakes (*latkes*) fried in hot oil (perhaps to symbolize the sacred oil of the ancient Temple), the dispensing of Hanukkah *gelt* (money) to children, gift giving, and the children's game of *dreidl* spinning —a game of chance played with a four-sided top.

Hanukkah, like Passover and Purim, is more a festive celebration than a solemn commemoration, and the traditions and customs surrounding the holiday reflect this spirit. Nevertheless, there is a serious underlying theme to Hanukkah, one that resonates throughout the celebration and serves as the inspiration for many of the literary selections included in this section. In its largest sense, Hanukkah pays tribute to the importance of religious freedom, to Jewish survival, and to the possibility of victory against overwhelming odds. As such, it is also a metaphor for the entire history of the Jewish people in the diaspora, their perseverance, and their determination to resist assimilation.

The selections that follow, which date from the eleventh century to the present, express these themes, as well as the joy inherent in the celebration of Hanukkah, usually among family and friends. As one of the characters from Theodor Herzl's short story "The Menorah" observes, "there was something intimate and homelike about the holiday." For many of the twentieth-century American authors represented in this section, however, Hanukkah — with its inherently anti-assimilationist theme — often engenders questions of identity and belonging as well, issues that inevitably arise in a country where the holiday is often linked with and compared to Christmas.

The earliest example of literary work devoted to Hanukkah custom and belief in this section is Yehuda Halevi's liturgical poem "Festival of Lights." Intended for the Sabbath of Hanukkah, the poem focuses on the symbol of light (the light of God, man, creation, and salvation) and the linking of that imagery with the miracle of the sacred oil. Halevi's poem is dedicated to the "light" and glory of God, for Halevi, like the Talmudic sages, did not wish to venerate the glories of war or the feats of the Maccabees. By the nineteenth century, however, Jews worldwide began to perceive the victory of the Maccabees as one of the more meaningful symbols of Jewish sovereignty. Emma Lazarus, for example, in both "The Feast of Lights" and "The Banner of the Jew," evokes the image and spirit of the Maccabees — their "glorious Maccabean rage" — in an effort to exhort fellow Jews to strive for peoplehood and to preserve their unique identity. With similar reference to the deeds of the Maccabees, Saul Tchernichovsky exhorts those Jews "who live and live not . . . who spurn their heritage," to emulate past Jewish heroes, to arise from their lethargy and reclaim what is rightfully theirs.

As do several other late twentieth-century American authors whose work appears in this section (Norma Rosen, Nathan Englander, and Anne Roiphe), poet Alan Shapiro probes the relationship of American Jews to their majority culture, a relationship that appears especially problematic during the winter holidays. Shapiro, in his poem "A Christmas Story," captures the pain, longing, and confusion of a young American Jew who views his family's "stunted" menorah with its "nine thin candles" as poor competition for the Christmas tree in his friend's house, "a pyramid of flames and glittering candles." Not for him, not yet anyway, is there any notion of "the spirit of the Lord," but only the image of a God whose heart "kept hardening."

Like Shapiro, essayists Roiphe and Rosen, in their works included here, explore the ambiguities and difficulties that confront Jews in a culture dominated by images of Christmas. Both writers express similar dilemmas prompted by their own successful cultural integration. Like many other twentieth-century American Jews, Roiphe and Rosen had moved increasingly further away from the immigrant past of their parents and grandparents and had begun to lose their distinctive religious and cultural identity. As Roiphe states, "ignorance about Judaism is the ice on the slippery slope to total assimilation . . . an identity that is shallow, materialistic, unrooted, and anxious." Similarly, Rosen describes her family as "comfortably going down forgetfulness road." Wishing to "reclaim" their ties to the traditions of Judaism, both begin the task of renewing their connections to community, history, and self. Celebrating Hanukkah with her family allows Roiphe to feel "part of the continuity," which enables her to experience her own sense of "rooted" identity. By recalling the story of the Maccabees, Rosen becomes reconnected: "Like the original cruse, which had oil for only one night yet burned for eight, we have managed to rekindle ourselves."

Growing up in the 1930s, Chaim Potok ("Miracles of a Broken Planet") was troubled by another sort of identity crisis. Reading the daily reports of escalating violence against Jews in Europe, the young Potok is unable to reconcile the image of a God who could perform ancient miracles with a contemporary deity who now presides over a "broken planet." "Where was God," the young Potok recalls thinking as the Hanukkah menorah is lit, while synagogues burned? The only meaningful miracles, Potok comes to realize with the help of his father, will be those made by man.

A very different ideology is presented by Isaac Bashevis Singer, in his short story "Hanukkah in the Poor House." Singer's narrator, although in his nineties and destitute, refuses to rebuke God for the state of the world or for his own life of deprivation: "According to the law, we should praise God for our misfortunes as well as our good fortunes." Traveling from one poor house to the next, he lights his Hanukkah lamp even when it is not Hanukkah, because it lifts his spirits and because, as he puts it, "love comes from the soul and souls radiate light."

Two late-twentieth-century stories conclude this section: Rebecca Goldstein's "Gifts of the Last Night" and Nathan Englander's "Reb Kringle." In Goldstein's poignant tale, a middle-aged professor encounters a famous (although now aging) Jewish writer in a lonely coffee shop on the last night of Hanukkah. Although the two appear at first to be adversaries, they eventually — almost unwittingly — help each other to realize the spirit and meaning of the holiday. Englander's "Reb Kringle" is as much about Christmas as it is about Hanukkah — or more precisely, it is a story about a Jew at Christmas and the conflicts that result. In this painfully funny tale, an observant Jew is forced by circumstance and financial need to take a job as Santa Claus every December. With his long white beard and ample belly, he makes a perfect Santa — except for his personal beliefs and the *yamulke* he manages to hide under his red hat. The irony of the situation is eventually too great for him to bear, and "Rabbi Santa," as he is mockingly called by a co-worker, finally snaps. Coexistence, it seems, between the Jewish and gentile worlds — at least at Christmas — is not easily achieved.

Although Englander, Shapiro, and others emphasize the difficulties encountered by Jews living outside of Israel during the Hanukkah celebration, the fact that the holiday has had to compete with Christmas is not altogether negative. Essentially a minor holiday, Hanukkah has increased in importance at least in part because of its association with the most celebrated of Christian festivals. As many of the more recent selections in this section indicate, this "conflict" between Christmas and Hanukkah has also motivated many Jews to reevaluate and renew their connection to their tradition and culture. The "Maccabean spirit," as the reader will discover, continues to thrive in unexpected ways and with unanticipated results.

# Poetry

# 🌿 Festival of Lights

YEHUDA HALEVI


Always through Your light, bright Lord,    do we see light.

  Hope — pointing the way for the people
  Throughout the night, how long will its beam shine
  and sin follow it?
Oh may it be crowned with light,     like fire and light!


  Encircle the bare head with sacred ornament,
  The torn robe — replace it
  With priestly robes, allow the seed of the first light
To blossom anew, as in "let there be light"      and there was light.


  May Your sign strengthen shaking knees,
  Let the angel precede them,
  And may soon the day dawn
When salvation envelops the pious and humiliation those      who
                                           despise the light!


  He who, as a servant, yearns for shade,
  Surround him with the light of Your salvation,
  And call to him: "Where there is dark,
How long will you remain there? Come, be cheerful!      There was
                                                light!"


  "Grace, grace" — exclaim! Make palm trees
  Grow in rows of two, so that
  In the Temple the oil will flow,
To light lights for Him, who is bright,      to His glory!


*Translated by Thomas Kovach, Eva Jospe, and Gilya Gerder Schmidt*

## 🐝 The Banner of the Jew

EMMA LAZARUS

Wake, Israel, wake! Recall to-day
    The glorious Maccabean rage,
The sire heroic, hoary-gray,
    His five-fold lion-lineage:
The Wise, the Elect, the Help-of-God,
The Burst-of-Spring, the Avenging Rod.

From Mizpeh's mountain-ridge they saw
    Jerusalem's empty streets, her shrine
Laid waste where Greeks profaned the Law,
    With idol and with pagan sign.
Mourners in tattered black were there,
With ashes sprinkled on their hair.

Then from the stony peak there rang
    A blast to ope the graves: down poured
The Maccabean clan, who sang
    Their battle-anthem to the Lord.
Five heroes lead, and following, see,
Ten thousand rush to victory!

Oh for Jerusalem's trumpet now,
    To blow a blast of shattering power,
To wake the sleepers high and low,
    And rouse them to the urgent hour!
No hand for vengeance — but to save,
A million naked swords should wave.

O deem not dead that martial fire,
    Say not the mystic flame is spent!
With Moses' law and David's lyre,
    Your ancient strength remains unbent.
Let but an Ezra rise anew,
To lift the Banner of the Jew!

A rag, a mock at first—erelong,
  When men have bled and women wept,
To guard its precious folds from wrong,
  Even they who shrunk, even they who slept,
Shall leap to bless it, and to save.
Strike! for the brave revere the brave!

## ?≈ The Feast of Lights

EMMA LAZARUS


Kindle the taper like the steadfast star
    Ablaze on evening's forehead o'er the earth,
And add each night a lustre till afar
    An eightfold splendor shine above thy hearth.
Clash, Israel, the cymbals. touch the lyre,
    Blow the brass trumpet and the harsh-tongued horn;
Chant psalms of victory till the heart take fire,
    The Maccabean spirit leap new-born.

Remember how from wintry dawn till night,
    Such songs were sung in Zion, when again
On the high altar flamed the sacred light,
    And, purified from every Syrian stain,
The foam-white walls with golden shields were hung,
    With crowns and silken spoils, and at the shrine,
Stood, midst their conqueror-tribe, five chieftains sprung
    From one heroic stock, one seed divine.

Five branches grown from Mattathias' stem,
    The Blessed John, the Keen-Eyed Jonathan,
Simon, the fair, the Burst-of-Spring, the Gem,
    Eleazar, Help-of-God; over all his clan
Judas the Lion-Prince, the Avenging Rod,
    Towered in warrior-beauty, uncrowned king,
Armed with the breastplate and the sword of Good,
    Whose praise is: "He received the perishing."

They who had camped within the mountain-pass,
    Couched on the rock, and tented neath the sky,
Who saw from Mizpah's heights the tangled grass
    Choke the wide Temple-courts, the altar lie
Disfigured and polluted — who had flung
    Their faces on the stones, and mourned aloud
And rent their garments, wailing with one tongue,
    Crushed as a wind-swept bed of reeds is bowed,

Even they by one voice fired, one heart of flame,
    Though broken reeds, had risen, and were men,
They rushed upon the spoiler and o'ercame,
    Each arm for freedom had the strength of ten.
Now is their mourning into dancing turned,
    Their sackcloth doffed for garments of delight,
Week-long the festive torches shall be burned,
    Music and revelry wed day with night.

Still ours the dance, the feast, the glorious Psalm,
    The mystic lights of emblem, and the Word.
Where is our Judas? Where our five-branched palm?
    Where are the lion-warriors of the Lord?

Clash, Israel, the cymbals, touch the lyre,
    Sound the brass trumpet and the harsh-tongued horn,
Chant hymns of victory till the heart take fire,
    The Maccabean spirit leap new-born!

## 🎋 A Night in Hanukkah

SAUL TCHERNICHOVSKY

Shadows and shades of death hold sway this night,
Heaven and earth are darkened like the grave,

The winds in the forest dance about the trees,
An instant calm, then thundering from all sides,
And moaning softly to awake the dead,
Crying pitifully, heaving sighs;
But in the dark night and its howling storm,
The city, wrapped in snow, prepares for sleep.

Over the housetops on the wings of the wind
Hover dark hosts — the shadows of the night,
Lifeless and still, that were a mighty band,
Staring with sockets that were anguished eyes:
"Lo! These are our Maccabees! These heaps of bones,
These shriveled hands, these bloodless arteries,
These blighted brains — 'tis a miracle they live,
Who live and live not, aged ere their time —
Sans strength or power, but with craven cowardice
Bent double like a willow o'er the brook;
They have not seen God's light, their life's a coin,
Their hapless soul knows not what beauty is;
In chains of the king's law, dogma and its bonds.
This errant folk plod on and sin for bread.

"We breathed our last in the hot and fiery waste,
In a land of drought where leopards prowl the hills;
From thirst, from famine, pricked by the sword of death,
Rent by the lion's jaws and beasts of prey,
On crosses by the wayside crucified,
Sword in hand we fell on the battlefront, —
We died, but thought that they who came after us,
Sword in hand, they would avenge our blood,
That day the horn would sound in Lebanon,
The strong arise, banners unfurled to Zion!
Was it for *these* we hoped? A race unschooled

To freedom, feeling not its iron bonds,
Unruffled when the wonted stone are thrown;
A nation of slaves who spurn their heritage
Surely will be cut off; their sword of pride
Rust has worn away."

Ere the last lamp of the Feast of Lights is out,
While the crickets chirp, the townsfolk turn to bed;
Then their desires awake, take human form,
Their ardor, hatred, anger and their strife
For honor, gods or a tiny loaf of bread.
The tempest groans — dread cries of the jungle depths,
The forest trees moan — dying men that sigh —
And bend their crown and shake their leafless boughs,
And rear their naked trunks toward the clouds.

*Translated by L. V. Snowman*

# 🏵 Chanukah Lights

PHILIP M. RASKIN

I kindle my eight little candles,
  My Chanukah candles, and lo!
Visions and dreams half forgotten
  Come back of the dim long ago . . .

I musingly gaze at my candles,
  And see in their quivering flames,
Written in fiery letters,
  Immortal indelible names.

The names of valorous Hebrews
  Whose soul no sword could subdue;
A battlefield stretches before me,
  Where many are conquered by few.

Defeated lies Syria's army,
  Judea's proud foe, in the field;
And Judas, the great Maccabaeus,
  I see in his helmet and shield.

His eyes are like stars in the desert,
  Like music each resonant word:
"We fought and we conquered the tyrant,
  "'For People and Towns of the Lord!'"

He speaks, and the hills are repeating,
  'For People and Towns of the Lord,'
The groves and the towers re-echo,
  'For People and Towns of the Lord.'

Swiftly the message is spreading,
  Judea, Judea is free!
The lamp in the Temple rekindled,
  And banished idolatry!

My eight little candles expire,
    Around me spreads darkness of night,
But deep in my soul is still burning,
    The ages-old miracle light . . .

# 🎋 Hanukkah

from *Meditations on the Fall and Winter Holidays*

CHARLES REZNIKOFF

The swollen dead fish float on the water;
the dead birds lie in the dust trampled to feathers;
the lights have been out a long time and the quick gentle hands that
    lit them —
rosy in the yellow tapers' glow —
have long ago become merely nails and little bones,
and of the mouths that said the blessing and the minds that thought
    it
only teeth are left and skulls, shards of skulls.
By all means, then, let us have psalms
and days of dedication anew to the old causes.

Penniless, penniless, I have come with less and still less
to this place of my need and the lack of this hour.
That was a comforting word the prophet spoke:
Not by might nor by power but by My spirit, said the Lord;
comforting, indeed, for those who have neither might nor power —
for a blade of grass, for a reed.

The miracle, of course, was not that the oil for the sacred light —
in a little cruse — lasted as long as they say;
but that the courage of the Maccabees lasted to this day:
let that nourish my flickering spirit.

Go swiftly in your chariot, my fellow Jew,
you who are blessed with horses;
and I will follow as best I can afoot,
bringing with me perhaps a word or two.
Speak your learned and witty discourses
and I will utter my word or two —
not by might nor by power
but by Your spirit, Lord.

# These Candle Lights

ABRAHAM M. KLEIN

Dead heroes ride the chariots of the wind;
Jew-phantoms light the candles of the sky;
Old war-cries echo in my memory;
The ghosts of five brave brothers stalk my mind.
And this because my father and his kind
Are lighting heirloom'd candelabra, aye,
Are singing praises to the One on High,
This night in which past battles are enshrined!
As sweet as were the sweet songs of degrees
That David sang rejoicing, in this rite
My sire rejoicing sings; and as the sight
Of almond blooms that burst on spring-time trees
Is sight of this menorah, and of these
Eight blossoms breaking on a winter night!

## ❧ Hanukkah

I Maccabees 2:17–23

RUTH BRIN

The light of freedom burns bright and hot
at the crossroads of decision.

In the market place at Modin
Mattathias stood in the heat and the light
for only an instant.

He heard the offer of the tyrant:
silver and gold, honor and the king's friendship,
but he, in his freedom, chose another way.

Without hesitation, he chose the law of God
for himself and his family,
though it meant warfare and death.

When we sing the holiday blessings
let us ponder the solemn choices of those men
who fathered our freedom,

When we light the Hanukkah candles
let us remember the grave choices
freedom illuminates for us.

## ❧ A Christmas Story

ALAN SHAPIRO

*And the Lord said to Moses, "When you go back to Egypt, see that you do before Pharaoh all the miracles which I have put in your power; but I will harden his heart, so that he will not let the people go."*
— Exodus 4:21


It wasn't only envy but also a vague desire
to make amends, to glorify the baby Jesus
and my friend Charlie (who said the Jews had killed him)

that made me sneak into my parents' bedroom
Christmas morning before anyone was awake
to phone Charlie about all the presents

I hadn't received, the tree we didn't have.
Quietly as Santa (whom we must have also killed)
I took the phone down from my father's bedside table

and slipped under the bed into the cramped dark
of springs all intricately crossed and swollen
against me where my father slept. A long time

I lay there cradling the phone; I dialed
when either parent shifted or snored, afraid
that they somehow would answer at the other end;

or hear Charlie's father yelling "Charlie make it quick"
and the forbidden prayer I whispered to him then
of every toy I had ever owned, or seen,

imagining that he imagined all of them right here
under a tree like his, and not the stark menorah,
our stunted version, with its nine thin candles

solemn as school, or the inkstand and underwear —
more chores than gifts — which I received for Chanukah.
No, it was Christmas here under my parents' bed,

it was His manger, and His death was as far from me
as I was from my own house carolling a holy
inventory to my friend. Then he was gone.

The springs became cold law against me as I was hauled
out clinging to the receiver like a hooked fish
to where my father waited, stern as the candles,

fisher of Jews: you want to be a goy, he said,
be a goy, and sent me to my room for the whole day
where it was Chanukah. And I was more a Jew

the more I pictured to myself all of the presents
I had seen at Charlie's house the day before,
a king's treasure, from which the tree ascended

in a pyramid of flames and glittering angels.
On my bare walls, all day, I had to build it
higher and brighter, as though it were a burden

I could not put down, could never escape —
driven to build it all day by a heart
the God of my father, the Lord our God, kept hardening.

# Memoir

# 🦋 A Generation Reclaims Hanukkah

NORMA ROSEN

The way they tell it in my family, at first there was no Hanukkah. My immigrant grandparents, once pious, felt overwhelmed, it seemed, by six children clamoring for melting-pot America. In December, presents were exchanged. It wasn't Christmas, but it wasn't Hanukkah either. The calendar obliged: it juxtaposed, or even overlapped, the holidays.

Assimilation? Hardly. The family dinner was likely to be pot roast and potato pancakes, called by their Yiddish name, latkes. Slippage. What happened after that is the story of how an immigrant family, by its third generation, reclaimed traditions abandoned in its first.

One aunt married a more religiously observant man; then another did, and then I did. By the time my children were born, Hanukkah was firmly in place. Not just traditional food and presents at the right time, but candles in a menorah for eight days, songs and spinning the dreidel, at which my husband had excelled as a boy. And the story of Hanukkah: how the Maccabees led a band of Jews in revolt against enforced conversion to Hellenic gods, and won, despite great odds. When a cruse of sacramental oil sufficient for one day was lit in the rededicated Temple in Jerusalem, it burned, the story goes, for eight.

My husband's memories from his Vienna boyhood became part of our children's. His are simple and straightforward: the blessing of the Hanukkah candles, each night one more added to the menorah and illuminated, until at last all eight blaze at once; the giving of Hanukkah gelt, small amounts of money, to the children to bet on the outcome of dreidel-spinning.

Our two streams blended in the children, and the children's memories are now also mine: They light the candles, which in turn illuminate me.

My husband taught the blessings and the songs to all of us together. I fumbled at the piano, sight-reading while we sang, loud, to cover the mistakes. "Maoz Tzur" ("Mighty Rock"), and whatever else seemed appropriate from a secondhand songbook for religious festivals. My mother flung herself into making latkes, cheering on her grandson, who hung around the stove, an appreciative gobbler-up of delicious pancakes hot and crisp from the frypan.

My mother knows the secret of keeping potatos snowy white throughout their tedious, knuckle-skinning preparation on the grater (no blender or food processor for her: texture is everything). Hers don't blacken. Mine do, just as matzo balls, when I'm foolish enough to try them on Passover, explode as soon as put to boil in the pot, making the cooking water resemble a kind of kosher egg-drop soup. (When you're good at reverse cooking alchemy, as I am, you have to be careful where you lay your hands on holidays whose message is transcendence.)

Later, we had the good fortune to be invited as a family to a neighboring family's Hanukkah zimria, a songfest. Though the food was always good, the thrilling center of it was the communal singing. These friends had gathered and copied for their guests a treasure of songs, well beyond "I Had a Little Dreidel." We sang them in parts and rounds to the accompaniment of a piano, a guitar, and finger cymbals passed around so that even the most unmusical could take a turn at clopping out the rhythm. The host's gorgeous baritone (in his pre-parent days it had graced the Christmas programs of the Collegiate Chorale) led the motley enthusiasts.

In Hebrew school the children made menorahs. Let my son's words describe his: "A yam-shaped slab of clay into which I poked holes with a pencil, then slathered on gold paint. I considered it a work of art." So did I. And we managed to use it alongside our storebought menorah year after year (as we used my daughter's blue- and-gold-painted clay candleholders on Friday nights) without burning down the house.

The children are now grown. My daughter, playing over Hanukkah memories, lists as favorites the candle-lighting, singing, and dreidel-spinning. Conspicuously omitted are the eight days of present-giving. I think I know why. Some sense must have seeped through of our wondering what on earth to give the children — every night a present? — after the second or third. She spotted the real and separated it from the false, even though we stopped this routine when the children were big enough to appreciate a single gift on the first night alone.

My son, however, remembers that on one of those multiple nights he received a present for which he had "a true hungry desire": a sort of machine that heated up plastic squares to make dinosaurs pop out. He played with that toy for weeks or months (he seems to think it went on for years — a mystical megalosaurian experience). Would I have wanted us to pass that up? Of course not. The senses are memory's mulch, and the dinosaur trail leads back to the meaning of Hanukkah lights as surely as Proust's tea-dipped madeleine leads back to love.

I've called my husband's Hanukkah memories simple. They are not. His parents were caught in the Holocaust. At fourteen, he escaped Vienna on a children's transport, and never saw his parents or home again.

My husband remembers that in his family the dreidel was homemade, a scrap of metal baked in the oven. What's a dreidel? It's a top with a spinning-point below and a grasper-point above. In between is a four-sided body, each side bearing a Hebrew letter — nun, gimel, hay, and shin — an acronym for the Hebrew sentence: "Nes gadol hayah sham": "A great miracle happened there." Spin it and bet on the outcome — which of the four letters will fall face up?

Is this encouraging gambling in the young? Perhaps. But neither our children nor those of friends have become gamblers. (Thus far, one must always say, a form of knocking wood, and what's wrong with a very small hedge against the evil eye, which is so very large?) Maybe there is something about sharing a bit of gambling in a lit-up family celebration that takes away the urge to indulge that impulse elsewhere. I hope so.

We combined. Between us we reclaimed Hanukkah: my husband from a murderous time of madness in Europe, I from a family in America comfortably going down forgetfulness road. A branch of the family that might have seeped through the cracks of time and sifted itself out of Jewish memory entirely somehow has renewed and extended itself (thus far) into a Jewish future. Like the original cruse, which had oil for only one night yet burned for eight, we have managed to rekindle ourselves.

Perhaps here is a clue to the connection between gambling and Hanukkah. Wasn't the whole thing a gamble? Against great odds? Isn't survival always a gamble, and the survival of the Jews in this century the greatest gamble of all? What are the odds on miracles? My husband showed our children how to spin the dreidel, and then, giving the whole thing an extra bravura dimension, how to flip it upside down to make it land on its head, where it continues its spinning. If that isn't against all the odds, I don't know what is.

## 🐾 Miracles for a Broken Planet

CHAIM POTOK

Hanukkah is the Festival of Lights. It commemorates an ancient Jewish rebellion against oppression, during which the Temple in Jerusalem was miraculously recaptured from pagan hellenizers and rededicated to the worship of God. The candles of Hanukkah celebrate that rededication. They also help brighten the long winter nights.

But I remember a Hanukkah when darkness almost overpowered the light.

It was the first week of November 1938. The final years of the Depression lay like a polluting mist across the streets of New York. On afternoons when it did not rain I would play on the sidewalk in front of the plate-glass window of the candy store near our apartment house. The bubble of darkness on the other side of the world bumped only vaguely against my consciousness. I was very young then, interested more in Flash Gordon and Buck Rogers than Adolf Hitler.

One afternoon I was near the candy store, in the cardboard box that was my rocket ship, when an elderly couple walked slowly by; I caught some of their frightened words. Before supper that evening I saw my mother standing over the kitchen sink, her head bowed, and heard her whispering agitatedly to herself. Later, my father came home from work, drenched in weariness; he turned on the radio and became wearier still.

That night I lay awake in my bed and saw the pieces of the day come together and form a portrait of terror.

A Jewish boy had shot a German, the old people had said. We will pay dearly for it, very dearly.

The boy had been sent by his parents to live with his uncle in Paris, my father had murmured. Then his parents were deported to Poland.

The boy went out of his mind, my mother had said in a voice full of fear. He did not know what he was doing.

He wanted to kill the German ambassador, my father had said. He wanted the world to know about the suffering of Germany's Jews. Inside the embassy he made a mistake and shot and wounded a subordinate instead.

He was out of his head with grief, my mother had said. He could not have known what he was doing.

I lay very still in my bed, thinking of the boy who had shot the German and wondering what the Germans would do to the Jews. Two days later the subordinate died.

In the weeks that followed I dreamed about the synagogues that were burning all over Germany, about the Jews who were being sent to concentration camps, about the looted stores and smashed shopwindows. One day I stood in front of our apartment house and imagined our street littered with glass, shattered glass everywhere, the plate-glass window of the candy store splattered across the sidewalk, the store itself burned and gutted. I imagined the entire block, the neighborhood, the city heaped with broken glass and thick with the stench of fire. The days of that November and December began to go dark, until it seemed all the world would soon be of shades of darkness: dark sun and dark moon, dark sky and dark earth, dark night and dark day. I was a child then, but I still remember that darkness as a malevolence I could touch and smell, an evil growth draining my world of its light.

My world seemed thick with that darkness when Hanukkah came that year on the twenty-fifth of December.

I remember my father chanting the blessings over the first candle on the first night of the festival. He was short and balding, and he chanted in a thin, intense voice. I stood between him and my mother, gazing at the flame of the first night's candle. The flame seemed pitiful against the malignant darkness outside our window. I went to bed and was cold with dread over the horror of the world.

The next night two candles were lighted. Again my father chanted the blessings before the lighting and the prayer that follows when the candles are burning: "We kindle these lights on account of the miracles, the deliverances, and the wonders which Thou didst work for our fathers. . . . During all eight days of Hanukkah these lights are sacred. . . . We are only to look at them, in order that we may give thanks unto Thy Name for Thy miracles, Thy deliverance and Thy wonders."

I wanted a miracle. But there were no miracles during that Hanukkah. Where was God? I kept dreaming of burning synagogues.

On the eighth and final night of the festival I stood with my parents in front of the burning candles. The darkness mocked the light. I could see my parents glancing at me. My mother sighed. Then my father murmured my name.

"You want another miracle?" he asked wearily.

I did not respond.

"Yes," he said. "You want another miracle." He was silent a moment.

Then he said, in a gentle, urging voice, "I also want another miracle. But if it does not come, we will make a human miracle. We will give the world the special gifts of our Jewishness. We will not let the world burn out our souls."

The candles glowed feebly against the dark window.

"Sometimes I think man is a greater miracle-maker than God," my father said tiredly, looking at the candles. "God does not have to live day after day on this broken planet. Perhaps you will learn to make your own miracles. I will try to teach you how to make human miracles."

I lay awake a long time that night and did not believe my father could ever teach me that. But now, decades later, I think he taught me well. And I am trying hard to teach it to my own children.

## ∂𝕒 Taking Down the Christmas Tree

ANNE ROIPHE

In December of 1978, the New York Times asked me to write a small piece on a Christmas theme for the home section of the paper. I dashed off an essay on being Jewish and having a Christmas tree. The Times published it the Thursday before the holiday. I had thought this a small, unimportant piece, a kind of family musing that would melt in the mind of the reader like a snowflake on the tongue. I have made misjudgments in my life but none so consequential for me as this one.

The phones rang at the New York Times — it seemed as if all the officers of all the major Jewish organizations were complaining to their personal friends at the Times about my piece. Housewives, rabbis, lawyers, doctors, businessmen, all but Indian chiefs phoned or wrote in, furious that the paper had published an article that advocated assimilation, displayed ignorance of Judaism, and seemed to express contempt for the Jewish way of life. At our house the phone calls began on Thursday at noon and lasted for weeks. . . .

What I wrote in the New York Times was this: every Christmas, my family bought a Christmas tree — and it seemed as if every Christmas we ran into the rabbi who lived across the street just as we were bringing the tree into our house. I always felt uncomfortable, embarrassed, and I didn't quite understand why. True, my family was Jewish, and all of us identified as such. But we had made a decision not to celebrate Chanukah — because we were secular Jews, because Chanukah had always seemed to me to be a holiday about an unacceptable miracle. God, I said, should have prevented the war in the first place, saved the lives of those who died in battle on both sides, instead of merely allowing a small can of oil an extended life. After the Holocaust, the miracle of the can of oil seemed pretty weak. At this point in my article, I made an embarrassing mistake. I confused the Romans with the Syrians and revealed to the readers of the New York Times that I had learned about Chanukah so many years before and had become so indifferent that even my grasp of Jewish history had grown weak. I aptly, if unconsciously, demonstrated the point that ignorance about Judaism is the ice on the slippery slope to total assimilation. In my essay, I concluded by stating that we celebrated Christmas because it was a way to come together as a family, to pause in our daily efforts, to be with each other, and to give something to each other. In honor or what? In honor of the family, I supposed.

The intense response to the piece made me realize that I had inadvertently offended many people. Rabbis were using the piece as the subject of their sermons, treating me as if I were a female Arafat. Every day, rabbis, scholars, and friends invited me to explore Judaism and see what it was that I had missed.

I accepted those invitations. . . .

My studies made me realize that I had not freely chosen to be less Jewish and more American. I hadn't known that assimilation was something that was happening to me and my family. I hadn't known that a tide of history had borne my family from Central Europe to the shores of the Lower East Side and up to the portals of the best colleges in the land. I had not understood the force of the dominant culture playing against my fragile identity, telling me that I would be more beautiful if I looked like a non-Jew, with straight blond hair and a short nose. I hadn't understood that, growing up in the forties, I had absorbed the anti-Semitism of the culture, and that's why I thought that people who spoke with accents were peculiar, that Jews were outsiders. I wanted to be inside with the others. And where were the others at Christmas? They were gathered around their Christmas tree.

Before I began to learn about Judaism, I didn't realize that assimilation had a dark side. I thought assimilation was a process as natural and inevitable as breathing. That's not quite true. I didn't think about it at all. I now realize that assimilation can produce an identity that is shallow, materialistic, unrooted, and anxious. Assimilation can deprive a person of the pleasure of belonging and the vitality that comes from real knowledge about and interest in that person's own community. To be American and nothing else is to be bland like a McDonald's hamburger, to be flat like the highways that cross Kansas, to be dull like our nightly TV programs. Americans can spout platitudes about the Constitution and brotherly love and the wonder of Paul Revere riding through the night, but the American identity, if it is not grafted onto something firm, turns to vapor, a substance that cannot sustain or nourish.

My studies of Judaism made me understand the conflicts my parents and I had faced. I realized that the concepts of Diaspora and melting pot are directly opposed and that my parents had chosen the melting pot for reasons that were legitimate enough for them.

When I was growing up, Christmas was the only holiday of the solstice that was important. My mother found it hard to resist the twinkling lights, the fir trees, the reindeer, and the presents that were all around her. At that time, no one celebrated Chanukah in a way that could compete with the apparent joyousness of Christmas. This was no small matter, because the power of Christmas — the carols, the Mass, and the commercial hoopla — was very great and made the American mainstream Christian world seem more appealing than the Jewish one. The choices individuals and families make about Christmas are significant statements about assimilation, about how these individuals and families will live as Jews in America and where they will stand on the tightrope between being Jewish and being American. When Jews resist Christmas, we affirm our own separate identity. When Jews resist Christmas, we reduce the hypocrisy in our lives and increase our personal security by deepening our roots within our own traditions. We claim our right to participate as equals and not just as a barely tolerated minority when we insist on not going along with the dominant culture.

I now see Chanukah not as a celebration of the miracle of the oil. (I still think that God must make a grander miracle to earn our amazement.) I see Chanukah as a time when, as we light the candles, we pause in awe before the Jewish people whose survival through adversity brings light into the darkness of the human soul. This view makes me Jewish in a different way from the way in which I was Jewish before. It makes me a part of the continuity while allowing me still to be myself, a modern American Jew filled with all the doubts and dark thoughts that are common to my times. Christmas is not the innocent matter that I had once thought.

## 🎄 **Hanukkah** A Brief Reminiscence

ILAN STAVANS

Hanukkah in Distrito Federal was a season of joy and reflection. The weeklong festival of light was celebrated not only at home and in school but also, indirectly, in our gentile neighborhood as part of the season of *posadas*. It would almost always fall several weeks before Christmas, so I have plentiful memories that unite Judas Maccabaeus with colorful piñatas, filled with oranges, *colación*, and bite-size pieces of sugar cane. In Yiddish school we performed humorous theater *shpiels*, patriotic in tone and spirit, re-enacting the plight of the Hasmoneans, who staged a guerilla war in Palestine in 165 B.C. when the Syrian ruler Antiochus IV stripped and desecrated Jerusalem's Holy Temple.

In my mind, the Jewish resistance was a mirror of the kind of uprising South American left-wing comandantes were famous for orchestrating in Bolivia, El Salvador, and Nicaragua. I would imagine the Hasmoneans as freedom fighters dressed in army fatigues and using Uzis. In fact, I remember playing Antiochus once — a role I thoroughly enjoyed — and also once Judas's father, Mattahias of Modin, a man with a beard very much like Fidel Castro's. As Antiochus I dressed like a Spanish conquistador and, simulating the voice of Presidente Luis Echeverría Alvarez, I pretended to conquer the temple, designed after the pyramid of the sun in Teotihuacán. At the end of the play we all sang classic Hebrew songs like *Hancrot Hallalu*, *Maoz Tsur*, and *Hava Narima* but in the style of ranchero ballads, sounding like El Mariachi Vargas de Tecalitlán, and using verbal puns to satirize Mexican and Israeli political events. In the early evening, my parents would give me and my siblings our presents (I still remember a beautiful *títere*, a puppet of a humble *campesino* with huge mustache, a bottle in one hand and a pistol in the other) and then we would light another one of the candles in the menorah, placing the candelabra in the dining room window sill.

Occasionally, our extended family gathered at my grandmother's house in Colonia Hipódromo, where the cousins sat in circles spinning the dreidel, a little top on which we gambled our Hanukkah money. (I remember that no matter how much I prayed for a miracle like the one that swept the Maccabees to redemption, I would never get the winning number and so, at the end of the evening I would be left with no assets to speak of and a bad temper.) After the game, as we would do on other Jewish holidays like Rosh Hashanah and Yom Kippur, we ate a Mexican meal, with Grandma's inevitable *pescado a la veracruzana*, chicken soup with *kneidlach*, the over-fried latkes accompanied by *mole poblano* and applesauce. By way of dessert, we would have delicious pastries that attempted to invoke the baking style of Eastern European Jewry but were really indigenous *bizcochos*.

As if this were not enough, at the end of the day we were often invited to join neighbors in their *posadas* and at this point, as I recall, numerous theological questions about the meaning of Hanukkah and Judaism in general were asked by our gentile acquaintances: Why eight candles? someone would ask. Did we personally kill Jesus Christ? Did we consider Him the messiah? Searching for replies often left me with a bizarre, uncomfortable aftertaste. No, I had not killed Jesus, and neither did we consider him the messiah. He is, my parents would state, another prophet of Biblical dimensions, and a nationalistic one at that. But our gentile friends would not take these answers at face value. Their facial gestures evidenced puzzlement. They liked us, no doubt, and perhaps a few even loved us — but we were clearly from another planet.

I only attached the term "exotic" to my Hanukkah when I emigrated to Manhattan and described these fiestas to non-Yiddish-speaking American-Jewish friends whose knowledge of the Hispanic world was limited to a couple of novels by Gabriel García Márquez, to Don Francisco's popular TV show, and to a short rendezvous to the touristy beaches of Acapulco. What did strike me as singular about the holiday while still a child was that it belonged not only to me, a Mexican Jew, but to an endless chain of generations. My parents and teachers had made me an integral part of a small transnational and multilingual group — unique, abstract, marginal — dispersed across different corners of the globe and alive for many centuries. Millions of kids before me had spun the dreidel on this holiday and millions more would do so in many years to come. I saw myself as a passing bridge, a peon, a crucial component in an infinite chain. The accident of my Hispanic birth had only added a different cultural flavor to the affair. I was, all Jewish children are, time-traveling Maccabees reenacting a cosmic festival of self-definition. These thoughts made me stronger, a superhero with a mission: to smile was to remember, to insert myself in history.

# Fiction

# ❧ The Menorah

THEODOR HERZL

Once there was a man who deep in his soul felt the need to be a Jew. His material circumstances were satisfactory enough. He was making an adequate living and was fortunate enough to have a vocation in which he could create according to the impulses of his heart. You see, he was an artist. He had long ceased to trouble his head about his Jewish origin or about the faith of his fathers, when the age-old hatred reasserted itself under a fashionable slogan. Like many others, our man, too, believed that this movement would soon subside. But instead of getting better, it got worse. Although he was not personally affected by them, the attacks pained him anew each time. Gradually his soul became one bleeding wound.

This secret psychic torment had the effect of steering him to its source, namely, his Jewishness, with the result that he experienced a change that he might never have in better days because he had become so alienated: he began to love Judaism with great furor. At first he did not fully acknowledge this mysterious affection but finally it grew so powerful that his vague feelings crystalized into a clear idea to which he gave voice: the thought that there was only one way out of this Jewish suffering— namely, to return to Judaism.

When his best friends, whose situation was similar to his, found out about this, they shook their heads and thought that he had gone out of his mind. How could something that only meant an intensification and deepening of the malady be a remedy? He, on the other hand, thought that the moral distress of modern Jews was so acute because they had lost the spiritual counterpoise which our strong forefathers had possessed. People ridiculed him behind his back, some even laughed right in his face, but he did not let the silly remarks of people whose judgment he had never before had occasion to value throw him off his course, and he bore their malicious or good-natured jests with equanimity. And since his behavior otherwise was not irrational, people in time left him to his whim, although some used a stronger term, *idée fixe*, to describe it.

In his patient way our man over and over again displayed the courage of his convictions. There were a number of changes which he himself found hard to accept, although he was stubborn enough not to let on. As a man and an artist of modern sensibilities he was deeply rooted in many non-Jewish customs, and he had absorbed ineradicable elements from the cultures of the nations among which his intellectual pursuits had taken him. How was this to be reconciled with his return to Judaism? This gave rise to many doubts in his own mind about the soundness of his guiding idea, his *idée maîtresse*, as a French thinker has called it. Perhaps the generation that had grown up under the influence of other cultures was no longer capable of that return which he had discovered as the solution. But the next generation, provided it were given the right guidance early enough, would be able to do so. He therefore tried to make sure that his own children, at least, would be shown the right way; he was going to give them a Jewish education from the very beginning

In previous years he had let the festival which for centuries had illuminated the marvel of the Maccabees with the glow of candles pass by unobserved. Now, however, he used it as an occasion to provide his children with a beautiful memory for the future. An attachment to the ancient nation was to be instituted early in these young souls. A menorah was acquired, and when he held this nine-branched candelabrum in his hands for the first time, a strange mood came over him. In his remote youth, in his father's house, such little lights had burned and there was something intimate and homelike about the holiday. This tradition did not seem chill or dead. The custom of kindling one light with another had been passed on through the ages.

The ancient form of the menorah also gave him food for thought. When had the primitive structure of this candelabrum first been devised? Obviously, its form had originally been derived from that of a tree: the sturdy stem in the center; four branches to the right and four to the left, each below the other, each pair on the same level, yet all reaching the same height. A later symbolism added a ninth, shorter branch which jutted out in front and was called the *shammash* or servant. With what mystery had this simple artistic form, taken from nature, been endowed by successive generations? And our friend, who was, after all an artist, wondered whether it would not be possible to infuse new life into the rigid form of the menorah, to water its roots like those of a tree. The very sound of the name, which he now pronounced in front of his children every evening, gave him pleasure. Its sound was especially lovely when it came from the mouth of a child.

The first candle was lit and the origin of the holiday was retold: the miracle of the little lamp which had burned so much longer than expected, as well as the story of the return from the Babylonian exile, of the Second Temple, of the Maccabees. Our friend told his children all he knew. It was not much but for them it was enough. When the second candle was lit, they repeated what he had told them, and although they had learned it all from him, it seemed to him quite new and beautiful. In the days that followed he could hardly wait for the evenings, which became ever brighter. Candle after candle was lit in the menorah, and together with his children the father mused upon the little lights. At length his reveries became more than he could or would tell them, for his dreams would have been beyond their understanding.

When he had resolved to return to the ancient fold and openly acknowledge his return, he had only intended to do what he considered honorable and sensible. But he had never dreamed that on his way back home he would also find gratification for his longing for beauty. Yet what befell him was nothing less. The menorah with its growing brilliance was indeed a thing of beauty, and inspired lofty thoughts. So he set to work and with an expert hand sketched a design for a menorah which he wanted to present to his children the following year. He made a free adaptation of the motif of the eight arms of equal height which projected from the central stem to the right and to the left, each pair on the same level. He did not consider himself bound by the rigid traditional form, but created again directly from nature, unconcerned with other interpretations which, of course, continued to be no less valid on that account. What he was aiming for was vibrant beauty. But as he brought new motion into the rigid forms, he still observed their tradition, the refined old style of their arrangement. It was a tree with slender branches; its ends opened up like calyxes, and it was these calyxes that were to hold the candles.

With such thoughtful occupation the week passed. There came the eighth day, on which the entire row of lights is kindled, including the faithful ninth candle, the *shammash*, which otherwise serves only to light the others. A great radiance shone forth from the menorah. The eyes of the children sparkled. For our friend, the occasion became a parable for the enkindling of a whole nation. First one candle; it is still dark and the solitary light looks gloomy. Then it finds a companion, then another, and yet another. The darkness must retreat. The young and the poor are the first to see the light, then the others join in, all those who love justice, truth, liberty, progress, humanity and beauty. When all the candles are ablaze everyone must stop in amazement and rejoice at what has been wrought. And no office is more blessed than that of a servant of light.

*Translated by Henry Zohn*

## ೫ Hanukkah in the Poorhouse

ISAAC BASHEVIS SINGER

Outside there was snow and frost, but in the poorhouse it was warm.
Those who were mortally ill or paralyzed lay in beds. The others were
sitting around a large Hanukkah lamp with eight burning wicks. Good-
hearted citizens had sent pancakes sprinkled with sugar and cinnamon to
the inmates. They conversed about olden times, unusual frosts, packs of
wolves invading the villages during the icy nights, as well as encounters
with demons, imps, and sprites. Among the paupers sat an old man, a
stranger who had arrived only two days before. He was tall, straight, and
had a milk-white beard. He didn't look older than seventy, but when the
warden of the poorhouse asked him his age, he pondered a while, counted
on his fingers, and said, "On Passover I will be ninety-two."

"No evil eye should befall you!" the others called out in unison.

"When you live you get older not younger!" the old man said.

One could hear from his pronunciation that he was not from Poland
but from Russia. For an hour or so he listened to the stories which the
other people told, while looking intensely at the Hanukkah lights. The
conversation turned to the harsh decrees against the Jews and the old man
said, "What do you people in Poland know about harsh decrees? In com-
parison to Russia, Poland is Paradise."

"Are you from Russia?" someone asked him.

"Yes, from Vitebsk."

"What are you doing here?" another one asked.

"When you wander, you come to all kinds of places," the old man
replied.

"You seem to speak in riddles," an old woman said.

"My life was one great riddle."

The warden of the poorhouse, who stood nearby, said, "I can see that
this man has a story to tell."

"If you have the patience to listen," the old man said.

"Here we must have patience," the warden replied.

"It is a story about Hanukkah," said the old man. "Come closer, because I like to talk, not shout."

They all moved their stools closer and the old man began.

"First let me tell you my name. It is Jacob, but my parents called me
Yankele. The Russians turned Yankele into Yasha. I mention the Russians
because I am one of those who are called the captured ones. When I was

a child Tsar Nicholas I, an enemy of the Jews, decreed that Jewish boys should be captured and brought up to be soldiers. The decree was aimed at Russian Jews, not at Polish ones. It created turmoil. The child catchers would barge into a house or into a cheder, where the boys studied, catch a boy as if he were some animal, and send him away deep into Russia, sometimes as far as Siberia. He was not drafted immediately. First he was taken to a peasant in a village where he would grow up, and then, when he was of age, he was taken into the army. He had to learn Russian and forget his Jewishness. Often he was forced to convert to the Greek Orthodox faith. The peasant made him work on the Sabbath and eat pork. Many boys died from the bad treatment and from yearning for their parents.

'Since the law stipulated that no one who was married could be drafted for military service, the Jews often married little boys to little girls to save the youngsters from being captured. The married little boy continued to go to cheder. The little girl put on a matron's bonnet, but she remained a child. It often happened that the young wife went out in the street to play with pebbles or to make mud cakes. Sometimes she would take off her bonnet and put her toys in it.

"What happened to me was of a different nature. The young girl whom I was about to marry was the daughter of a neighbor. Her name was Reizel. When we were children of four or five, we played together. I was supposed to be her husband and she my wife. I made believe that I went to the synagogue and she prepared supper for me, a shard with sand or mud. I loved Reizel and we promised ourselves that when we grew up we really would become husband and wife. She was fair, with red hair and blue eyes. Some years later, when my parents brought me the good tidings that Reizel was to marry me, I became mad with joy. We would have married immediately; however, Reizel's mother insisted on preparing a trousseau for the eight-year-old bride, even though she would grow out of it in no time.

"Three days before our wedding, two Cossacks broke into our house in the middle of the night, tore me from my bed, and forced me to follow them. My mother fainted. My father tried to save me, but they slapped him so hard he lost two teeth. It was on the second night of Hanukkah. The next day the captured boys were led into the synagogue to take an oath that they would serve the Tsar faithfully. Half the townspeople gathered before the synagogue. Men and women were crying, and in the crowd I saw Reizel. In all misery I managed to call out, 'Reizel, I will come back to you.' And she called back, 'Yankele, I will wait for you.'

"If I wanted to tell you what I went through, I could write a book of a thousand pages. They drove me somewhere deep into Russia. The trip lasted many weeks. They took me to a hamlet and put me in the custody of a peasant by the name of Ivan. Ivan had a wife and six children, and the whole family tried to make a Russian out of me. They all slept in one large bed. In the winter they kept their pigs in their hut. The place was swarming with roaches. I knew only a few Russian words. My fringed garment was taken away and my sidelocks were cut off. I had no choice but to eat unkosher food. In the first days I spat out the pig meat, but how long can a boy fast? For hundreds of miles around there was not a single Jew. They could force my body to do all kinds of things, but they could not make my soul forsake the faith of my fathers. I remembered a few prayers and benedictions by heart and kept on repeating them. I often spoke to myself when nobody was around so as not to forget the Yiddish language. In the summer Ivan sent me to pasture his goats. In later years I took care of his cows and horse. I would sit in the grass and talk to my parents, to my sister Leah, and to my brother Chaim, both younger than I, and also to Reizel. Though I was far away from them, I imagined that they heard me and answered me.

"Since I was captured on Hanukkah I decided to celebrate this feast even if it cost me my life. I had no Jewish calendar, but I recalled that Hanukkah comes about the time of Christmas — a little earlier or later. I would wake up and go outside in the middle of the night. Not far from the granary grew an old oak. Lightning had burned a large hole in its trunk. I crept inside, lit some kindling wood, and made the benediction. If the peasant had caught me he would have beaten me. But he slept like a bear.

"Years passed and I became a soldier. There was no old oak tree near the barracks and you would be whipped for leaving the bunk bed and going outside without permission. But on some winter nights they sent me to guard an ammunition warehouse, and I always found an opportunity to light a candle and recite a prayer. Once a Jewish soldier came to our barracks and brought with him a small prayer book. My joy at seeing the old familiar Hebrew letters cannot be described. I hid somewhere and recited all the prayers, those of the weekdays, the Sabbath, and the holidays. That soldier had already served out his term, and before he went home, he left me the prayer book as a gift. It was the greatest treasure of my life. I still carry it in my sack.

"Twenty-two years had passed since I was captured. The soldiers were supposed to have the right to send letters to their parents once a month, but since I wrote mine in Yiddish, they were never delivered, and I never received anything from them.

"One winter night, when it was my turn to stand watch at the warehouse, I lit two candles, and since there was no wind, I stuck them into the snow. According to my calculation it was Hanukkah. A soldier who stands watch is not allowed to sit down and certainly not to fall asleep, but it was the middle of the night and nobody was there, so I squatted on the threshold of the warehouse to observe the two little flames burning brightly. I was tired after a difficult day of service and my eyelids closed. Soon I fell asleep. I was committing three sins against the Tsar at once. Suddenly I felt someone shaking my shoulder. I opened my eyes and saw my enemy, a vicious corporal by the name of Kapustin — tall, with broad shoulders, curled mustache, and a thick red nose with purple veins from drinking. Usually he slept the whole night, but that night some demon made him come outside. When I saw that rascal by the light of the still-burning Hanukkah candles, I knew that this was my end. I would be court-martialed and sent to Siberia. I jumped up, grabbed my gun, and hit him over the head. He fell down and I started running. I ran until sunrise. I didn't know where my feet were carrying me. I had entered a thick forest and it seemed to have no end.

"For three days I ate nothing, and drank only melted snow. Then I came to a hamlet. In all these years I had saved some fifteen rubles from the few kopeks that a soldier receives as pay. I carried it in a little pouch on my chest. I bought myself a cotton-lined jacket, a pair of pants, and a cap. My soldier's uniform and the gun I threw into a stream. After weeks of wandering on foot, I came to railroad tracks. A freight train carrying logs and moving slowly was heading south. It had almost a hundred cars. I jumped on one of them. When the train approached a station, I jumped off in order not to be seen by the stationmaster. I could tell from signs along the way that we were heading toward St. Petersburg, the capital of Russia. At some stations the train stood for many hours and I went into the town or village and begged for a slice of bread. The Russians had robbed me of my best years and I had the right to take some food from them. And so I arrived in Petersburg.

"There I found rich Jews, and when I told them of my predicament they let me rest a few weeks and provided me with warm clothes and the fare to return to my hometown, Vitebsk. I had grown a beard and no one would have recognized me. Still, to come home to my family using my real name was dangerous because I would be arrested as a deserter.

"The train arrived in Vitebsk at dawn. The winter was about to end. The smell of spring was in the air. A few stations before Vitebsk Jewish passengers entered my car, and from their talk I learned that it was Purim. I remembered that on this holiday it was the custom for poor young men to put on masks and to disguise themselves as the silly King Ahasuerus, the righteous Mordecai, the cruel Haman, or his vicious wife, Zeresh. Toward evening they went from house to house singing songs and performing scenes from the book of Esther, and the people gave them a few groschen. I remained at the railroad station until late in the morning, and then I went into town and bought myself a mask of Haman with a high red triangular hat made of paper, as well as a paper sword. I was afraid that I might be recognized by some townspeople after all, and I did not want to shock my old parents with my sudden appearance. Since I was tired, I went to the poorhouse. The poorhouse warden asked me where I came from and I gave him the name of some faraway city. The poor and the sick had gotten chicken soup and challah from wealthy citizens. I ate a delicious meal—even a slice of cake—washed down by a glass of tea.

"After sunset I put on the mask of the wicked Haman, hung my paper sword at my side, and walked toward our old house. I opened the door and saw my parents. My father's beard had turned white over the years. My mother's face was shrunken and wrinkled. My brother Chaim and my sister Leah were not there. They must have gotten married and moved away.

"From my boyhood I remembered a song which the disguised Haman used to sing and I began to chant the words:

> I am wicked Haman, the hero great,
> And Zeresh is my spiteful mate,
> On the King's horse ride I will,
> And all the Jews shall I kill.

"I tried to continue, but a lump stuck in my throat and I could not utter another word. I heard my mother say, 'Here is Haman. Why didn't you bring Zeresh the shrew with you?' I made an effort to sing with a hoarse voice, and my father remarked. 'A great voice he has not, but he will get his two groschen anyhow.'

"'Do you know what, Haman,' my mother said, 'take off your mask, sit down at the table, and eat the Purim repast with us.'

"I glanced at the table. Two thick candles were lit in silver candlesticks as in my young days. Everything looked familiar to me—the embroidered tablecloth, the carafe of wine. I had forgotten in cold Russia that oranges existed. But on the table there were some oranges, as well as mandelbread, a tray of sweet and sour fish, a double-braided challah and a dish of poppy cakes. After some hesitation I took off my mask and sat down at the table. My mother looked at me and said, 'You must be from another town. Where do you come from?'

"I named a faraway city. 'What are you doing here in Vitebsk' my father asked. 'Oh, I wander all over the world.' I answered. 'You still look like a young man. What is the purpose of becoming a wanderer at your age?' my father asked me. 'Don't ask him so many questions,' my mother said. 'Let him eat in peace. Go wash your hands.'

"I washed my hands with water from the copper pitcher of olden days and my mother handed me a towel and a knife to cut the challah. The handle was made of mother-of-pearl and embossed with the words 'Holy Sabbath.' Then she brought me a plate of kreplach filled with mincemeat. I asked my parents if they had children, and my mother began to talk about my brother Chaim and my sister Leah. Both lived in other towns with their families. My parents didn't mention my name but I could see my mother's upper lip trembling. Then she burst out crying and my father reproached her. 'You are crying again? Today is a holiday.' 'I won't cry any more' my mother apologized. My father handed her his handkerchief and said to me, 'We had another son and he got lost like a stone in water.'

"In cheder I had studied the book of Genesis and the story of Joseph and his brothers. I wanted to cry out to my parents: 'I am your son.' But I was afraid that the surprise would cause my frail mother to faint. My father also looked exhausted. Gradually he began to tell me what happened on that Hanukkah night when the Cossacks captured his son Yankele. I asked 'What happened to his bride-to-be?' and my father said, 'For years she refused to marry, hoping that our Yankele would return. Finally her parents persuaded her to get engaged again. She was about to be married when she caught typhoid fever and died.'

"'She died from yearning for our Yankele,' my mother interjected. The day the murderous Cossacks captured him she began to pine away. She died with Yankele's name on her lips.'

"My mother again burst out crying, and my father said, 'Enough. According to the law, we should praise God for our misfortunes as well as for our good fortunes.'

"That night I gradually revealed to my parents who I was. First I told my father, and then he prepared my mother for the good news. After all the sobbing and kissing and embraces were over, we began to speak about my future. I could not stay at home under my real name. The police would have found out about me and arrested me. We decided that I could stay and live in the house only as a relative from some distant place. My parents were to introduce me as a nephew—a widower without children who came to live in their house after the loss of his wife. In a sense it was true. I had always thought of Reizel as my wife. I knew even then that I could never marry another woman. I assumed the name of Leibele instead of Yankele.

"And so it was. When the matchmakers heard that I was without a wife, they became busy with marriage propositions. However, I told them all that I loved my wife too much to exchange her for another woman. My parents were old and weak and they needed my care. For almost six years I remained at home. After four years my father died. My mother lived another two years, and then she also died and was buried beside him. A few times my brother and sister came to visit. Of course they learned who I really was, but they kept it a secret. These were the happiest years of my adult life. Every night when I went to sleep in a bed at home instead of a bunk bed in the barracks and every day when I went to pray in the synagogue, I thanked God for being rescued from the hands of the tyrants.

"After my parents' deaths I had no reason to remain in Vitebsk. I was thinking of learning a trade and settling down somewhere but it made no sense to stay in one place all by myself. I began to wander from town to town. Wherever I went I stopped at the poorhouse and helped the poor and the sick. All my possessions are in this sack. As I told you, I still carry the prayer book that the soldier gave me some sixty-odd years ago, as well as my parents' Hanukkah lamp. Sometimes when I am on the road and feel especially downhearted, I hide in a forest and light Hanukkah candles, even though it is not Hanukkah.

"At night, the moment I close my eyes, Reizel is with me. She is young and she wears the white silk bridal gown her parents had prepared for her trousseau. She pours oil into a magnificent Hanukkah lamp and I light the candles with a long torch. Sometimes the whole sky turns into an other-worldly Hanukkah lamp, with the stars as its lights. I told my dreams to a rabbi and he said, 'Love comes from the soul and souls radiate light.' I know that when my time comes, Reizel's soul will wait for me in Heaven. Well, it's time to go to sleep. Good night, a happy Hanukkah."

# ৯৯ Gifts of the Last Night

REBECCA GOLDSTEIN

That the winds had taken possession of Manhattan on this last night of Chanukah; that they were roaming the wide avenue, snarling and hissing like a pack of demons unloosed from Gehenna: this was not the way she would ever have described the situation. Pearl Pinsky had little use for metaphor and none at all for old-world hocus-pocus.

The simple facts: It was late December, early dusk, and cold. Devilishly cold. Those winds.

Pearl had been waiting for almost an hour at her bus stop, not far from Columbia University. Classes were suspended for the winter recess, and the neighborhood felt eerily emptied. She stood on the corner all by herself, as the savage evening deepened around her into demented night. Her eyes, streaming cruelly from the cold behind her bifocals, were the lone eyes fixed on the dimming west, from where she expected to see, momentarily, the bright headbeams rounding the corner from Riverside Drive.

Meanwhile it only got darker, and the imps of the air were whooping it up with the ends of the long knitted scarf Pearl was vainly attempting to keep wound across her face, breathing open-mouthed into the woolly fluff to generate some warmth.

It was an incongruous scarf to be seen on a middle-aged woman of an otherwise serious cast. Splattered with primary colors, it was like something a little child might have worn, or perhaps even have painted. So that he knew at first glance that this was a woman who gave little thought to appearances.

Beyond the point at which Pearl had given up all hope of seeing her bus tonight; at exactly the moment at which she had even despaired of finding a taxi on this lonely stretch of Broadway, abandoned to godless gusts; just then she turned and noticed a little plain restaurant. Nothing fancy, nothing trendy. To say it was modest is already to overdo it. Not a glance of the brilliance of the festive season fell upon it. Not a single colored lightbulb glimmered, not a glitter of a word had been hung to wish a patron or a passerby a merry this or a happy the other. Squeezed in as it was, between the corner and a dazzlingly done-up Gap store, aglow with a white star and a sentimental message, a person might almost not have noticed it at all, but Pearl had noticed. The winds themselves had taken hold and almost lifted her bodily from the pavement — she was, after all, not so much to lift, a short woman, full-figured, but still, not weighing more than maybe 1 1 5 pounds — and had urgently nudged her through the door, slamming it shut behind her, so that again all was calm within the ill-lit establishment, where a lone customer sat eating his apple sauce.

He looked up, his spoon poised on its way to his open mouth, and stared intently at the bedraggled female suddenly deposited before his gaze. The intelligent high forehead, black-framed glasses, and slightly sagging jowls; the bulging book satchel, incongruous scarf, and unraveling skirt drooping from beneath her coat: he took note of all the telling details, but of the scarf most of all. He was a writer.

Pearl endured the writer's scrutinizing unaware. The overheated air of the restaurant, hitting the frozen lenses of her bifocals, had completely misted them over. She took them off and began to rub them vigorously with one end of her woolen scarf, taking care to do a thorough job of it, since she hated for obscurity of any sort to come between her and the world. So the writer had a few good long minutes in which to arrange his observations and hazard his deductions.

Her age he guessed exactly. It was what she looked, and a woman who wore such a scarf would have taken no pains to disguise the truth.

Years ago, when the writer had been a man in all his vigor, he used to feel a certain mild outrage with such a woman as this, who took so little care to acknowledge and augment the feminine principle within her. This had been a great theme for him, both in his work and in his life: namely, the feminine principle. With him, it had never simply been a matter of a love affair, of which he had had a not insignificant number. Rather it had been a matter of paying homage to the feminine principle, wherever he had happened to find it realized, and available, in this or that particular lady of his acquaintance.

He had been born to a woman who had known, even while he had not yet vacated her womb, that her firstborn would be a boy child of remarkable genius, destined to transform, at the least, the century. Nothing in his childhood had dimmed his mother's certainty, which had, quite naturally, been duplicated in him. The consequence was that he had been the sort of man who couldn't feel the insistent urgings of his manhood without at the same time endowing them with universal themes and erecting them into a theory of art and of life.

The exact details of this theory we can forget, because even the writer had by now forgotten them. They had gone the way of the urgings. So that now he could examine this woman and take in the telling details with nothing of his old outrage.

All evening long he had been acquiver with anticipation since tonight was the very last night of Chanukah, and he could not suppress his sense that the universe was not altogether indifferent. It had been the tradition, when he had been a boy, that each successive night of Chanukah his presents from his parents had gotten progressively more wonderful, a practice grounded in sound theology. After all, the ancient miracle of the little holy lamp that had continued to burn on such meager fuel: this miracle had gotten better and better with each passing day.

He couldn't remember now whether his sisters, too, had received gifts of mounting extravagance. His parents had been over-worked immigrants, their circumstances cramped. Maybe the sisters had received joint presents, as would have suited what had seemed to him to be their joint existence. He, the supremely only son, had simply thought of the three — Ida, Sophie, and Dorothy — as "the sisters."

But the presents that it had been his to receive on those last nights of the magical Chanukah of his childhood: these he could recall in loving detail until this day. When he had been five years old, he had received a tiny violin, sized just right for his little cheek and shoulder. When he had been six it had been the entire set of the *Book of Knowledge* encyclopedia, all of whose twenty-five volumes, with appendix, he had read by the time he was eight. In fact, it had been of his beloved *Book of Knowledge*, with its many magnificent pages of full-colored plates, that he had now been thinking, when the restaurant door was flung open and his attention diverted. So that when Pearl Pinsky finally returned her de-fogged bifocals to the bridge of her nose — not a bad nose, he had noted, though a little wide — she found an old man's watery, red-rimmed eyes avidly fixed upon her

By this time, the writer knew what he knew, and he closed his mouth around a smile as if he and this woman were on old familiar terms with one another.

"Do I know you?" asked Pearl.

"Such winds," responded the writer, with a sympathetic little shiver. "Snarling and hissing like a pack of demons unloosed from Gehenna."

"Gehenna!" the woman gave a short little hoot of a laugh. She had a high-pitched voice, more girlishly sweet than he would have anticipated, with just a hint of the plaintive to curdle it. Without any ceremony, she came over and sat herself down opposite the writer at his little Formica table against the wall. "Gehenna" she repeated as she placed her bookbag and purse on the floor between her feet. "I thought it was supposed to be hot in Gehenna!"

"You thought wrong," the writer answered, and at last took the spoonful of apple sauce into his mouth.

Pearl was inclined to hoot once again, but she only snorted, and rather gently at that. The man across from her — palsied and bent, with only his imperious nose and vivid eyes still undiminished — was about the same age that her own father would have been, although her father would have had even less use than she for the quaint choice in metaphor just voiced. Simon Pinsky had been all sorts of things in his lifetime, including the editor of a Jewish anarchist newspaper, which had had its heyday when Pearl had been a child. She and her anarchist father had been comrades till the end, and Pearl had always felt most comfortable with men of Simon's generation.

"You know, it's a funny thing," she confided, after she had given her order for tomato soup to the young waitress. "I wait at this corner almost every evening for my bus, and I never once noticed this restaurant."

"You're probably preoccupied. You strike me as a very preoccupied person."

He stared at her for some moments more. "I wonder," he began slowly.

"Yes?" Pearl prompted.

"I wonder if you even realize what tonight is."

She looked at him blankly.

"It's the eighth night of Chanukah — the very last night — the best night!" He finished on a high note, almost a squeak. A spray of spittle punctuated his excitement.

"Well, you're right there." Pearl answered, frankly taken aback.

The old man was leaning toward her, his striped tie in his apple sauce, his eyes, protuberant to begin with, gazing into hers with strange meaning. "I mean you're right that I wasn't aware."

"I knew it! I knew you had forgotten!"

"It doesn't mean all that much to me."

"You think you have to tell me that? You think I can't figure that out for myself?" he demanded in an aggrieved tone. He sat back in a sulk.

"So why's the last night the best night?" Pearl asked him. Her father had also had a quirky temper, as had many of the men of his generation whom Pearl had known, so she was an old pro when it came to this kind of appeasement. "I never heard that one," she threw in for good measure.

He didn't want to admit to her that the source of his pronouncement was only the order in which he had received his Chanukah presents as a boy. She was clearly a very intelligent woman. He wouldn't be surprised to learn that she was a lady professor. But still she was also, just as clearly, a person completely ignorant on the subject of Jewishness, so that he could lie to her if he wanted, which he did want.

"It's part of the religion," he said, and took another spoonful of his apple sauce.

"So, if this is the best night, you should at least have some potato latkes to go with that apple sauce," she said, smiling so girlishly sweet that he immediately repented. It was a mean trick to mislead a person about her own religion.

"You know what, Miss?"

"Pearl," said Pearl.

"Pearl. I have a little something for you."

He reached down into his pants pocket, fumbling around until he pulled out a little black book and handed it across the table to her. It was cheap imitation black leather, embossed with gold Hebrew letters.

"It's a Jewish calendar," he said, smiling with the sudden pleasure of his own generosity. "Organizations are always sending them to me, whether I send them back a donation or not. This one happens to be the nicest, but I have others. Take it, it's hardly even used. One or two appointments I had in September, I penciled them in, but I'm not so much in demand as I used to be. It's almost as good as new, Pearl. And all the Jewish holidays they've got printed up, even the exact moment of the sunset when they start. This way you'll at least know when you're not observing."

"Well, thank you." Pearl said, her voice gone more girlish than ever. "Will you inscribe it for me?" she asked, a little shyly.

"With pleasure!" he answered. He was, after all, a writer. It wasn't the first time in his life his autograph had been shyly requested. Women, young and old, single and married, used to flock when he had given readings, and then they would line up afterwards to have him sign copies of his stories that they had clipped out from the Jewish dailies.

Pearl began to fish around in her purse for something to write with, but he quickly produced his own beautiful silver fountain pen, a gift he had received many years ago from one of his wealthier girlfriends.

"Chanukah, 19___," Pearl read. "With my best wishes on the last night —I. M. Feigenbaum."

Pearl looked up, her intelligent high forehead creased into wondering disbelief, her bifocals slipping down to the very tip of her short wide nose. "I. M. Feigenbaum? Are you *the* I. M. Feigenbaum? I. M. Feigenbaum, the *writer?*"

"You know me?" the writer whispered, barely able to control his quivering voice. "You know me?"

Did Pearl Pinsky know I. M. Feigenbaum? And how she knew I. M. Feigenbaum! His brief heyday had coincided with the brief heyday of her father's paper, and sometimes Simon would receive a manuscript or a short story from the young author. Pearl's father had detested the writer I. M. Feigenbaum. It was not simply that this upstart was a sentimental bourgeois, whose writing did not even acknowledge the great class struggles of the day. It was far worse. His stories wallowed in superstition and obscenity, unnatural lusts alternating with old-world hocus-pocus, and Simon Pinsky had regarded each and every page from the pen of I. M. Feigenbaum as a profound and personal insult.

"Don't defile our trash cans with it!" Simon Pinsky would command his wife, who helped out with the editing. Our garbage is too good to be associated with it! Flush it down the toilet, Hannah!"

Simon Pinsky, as radical as he had been in his politics, had also had an almost rabbinical aversion to vulgarity. To hear him utter such a word as "toilet" was painful for his wife and daughter. (A secret: Hannah Pinsky, an otherwise dutiful wife, had saved each and every one or those rejected manuscripts.) In any case, such was the effect that the writer I. M. Feigenbaum used to have on Simon Pinsky.

Pearl's was a forthrightly truthful personality. When she knew something, her procedure was to come right out and say it. It was in her nature, therefore, to explain precisely how it was that she came to know so well the name of I. M. Feigenbaum.

But for once in her life, she held her tongue. Staring across the little formica table at the trembling old man, whose face was luminous with the wonder of this extravagant gift, Pearl Pinsky blessedly held her tongue.

# ❧ Reb Kringle

## NATHAN ENGLANDER

Buna Michla stuck her head into the men's section of the sanctuary, hesitant, even though her husband was the only man there.

"Itzi," she said.

He was over by the ark, changing the bulb in the eternal light, pretending that he hadn't heard.

"Itzi, the children. Think of all the children."

"Bah!" He screwed in the bulb with his handkerchief and the eternal light flickered once before resuming its usual glow. Reb Yitzhak folded his hankie carefully and, slipping a hand under his caftan, stuffed it into his back pocket.

"Itzi!"

He turned to face her. "I should worry over the children? These are my children, all of them, that I should worry over them and their greed?"

She walked to the heart of the sanctuary and sat in the front row of the easterly-facing benches. You should worry maybe over your shul. You should worry over the mortgage that is due." Buna took a deep breath. It was satisfying to yell at this stubborn man.

"How many people pray here, Yitzeleh? How many prayers go up to heaven from under this roof?"

"There are thirty-one people who pray here three times a day and I don't know how many prayers reach heaven. If I knew such things I would also know a better way to pay the rent."

"And what of the roof under which we sleep?"

"Yes, Buna. And I would know also how to pay for the roof."

"How to pay you already know," she said. "Four weeks work is food in our mouths, so what's the question? For eleven months you won't be forced to smile."

Reb Yitzhak considered his wife's statement. Every year it was the same argument and every year he lost. If only he had been born a wiser man — or married a simpler woman. He put his fingers into his long white beard and slowly worked them down toward its jagged end.

"It's a sin, this job," was all he came up with.

"It is absolutely not a sin. Where does it say that playing with goyishe children is a sin? There is no rule against playing games with them."

"Playing! You haven't seen, Buna. Anyone who has seen would never call such mayhem playing. Not since the time of Noah has the world seen such boundless greed."

"So it's not playing. Fine. But you're going. And you will be jolly and laugh like the bride's father at a wedding — miserable or not."

Reb Yitzhak took off his caftan and made his way down to the basement, leaning against the banister with every step. He was a heavy man, big in the belly, and his sciatica was acting up. The rickety wood stairs groaned as he headed down into the darkness, where he grabbed at the air in search of the frayed string and the lone sixty-watt bulb.

The oil burner sat under a web of rusted pipes that spread across the low ceiling. Behind the burner, there was a turn in the basement leading to a narrow dead end of storage space. It was the farthest place from anything, the best place to keep the Passover dishes so that they shouldn't be contaminated during the rest of the year.

He pulled the sheets off the boxes, all of which were marked PESACH, in Hebrew with a big black marker. He couldn't make out the word since the light from the bulb barely reached that part of the room. But Reb Yitzhak didn't need to see so well. What he was looking for was recognizable by feel. The box he needed was fancy, not like the kind one brings home from the alley behind the supermarket, the sides advertising cereals and toilet paper, boxes living already a second life. This one had a top to it, the kind that could be lifted off, like a hatbox but square. This box felt smooth to the touch, overlaid with satin. When his fingers brushed against it he knew.

As he picked up the box, Reb Itzik employed the Back-Saver Erect Spine Lift, counting out the positions. "One, feet apart; two, bend knees," exactly as Dr. Mittleman had shown him.

Trudging up the stairs and directly to the front door, Itzik stopped and put the cumbersome package down.

"Ach," he said, "subway tokens."

"They're on the shelf in the foyer where they sit every day for the last forty years." Buna came in from the kitchen, wringing her hands on a towel and ready to show this mule of a man where was a token and the shelf and also, if need be, the front door.

"To get to the subway you remember?" she asked, daring him to show even the slightest bit of resistance. "You want I should get dressed and ride all the way into the city with you?"

Reb Yitzhak didn't want that at all.

Putting on caftan and coat and lifting the satin box, he gave Buna Michla his best look of despair — a look she saw only twice a year. First when it came time to carry up all the Passover dishes from the basement and, second, from the doorway, when he went off to the department store at the start of the holiday rush. So sad was the look that she lost her resolve not to chide him — she could not stand when he indulged himself to such a degree.

"Do they make you work on Shabbos?" she said. "Do they force you to go around with your head uncovered or deny you proper respect?" She undid the lock for him. "Like a king on a throne they treat you."

Itzik lifted up his box and fumbled with the door. "I pity such a king."

Leaning against a public telephone on the sidewalk and taking a moment to catch his breath, Itzik was surprised to see a new man yank open the gate of the service elevator at the department store. Ramirez, who had been there every year from the start, from the day Reb Itzik had surfaced with the employment agency slip in his hand, was now gone. He had been Reb Itzik's one friend at the job and had always kept an eye out on "the rabbi's behalf." Without Ramirez there chewing on a cigar and offering immediate consolation, Itzik gave in to a moment of virtual despair. He felt abandoned. But at least one of them was free of the place.

Itzik approached the freight elevator, scowling at the Salvation Army worker who shook out Christmas tunes with wooden-handled bells — his last chance to be grumpy that day. The elevator man, not much older than a boy, gave Itzik a slow looking over, working his way up from the orthopedic shoes and taking his time with the long white beard. Itzik didn't flinch. He was used to it, prepared for the thousands of looks and inane questions, tugs and sticky fingers, that he was in for during the coming days.

"Floor?" the man asked, motioning with his thumb.

"Eight," Reb Itzik said.

"I heard about you," the elevator man told him, shoving the empty garbage dollies to the back wall. "You that Rabbi Santa."

"Yes." Itzik answered. "I'm the infamous Reb Santa."

The elevator man began to cough into his fist.

"Damn," he said. "I thought they were shitting me. That you was a myth."

"I exist, yes, for real," Reb Itzik said.

"Seems so." the man said. He began to pull the gate closed behind Reb Itzik and hesitated midway, "Don't you want to go in through the chimney?"

Reb Itzik turned to face the street.

"Such jokes my friend Ramirez got tired of making when you were still too small to reach the buttons."

The elves were in place, stationed every few feet throughout the giant room and continuing along the line of children that reached out into the hallway and past the tiny café, then snaked around the back of the passenger elevators and onto the staircase to the seventh floor. The room itself was decked with flashing lights and fake trees, hollow gifts with colored bows and giant paper candy canes that all the curious children ventured to lick, one germy tongue after another. There were elves posted on each side of Itzik, one — a humorless, muscular midget — wore a pair of combat boots that gave him the look of elf-at-arms. His companion might have been a twin. He wore black high-tops but had the same vigilant paramilitary demeanor.

Sitting in the chair, resting his hands on the golden armrests and leaning back against the plush cushions, Itzik was forced to admit that Buna was right. Poised in front of hundreds of worshiping faces and with a staff of thirty at his beck and call, it did indeed seem, looking down from his giant gilt chair, that he was a king on a throne.

Itzik had arranged for his support elves to keep up a steady stream of Merry Christmases. He was not one of the provincial Jews who had never crossed the Royal Hills bridge into Manhattan, the naives who'd never dealt with the secular world; it was not the first time he'd put on the suit, and he very well knew the holiday kept him afloat. But even after all those years, the words "Merry Christmas" remained obscene to him.

The first child was an excited little girl. Small enough that she was there to see Santa, to get a pinch on the cheeks and a picture to put up on the refrigerator door — not yet a rapacious little beast with a list of demands who would have a seizure if he did not promise everything he was asked.

Itzik fell into character and gave a nod to the elf manning the crimson cord. The little girl rushed toward him like a bull in a chute, her mother prodding her regardless, and the immense crowd taking a baby step toward him, beginning with the front and then spreading backward in a seemingly endless wave.

"Ho, ho, ho," Itzik said, offering a hand as the girl was lowered into his lap. The girl beamed appropriately, bathed in the light of popping flashes and the glory of receiving the first ho, ho, ho of the year.

"What's your name?"

"It's Emily, Santa. I wrote you a letter."

"Yes, of course. The letter from Emily." He tapped his foot against the platform. "Well, remind Santa again: Have you been a good little girl?"

By twenty minutes to lunch, Itzik was sure that his very spirit was being challenged, as if God had become sadistic in his tests of the human soul. Both his pant legs were wet with the accidents of children who showed their excitement like puppies. The sciatica was broken glass running up and down the nerve in the back of his thigh and one boy — a little Nazi, that one — had pulled out a pair of safety scissors and gone after his beard.

"Get on up there," said the elf on winter break from Tulane. She lowered a curly-headed tyke onto Itzik's left knee, his bottom lip flapping as he primed his crying machine.

"Don't cry, boychik. Tell me where's your mother."

"She's waiting for me at the Lancôme counter." And then, after a pause. "She's getting her face done."

"Her face done?" Ytazik said.

"Yes," the boy said.

"So, nu?" Itzik said. "Have you been good this year?"

The boy nodded.

"Did you pay federal and state taxes, both?"

The boy shook his head, no.

"I can find it in my heart to forgive you." Itzik said. "But Santa isn't the IRS."

The boy didn't laugh. The elves didn't laugh. Tulane actually sneered.

Reb Itzik ran his hand along the length of his beard and extended his free leg.

"What can I do you for?" he asked.

"Mountain bike." said the boy.

"And?"

"Force Five Action Figures."

"And?"

"Doom — the Return of the Deathbot: Man Eater: Stop That Plague: and Gary Barry's All Star Eye on the Prize — all on CD-Rom."

"Anything else?" This appeared to be, aside from the sappy children in search of world peace, the shortest appointment of the day.

"Come on," Itzik said, "out with it." The lip was starting to move and Itzik knew if he didn't get that last wish soon, he was in for a tantrum. "How about it?"

"A menorah," said the boy, and the tears started anyway and then stopped in a fine show of strength. It was Santa, at first stunned, then desperately trying to recall a toy by that name, who found himself bordering on a fit.

"A what?" he said, way too loudly. Then, sweet, nice, playing the part of Mr. Kringle, "A what did you say?"

"A menorah."

"And what would a nice Christian boy want with a menorah?"

"I'm Jewish, not Christian. My new father says we're having a real Christmas and a tree, and not any candles at all — which isn't fair because my last father let me have a menorah and he wasn't Jewish." And the tears started running along with his nose.

"Why won't this new daddy let you light candles?"

"Because he says there's not going to be Chanukah this year."

Itzik gasped, and the boy, responding, began to bawl.

"Calm down there, little one. Santa's right here." Reaching back and squirming in his chair. Itzik produced a clean hankie. "Blow," he said, holding it to the child's nose. The child blew with some force. "Now don't you worry about a thing. You ask Santa for Chanukah, you get it." He tried his best to sound cheery; but he could feel the fury rattling in the back of his voice. "You just tell me your address and I'll bring you the candles myself!"

The boy had quieted down some, but did not answer.

"Upper West or East?" Santa asked.

The boy emitted a high-pitched "Neither."

"Not in the Village, I hope," Santa said.

"We'll be in Vermont for Christmas. We have to drive all the way there so we can go to his stupid parents' church." Right then, Itzik knew, in an already fading flash of total clarity, that the farce had finally come to an end.

"Church," he said, his voice booming. "Church and no Chanukah!" Itzik yelled, scooping the boy off his knee and getting to his feet. Itzik, glaring, held the child under his arm. The elf with the high-tops took the boy and stood him up on the platform as Itzik again yelled. "No Chanukah!"

This Buna would understand: hearing this she would understand why, the whole thing, the job and the costume and the laughter was a sin. It was blasphemy! And then he screamed, loud and long, because of the cramps in his legs and the sciatic nerve that felt as if it had been stretched and released like the hemp cord of an archer's bow.

"Where is this mother?" he called out over the crowd. Grabbing the boy and risking a pinch to the already inflamed nerve, Itzik lifted him by the arm off the ground. "Where is this mother?" Itzik demanded, the boy dangling like a purse in his hand. He wanted this grinch of a man brought forth, presented to him in judgment.

The boy wiggled his way free. He took a cellular phone from his pocket and called his mother on the first floor.

Itzik, conscious of the phone, began to feel guilt for scaring the child. He was still furious but also ashamed. He lowered his eyes and found the throng of holiday shoppers and the startled tots, eyes wide, staring back. Itzik, seeking a friendly face, a calm face, found none. He knew he had crossed the boundaries of propriety, and he was far past the point where he could sit back down and nod toward the elf in the combat boots to set loose the next child in line. He grabbed the pompom hanging down from his head and yanked off his hat, revealing a large black yarmulke.

"This," he yelled from deep down in his ample belly, "is not a fit job for a Jew."

A woman toward the middle of the room fainted dead away without letting go of the hand of her wailing daughter. She fell atop a padded rope that pulled down the brass-plated poles, spreading panic through the already jittery crowd, which began to knock over the aluminum trees and towering candy canes. The elves scurried, cursing and shrieking, unprepared by their half-day course for such an emergency. And one elf, the undercover security elf, clasped the earplug in his pointed ear and began to whisper furiously into his green velvet collar, an action that brought on the entrance of two more elves, one big and black, the other smaller, stockier, and white as the fake snow.

The pair tackled the Jewish Santa, the impostor, only kept on by the store out of fear. It had been a bad idea from the beginning, authentic beard or not; a very terrible idea from the very first year. And they would have been rid of him, too, would have been rid of Itzik ten times over, if not for the headlock that management was in. The department store had only in September paid out two-point-three million dollars for giving the boot to HIV Santa, and it didn't have a penny more for Reb Santa or Punjabi Santa — didn't yet have an inkling about how to handle the third application from Ms. Santa that had, this time, been submitted by her counsel.

As Itzik was hustled away, his replacement, tuna-fish sandwich still in hand, was pushed in through a side door. The boy's mother fought her way in from the back of what had been the line. Wielding her shopping bags like battle-axes, she moved toward her son. She called his name with the force of a terrified parent, so loudly that it carried over the echoing hysteria of the crowd, so that Itzik heard it and knew to whom the voice belonged. Reaching the boy, she stroked his hair, and finding the throne empty and her son seemingly unharmed, she asked the question to which every mother fears the answer.

"Matthew dear, tell me the truth. Did Santa Claus touch you?"

They held him in a storeroom, in a chair neither gilt nor comfortable. The chair was in a clearing surrounded by towering walls of boxes that looked more precarious than the walls of Jericho on Joshua's sixth pass. Itzik sat with his suit undone, the patent-leather belt hanging at his sides along with his ritual fringes. The pale security guard, a bitter elf, chided him for his lack of professionalism in the face of duty, telling Itzik he was lower than the Muscatel Santas on the street — a travesty in red.

"Better than to hang up my beard on a hook every night," Itzik said. He waited with the elf for the chief Santa to arrive.

Chief Santa was as much of a shock to Reb Itzik as Reb Itzik was to all the children, for the wizard behind this Christmas empire was not fat or jolly or even a man, but a small thin-lipped woman, without the slightest paunch from which to laugh, whose feet had clearly never donned a curly-toed bootee.

She handed him an envelope.

"Check," she said with such great force that Itzik half expected to see a waiter rush through the door.

"You," she said, the thin lips so white with tension that her face seemed an uninterrupted plane below the nose. "You are a disgrace to the profession! And as far as we, and all of our one-hundred-and-six satellite stores are concerned, you are no longer Santa Claus."

It's not as simple as that, he wanted to tell her. Granting wishes that you don't have to make good on is simple. Believing every child who says he wasn't naughty but nice also can be done with little effort. But telling the man in the red suit — the only one in your employ with a real belly, the only one whose beard does not drip glue — that he is not Santa Claus is another matter completely. That, this woman hadn't the power to decide: Reb Yitzhak from Royal Hills, Brooklyn, hadn't the power to decide. The only one who could make such a decision was Buna Michla herself, and she had said that Itzik would finish out the year. This was the truth, he knew, as well as he knew that, sciatica or not, he would be carrying Passover dishes up from the basement again in the spring.

Itzik considered what would be worse as he rode down the freight elevator. He leaned the satin box against an empty garment rack, the naked hangers banging against each other like bones. He pictured himself riding the subway the next morning with the apology Buna Michla had coached him on, or rejected and cleaning the pews in his costume with Buna standing over him. She'd see to it. Itzik was Santa until the end of the season, whether he lost his throne or not.

# Purim

## The Gift of Esther

# 🎋 Introduction

*And these days of Purim shall never cease among the Jews,*
*and the memory of them shall never perish among their descendants.*
— The Book of Esther 9.28
*So many Hamans but only one Purim.*
— Yiddish Proverb

The rationale for the celebration of Purim, as well as the story of Purim itself, is found in the biblical Book of Esther. Most scholars, however, attribute the story — with its high drama, happy ending, and archetypal heroes and villains — more to legend than to fact. In truth, there is little historical evidence to validate either the narrative or the existence of the characters involved. Nevertheless, the account of the near annihilation of the Jews and their last minute salvation by the beautiful and courageous Queen Esther has come to symbolize for Jews throughout the world the threat of anti Semitism, the triumph of good over evil, and the human capacity to change the course of history.

According to the story recounted in the Book of Esther, there existed a large, prosperous, and well-integrated Jewish community in Persia sometime around the fifth century B.C.E. The land was ruled by a King named Ahasuerus, who — after having banished his first wife for failing to obey him — holds a contest to find a new Queen. The King is enchanted by the beautiful Esther, who becomes his wife without revealing her Jewish identity. Her cousin and guardian, Mordecai, one of the King's courtiers, fearing for her safety, manages to keep watch over Esther. Unfortunately, Mordecai runs into difficulty with the King's chief advisor, Haman. Enraged when Mordecai refuses to bow before him, Haman convinces the King to issue a decree ordering the death of all Jews. Overhearing these plans, Mordecai asks Queen Esther to appeal to the King on behalf of her people. At first reluctant, Esther eventually conceives of a plan whereby she is able to reveal to the King her Jewish identity and plead for her life and those of her people. Unaware that his decree meant the death of his beloved Queen, Ahasuerus has Haman (and his ten sons) killed, allows the Jews to defend themselves against their attackers, and installs Mordecai as his new chief minister. Everyone lives happily ever after.

Although the triumph of the Persian Jews over their enemies is the basis for the celebration of Purim, the holiday derives its name from the actions of Haman, the story's chief villain. The word *purim* (or *pur* in the singular) is the Hebrew word for "lots," which Haman was said to have drawn to determine the date of the execution of the Jews. Today Purim is celebrated on the 14th of *Adar*, the day after the Persian Jews defeated their enemies, the day they "rested . . . and made . . . a day of feasting and merrymaking" (Esther 9.17). In Jerusalem (once a walled city) Purim is celebrated a day later because — according to the Book of Esther — there was an additional day's battle in the fortress city of Sushan. Hence the 15th of *Adar*, known as "Sushan Purim," is the day Purim is observed in any present or former walled city.

In spite of the melodramatic nature of the story and despite its lack of historical legitimacy, it is easy to understand its very real psychological appeal. The Book of Esther makes for fascinating reading today, not only because of the dramatic events it recounts, but also because of the underlying themes it embodies: persecution, heroism, retribution, and survival. The book contains, for example, a vivid portrayal of genocidal mania: the desire to destroy the entire Jewish population through another sort of "final solution." In his reasoning to convince the King to adopt his plan to annihilate the Jews, Haman makes use of a familiar anti-Semitic argument: "'There is a certain people, scattered and dispersed among the other peoples in all the provinces of your realm, whose laws are different from those of any other people and who do not obey the King's laws; and it is not in Your majesty's interest to tolerate them'" (Esther 3.8). Jews were "different," Haman maintains, and therefore should not be "tolerated."

The story of Purim, however, is also a metaphor for Jewish survival through human rather than divine action, as The Book of Esther is the only book in the Bible that contains no mention of God. Unlike events commemorated on other holidays, there are no miracles associated with the celebration of Purim: no parting seas, no plagues, no "miracle" lamp. The players are all human, and events are motivated solely by the characters' courageous actions and quick thinking. Mordecai is portrayed as defiant, intelligent, and the prime-mover in subverting Haman's plot. Esther, equally resourceful, undergoes considerable personal risk (the Queen was not permitted to appear before the King unless summoned by him) in her attempt to save her people. Moreover, the Jewish population itself rises up (with the consent of the King but with no army to support them) to defeat those who would annihilate them. In short, it is the proud story of personal and collective heroism, another lesson in the long history of Jewish survival.

Today, Purim, a favorite of children, is a boisterous, high-spirited, and exuberant holiday. Although customs vary from country to country, it is traditionally celebrated with parades, costumes, noisemakers, skits, and a festive meal. In synagogues, the Book of Esther (referred to as the *megillah*, or "scroll" of Esther) is read, often to the accompaniment of a raucous congregation. At the mention of Haman's name, congregants boo, hiss, whistle, and generally try to make as much commotion as possible through the use of traditional noisemakers, called *graggers*, or *rashanim* in Hebrew. Behind this clamor and frivolity, however, there is a serious message: in the face of evil, one must not remain silent. Objections must be voiced loudly and collectively.

Many congregations also stage a *Purimspiel* or "Purim Skit" performed by children and adults alike, a tradition dating back to the middle ages. Although these tend to be more farce than serious theater, several critics have traced the beginning of Yiddish drama to these early plays. In the home, there is a holiday meal, often followed by a family *Purimspiel*. Among the traditional foods associated with Purim are three-cornered pastry called in Yiddish *hamentashen*, translated as "Haman's pockets," but more representative of the three-cornered hat supposedly worn by Haman. In Hebrew these are referred to as *oznei Haman*, "Haman's ears," the title of Maxine Kumin's poem reprinted below.

All the literary selections reprinted in this section relate in one form or another to the mythology (if not the food) associated with Purim. Yehuda Halevi's poem, "The Banquet of Esther," is a retelling in verse of the entire Purim story, whereas in "Satan and Haman" Philip M. Raskin concentrates on the character of Haman, who is seen as the earth-bound counterpart to Satan. Raskin's short poem in the form of a Talmudic parable portrays a God whose extreme faith in the goodness of the Jews allows him to trick a Satan too willing to condemn God's chosen people. Abraham Linik's "Esther" focuses on the actions of its title character, although the poem concludes with a larger reference to the perpetual danger faced by all who are condemned to live in exile. Abraham M. Klein's "Five Characters" delineates the major players in the Purim story, while his "Festival" is more concerned with the holiday's traditional celebration than with its history. Purim, which usually occurs in late February or early March, has generally been linked with the onset of Spring, and the poems of both Jessie Sampter and Ruth Brin make that association clear. By contrast, Menahem Stern's "Purim in Winter" alludes to the relationship of winter and Purim—the cold, harsh reality of what always lies in wait for those unprotected.

Only Maxine Kumin, the late-twentieth-century American poet, explores some of the subtext and sheer improbability of the Purim story in her poem "Haman's Ears." Kumin describes Esther as a "reluctant heroine," little more than an ancient beauty pageant contestant, a "happy know-nothing." What justice is there, she asks, in hanging Haman's ten sons "for the sins of the father"? And did the Jews really slay seventy-five thousand of their enemies "with the stroke of the sword"? But these are questions she would rather not pose to her children—not when they are still young and certainly not during the Purim festivities.

The short excerpt from Israel Zangwill's memoir *Children of the Ghetto*, entitled "Purim in England," presents a brief but colorful view of festivities surrounding the holiday in turn-of-the-century London. As tradition dictates, there is a carnival-like atmosphere here: the *Purimspiel* is enacted, luscious foods are consumed, disguises are donned, and everyday reality is—at least for an evening—abandoned.

The two additional memoirs included in this section (Isaac Bashevis Singer's "The Purim Gift" and Bella Chagall's "Purim Gifts") share more than similar titles. Both are set at the end of winter, with the promise of spring close by. Both emphasize the gift-giving tradition associated with Purim. Both are told from the perspective of a young narrator. Chagall's memories are recounted through a child's consciousness: wondering, excited, slightly rapacious. Singer's narrator is more thoughtful, introspective, and questioning. Life, he understands, is ambiguous. The occasion of Purim—with its bright colors, parades, costumes, and disguises—seems to belie his everyday existence with his mother and puritanical rabbi father. But this contradiction, the young Singer concludes, is probably part of God's plan. The Purim "gift" of the story's title is the gift of knowledge, the gift of knowing that the world, for all its paradoxes—and possibly because of them—is a glorious place.

This section concludes with a story by I. L. Peretz and an excerpt from a novel by American Tova Mirvis. Peretz's story "Purim Players," written in Yiddish in the nineteenth century, has a moral tone, but one consistent with the themes of Purim: role playing, deception, gift giving, and even retribution. Things are seldom what they seem in the world Peretz describes, especially during Purim. The excerpt from Mirvis's *The Ladies Auxiliary*, set in the American South at the end of the twentieth century among a neighborhood of Orthodox Jews, vividly conveys the carnival-like atmosphere of the Purim *seudah*, or festive meal. Underlying the celebration, however, is a more somber mood, as the realities of keeping this close-knit (and perhaps obsolete) religious community intact begin to manifest themselves. The Haman they face is within, more subtle to be sure but no less insidious, no less a threat to religious identity.

Purim, which occurs during the last days of winter, celebrates a reversal of fortune, an end to persecution. It recalls a moment of total victory, an occasion rare enough in Jewish history. More than anything else, however, the story of Purim perpetuates the hope for a day without fear, for a time when Jews will no longer be threatened by irrational hatred and violence. It is ultimately unimportant if the original tale lacks historical accuracy, for it stands not so much as a story about a particular time and place, but rather as a wish for a time that will be.

Although the ancient sages were at first hesitant to acknowledge the legitimacy of Purim, they eventually embraced the holiday completely. Tradition holds that when the Messiah comes, even if all other holidays are abandoned, Purim will continue to be celebrated!

# Poetry

# 🪰 The Banquet of Esther

YEHUDA HALEVI

While copious flowed the banquet wine,
　　The king addressed his lovely queen.
　　"But ask, and all thou wilt I'll give."
　　　　Her tears now supplicate him.

"O king, my lord, I humbly crave
　　My life, and more my people's life.
　　For we are sold to bitter foe
　　　　Since thou didst yield before him."

"What other wish could now be mine,
　　With violence so rank afoot?
　　Could I betray my kin to fangs
　　　　Of beast that would devour him?"

The king cried out: "What subject this,
　　Or who in all my broad domain,
　　Or who among my creditors
　　　　Dare ween you're sold to please him?"

She spake, "This Haman fell, malign,
　　Who voids his venom on my folk."
　　O woe unto the evil man;
　　　　His plotting shall undo him.

The king in wrath his garden paced;
　　Returned, sees Haman abject, vile.
　　The very skies revealed his guilt,
　　　　And earth rose up against him.

A faithful chamberlain said, "See
　　His gallows made for Mordecai."
　　The king cried out, "Hang Haman high!"
　　　　The gallows loomed before him.

Queen Esther urged her people's plight;
    The edict dire must be annulled.
For how could one smite Israel!
    Unless God planned to heal him?

Forthwith an edict was prepared
    To arm the Jews against their foes.
Good Mordecai in power grew;
    The peace of God possessed him.

His people breathed fair freedom's air
    When he was made Chief Minister
With honors great, in Haman's place
    Of power to succeed him.

Then Persia's Jews in self defence
    Rose up to guard themselves from hurt.
Through Haman's machinations foul
    His sons met death beside him.

Parshandatha, Dalfon, Aspatha,
    Poratha, Adalia, Aridatha,
Parmashta, Arisai, Aridai, Vaizatha.
    The earth would not receive him.

Delivered from the yawing grave,
    The Jews hurled back each fell assault.
God's succor strong upheld the weak
    And poor with none to aid him.

Be this now writ indelibly
    That age to age may ne'er forget,
And he who reads may sing, "Let man
    Rejoice when God protects him."

So feast, good friends, go eat and drink;
    Purim shall be your merry feast.
But in your joy seek out the poor
    With gifts; do not forget him.

From ancient time God's providence
   Has borne me o'er engulfing tides.
  For this my spirit counsels me,
    The hope is God; await Him.

*Translated by David de Sola Pool*

## 🎋 Satan and Haman

(After the Talmud)

PHILIP M. RASKIN

When the Persian Haman
     Thrilled and throbbed with joy,
At the gladsome prospect
     Israel to destroy;

Satan, likewise joyful,
     Brought to God the news,
Bade Him sign the verdict
     To destroy the Jews.

The Almighty answered:
     "Thy request is good,
But my seal, ere signing,
     Must be dipped in blood.

Bring some human blood, then,
     Shed by Jewish hands."
Forthwith sped old Satan
     Over sea and lands,

Searching every highway,
     Every cave and wood;
But, alas, he could not
     Find such human blood.

Then, to God returning,
     He brought back the tale:
"Cowards are Thy people,
     And of hearts too frail."

# 🎋 Purim in Palestine

JESSIE E. SAMPTER

Flowers in the crannies
   And vines that trail the walls,
And down among the lemon trees
   The piping Bulbul calls!

It's springtime here at Purim,
   The very heart of spring,
With days that shine but do not burn,
   When gardens bloom and sing.

We're putting up a scaffold
   In the cruel old-fashioned way,
But we're only going to hang on it
   A curtain for our play.

Don't bother hanging Haman,
   Nor hating anything,
When we're planning for our festival
   In Palestine, in spring.

We're glad that Haman hated,
   And we're glad that he was hung,
Because it's fun that Purim brings
   When you're a Jew and young.

We hold no grudge against him,
   And we're glad he lived and raged,
Because without old Haman, how
   Could Purim plays be staged?

## 🐝 Five Characters

ABRAHAM M. KLEIN

### I Ahasuerus

Set in the jeweled fore-part of his crown
   A naked innuendo cameo
   Of his loved empress shone in purple glow . . .
And when a ray of light was on it thrown,
It smiled as if it knew what was not known . . .
   The king arose, and swaying to and fro
   Raised up his goblet, quaffed it . . . Let wine flow!
And then he sank upon his cushioned throne.
   Drink! drink, my satraps! drink my nobles! drink!
And let me fill again this cup of mine . . .
   He rose again but once again to sink,
And drooped his head, his whole crown making shine,
   And stared into the bottom of his drink,
And saw his Vashti smiling from the wine . . .

### II Vashti

The chamberlain burst on the royal feast
   Of Vashti, and he caught the women flushed
   With wine and maiden-pleasure. They all blushed . . .
But Vashti did not blush, not in the least.
The chamberlain, as solemn as a priest,
   Delivered the king's oracle, and hushed
   The hall. Then Vashti's blood boiled, rushed
Into her face, but she was pale as East
   Before the worshippers may praise the dawn,
As pale as Shushan-lilies in moonlight —
   'The king shall not see me, a naked swan . . . '
She faltered, weeping almost, but not quite.
   The chamberlain looked closer; deathly wan
She was not pale. No. She was leprous, white . . .

## III Esther

Queen Esther is out walking in the garden,
    Yet all the wise men, knowers of the seasons,
    Are watching for some new Star's sudden naissance,
While Esther is out walking in the garden . . .
Hadassah is out walking in the garden,
    And every rose is wafting forth its reasons
For love of life, and the entire pleasance
Is whispering the secrets of her pardon . . .
    The king has seen his queen, alone, and facing
His palace and the moonlight. He does lust her,
    — So beautiful and mine — His wild love racing
Into his lips, how Persian-hot he kissed her,
    Giving her his scepter, and embracing:
'What wilt thou? What is thy request, my Esther? . . . '


## IV Mordecai

He reverenced no idol, nor of gold,
    Nor silver, certainly not one of flesh.
    He was not snared within the common mesh
Of hero-worshipping, by being told . . .
Had he not justly loyally revealed
    The plot of Bigthana and loud Teresh?
    Were they not hung upon a single leash
From either end? Had he not thus unsealed
    The king's death? Was he not a king's grandson?
So Mordecai was bold and cringeless proud.
    And now when Haman passed, though everyone
Fell prostrate in a belly-walking crowd,
    Haman and Mordecai erect alone,
No one could tell for whom the people bowed . . .

## V  Haman

How lividly he looks, obliviously! . . .
　　How eagerly he stares at endlessness,
　　Enchanted by the accolade-caress
Of hempen rope swung from a gallows-tree . . .
Whenever breezes shake him carelessly,
　　Dangling, he remonstrates a brief distress
　　By clicking teeth, and gurgling to express
A last thought . . . Starkness stiffens cap-à-pie.
　　And that is Haman whom the king delights
To honour . . . He has raised him and assigned
　　Him place amongst the high . . . the raven-flights.
There's his coveted horse. — Where? — Are you blind?

　　Do you not see him sway in starting plights,
Curvetting on the Charger of the Wind?

## ⁂ Festival

ABRAHAM M. KLEIN

Ho, maskers, fix your noses, strike a posture,
Squeak out your ditties in a thin falsetto,
Flutter your torn hermaphroditic vesture,
And dance the dances of the vinous ghetto.

If you are thirsty, lift your masks with caution,
And drink this adloyada wine; if hungry,
Here are the cakes, and here the haman-taschen;
Guzzle and glut, or leave your host most angry.

To-night God loves his Jews a trifle tipsy;
He looks upon the sober with displeasure;
Trundle your bones in joyful epilepsy,
Carol the catches of a lusty measure . . .

Tell us, Ahasuerus, anent your harem,
What does a maid to make her royal booty?
How many in a bed-room is a quorum?
Wherefore did Vashti Queen refuse her duty?

Zeresh, mimic your consort's antic bellows
The time you crowned him with the pot mephitic?
Mimic him, too, upon the lofty gallows,
Gallows designed for Mordecai, semitic.

Rattle, you rattlers, at the name of Haman,
Ordure to be expelled with sonal senna;
The young men curse him, and the old cry Amen, —
And he becomes a whisper in Gehenna.

## 🦋 Purim in Winter

MENAHEM STERN

Rows of naked trees on the hill —
Their leafless branches and twigs
Swing at the gray, angry sky
That hangs over the park.

The wind drives with might
As if it wanted to turn
The hilly park into blight

In the evening
The wind being more aroused
Tries furiously to sweep the sky
From the stars that lie
Like crumbs over a palace floor
After a festive meal . . .

But with the coming of night
The wind calms down
And falls asleep
In winter's icy arms.

# 🌸 Ceremony of Spring

RUTH F. BRIN

From the whispering past comes word of the ancient rites of spring,
Tales of the goddess who sought her beloved in the underworld:

Carnival was held to gladden the hearts of the ancient deities of
 earth,
To beg from the mother-goddess fruitfulness for field and flock and
 woman alike.

It is written that the daughters of Jerusalem searched the dark city
 for the lover of the fairest woman,
That the maidens of Israel wept on the mountains for the daughter
 of Jephtha.

We know the earth needs neither ritual nor goddess to bring the
 seasons;
In due course the rotating globe will turn its cold face to the sun.

Yet the past whispers to us when we celebrate Esther, who walked
 in danger to give her people life,
When bright new dress and spicy cakes gladden the children as they
 once were made to gladden the goddess.

When we crouch in the black earth planting seeds, hoping for
 crops,
We make the gestures of the most ancient ceremony of spring.

God, whose life is eternal and whose light never sets,
God, who sustains in mercy the changing seasons and our changing
 souls,

I will go down to the depths of my soul to search for You,
To offer You seasonal ceremony, springtime prayer:

I will rejoice in You more than I rejoice in flower and fruit and
field.
My heart will quicken with You more than my step quickens on the
fresh grass.

I will trust in You more than I trust in the coming of summer.
I will know the warmth of Your love more than I know the heat of
the sun.

For I know that the seasons are Yours and the earth is Yours,
You are our blessing and our hope, and we are Your possession.

## ❧ Esther

ABRAHAM LINIK

And Esther put on her royal rubies,
And the joyful gaze of her eyes,
But in her heart there was night.
On pain of death she will approach
The throne.
And he who forced this bitterness
Upon her people, his cunning web
She will expose.

In sackcloth and ashes Mordecai waits.
And day steps into night.
Bitter is the air of exile,
Like poisoned wine.

## ੨ Haman's Ears

MAXINE KUMIN

Notice this time again how the Jew comes in, in disguise:
Moses, floating on rushes in the Nile's muddy backwash
and now at this season, Esther, Esther of the sloe eyes
warned by her worried uncle to hold back her origins.

It is almost spring. The snow sinks down like an ashpit
in Boston, Massachusetts. I take down the book
and I read how Ahasuerus put away Vashti his queen
for something unspecified (she did not come when he beckoned).
And after the lady was banished, his royal wrath pricking him still,

the King sent couriers out for virgins that he could pluck.
And here in the wings waits Esther (I am reading out of the book),
*a maiden of beautiful form and fair to look on.*

That was in Persia, five centuries, as they say in the temple,
b.c.e. — before the common era. And in Shushan the castle,
it was a golden time of bounty measured in marble,
*in cords of fine linen and purple,* and bickering concubines.

The rest happens quickly. You can read it there for yourself.

Salome asked for John's head on a platter. We eat these pastries
which were, in my childhood, called Haman's ears.
I suppose that the devil has ears like Pan's, and cloven hoofs,
and canters about with the leer of a satyr.

I learn, but too late to destroy the image, that *tashen*
means pockets. Dustmen's pockets, I think; or the mailman's
pouch. And in it, a secret edict wangled out of the King:
wipe out the Jews. They are too proud to bow down.

Esther, that happy know-nothing, begs Mordecai to get dressed.
Why do you tear up your tunic? Why do you lie down in dirt?
And even after he tells her, poor uncle, he has to blackmail her.
Why should she rescue her people, except to save her own skin?
She didn't ask for the part, this reluctant heroine.

In Sunday school there is a party, something like Hallowe'en.
The girls dress up as Esther, the passionate Queen,
anointed to come into his presence, and jeweled, but shy,
and every small boy is the King.
No one wants to wear sackcloth and worry like Mordecai.
After all, he is only the uncle, he has his troubles.

And unlike that night of spirits, filled up with witches and satans,
no little American Jew wants to be Haman.
As the story is told them, the children have shakers they rattle
to drown out so much as the sound of his name.

I have not heard my children question, as it is written:
the Jews smote all their enemies with the stroke of the sword
and did what they would unto those that hated them.
Seventy and five thousand they slew. And Haman's ten sons
—for the sins of the father are so visited—they hanged
on the gallows. I do not read them this message.

The evening is merry. We lounge at the supper table.
I say it is time for dessert and pass round the hamantashen
After all, after all,
what do the children know?
That the King was a good man, rich, strong, and noble,
and Haman, well, he was a nazi
and what Esther did was good.
Even in Persia, in perfumes and bangles and silk stuff
she remembered that she was a Jew.
They know enough.

# Memoir

# Purim in England

from *Children of the Ghetto*

ISRAEL ZANGWILL

At Purim a gaiety, as of the Roman carnival, enlivened the swampy Wentworth Street, and brought a smile into the unwashed face of the pavement. The confectioners' shops, crammed with "stuffed monkeys" and "bolas" (balls), were besieged by hilarious crowds of handsome girls and their young men, fat women and their children, all washing down the luscious spicy compounds with cups of chocolate; temporarily erected swinging cradles bore a vociferous many-colored burden to the skies; cardboard noses, grotesque in their departure from truth, abounded. The Purim *Spiel*, or Purim play, never took root in England, nor was Haman ever burnt in the streets, but *Shalah Monot*, or gifts of the season, passed between friends, and masquerading parties burst into neighbors' houses.

## ⁂ Purim Gifts

from *Burning Lights*

BELLA CHAGAL

A white snow, a pale sun. With the early morning Purim has come. A thin frost has carved white horses with heroic riders on the window panes. A little wind brings the tidings: today is a holiday!

My brother Abrashke and I have run to meet it. We received Purim money. The copper coins clinked in our hands. We ran to the meat market on the square. We found it already full of stir like a fair.

The old, dilapidated tables were blanketed with white hole-riddled tablecloths, as with snow blown in. The tables were set as for a wedding. Women and children stamped around the tables, as the men do in shul during the ceremony of hakkafot. The tables were dazzling, bewitching.

A whole world of little beings of frozen candy was spread on the tables. Little horses, sheep, birds, dolls, and cradles — their red-yellow dots seemed to wink at us, to show that they were still alive, that they were not yet quite dead. Little golden fiddles looked as though they had fallen asleep while playing a last melody. Mordecais and Ahasueruses on horseback seemed to be raising themselves in the saddle.

The cold sun occasionally cast his rays on all these dreamlike Purim gifts and hardly warmed their coats of sugar. Abrashke and I elbowed up close to the tables, as if we were trying to rescue the frozen toys with our own breath. We wanted to take them all with us. On the street here, wouldn't they be frozen to death?

"Children, let's get on with it! Choose your presents and go home!" The freezing vendor interrupted our dreams.

As though it were easy to choose! Our hearts pounded. We looked at the Purim toys, hoping that they themselves would tell us which of them wanted to go with us, which to remain.

How could one let them go out of one's hands? And what should we take? A big horse or a small one? My friend Zlatke might think that in giving her the bigger horse I wanted to show off, yet she would be more pleased with it than with the smaller one. So I touched the little horse in front and in back.

"Bashke, what are you doing? It's dangerous to touch it!" my brother teased me.

I let go of the horse, as though I feared that it might bite me. My teeth were chattering, either from cold or from the temptation of the thought whispering to me that all these little horses and little violins were the sweetest of all sweets, and that it would feel good to be crunching them alive in one's mouth.

"If you wish, I'll deliver your Purim presents," said a tall, scrawny boy coming up to us.

"Sure, yes — come with us!"

His round, sad eyes, the eyes of a much-beaten dog, drew us after him. And like a dog he ran in front of us.

"What's your name?" we asked him.

"Pinye."

Pinye? That is a strange name, like a bird's.

"Can you whistle?"

At home we spread our Purim gifts on two plates, one plate for Abrashke and the other for me.

The little sugar animals seemed to come back to life in the warm air. Their little cheeks began to glisten. Frightened, I blew on them, so that they should not melt from the heat. That would be the last straw — that our presents should melt, fall apart in little bits. More than once we changed the places, picked among the presents, sorted them. I clung particularly to the little candy violin. It nestled in my fingers, stroked them, like a toy bow, as if it were trying to play a melody on them.

"And if I send the little violin to my friend, it will surely never come back to me," I thought, feeling a stab in my heart.

But Pinye, the errand boy, was shuffling his feet, waiting for our presents. Trembling with emotion, we gazed for the last time on our plates, wrapped them each in a kerchief, and gathered together the corners.

"Pinye, see, here are our Purim gifts. But you mustn't run, mind you! Better walk slowly! You must not — God forbid — slip on the wet snow with the plates. And don't turn around! You might be pushed! What is the matter, are you asleep? Why do you look at us as in a dream?" And we shook the boy by his shoulders.

Pinye started from his place and at once began to run. The plates shook in his hands.

"Don't rush like that, Pinye! Have you no time? What's the hurry? Watch out, hold fast to the corners of the kerchiefs!" we shouted after him.

Oh, he'll make trouble, that boy, I said to myself. He has such long legs! Our presents will tumble over on one another. And suppose an ear of the horse breaks off on the way, or the top of the curved little violin falls off? What will our friends think? That we sent them broken presents?

"Where are you, Pinye?"

But Pinye has vanished.

Right now, I keep thinking, Pinye has turned into the little street where my friend Zlatke lives. The black latch of the door is lifted from inside, and from behind the door Zlatke appears, as though she had been waiting for the messenger.

"Are the two for me?" And Zlatke stretches out both hands.

"No, this one is yours!" And Pinye probably confuses our plates.

Zlatke snatches the little plate from Pinye's hands and runs to her bedroom. Pinye remains standing there.

In the kitchen, Zlatke's mother is busying herself. With a long iron fork she lifts a big black pot and pushes it into the oven. Pinye's tongue hangs out of his mouth. He wants to eat. The roasted meat and potatoes smell so good.

"Zlatke, why does it take so long? Have you fallen asleep there, or what? Ai, what children get excited about! Going wild over nothing!"

Zlatke's mother turns to the boy with a cry. "What are you standing for, you ninny? For the same money you can sit down!"

Zlatke is somewhat fat, with short little legs, and she wears her hair in a long, heavy pigtail on her back. And she always walks so slowly that I get bored looking at her. Even her big eyes stare as if frozen in her face. Before she gets through with the Purim gifts, the Messiah himself might come. She probably examines my plate from all sides, touches the little horse and the golden lamb. She puts them to her nose, to her ears.

Her long pigtail wiggles on her back as though it were helping her to think. She is unable to fix her attention on anything. And suppose Zlatke wants to keep the whole plate?

Oh, why do I think up such false accusations? I shame myself. Probably Zlatke runs to the drawer where she keeps her own presents, spreads out her little horses and lambs, and compares them with mine.

"She is taking the sweet little violin from my plate!" I think with pounding heart.

And what will she put in its place? Oh, why doesn't the boy come back? He has vanished as though forever! I begin to question Abrashke: "Do you think Pinye has already been at my friend's?"

But my brother teases me. He thinks that being older than I, and a boy to boot, he can make fun of me. So he bursts into laughter.

Let him laugh, by all means! I know nevertheless that he too is waiting for Pinye, that he is dying to see what has remained on his plate, and what gifts for him have been added on it. To whom is he boasting? Don't I see that he keeps looking out of the window, watching for the return of our Pinye?

"You know, Bashke," he says, "Pinye probably won't be back for at least an hour. You know that my friend Motke lives on the other side of the river. And by the time that dreamy Pinye crosses the bridge, we shall be falling asleep. How can you expect him not to stop to have a look at what is going on in the river? Perhaps the ice has begun to break!"

And what if Abrashke is right? I am bursting with grief.

"Pinye is capable of anything," I agree with my brother. "That's all he has to do — inspect the whole river! He won't even be back for the meal!"

"You dumb cluck, you believe everything! I've just made that up!" My brother is now rolling with laughter.

Suddenly he pushes me to one side and like a cat scrambles down all the stairs that lead to the kitchen. Pinye is knocking at the door.

"Ah, you brats, why do you make so much noise?" the fat cook yells at us. "You idlers! All day long you roam about here — you don't give me a chance to do anything. Out of the kitchen!"

We drag Pinye into the house. First we look into his eyes, then into the plates. He has probably seen what kind of presents have been sent us in exchange for ours.

Well, the little violin must be gone! I read it in Pinye's sad eyes. I open the kerchief on my plate. Yes, she did take the pretty little violin! And I have no other violin, and I don't need the doll she has given me. I've got two like it. Abrashke has given me his. And that's what made her fuss for a whole hour! In anger I bite my lips.

What? He is laughing again, Abrashke, and even that silly Pinye too! I can't look at them any more.

Abrashke is lucky. He can afford to be in a good mood. Motke has put a big horse on his plate. In his enthusiasm, Abrashke neighs like a real horse.

Weeping, I run to the kitchen.

"Why do you make such a long face?" The cook throws the words at me while chopping onions. "What is the matter, did you get a bad Purim gift?" And she keeps on babbling in her usual fashion, as though she were chopping the onions with her tongue, and she spatters me with wet crumbs. "What a misfortune that is! May you have no greater grief until your hundred-and-twentieth year! Silly girl, you'll surely forget about it before your wedding!"

Whether because of the onions or because of her words, my eyes begin actually to drop tears.

"Here, take your little Haman-tash." And the cook squeezes into my hands a triangular cake, bursting with heat and with the poppyseed with which it is stuffed.

My hands at once become wet and warm as though somebody had kissed them.

"You see, Bashutke, there was no reason for crying!" Sasha cheers me with her smile. "You know what? Just wait a while — when I'm through with my work, I'll run out for a minute and exchange your doll for a violin."

"Darling Sasha!" I creep into her skirts, stuffed underneath like a whole wardrobe, and wipe my eyes on her sleeves.

"That's enough, Bashutke, go now, let me work! It will be mealtime soon! Why do you keep spinning around me, you crazy girl?" And she pushes me away gently.

In the dark rear shop I bump into something hard. Aha, a woven basket! This must be mother's Purim gifts prepared for our uncles and aunts. A basket packed full of good things! How can mother send them away so improvidently? The basket will have bottles of red and white wine, bottles of sweet syrups, big pears, wooden boxes with cigars heaped on one another like blocks; there will be cans of sprats and sardines, and amidst all this a new red tablecloth with painted flowers.

Mother has been busy in the shop, as always, and probably has forgotten her Purim presents. Doesn't she even think of them? The basket will soon be carried away! And isn't she waiting at all for the presents that she will get?

I imagine my good Aunt Rachel's delight over mother's presents: "Lord of the Universe! So many good things! And all that for me! Ah, Alta, you'll spoil me altogether!"

My aunt's weak heart is choked with joy. She sniffs at the basket; she seems instantly to be made drunk by all the good smells, for she closes her eyes. Then she awakens as if from a dream. She feels the tablecloth, lifts it in the air, strokes it. She might be saying a benediction: "Thank you, Altinke! May God in heaven grant you many healthful and happy years! How could you guess so truly? I really needed a new tablecloth for Pesach, to honor my guests."

And suddenly my aunt fancies that a speck of dust has fallen on the new tablecloth. She blows away the speck, and fearing that the table-cloth may become soiled before the Passover, she carefully lays it in its folds.

How many baskets with presents have been carried through the streets from one house to another! And the things they were filled with! The scrawny woman messengers were hardly able to hold them up.

"Is Itchke at home?"

I suddenly hear an unfamiliar voice in the kitchen. In the doorway stands a little old Jewish woman, wrapped in a big shawl. In her hands she holds a yellowed candy horse as one holds a little live chicken.

"Bashinke, gut yom-tov!" And she smiles at me with her thin lips. "Is Itchke in? There's a Purim present for him!"

She lifts the little horse. She wants to show me how big and beautiful her present is. And indeed, the little horse almost seems to be bigger and fatter than she is.

A strange woman, like someone just out of a madhouse. Was she really once my brother Itchke's nurse? Now he is tall and big — how could he have had this little woman for a nurse?

My brother has for many years been living abroad, studying medicine, but the old woman comes every Purim to bring him a gift. The dried-up nurse always explains that she wants to have a look at her Itchke.

Mother presses a silver coin into her hand and tells her in a low voice, as though fearing to frighten her, that Itchke is not at home, and that she can take back her little horse: the present may come in handy next year, God willing. And actually the little horse grows yellower and yellower every year.

One day the old woman found Itchke at home. But when she saw in the doorway a grown-up young man, she was so frightened that she ran out of the kitchen as if someone were chasing her. She even forgot to hand him the little horse.

No one stopped her. And since then she has not returned.

Mother distributes gifts among the people she employs in the house and in the shop. Something glistens in her fingers. A pair of golden ear-rings and a ring stick out from their tissue paper — presents for the maids. At every holiday they receive golden things. And they are happy to think that they are collecting jewelry, although they have never married.

I look at our bookkeeper. Usually quiet, wordless, he now becomes talkative and his mustache quivers. His hands stroke a new silver watch.

Huneh, the clerk, quietly folds a white silken kerchief that mother has given him for his young wife.

Unlike him, Rose, the salesgirl, fills the shop with her loud enthusiasm, turns about before the mirror, boasts to everyone of her beautiful medallion, her Purim present. The cashier has received some money. Although she is busy all day long with a box full of money, she has found herself short of funds.

The watchmaker receives some bottles of wine — he has enough watches in his table drawer. The faces of all of them are radiant, as though a wedding were being celebrated in the shop.

"Close the shop! It will soon be dinnertime!" Father's voice breaks into the noisy gathering.

*Translated by Norbert Guterman*

# The Purim Gift

from In My Father's Court

ISAAC BASHEVIS SINGER

Our home was always half unfurnished. Father's study was empty except for books. In the bedroom there were two bedsteads, and that was all. Mother kept no foods stocked in the pantry. She bought exactly what she needed for one day, and no more, often because there was no money to pay for more. In our neighbors' homes I had seen carpets, pictures on the walls, copper bowls, lamps, and figurines. But in our house, a rabbi's house, such luxuries were frowned upon. Pictures and statuary were out of the question; my parents regarded them as idolatrous. I remember that in the heder I had once bartered my Pentateuch for another boy's, because the frontispiece of his was decorated with pictures of Moses holding the Tablets and Aaron wearing the priestly robe and breastplate—as well as two angels. Mother saw it and frowned. She showed it to my father. Father declared that it was forbidden to have such pictures in a sacred book. He cited the Commandment: "Thou shalt not make unto thee any graven image, or any likeness . . ."

Into this stronghold of Jewish puritanism, where the body was looked upon as a mere appendage to the soul, the feast of Purim introduced a taste of luxury.

All the neighbors sent shalach-monos—Purim gifts. From early afternoon the messengers kept coming. They brought wine, mead, oranges, cakes, and cookies. One generous man sent a tin of sardines; another, smoked salmon; a third, sweet-and-sour fish. They brought apples carefully wrapped in tissue paper, dates, figs—anything you could think of. The table was heaped with delicacies. Then came the masked mummers, with helmets on their heads and cardboard shields and swords, all covered with gold or silver paper. For me it was a glorious day.

But my parents were not pleased with this extravagance. Once a wealthy man sent us some English ale. Father looked at the bottle, which bore a colorful label, and sighed. The label showed a red-faced man with a blond mustache, wearing a hat with a feather. His intoxicated eyes were full of a pagan joy. Father said, in an undertone, "How much thought and energy they expend on these worldly vanities."

Later in the day Father would treat the Hasidim with the wine. We did not eat the Warsaw cakes, for we were never certain just how conscientious Warsaw Jews were about the dietary regulations. One could not know whether the pastries had been baked with chicken fat and must therefore not be eaten together with any milk foods.

The mummers, too, were disposed of quickly, for the wearing of masks and the singing of songs smacked of the theater, and the theater was *tref*—unclean. In our home, the "world" itself was *tref*. Many years were to pass before I began to understand how much sense there was in this attitude.

But Krochmalna Street did not wish to take note of such thoughts. For Krochmalna Street, Purim was a grand carnival. The street was filled with maskers and bearers of gifts. It smelled of cinnamon, saffron and chocolate, of freshly baked cakes and all sorts of sweets and spices whose names I did not know. The sweetshops sold cookies in the shapes of King Ahasuerus, Haman the Wicked, the chamberlain Harbona, Queen Vashti, and Vaizatha, the tenth son of Haman. It was good to bite off Haman's leg, or to swallow the head of Queen Esther. And the noisemakers kept up a merry clamor, in defiance of all the Hamans of all the ages.

Among betrothed couples, and boys and girls who were "going with each other," the sending of Purim gifts was obligatory. This was part of the customary exchange of engagement presents. Because of one such Purim gift, an argument arose that almost led to a Din Torah in our house.

A young man sent his betrothed a silver box, but when she opened it —in the presence of her sister and her girl friends, who were impatiently awaiting the arrival of the gift—she found it contained a dead mouse! She uttered an unearthly shriek and fainted. The other girls screeched and screamed. After the bride-to-be had been revived with compresses of cold water and vinegar, and her friends had collected their wits, they began to plot revenge. The bride-to-be knew the reason for her boyfriend's outrageous deed. Several days before, they had quarreled. After much talk and discussion, the young women decided to repay the malicious youth in kind. Instead of a dead mouse, however, they sent him a fancy cake— filled with refuse. The baker was party to the conspiracy. The girls of Krochmalna Street looked upon this conflict as a war between the sexes, and Krochmalna Street had something to laugh about that Purim. The strange part of it was that the young man, although he had committed a revolting act, had not expected an equally odious retaliation, and was no less stunned than his fiancée had been. People quickly added imaginary incidents. The girls of Krochmalna Street always believed in laughing. One often heard bursts of uncontrolled laughter that might have come from an insane asylum. This time they chortled and chuckled from one end of the street to the other. The young man, too, had been surrounded by friends at the festive Purim meal. He, too, had been aided and abetted in his prank.

Yes, that Purim was a merry one. But the next morning everyone had sobered up and the warring clans came to us for a Din Torah. The room was jammed full with people. The bride-to-be had brought her family and her girl friends, and the groom was accompanied by his relatives and cronies. All of them were shouting as they climbed up the stairs, and they kept on shouting for half an hour or more, and my father had yet to learn who was the accuser, who the defendant and what the tumult was about. But while they were yelling, screaming, hurling insults and curses, Father quietly pored over one of his books. He knew that sooner or later they would grow calm. Jews, after all, are not bandits. In the meanwhile, before more time had been wasted, he wanted to know what Rabbi Samuel Eliezer Edels meant by the comment in his book, The Maharsha: "And one might also say . . ."

I was present in the room and soon knew all about the affair. I listened attentively to every insult, every curse. There was quarreling and bickering, but every once in a while someone ventured a mild word or the suggestion that it was senseless to break off a match for such foolishness. Others, however, raked up the sins of the past. One minute their words were wild and coarse, but the next minute they had changed their tune and were full of friendship and courtesy. From early childhood on, I have noted that for most people there is only one small step between vulgarity and "refinement," between blows and kisses, between spitting at one's neighbor's face and showering him with kindness.

After they had finished shouting, and everyone had grown hoarse, someone at last related the entire story to my father. Father was shocked.

"Shame! How can anyone do such things? It is a violation of the law: 'Ye shall not make your souls abominable . . .'"

Father immediately cited a number of biblical verses and laws. First, it was impious; second, it was loathsome; third, such acts lead to anger, gossip, slander, discord, and what not. It was also dangerous, for the victim, overcome by nausea, might have become seriously ill. And the defilement of edibles, the food which God had created to still man's hunger and over which benedictions were to be recited, was in itself a sacrilege. Father recalled the sage who used to say that he merited long life if only because he had never left bread crumbs lying on the ground. He reminded them that, in order for a cake to be baked, someone had to till the soil and sow the grain, and then rain and dew had to fall from heaven. It was no small thing that out of a rotting seed in the earth a stalk of wheat burst forth. All the wise men of the world together could not create such a stalk. And here, instead of thanking and praising the Almighty for His bounty, men had taken this gift and used it to provoke their neighbors — had defiled what He had created.

Where formerly there had been an uproar, silence now reigned. The women wiped their eyes with their aprons. The men bowed their heads. The girls bashfully lowered their eyelids. After Father's words there was no more talk of a Din Torah. A sense of shame and solemnity seemed to have overcome everyone. Out of my father's mouth spoke the Torah, and all understood that every word was just. I was often to witness how my father, with his simple words, routed pettiness, vain ambition, foolish resentment, and conceit.

After Father's admonition the bride- and groom-to-be made peace. The mothers, who just a few minutes before had hurled insults at each other, now embraced. Talk of setting a date for the wedding was heard. My father received no fee, for there had been no actual Din Torah. His words of mild reproach had damaged his own livelihood. But no matter, for the weeks between Purim and Passover were a time of relative prosperity for us. Together with the Purim delicacies, the neighbors had sent a half ruble or a ruble each. And soon the pre-Passover sale of leavened bread would begin.

When the study had emptied, Father called me over and cautioned me to take heed of what may happen to those who do not study the Torah but concern themselves only with the vanities of this world.

The next Sabbath, after the *cholent*, the Sabbath stew, I went out on the balcony. The air was mild. The snow had long since melted. The pavements were dry. In the gutter flowed little streamlets whose ripples reflected the blue of the sky and the gold of the sun. The young couples of Krochmalna Street were starting out on their Sabbath walks. Suddenly the two who had sent each other the ugly gifts passed by. They walked arm in arm, chatting animatedly, smiling. A boy and his girl had quarreled — what of it?

I stood on the balcony in my satin gabardine and my velvet hat, and gazed about me. How vast was this world, and how rich in all kinds of people and strange happenings! And how high was the sky above the rooftops! And how deep the earth beneath the flagstones! And why did men and women love each other? And where was God, who was constantly spoken of in our house? I was amazed, delighted, entranced. I felt that I must solve this riddle, I alone, with my own understanding.

*Translated by Channa Kleinerman Goldstein, Elaine Gottlieb, and Joseph Singer*

# Fiction

# ❧ from The Book of Esther

### 1

It happened in the days of Ahasuerus — that Ahasuerus who reigned over a hundred and twenty-seven provinces from India to Nubia. In those days, when King Ahasuerus occupied the royal throne in the fortress, Shushan, in the third year of his reign, he gave a banquet for all the officials and courtiers — the administration of Persia and Media, the nobles and the governors of the provinces in his service. For no fewer than a hundred and eighty days he displayed the vast riches of his kingdom and the splendid glory of his majesty. At the end of this period, the king gave a banquet for seven days in the court of the king's palace garden for all the people who lived in the fortress Shushan, high and low alike. [There were hangings of] white cotton and blue wool, caught up by cords of fine linen and purple wool to silver rods and alabaster columns; and there were couches of gold and silver on a pavement of marble, alabaster, mother of pearl, and mosaics. Royal wine was served in abundance, as befits a king, in golden beakers, beakers of varied design. And the rule for the drinking was, "No restrictions!" For the king had given orders to every palace steward to comply with each man's wishes. In addition, Queen Vashti gave a banquet for women, in the royal palace of King Ahasuerus.

On the seventh day, when the king was merry with wine, he ordered Mehuman, Bizzetha, Harbona, Bigtha, Abagtha, Zethar, and Carcas, the seven eunuchs in attendance on King Ahasuerus, to bring Queen Vashti before the king wearing a royal diadem, to display her beauty to the peoples and the officials; for she was a beautiful woman. But Queen Vashti refused to come at the king's command conveyed by the eunuchs. The king was greatly incensed, and his fury burned within him. . . .

### 2

Some time afterward, when the anger of King Ahasuerus subsided, he thought of Vashti and what she had done and what had been decreed against her. The king's servants who attended him said, "Let beautiful young virgins be sought out for Your Majesty. Let Your Majesty appoint officers in every province of your realm to assemble all the beautiful young virgins at the fortress Shushan, in the harem under the supervision of Hege, the king's eunuch, guardian of the women. Let them be provided with their cosmetics. And let the maiden who pleases Your Majesty be queen instead of Vashti." The proposal pleased the king, and he acted upon it.

In the fortress Shushan lived a Jew by the name of Mordecai, son of Jair son of Shimei son of Kish, a Benjaminite. [Kish] had been exiled from Jerusalem in the group that was carried into exile along with King Jeconiah of Judah, which had been driven into exile by King Nebuchadnezzar of Babylon. — He was foster father to Hadassah — that is, Esther — his uncle's daughter, for she had neither father nor mother. The maiden was shapely and beautiful; and when her father and mother died, Mordecai adopted her as his own daughter.

When the king's order and edict was proclaimed, and when many girls were assembled in the fortress Shushan under the supervision of Hegai, Esther too was taken into the king's palace under the supervision of Hegai, guardian of the women. The girl pleased him and won his favor, and he hastened to furnish her with her cosmetics and her rations, as well as with the seven maids who were her due from the king's palace; and he treated her and her maids with special kindness in the harem. Esther did not reveal her people or her kindred, for Mordecai had told her not to reveal it. Every single day Mordecai would walk about in front of the court of the harem, to learn how Esther was faring and what was happening to her.

When each girl's turn came to go to King Ahasuerus at the end of the twelve months' treatment prescribed for women (for that was the period spent on beautifying them: six months with oil of myrrh and six months with perfumes and women's cosmetics, and it was after that that the girl would go to the king), whatever she asked for would be given her to take with her from the harem to the king's palace. She would go in the evening and leave in the morning for a second harem in charge of Shaashgaz, the king's eunuch, guardian of the concubines. She would not go again to the king unless the king wanted her, when she would be summoned by name. When the turn came for Esther daughter of Abihail — the uncle of Mordecai, who had adopted her as his own daughter — to go to the king, she did not ask for anything but what Hegai, the king's eunuch, guardian of the women, advised. Yet Esther won the admiration of all who saw her.

Esther was taken to King Ahasuerus, in his royal palace, in the tenth month, which is the month of Tebeth, in the seventh year of his reign. The king loved Esther more than all the other women, and she won his grace and favor more than all the virgins. So he set a royal diadem on her head and made her queen instead of Vashti. The king gave a great banquet for all his officials and courtiers, "the banquet of Esther." He proclaimed a remission of taxes for the provinces and distributed gifts as befits a king.

When the virgins were assembled a second time, Mordecai sat in the palace gate. But Esther still did not reveal her kindred or her people, as Mordecai had instructed her; for Esther obeyed Mordecai's bidding, as she had done when she was under his tutelage.

At that time, when Mordecai was sitting in the palace gate, Bigthan and Teresh, two of the king's eunuchs who guarded the threshold, became angry, and plotted to do away with King Ahasuerus. Mordecai learned of it and told it to Queen Esther, and Esther reported it to the king in Mordecai's name. The matter was investigated and found to be so, and the two were impaled on stakes. This was recorded in the book of annals at the instance of the king.

## 3

Some time afterward, King Ahasuerus promoted Haman son of Hammedatha the Agagite; he advanced him and seated him higher than any of his fellow officials. All the king's courtiers in the palace gate knelt and bowed low to Haman, for such was the king's order concerning him; but Mordecai would not kneel or bow low. Then the king's courtiers who were in the palace gate said to Mordecai, "Why do you disobey the king's order?" When they spoke to him day after day and he would not listen to them, they told Haman, in order to see whether Mordecai's resolve would prevail; for he had explained to them that he was a Jew. When Haman saw that Mordecai would not kneel or bow low to him, Haman was filled with rage. But he disdained to lay hands on Mordecai alone; having been told who Mordecai's people were, Haman plotted to do away with all the Jews, Mordecai's people, throughout the kingdom of Ahasuerus.

In the first month, that is, the month of Nisan, in the twelfth year of King Ahasuerus, pur—which means "the lot"—was cast before Haman concerning every day and every month, [until it fell on] the twelfth month, that is, the month of Adar. Haman then said to King Ahasuerus, "There is a certain people, scattered and dispersed among the other peoples in all the provinces of your realm, whose laws are different from those of any other people and who do not obey the king's laws; and it is not in Your Majesty's interest to tolerate them. If it please Your Majesty, let an edict be drawn for their destruction, and I will pay ten thousand talents of silver to the stewards for deposit in the royal treasury."

Thereupon the king removed his signet ring from his hand and gave it to Haman son of Hammedatha the Agagite, the foe of the Jews. And the king said, "The money and the people are yours to do with as you see fit."

On the thirteenth day of the first month, the king's scribes were summoned and a decree was issued as Haman directed, to the king's satraps, to the governors of every province, and to the officials of every people, to every province in its own script and to every people in its own language. The orders were issued in the name of King Ahasuerus and sealed with the king's signet. Accordingly, written instructions were dispatched by couriers to all the king's provinces to destroy, massacre, and exterminate all the Jews, young and old, children and women, on a single day, on the thirteenth day of the twelfth month — that is, the month of Adar — and to plunder their possessions. The text of the document was to the effect that a law should be proclaimed in every single province; it was to be publicly displayed to all the peoples, so that they might be ready for that day.

The couriers went out posthaste on the royal mission, and the decree was proclaimed in the fortress Shushan. The king and Haman sat down to feast, but the city of Shushan was dumfounded.

4

When Mordecai learned all that had happened, Mordecai tore his clothes and put on sackcloth and ashes. He went through the city, crying out loudly and bitterly, until he came in front of the palace gate; for one could not enter the palace gate wearing sackcloth. — Also, in every province that the king's command and decree reached, there was great mourning among the Jews, with fasting, weeping, and wailing, and everybody lay in sackcloth and ashes. — When Esther's maidens and eunuchs came and informed her, the queen was greatly agitated. She sent clothing for Mordecai to wear, so that he might take off his sackcloth; but he refused. Thereupon Esther summoned Hathach, one of the eunuchs whom the king had appointed to serve her, and sent him to Mordecai to learn the why and wherefore of it all. Hathach went out to Mordecai in the city square in front of the palace gate; and Mordecai told him all that had happened to him, and all about the money that Haman had offered to pay into the royal treasury for the destruction of the Jews. He also gave him the written text of the law that had been proclaimed in Shushan for their destruction. [He bade him] show it to Esther and inform her, and charge her to go to the king and to appeal to him and to plead with him for her people. When Hathach came and delivered Mordecai's message to Esther, Esther told

Hathach to take back to Mordecai the following reply: "All the king's courtiers and the people of the king's provinces know that if any person, man or woman, enters the king's presence in the inner court without having been summoned, there is but one law for him — that he be put to death. Only if the king extends the golden scepter to him may he live. Now I have not been summoned to visit the king for the last thirty days."

When Mordecai was told what Esther had said, Mordecai had this message delivered to Esther: "Do not imagine that you, of all the Jews, will escape with your life by being in the king's palace. On the contrary, if you keep silent in this crisis, relief and deliverance will come to the Jews from another quarter, while you and your father's house will perish. And who knows, perhaps you have attained to royal position for just such a crisis." Then Esther sent back this answer to Mordecai: "Go, assemble all the Jews who live in Shushan, and fast in my behalf; do not eat or drink for three days, night or day. I and my maidens will observe the same fast. Then I shall go to the king, though it is contrary to the law; and if I am to perish, I shall perish!" So Mordecai went about [the city] and did just as Esther had commanded him.

5

On the third day, Esther put on royal apparel and stood in the inner court of the king's palace, facing the king's palace, while the king was sitting on his royal throne in the throne room facing the entrance of the palace. As soon as the king saw Queen Esther standing in the court, she won his favor. The king extended to Esther the golden scepter which he had in his hand, and Esther approached and touched the tip of the scepter. "What troubles you, Queen Esther?" the king asked her. "And what is your request? Even to half the kingdom, it shall be granted you." "If it please Your Majesty," Esther replied, "Let Your Majesty and Haman come today to the feast that I have prepared for him." The king commanded, "Tell Haman to hurry and do Esther's bidding." So the king and Haman came to the feast that Esther had prepared.

At the wine feast, the king asked Esther, "What is your wish? It shall be granted you, and what is your request? Even to half the kingdom, it shall be fulfilled." "My wish," replied Esther, "my request — if Your Majesty will do me the favor, if it please Your Majesty to grant my wish and accede to my request — let Your Majesty and Haman come to the feast which I will prepare for them; and tomorrow I will do Your Majesty's bidding."

. . . . . . . . . . . . . . . . . . . . . . . . . . . . . . . .

## 7

So the king and Haman came to feast with Queen Esther. On the second day, the king again asked Esther at the wine feast, "What is your wish, Queen Esther? It shall be granted you. And what is your request? Even to half the kingdom, it shall be fulfilled." Queen Esther replied: "If Your Majesty will do me the favor, and if it pleases Your Majesty, let my life be granted me as my wish, and my people as my request. For we have been sold, my people and I, to be destroyed, massacred, and exterminated. Had we only been sold as bondmen and bondwomen, I would have kept silent; for the adversary is not worthy of the king's trouble." Thereupon King Ahasuerus demanded of Queen Esther, "Who is he and where is he who dared to do this?" "The adversary and enemy," replied Esther, "is this evil Haman!" And Haman cringed in terror before the king and the queen. The king, in his fury, left the wine feast for the palace garden, while Haman remained to plead with Queen Esther for his life; for he saw that the king had resolved to destroy him. When the king returned from the palace garden to the banquet room, Haman was lying prostrate on the couch on which Esther reclined. "Does he mean," cried the king, "to ravish the queen in my own palace?" No sooner did these words leave the king's lips than Haman's face was covered. Then Harbonah, one of the eunuchs in attendance on the king, said, "What is more, a stake is standing at Haman's house, fifty cubits high, which Haman made for Mordecai — the man whose words saved the king." "Impale him on it!" the king ordered. So they impaled Haman on the stake which he had put up for Mordecai, and the king's fury abated.

## 8

That very day King Ahasuerus gave the property of Haman, the enemy of the Jews, to Queen Esther. Mordecai presented himself to the king, for Esther had revealed how he was related to her. The king slipped off his ring, which he had taken back from Haman, and gave it to Mordecai; and Esther put Mordecai in charge of Haman's property.

Esther spoke to the king again, falling at his feet and weeping, and beseeching him to avert the evil plotted by Haman the Agagite against the Jews. The king extended the golden scepter to Esther, and Esther arose and stood before the king. "If it please your Majesty," she said "and if I have won your favor and the proposal seems right to Your Majesty, and if I am pleasing to you — let dispatches be written countermanding those which were written by Haman son of Hammedatha the Agagite, embodying his plot to annihilate the Jews throughout the king's provinces. For how can I bear to see the disaster which will befall my people! And how can I bear to see the destruction of my kindred!"

The King Ahasuerus said to Queen Esther and Mordecai the Jew, "I have given Haman's property to Esther, and he has been impaled on the stake for scheming against the Jews. And you may further write with regard to the Jews as you see fit. [Write it] in the king's name and seal it with the king's signet, for an edict that has been written in the king's name and sealed with the king's signet may not be revoked."

. . . . . . . . . . . . . . . . . . . . . . . .

## 9

And so, on the thirteenth day of the twelfth month—that is, the month of Adar—when the king's command and decree were to be executed, the very day on which the enemies of the Jews had expected to get them in their power, the opposite happened, and the Jews got their enemies in their power. Throughout the provinces of King Ahasuerus, the Jews mustered in their cities to attack those who sought their hurt; and no one could withstand them, for the fear of them had fallen upon all the peoples. Indeed, all the officials of the provinces—the satraps, the governors, and the king's stewards—showed deference to the Jews, because the fear of Mordecai had fallen upon them. For Mordecai was now powerful in the royal palace, and his fame was spreading through all the provinces; the man Mordecai was growing ever more powerful. So the Jews struck at their enemies with the sword, slaying and destroying; they wreaked their will upon their enemies.

In the fortress Shushan the Jews killed a total of five hundred men. They also killed Parshandatha, Dalphon, Aspatha, Poratha, Adalia, Aridatha, Parmashta, Arisai, Aridai, and Vaizatha, the ten sons of Haman son of Hammedatha, the foe of the Jews. But they did not lay hands on the spoil. When the number of those slain in the fortress Shushan was reported on that same day to the king, the king said to Queen Esther, "In the fortress Shushan alone the Jews have killed a total of five hundred men, as well as the ten sons of Haman. What then must they have done in the provinces of the realm! What is your wish now? It shall be granted you. And what is your request? It shall be fulfilled." "If it please Your Majesty," Esther replied, "Let the Jews in Shushan be permitted to act tomorrow also as they did today; and let Haman's ten sons be impaled on the stake." The king ordered that this should be done, and the decree was proclaimed in

Shushan. Haman's ten sons were impaled: and the Jews in Shushan mustered again on the fourteenth day of Adar and slew three hundred men in Shushan. But they did not lay hands on the spoil.

The rest of the Jews, those in the king's provinces, likewise mustered and fought for their lives. They disposed of their enemies, killing seventy-five thousand of their foes; but they did not lay hands on the spoil. That was on the thirteenth day of the month of Adar; and they rested on the fourteenth day and made it a day of feasting and merrymaking. (But the Jews in Shushan mustered on both the thirteenth and fourteenth days, and so rested on the fifteenth, and made it a day of feasting and merrymaking.) That is why village Jews, who live in unwalled towns, observe the fourteenth day of the month of Adar and make it a day of merrymaking and feasting, and as a holiday and an occasion for sending gifts to one another.

Mordecai recorded these events. And he sent dispatches to all the Jews throughout the provinces of King Ahasuerus, near and far, charging them to observe the fourteenth and fifteenth days of Adar, every year — the same days on which the Jews enjoyed relief from their foes and the same month which had been transformed for them from one of grief and mourning to one of festive joy. They were to observe them as days of feasting and merrymaking, and as an occasion for sending gifts to one another and presents to the poor. The Jews accordingly assumed as an obligation that which they had begun to practice and which Mordecai prescribed for them.

For Haman son of Hammedatha the Agagite, the foe of all the Jews, had plotted to destroy the Jews, and had cast pur — that is, the lot — with intent to crush and exterminate them. But when [Esther] came before the king, he commanded: "With the promulgation of this decree, let the evil plot, which he devised against the Jews, recoil on his own head!" So they impaled him and his sons on the stake. For that reason these days were named Purim, after pur.

In view, then, of all the instructions in the said letter and of what they had experienced in that matter and what had befallen them, the Jews undertook and irrevocably obligated themselves and their descendants, and all who might join them, to observe these two days in the manner prescribed and at the proper time each year. Consequently, these days are recalled and observed in every generation: by every family, every province, and every city. And these days of Purim shall never cease among the Jews, and the memory of them shall never perish among their descendants.

Then Queen Esther daughter of Abihail wrote a second letter of Purim for the purpose of confirming with full authority the aforementioned one of Mordecai the Jew. Dispatches were sent to all the Jews in the hundred and twenty-seven provinces of the realm of Ahasuerus with an ordinance of "equity and honesty:" These days of Purim shall be observed at their proper time, as Mordecai the Jew — and now Queen Esther — has obligated them to do, and just as they have assumed for themselves and their descendants the obligation of the fasts with their lamentations.

And Esther's ordinance validating these observances of Purim was recorded in a scroll.

# ఔ Purim Players

### I. L. PERETZ

I live in a quiet house, far from the rush and roar of the Grzybow and from the turbulent, seething Nalewkis. Sometimes the cry of a shopkeeper or a stallholder calling his wares strays into my room, or the sound of a carpenter sawing, or a smith hammering, or a servant-girl beating the carpets. Else my room would be as quiet as in some remote country village, and I could sit all day at my desk writing, absolutely undisturbed. As it is, as soon as the slightest sound penetrates from outside, my muse is alarmed and flies away.

The only thing that is then left for me to do is to go to the window and look out, to see what my neighbors are doing.

There is a well-to-do couple on the second floor opposite. I saw the furniture when they moved in, a piano player, and Turkish and Japanese furniture, as well as some made here in Poland, everything new and of the best.

He wore a silk hat, she a lovely flowered frock. Everything was new, except his face, which looked a little oldish. They walked arm in arm. On the steps they stopped, laughed, and kissed.

I don't know what goes on inside their love nest. They have thick double curtains at the windows.

Once a gipsy with a barrel-organ had come down our street, and a gipsy girl had danced. It was such a plaintive, heartbreaking melody. The curtains had parted, and I saw a blonde head look out. Then a bald head joined her, and kissed the blonde head.

But it was not his wife's head. It was the servant-girl's — a girl from the country, who had brought the smell of the fields with her.

There are no curtains on the first floor. I can see everything that goes on there.

All the week round there is nobody there. She is busy in the shop, he is out in the street at his job. The old-fashioned upholstered furniture is hidden under dust-sheets. Sometimes the servant-girl comes in from the kitchen with her shawl over her head and a basket over her arm, looks into the mirror on the wall, and holds a consultation with herself whether to go into the street like that, or to wash her face first. But the face seems to please her as it is. I can see the satisfied smile on it. But she does tuck her hair in under the shawl. Then she seems to have second thoughts, and she runs back into the kitchen, and comes out with her hair and face shining. She must have put butter or fat on. Now her hair lies flat under the shawl, and even the bits that show lie straight.

The servant-girl has gone. A mouse creeps out of the big wardrobe, and looks round with bright eyes on every side. The sofa, the chairs, the table are all silent and still. The silver tray and the glasses on it standing in the silver cupboard are motionless. The spice-box and the *Chanukah* lamp don't stir. Not a sound! The mouse disappears into the kitchen. And the room stays quiet and still till the evening.

Then they both come home, eat, and disappear into the bedroom.

There is a *mizrach* hanging on the wall, with terrible lions on it—and a Hebrew calendar. Several Hebrew books lie on top of the wardrobe. There is no bookcase, and there are no bookshelves. The books are familiar. An ivory-bound prayer book with Yiddish translation—a wedding present. A *Tze'enu Urenu*, stouter, and much-used. An *Orach Chaim*, and a few slimmer volumes—a *Hagaddah*, a *Megillah*—the Five Books of Moses, two *machzorim*. And that's about all. The complete library of a simple "unlearned" man.

All the week round the place is quiet and still. But on Friday it is full of bustle. She is busy all day cooking and baking and getting ready for the Sabbath.

When Passover approaches she never seems to stop—she and the servant-girl, scrubbing floors and cupboards, washing and cleaning, cooking and baking—at it all the time.

On *Succoth* the smell of fresh soft cheese, butter, and raisins comes into my room. He brings the foliage for the *succah*, and arranges it carefully, so that there shouldn't be too much sun nor too much shade. And then, climbing about the *succah* he fell off the ladder, and luckily escaped serious injury. He picked himself up and went humming happily to the cupboard and brought out his *lulav* and *ethrog*.

On the Sabbath they take a nap after the midday meal, and then visitors come, and they offer them conserves and fruit.

That's when I see their furniture without the dust-sheets. Yellow birds and green leaves.

How I envied this plain simple man!

The story of Genesis and the secret doctrines of the Lord were not his affair. No more than high politics were. All he asked was that God might help him to make his living! He did his share towards it. They had no children, or the children might have grown up and married, and were living on their own. They had only to wait for the Messiah.

He had no wide horizons; but instead he had a straight sure road from the cradle to the grave. There was no worm of doubt gnawing away at his mind. There were no questions worrying him to which there was no ready answer. Past generations had worked out all the answers for him. They had left him a last will and testament, which set out his line of conduct — when to sleep, when to eat, when to scrub and clean, when to drink wine, when to sit hunched up, and when to sit at ease. He had been instructed when to pray to God, and what to ask of God, what to wish people on occasions — a straight course for the whole of his life! And a faithful wife for his bosom — for a hundred and twenty years.

If he is not sure about anything he asks the rabbi. The ground never slips from under his feet. His heaven will not fall; his world stands firm and will remain standing firm to the end. What comes after the end — he leaves that to God.

You will never catch this man telling a lie. Because he never speaks with certainty. Always he says — "If God spares me" — "If God pleases" — "If God wills," then he will do this or he will do that.

Such a man, provided he is well, and makes ends meet, and his wife is bearable, is a happy man! He has nothing to be ashamed of. His window stands open in summer; and there are no curtains in winter to hide what goes on inside. Heaven and earth are welcome to look in and see!

I am sure he has no bell at his door, and no lock either. He doesn't shut himself in — people don't have to ring first when they want to come to see him, to give him time to hide what he doesn't want them to see.

So I look quite unashamedly from my window into his quiet, happy room.

It is particularly gay and happy in his room today. It's Purim!

What is there about Purim that makes him so happy? Why is he laughing all over his face? What is amusing him? Yes, of course, it's the Purim players! They've just come, dressed up, cracking jokes, and he is glad of the opportunity to have a good laugh.

I still remember the Purim plays of my childhood. A young whippersnapper would come dashing in, with a beard and earlocks stuck on his face, and a Galician hat on his head. He was dressed up as a village Jew, who talks nothing but Hebrew, and all his Hebrew is full of the most absurd mistakes — nothing he says makes sense. Then a Chassid (dressed up for the part, of course) would rush in, waving his arms about, with all sorts of wild gestures and funny mannerisms, banging the table and the walls, skipping about like a young goat, and then doing a wild dance that made you giddy!

And all the Purim players said and say the same thing:

Today is Purim,
Tomorrow is nowt!
Give me a cake,
And kick me out!

I turn to the second floor. There is a sound of music coming through the windows. But these are no Purim players! This is no Purim music! It's a ball for the poor! I got a ticket, too. The pianola provides the music. But there's a fiddle too. The dancers take the beat from the fiddle rather than from the pianola.

I know that fiddle! I know the thin, bony hand of the violinist, clasping her instrument against her hollow, wheezy bosom. I have never seen her eyes, because God forgot to open them.

She plays as if in a dream! And then she lets herself be led as in a dream to the table, where they give her food.

When the ball is over she finds her way alone up to her room on the fourth floor.

On the first floor they dole out a few small coins to poor people. Sometimes with a drink of brandy and a piece of Purim cake.

On the second floor they are busy dancing. Their troubled conscience is trying to find some quiet and peace. Both the religious and the nonreligious are doing what they can to fill in the pit that has been dug between rich and poor. The old type of charity was more economical.

My simple neighbor on the first floor eats a meal that costs a *rouble*, and he distributes five or six in charity; at the ball on the second floor the party dress costs twenty-five *roubles*, and the poor get about twenty-five *kopeks* each out of the proceeds.

Poor sewing girls have been working hard to make these dresses. And then when they have been worn at two or three balls they are sold, and poor brides wear them as wedding dresses.

There's something more — young men and young girls meet at these balls. So they can dispense with matchmakers. Another saving! Those who will may get enthusiastic about it! I can't!

In ancient Greece they traded in human beings. The salesman produced a score of girls and women in the open market, glamorously attired, seductively attractive. The merchant praised his wares to his customers. The girls paraded to show off their points, but they said nothing.

A girl spoke only under the first lash of the whip. Under the second lash she sang. Under the third she danced. The customer had to know that besides tiny, twinkling feet and hard, firm breasts a girl also had a heart.

Today the slave-girls speak and sing and dance without needing the slave-merchant's whip. They display their tiny, twinkling feet, and wear seductive dress to show a little and suggest more — the girl comes forward herself to sing and to dance — to sell herself.

The *shadchan* is only a liar, and since he deceives both parties he has neither of them on his conscience. But the mother who parades her daughter to the world has everything on her conscience — to say nothing of her daughter who lets herself be put up for sale!

I'll tell you a story about a dress.

One of these balls for the poor raised enough money to marry off a poor sewing girl, no longer young, who had nearly gone blind at her needle. All the people with whose sewing she had lost her sight collected a little money for her, and they found an old widower who married her for forty-five *roubles*.

They bought her a wedding dress. The bride didn't say a word the whole time — she went about as though it was not she who was getting married. She didn't want a husband, she didn't need a husband, she had no eyes to see him!

"She's like a log of wood, poor thing!" her girl friends said.

"She doesn't even say thank you," her patrons grumbled. "You put yourself out for her, and you get no appreciation!"

When they brought her the wedding dress she stared at the white silk rag — and then she started tearing her hair, tearing off her clothes, and she burst out crying.

It took them a long time to quiet her, to get her back to being a log of wood again, and they led her to the *chuppa*.

She had recognized the dress. She had remembered whom she had sewn it for! She had stolen into the synagogue to see how the rich girl looked in it under the wedding canopy. She had recognized the bridegroom!

That's how the world lives! Rich brides give their wedding dresses to poor brides, and poor brides give their bridegrooms to rich brides!

*Translated by Joseph Leftwich*

## ❧ from *The Ladies Auxiliary*

TOVA MIRVIS

On the eve of Purim, we went to shul, trying to get ourselves into the proper mood. The day before the holiday was a fast day, commemorating the danger the Jews had been in in Persia, and we were struck by the sudden change of mood, from somber and repentant to wild and free. We tried to loosen up, to push our worries to the backs of our minds and breathe in the joyousness of this one day of the year when we were commanded to be free-spirited, when nothing is supposed to be as it usually is; just as Haman's decree against the Jews was reversed and he was hanged on the same gallows he prepared for Mordechai, we celebrate this day where everything is turned upside-down.

The shul had been decorated with this theme in mind. In the seats in the front of the room where the board members usually sat, someone had placed stuffed animals wearing cartoon character masks. And there were streamers hanging from the ner tamid, a red-and-white polka dot tablecloth across the bima. Even the Rabbi was wearing a Hawaiian print shirt Mrs. Levy wore a pair of rhinestone-studded sunglasses, and she had encouraged Helen Shayowitz to tie a yellow ribbon in her hair. Tziporah Newburger had brought along a floppy rainbow-colored hat to wear over her wig, if she worked up the nerve. Batsheva was the only adult who wore a full-fledged costume, and by now, this wasn't surprising. She was dressed as Queen Esther, the heroine of the Purim story. Her hair was elaborately braided underneath a construction-paper gold crown, and she wore a long purple dress covered with tiny beads and sequins. Around her neck she had tied a silver, sparkly piece of fabric, creating a dramatic flourish behind her when she walked.

We tried, though, not to think about Batsheva as we listened to the reading of the Scroll of Esther. Achashverosh, the King of Persia, held a feast in Shushan, his capital city, and ordered his wife, Vashti, to appear. She refused, and in his drunkenness, he had her killed. The next morning, he awoke, filled with sorrow at what he had done. His minister Haman advised him to assemble all the maidens in the land and select a new queen. In the end he chose Esther, who, unbeknownst to him, was a Jew. Later, when Mordechai, Esther's uncle, would not bow down to Haman, Haman was furious and conspired to kill all the Jews of Persia. Hearing of this decree, Esther went before the king, revealed that she was Jewish, and pleaded for her people. The king granted her request, hanged Haman, and appointed Mordechai as minister in his place. The Jews of Persia took revenge on their enemies and they were joyous and happy.

This year, though, the story was transformed, and we saw Memphis as a modern-day Shushan. A terrible decree had been sent forth against us, and only we had the power to turn it around. As much as Batsheva thought she would save our daughters, we knew that we were really the Esthers of our story, good and righteous and beautiful, trying to save the community we had worked so hard for. Each time Haman's name was read, the shul erupted in boos and hisses, the sounds of graggers twirling back and forth, feet stamping, even a trumpet blaring. These were our attempts to blot out Haman's memory, to show that we could overcome any enemy who rose up to destroy us, and this year we added a special hope that we could wipe out all the troubles that were befalling us.

. . . . . . . . . . . . . . . . . . . . . . . . . . . . .

As our Purim celebrations continued throughout the day, a carnival-like feeling descended over the community. Our usually orderly neighborhood seemed to be painted with wilder, almost garish colors, deeper shadows, thicker brush strokes. Littering our yards were candy wrappers, curls of ribbon that had been used to tie shaloch manot, pieces of hot pink and orange tissue paper. Our husbands came home from work early and began drinking with their friends, a Purim mitzvah that was always scrupulously observed. We could barely recognize our children: boys were dressed as girls, girls as boys. They wore multicolored wigs and grotesque masks. Clown makeup had become smudged, turning once neat faces into blurs of white and red and yellow and blue.

When it was time for the seudah, our girls were getting ready to go to Batsheva's house. Batsheva had somehow convinced them to dress up in costumes, even though most of them had abandoned this practice by the time they entered high school. On this day when they could do whatever they wanted, they transformed themselves into punks, their hair teased high above their forehead, spray-painted with glitter and temporary green dye. They wore leather jackets, neon dresses, multiple strands of silver necklaces. They clipped rows of earrings onto their ears. They became rock stars, caked eyeshadow onto their lids, and painted their lips bright red. And there was nothing we could say. There was no sense, at least for this one day, of how things ought to be.

. . . . . . . . . . . . . . . . . . . . . . . . . . . . .

When all the girls had arrived, Batsheva's house was full of activity. Shira Feldman was the only one not there; she hadn't been in school for the few days before and when her friends called, Becky had said that she was under the weather. But her absence was quickly forgotten. The girls knew what was going on between Batsheva and us — there was no keeping secrets from them — and being at Batsheva's was their personal victory, an assertion that they could do what they wanted. They felt like it was finally their turn — after years of hearing the boys talk about the wild times they had at their rabbis' seudahs, they were now having a seudah of their own.

The seudah started out almost as any of ours did — Batsheva had made an effort to cook a nice meal, and she looked so proud of herself as she served it. She had made carrot soup and potato kugel and vegetable pies. The only unusual dishes were the vodka tofu and the pasta salad dyed green with food coloring, which she presented to the girls with a laugh, trying to encourage them to get into the topsy-turvy spirit of the day.

After eating, Batsheva started singing Purim songs, and the girls joined in, so much excess energy running through them. Then Batsheva stood up to dance. She wrapped her cape over her arms, so that when she raised them over her head, the silvery fabric shimmered. She grabbed Ayala's hand and lifted her onto her shoulders. Our girls got up too, their feet stomping loudly and their voices rising in pitch. In the middle of this exuberance, someone turned on the radio to a rock station. They were no longer celebrating God's deliverance of the Jews. Instead, they were dancing to rock songs, celebrating God knows what. Shira arrived somewhere in the middle of the dancing, but she barely spoke to anyone, nor did she join the other girls as they danced, doing moves we didn't know they knew, hips shaking, bottoms wiggling. The girls danced until they could no longer see straight and everything was a fast, uneasy blur. They collapsed exhausted onto the couch and floor, catching their breaths, their heads still spinning.

The high school boys hadn't been invited to Batsheva's, or at least none of the girls would admit to telling them to stop by, but as the dancing stopped, they arrived. They gathered on Batsheva's front yard, and when the girls realized that they were there, they went out to join them. Soon the entire party had moved outdoors. Our children were milling around Batsheva's yard, sitting on the porch, a few bottles of beer that the boys had brought with them visible here and there. The girls were so happy to see the boys that Batsheva told them they could come inside and continue the party there; if they were going to be outside together, they may as well be inside, she had said with a nervous laugh. When they shuffled into her house, she seemed overwhelmed — her house was wall to wall with high school kids and they were rowdy and carrying on. But Batsheva seemed determined not to ruin the fun, and she tried to laugh along with them and look the other way as they sprawled out on her couch and floor.

. . . . . . . . . . . . . . . . . . . . . . . . . . . . . . . . . .

While such things were going on, we were home wondering where our children were. Our husbands, drunk from their own Purim celebrations, had conked out, and we were left to handle this situation on our own. We kept glancing out our windows. It looked like there were too many people over at Batsheva's house, certainly more than the eighteen high school girls who were supposed to be there. But we couldn't be sure and we kept waiting, hoping they would show up. Every time we heard a creak, we were sure it was our children, and every time we were disappointed. When midnight passed with still no sign of them, Arlene Salzman and Becky Feldman decided that it was time to go over to Batsheva's. By this time, the neighborhood had quieted down, but even so, Arlene and Becky felt afraid to be out so late at night. The porch lamps seemed to glow an eerie yellow, and they worried that someone in costume might jump out at them from behind a tree or a drunken figure might chase them around the block.

When Arlene and Becky arrived at Batsheva's house the party had quieted down. A few boys appeared to be sneaking out, but when Batsheva opened the door, looking tired, only the girls were there. They were lying across her couch, sitting on the floor, deep in conversation. The room looked like there had been a wild party going on. The coffee table had been pushed aside and the throw pillows were on the floor. The confetti that had been sprinkled on the tablecloth was now on the sofa and in the girls' hair. There were plates of food scattered around the room and enough empty cups for a crowd much larger than just the girls.

"What is going on here?" Becky exclaimed. "Do y'all have any idea what time it is?"

"I don't know who you young ladies think you are," Arlene said, "but this is not a free-for-all."

Becky and Arlene looked around. None of the girls offered the excuses they had expected to hear, that they had lost track of time, that they were about to leave, that they had just been gathering up their things to go home. There was just a horrible creeping silence. Then it hit Becky.

"Where's Shira?" she asked.

Becky's sharp, nervous question snapped the girls out of the dreamy haze they had been in, the craziness of the past day coming to an end. They blinked as if they had just woken up and looked around.

"She must have gone home," Batsheva said. "I haven't seen her for a while."

"No, I would have heard her come in. She must still be here," Becky insisted.

Under normal circumstances, Becky might not have been so worried. There had been other times when Shira wasn't where she said she would be. But their relationship had hit an all-time low these past two weeks. Even though Becky had forbidden Shira to apply to any college besides Stern, she had done so anyway. That week her first acceptance had come, from Brown (who had even heard of such a school? What kind of nice Jewish girl went there?), and Shira had been thrilled. But Becky had heard too many stories about religious kids who went to college and were forced to read the New Testament and secular philosophy. And then the gradual decline: they would start eating in the nonkosher dining hall, first just a salad, then pizza, and soon they would go to parties on Friday nights and football games on Shabbos afternoons and live in coed dorms with coed bathrooms. By the end of the semester, religion would be thrown to the wind. Becky would not have this happen to her daughter. She tore Shira's acceptance letter to shreds and made Shira write a letter saying she wouldn't be attending.

Since then, Shira hadn't spoken to her. She refused to go to school. She wouldn't help prepare shaloch manot and she hadn't gone to megillah reading. All she did was stay in bed and watch television. As angry as Shira had been in the past, Becky saw that this was different, and she didn't know if there would be any turning back.

"Please tell me where my daughter is," Becky said again, her voice pleading.

Batsheva looked at the girls, but they too seemed to have no idea where Shira was. Faced with this silence, Batsheva turned to Ilana. She and Shira were best friends, and if anyone would know where Shira was, Ilana would. With everyone looking at her so intently, Ilana burst into tears.

"I didn't know what to do. She had already made up her mind. There was nothing I could say to convince her to stay," she wailed.

"What are you talking about?" Becky demanded.

"Ilana, if you know something you're not telling us, you're going to be in big trouble," her mother threatened.

Her voice shaking, Ilana described what had happened. Shira had arrived late to the party and wasn't in costume like the other girls. All she wore was a silver mask in the shape of a star. She tried to act like she was into the party but Ilana could tell something was wrong. When Shira pulled up her mask, her eyes were red and swollen.

"Come outside," Shira whispered. "I need to talk to you."

Ilana followed her outside, worried about her. "Shira, what's going on?" she asked.

"I'm leaving," Shira had said. "Matt and I are getting out of here."

Matt was Shira's non-Jewish boyfriend, the one Tziporah had seen at McDonald's. They had met at the mall and had started going out secretly. Matt was twenty-one, and according to Shira, they were in love. She didn't know where they were going, only that they wanted to be together and this was the only way. Even though Ilana had known about Matt, she never thought Shira would do something like this. She and Shira had spent hours complaining about the school, about their parents, about the community, but Ilana still couldn't imagine running away from it. As constricted as she felt, it was the only life she knew.

"Are you sure you want to do this? Maybe you can try it here a little longer," Ilana begged Shira. She was suddenly terrified for her friend, and she wished there was some way to stop her from leaving.

"I can't stand it anymore. If I don't go now, I'll never have the chance to get out of here. Matt will be here any minute. My stuff is already in his car."

Ilana started to cry and when Matt pulled up, she hugged Shira good-bye. Shira's tough demeanor shook, and she too began to cry as she got into Matt's car. As he pulled out of the driveway, Shira turned back and waved to Ilana. Ilana stood there watching them go, until the car had turned the corner and was out of sight.

"I'm sorry," Ilana said to her mother and Becky and all the girls who were staring at her. Batsheva was as surprised as everyone else. Her face went white and her eyes looked as if they would spring from her face. "But I didn't know what to do. She said she had to get out of here."

"What do you mean?" Becky asked, her voice nearing the point of hysteria. "What do you mean she left? And you let her go? You stood here and let her go?" Ilana started to cry harder and Becky turned her fury on Batsheva. "How could you do this? What's wrong with you? Is this what you wanted to do to us?"

Batsheva didn't say anything — she was too stunned to speak — and this only angered Becky more. She put her hands on Batsheva's shoulders, wanting to shake her, as if this strange woman in front of her was a phantom that had snuck in during the night and stolen away her daughter. If she could shake her, shake her harder and harder she might reverse this terrible nightmare. But instead, Becky let go of Batsheva and sank into a pile on the floor.

. . . . . . . . . . . . . . . . . . . . . . . . . . . . . . . . .

When Leanna Zuckerman heard that Shira had run off, the first thing that came to her mind was the conversation she had had with Batsheva at the Posh Nosh. Was this the price of freedom? she wondered. She looked down at her daughter, Deena, reading a book. She was such a good child, dutiful and sweet and studious. Maybe Batsheva had been right: the more restrictions you placed, the more the kids would rebel. Shira especially seemed to have so many rules and maybe that was why she'd run off. But if you let children do whatever they wanted, there was no way of knowing what would happen. Of course it was possible to strike a balance, but who knew where to find that perfect combination?

Mrs. Levy was home trying to busy herself with other tasks. She longed to lose herself in cooking, to allow the rhythmic beating of the electric mixer to soothe her. But everything seemed inconsequential. What good were homemade challahs and fresh apple cake if there were no children left? She was trying to save this community, but so far, nothing was working. Filled with the fear that maybe even she did not have what it took to fight this battle, she turned off the mixer, put down her spatula, sank into a chair, and prayed. She begged God to save this community that she had worked her whole life to build. With all that had happened, she could almost feel it sinking to the bottom of the Mississippi. This is how the Jews must have felt when the Holy Temple was destroyed. Like the martyrs who wept at the sight of their city in flames, Mrs. Levy realized that she would risk her life to preserve this Jerusalem of the South.

# Passover

## Celebration of Freedom

# ᙤ Introduction

*The LORD freed us from Egypt by a mighty hand, by an outstretched arm and awesome power, and by signs and portents. He brought us to this place and gave us this land, a land flowing with milk and honey.*
— Deuteronomy 26.8–9

Passover is the most universally celebrated Jewish holiday, just as the Seder — the traditional Passover meal during which the story of the Exodus from Egypt is recounted each year — is the single most significant home celebration of the year. Passover is also the holiday that is most deeply embedded in Jewish consciousness, as it celebrates the beginning of nationhood, the continuous survival of a people, and the importance of freedom.

The origins of Passover are complex. Scholars generally agree that the holiday began as an ancient spring ritual, or rather an amalgamation of two distinct festivals that occurred about the same time. Long before their enslavement in Egypt, nomadic Israelite shepherds observed a spring ceremony during the full moon of the month when the first kids and lambs of the flock were born. Just before nightfall, a sheep or goat was sacrificed, roasted, and eaten by the entire family. One of the early features of this spring festival was the spreading of blood of the sacrificial animal on the posts of the family's tent. As with other rituals associated with this ancient holiday, its purpose remains uncertain, but most probably it was a ceremony the ancients believed would bring good fortune and ward off evil spirits during the coming year. The festival and the festive meal were called *Pesach*, a word whose etymology is unclear. It is evident, however, that from its earliest beginnings this was a home celebration, unconnected to any sanctuary or priesthood.

Many years later, as the Jews left the desert, settled in Palestine, and became more of an agrarian society, they observed another form of spring ritual related to the harvesting of wheat and barley. The harvest season began with the cutting of the first barley and ended with the reaping of the last wheat, seven weeks later. Upon the initial cutting of the barley, or Omer, the first sheaf was brought to the sanctuary and offered as a gift to God. The ceremony of the Omer, as it became known, continued for the entire seven weeks, terminating with the conclusion of the harvest. Before the start of the harvest, the Jews would remove all the old dough and leavened bread in their possession. It is uncertain whether this was an effort to get rid of any products thought to contain impurities or—more likely—a symbolic gesture to assure a productive harvest. In any event, the practice became known as "The Festival of Matzos" (unleavened bread), and evolved into one of the essential features of the ceremony of the Omer.

It was not until much later that the *Festival of Matzos* and *Pesach* were gradually incorporated into the holiday we now celebrate, with a new interpretation that symbolically and irrevocably linked it with the story of the exodus of the Jews from Egypt. In time, the old agricultural significance of the holiday was forgotten, as *Pesach* came to represent a higher ideal, as well as an important historical occurrence. It was, after all, in the first month of spring (*Nisan*) that the Jews fled Egypt. Moreover, the concepts of human freedom and the awakening of the earth from its winter slumber are appropriate complements. And although *Pesach* remains a spring festival, with many spring symbols incorporated in the holiday, what was once merely a seasonal celebration in time came to commemorate the most significant event in early Jewish history.

As with other holidays, customs associated with old ceremonies gradually acquired new interpretations that defined and characterized the festival of Passover. The Hebrew word *Pesach* came to mean "passing over," as well as the name of the holiday, as it was said that the angel of death "passed over" the houses of the Jews when the firstborn of the Egyptians were slain. The blood of the sacrificed lamb, which once may have been spread on the family's tent post as a symbolic sacrifice to the ancient gods, was now interpreted as a sign to the angel of death not to visit Jewish homes. The quickly baked *Matzo*, or unleavened bread, once a symbolic offering, was said to have served as sustenance for the Jews fleeing Egypt. Thus *Pesach* and the *Festival of Matzos* were joined together to become Passover, the most important family holiday of the year.

Today Passover is celebrated by Jews throughout the world. Most Israelis and Reformed Jews in America observe the holiday for seven days, while Conservative and Orthodox Jews commemorate eight days. As in ancient times, Passover remains mostly a home celebration, with the ceremonial *Seder* meal as the highlight of the holiday. The *Seder*, which literally means "order," is more than a gathering of friends and family for a festive meal. It is, as Theodor Herzl states in his essay included in this section, "half ritual, half family festival." Its purpose is to retell and recall the Jewish exodus from Egypt in story, song, and with the eating of symbolic foods. The *Seder* traditionally ends with the words, "next year in Jerusalem," signifying the desire (literally or figuratively) for a reunification of all Jews in their homeland. The beauty and significance of Passover therefore lie both in the historical importance of the event it commemorates and in the spirit of continuity it celebrates.

Both these aspects characterize the selections that follow, beginning with a work by the medieval poet Solomon Ibn Gabirol. Best known for his liturgical poems, of which "Passover Psalm" is a good example, Gabirol here praises the powers and glory of God, who has kept his special covenant with the Jews and delivered them out of bondage.

The more contemporary poems included in this section, although varying greatly in style and form, are all poetic meditations on the meaning of Passover and its accompanying themes of freedom, peoplehood, and the importance of history. For several poets, such as Sam Goldemberg, Merle Feld, and Alan Shapiro, these motifs intermingle with personal memories of family gatherings. Others, such as Eleanor Wilner and Howard Nemerov, explore subjects and themes generally ignored in traditional Passover literature. Wilner's poem "Miriam's Song," for example, enters into the consciousness of Miriam, Moses's sister, who — as a mother and woman — empathizes with her Egyptian counterparts, recoiling in horror at the thought of the murder of firstborn sons. Nemerov tells the story of the Jewish exodus from the point of view of the ruler of Egypt in "Pharaoh's Meditation on the Exodus," imagining a conflicted Pharaoh who broods over his isolation, the death of his son, and the fate of the escaping Jews. Both Muriel Rukeyser and Marge Piercy link the Passover story with other events in Jewish history, both ancient and modern. Throughout their history Jews have repeatedly heard, in Rukeyser's words, the "music of passage" and have been obliged to possess, as Piercy states: "The courage to walk out of the pain that is known / into the pain that cannot be imagined." For both poets, Passover becomes a metaphor for centuries of wanderings and escapes, and a memorial to all those who, as Piercy states, "let go of every- / thing but freedom."

The personal essays in this section further explore the themes of freedom, survival, and continuity. The brief memoir by Herzl, the founder of the Zionist movement, dramatically demonstrates the need for peoplehood, as well as the ancient, mythic qualities of the festival. Herzl's "penitent," the focus of this short essay — with his self-voyage of separation, rebellion, and return — metaphorically replicates the journey of the Jews through the desert, with their wandering, temporary loss of faith, and ultimate entrance into the promised land. The excerpt from Faye Moskowitz's A Leak in the Heart also explores the themes of doubt and rebellion, although under very different circumstances and in a much lighter tone. Moskowitz's memoir is set against the backdrop of traditional family observance, and the description of her family's preparations for the holiday echo those of Letty Cottin Pogrebin, whose memories of Passover are also dominated by the image of her mother. "Passover always reminds me of my mother," Pogrebin begins her essay, and what follows is a tribute to her mother's often overlooked role in the annual ceremony.

Elizabeth Ehrlich, in the selection reprinted here from her memoir *Miriam's Kitchen*, juxtaposes childhood recollections of *Seders* in Brooklyn in the 1950s ("In the beginning there was Brooklyn, and it was Passover") with descriptions of those she now hosts for her own family more than forty years later. As a child she was aware of the gradual but clearly visible decline of Passover ritual in her family. As a young woman in college she decides not to return home for the holiday and sadly discovers that she has become "an exile from history." As an adult, however, with the encouragement of her husband and the help of her mother-in-law, Ehrlich — like Herzl's penitent — is able to retrieve her sense of Jewish identity and tradition, both of which manifest themselves most clearly in the Passover *Seders* she now hosts.

The two stories included in this section, Sholom Aleichem's "Home for Passover" and Allegra Goodman's "The Four Questions," both make obvious the psychological and emotional connection between home and Passover, although the implications of that association manifest themselves in very different ways. Aleichem's nineteenth-century story, set in eastern Europe, is the tale of a poor itinerant *melamed*, or teacher, attempting to return home in time for the start of the Passover celebration. In the process, he encounters difficulties of biblical proportions: a river swollen with floods and filled with floating icebergs, impassable roads, hostile or apathetic cart drivers and ferrymen — and of course his own incompetence. Throughout this comic tale of near disaster, Aleichem manages to subtly yet lovingly convey the importance of home, family, and holiday ritual.

Goodman's American characters also manage (with difficulty) to return "home" for Passover. When one reads this late-twentieth-century Passover story, however, one realizes how far the Jewish experience (at least the American Jewish experience as portrayed by Goodman) has evolved since the time of Aleichem's *shtetl* Jews. In this wry, satiric tale of a mostly dysfunctional family that has seemingly lost all but the most tenuous ties to the meaning and customs of Passover, Goodman depicts individuals concerned with their own needs, Jews without any sense of connection to history, and a joyless family *Seder*. Only in the story's concluding paragraph is there a recognition of all that has been lost, or more precisely, that which is ever-present but barely acknowledged: "the thundering of history."

It is this very sense of the importance of history that gives much of the literature in this section (and much of the Passover ritual as well) its meaning and resonance. Goodman's characters are hardly aware of their history, much less its power, although obviously Goodman understands the ramifications of their ignorance. For others, such as Herzl and Ehrlich, both of whom delineate a return to tradition in their works, as well as Goldemberg, Piercy, Rukeyser, and Wilner, the dominance of history — and one's connection to that history — becomes the primary theme of the Passover celebration.

# Poetry

## 🦋 Passover Psalm

### SOLOMON IBN GABIROL

Who is like unto Thee to uncover the deeps,
    And who hath Thy power to raise and cast down?
Show Thy marvellous love to the captive who weeps,
    O Worker of wonders, of awesome renown!

Thy children belovèd intoned a new song
    When Egypt's proud host found a watery grave,
There was praise from the saints in their jubilant throng
    When the wheels of the chariots clogged in the wave.

Thy fondlings storm-tossed were all weeping and tired
    When the great roaring flood-tides before them arose,
But Thy hand led them safe to the haven desired
    And the waters returned, overwhelming their foes.

The chariots of Pharaoh and all that great host
    God cast in the billows and covered them o'er,
But His people trod sea-bottom, coast unto coast,
    He admonished the sea and it dried like the shore.

Thus, Lord, do Thou Zion support and uphold,
    Arise, for the hour of her grace is at hand,
The day long appointed to sing as of old,
    God reigneth, His Kingdom forever shall stand.

*Translated by Israel Zangwill*

## 🦀 The Way Out

From *AKIBA*

**MURIEL RUKEYSER**

The night is covered with signs. The body and face of man,
with signs, and his journeys. Where the rock is split
and speaks to the water; the flame speaks to the cloud;
the red splatter, abstraction, on the door
speaks to the angel and the constellations.
The grains of sand on the sea-floor speak at last to the noon.
And the loud hammering of the land behind
speaks ringing up the bones of our thighs, the hoofs,
we hear the hoofs over the seethe of the sea.

All night down the centuries, have heard, music of passage.

Music of one child carried into the desert;
firstborn forbidden by law of the pyramid.
Drawn through the water with the water-drawn people
led by the water-drawn man to the smoke mountain.
The voice of the world speaking, the world covered by signs,
the burning, the loving, the speaking, the opening.
Strong throat of sound from the smoking mountain.
Still flame, the spoken singing of a young child.
The meaning beginning to move, which is the song.

Music of those who have walked out of slavery.

Into that journey where all things speak to all things
refusing to accept the curse, and taking

Akiba is the Jewish shepherd-scholar of the first and second century, identified with The Song of Songs and with the insurrection against Hadrian's Rome,
led in A.D. 132 by Bar Cochba (Son of the Star). After this lightning war, Jerusalem
captured, the Romans driven out of the south, Rome increased its military machine; by 135, the last defenses fell, Bar Cochba was killed, Akiba was tortured
to death at the command of his friend, the Roman Rufus, and a harrow was
drawn over the ground where Jerusalem had stood, leaving only a corner of wall.
The story in my mother's family is that we are descended from Akiba — unveri-
fiable, but a great gift to a child.

for signs the signs of all things, the world, the body
which is part of the soul, and speaks to the world,
all creation being created in one image, creation.
This is not the past walking into the future,
the walk is painful, into the present, the dance
not visible as dance until much later.
These dancers are discoverers of God.

We knew we had all crossed over when we heard the song.

Out of a life of building lack on lack:
the slaves refusing slavery, escaping into faith:
an army who came to the ocean: the walkers
who walked through the opposites, from I to opened Thou,
city and cleave of the sea. Those at flaming Nauvoo,
the ice on the great river: the escaping Negroes,
swamp and wild city: the shivering children of Paris
and the glass black hearses; those on the Long March:
all those who together are the frontier, forehead of man.

Where the wilderness enters, the world, the song of the world.

Akiba rescued, secretly, in the clothes of death
by his disciples carried from Jerusalem
in blackness journeying to find his journey
to whatever he was loving with his life.
The wilderness journey through which we move
under the whirlwind truth into the new,
the only accurate. A cluster of lights at night:
faces before the pillar of fire. A child watching
while the sea breaks open. This night. The way in.

Barbarian music, a new song.

Acknowledging opened water, possibility:
open like a woman to this meaning.
In a time of building statues of the stars,
valuing certain partial ferocious skills
while past us the chill and immense wilderness
spreads its one-color wings until we know

rock, water, flame, cloud, or the floor of the sea,
the world is a sign, a way of speaking. To find.
What shall we find? Energies, rhythms, journey.

Ways to discover. The song of the way in.

# 🐝 Pharaoh's Meditation on the Exodus

HOWARD NEMEROV

The thing is finished now, there is no more
Administration worth attending to,
And I have withdrawn to this inner room
To think, or dream. From the ridiculous
To death itself we have traveled in the space
Of ten days more or less (and my child dead),
But the damp stone may weep, the wall sweat blood
(And he may take his god and go elsewhere),
Since I no longer care? Why did I care?

To come from Midian, and need his brother's help
To turn a rod into a snake — there's no
Magician here who wouldn't be ashamed
To deal in parlor magic; yet his snake
Certainly swallowed theirs, and they were out
That many rods, and had their tempers up
Besides, that they could do what he could do.
So when he turned the water all to blood,
My idiots had to have fresh wells dug out
And turn them bloody too, assisting him
While seeming to compete; if he brought frogs,
And thousands of 'em, each wizard of mine
Must proudly add some six or seven frogs
To the total disaster and say it wasn't hard —
But luckily they stuck at the lice and flies
(Though by then we were past what luck could do).

The thing is finished, and I've had enough.
If the nation break, and the rude tribes
Flood in over the marches of the South;
If the commanders elaborate confusion
Because they have heard nothing; if one whole
Division has been drowned with its equipment —
It is nothing to me, it means nothing,

I will refuse to hear. All the last week
Things were bled white of meaning, and I say,
Enough! and have imposed my solitude
On kingdom and court, so that I may have time,
In this inner room, where I need not endure
Daylight or darkness but am soothed by lamps,
To think, should there be anything left to think.
Alone, in the cool silence of the stone,
Where only my heartbeats happen, and my thoughts
Follow the small flame's wavering against the wall
Until that meaningless motion is my thought,
It may be that the world outside has stopped,
The fountain dried up, and the brickwork broken
Under the insane silence of the sun
Centuries ago, and the whole course of the world
Shifted like sand; and I alone, the brain
In this room the skull of Egypt, am alive.

My first-born son is dead, the first-born sons
Of all Egypt are dead, but that's no matter.
I am astounded, but I do not weep.
How did that power come? Out of the desert?
Out of the empty land of Midian?
May he take his god and go back there
Again, and die there.
                            But he will not die.
I'll be the one to die, and when I do,
When they replace my gut with spices, wrap
My body in the rich cloth, and write me
Immortal on the soul's stone hull I sail
Beneath the world, into some inner room
Like this, where blue Polaris, through a shaft,
Shines coldly on my smile, Egypt and I
Shall triumph. And have I hardened my heart?
I harden it again, for the greatest virtues
Are cut from stone. And on the day I rise
Once more, driving my horses up the East,
Let him and all his people fear the whip
And run to their confusion through the world.

## ❧ Passover

LINDA PASTAN

I

I set my table with metaphor:
the curling parsley — green sign nailed to the doors
of God's underground; salt of desert and eyes;
the roasted shank bone of a Pascal lamb,
relic of sacrifice and bleating spring.
Down the long table, past fresh shoots of a root
they have been hacking at for centuries,
you hold up the unleavened bread — a baked scroll
whose wavy lines are indecipherable.


2

The wise son and the wicked, the simple son
and the son who doesn't ask, are all my son
leaning tonight as it is written,
slouching his father calls it. His hair is long:
hippie hair, hassid hair, how strangely alike
they seem tonight.
                            First Born, a live child cried
among the bulrushes, but the only root
you know stirs between your legs, ready
to spill its seed in gentile gardens.
And if the flowers be delicate and fair
I only mind this one night of the year
when far beyond the lights of Jersey
Jerusalem still beckons us, in tongues.


3

What black-throated bird
in a warm country
sings spirituals,
sings spirituals
to Moses now?

4
One exodus prefigures the next.
The glaciers fled before hot whips of air.
Waves bowed at God's gesture
for fugitive Israel to pass;
while fish, caught then behind windows
of water, remembered how their brothers once
pulled themselves painfully from the sea,
willing legs to grow
from slanted fins.
Now the blossoms pass from April's tree,
refugee raindrops mar the glass,
borders are transitory.
And the changling gene, still seeking
stone sanctuary, moves on.


5
Far from Egypt, I have sighted blood,
have heard the throaty mating of frogs.
My city knows vermin, animals loose in hallways,
boils, sickness, hail.
In the suburban gardens
seventeen-year locusts rise
from their heavy beds
in small explosions of sod.
Darkness of newsprint.
My son, my son.

# 🦋 Maggid

MARGE PIERCY

The courage to let go of the door, the handle.
The courage to shed the familiar walls whose very
stains and leaks are comfortable as the little moles
of the upper arm; stains that recall a feast,
a child's naughtiness, a loud blattering storm
that slapped the roof hard, pouring through.

The courage to abandon the graves dug into the hill,
the small bones of children and the brittle bones
of the old whose marrow hunger had stolen;
the courage to desert the tree planted and only
begun to bear; the riverside where promises were
shaped; the street where their empty pots were broken.

The courage to leave the place whose language you learned
as early as your own, whose customs however dangerous or demeaning, bind you like a halter
you have learned to pull inside, to move your load;
the land fertile with the blood spilled on it;
the roads mapped and annotated for survival.

The courage to walk out of the pain that is known
into the pain that cannot be imagined,
mapless, walking into the wilderness, going
barefoot with a canteen into the desert;
stuffed in the stinking hold of a rotting ship
sailing off the map into dragons' mouths,

Cathay, India, Siberia, goldeneh medina,
leaving bodies by the way like abandoned treasure.
So they walked out of Egypt. So they bribed their way
out of Russia under loads of straw; so they steamed
out of the bloody smoking charnelhouse of Europe
on overloaded freighters forbidden all ports —

out of pain into death or freedom or a different
painful dignity, into squalor and politics.
We Jews are all born of wanderers, with shoes
under our pillows and a memory of blood that is ours
raining down. We honor only those Jews who changed
tonight, those who chose the desert over bondage,

who walked into the strange and became strangers
and gave birth to children who could look down
on them standing on their shoulders for having
been slaves. We honor those who let go of everything but freedom, who ran, who revolted, who fought,
who became other by saving themselves.

# ❧ Miriam's Song

ELEANOR WILNER

Death to the first-born sons, always —
the first fruits to the gods of men.
She had not meant it so, standing in the reeds
back then, the current tugging at her skirt
like hands, she had only meant to save
her little brother, Moses,
red-faced with rage when he was given
to the river. The long curve of the Nile
would keep their line, the promised land
around the bend. Years later
when the gray angel, like the smoke trail
of a dying comet, passed by the houses
with blood smeared over doorways,
Miriam, her head hot in her hands, wept
as the city swelled
with the wail of Egypt's women.
Then she straightened up, slowly plaited
her hair and wound it tight around her head,
drew her long white cloak with its deep blue threads
around her, went out to watch the river
where Osiris, in his golden funeral barge,
floated by forever

as if in offering, she placed a basket on the river,
this time an empty one, without the precious cargo
of tomorrow. She watched it drift a little
from the shore. She threw one small stone in it,
then another, and another, till its weight
was too much for the water and it slowly turned
and sank. She watched the Nile gape and shudder,
then heal its own green skin. She went
to join the others, to leave one ruler
for another, one Egypt for the next.
Some nights you still can see her, by some river
where the willows hang, listening to the heavy tread
of armies, those sons once hidden dark

in baskets, and in her mind she sees her sister,
the black-eyed Pharaoh's daughter, lift the baby
like a gift from the brown flood waters
and take him home to save him, such a pretty
boy and so disarming, as his dimpled hands
reach up, his mouth already open
for the breast.

# 🐾 Haggadah

SAM GOLDEMBERG

The abundance of wine the ritual of those gentle grapes on my
    father's joyous table
humble is the yeast for the unleavened bread
the bruised loneliness of the table and its edges
the scattered history of my forefathers
in the scarcity of wine
in the zigzag
of their peddling legs
wheeling and dealing from the patched up Ukrainian landscape
to the mummified bone of a Peruvian graveyard

My grandfather is still the same old urn digger
on his way back from plundering graves
from the world above
from the world below
Ay ayayai the turning of his poncho into the wind
ay ayayai the broken echoes of his quena
My father's history walks down the dirt roads of my country
his exile spirals all the way around my tent
Ay ayayai the high noons of his shadow
Ay ayayai in his shofar the echo of a quena

To you father I give all the silence of my kaddish
the proud majesty of a wheat stalk that will never be unleavened
    bread in your hand
the northern seas that fling you door to door
from the world above
from the world below

Haggadah — the book containing the Seder Service for Passover Eve, and in
which the story of the Exodus is told.
    Shofar — the ram's horn sounded on the Jewish High Holy Days
    Quena — a reed flute made by the Incas
    kaddish — the prayer for the dead recited in the synagogue at public service

To you I give all the hinges of my wrapped up bone that you count
    and recount from inside the hidden spaces of my urn
Ay ayayai the twisted silence of your Yiddish words
Ay ayayai the broken echo of my words in Quechua

*Translated by David Unger and Isaac Goldemberg*

Quechua — the main indigenous language spoken in Peru

## 🦌 Broken Matzah

MERLE FELD

On the New Jersey transit train
I pulled my particularity
out of a brown paper bag:
one of four broken pieces of
buttered matzah.
Slowly, delicately
I proceeded with my dinner.

The young man across the aisle
in his dark business suit
pale skin, wavy black hair
looked to me Italian
but I admit I'm not good at that.

He seemed uncomfortable,
not so much with the chremzel
I carefully dipped into
a little puddle of sour cream,
nor even with my public
consumption of food —
probably I was brought up
to know better, but I was brought up
so long ago I've misplaced
some of my mother's niceties —

No, I think it was the matzah
that did it, it was the matzah
that singled me out,
the unmistakable display
of my particularity:
four broken pieces of buttered matzah.

Or maybe he didn't care at all
didn't notice
maybe his breathing didn't
become slightly irregular

maybe it was all
my imagination
or my breathing
becoming slightly irregular.

How like my mother I am, after all,
who trained us in our largely
Jewish Brooklyn neighborhood
not to wear our old playclothes
outside on Sundays
so as not to offend our Christian
neighbors on their way home from church.

In those days I took her at her word;
now I wonder as the train
pulls into Penn Station
if Marie Brady who lived across the street
ever noticed us in our Sunday finery,
ever thought it curious
that we dressed up on her Sabbath,
ever questioned our carefully guarded
particularity, ever saw close up
a buttered piece of matzah.

# ❧ On the Eve of the Warsaw Uprising

ALAN SHAPIRO

*At the end of the Passover service, a cup of wine is set aside*
*for the prophet Elijah. The messenger of God, he is appointed*
*to herald the era of the messiah.*

*Elijah come in glorious state*
*For thy glad tidings long we wait.*
*Ah me, ah me, when cometh he?*
*Hush! In good time cometh he.*

My uncle said, "This is Elijah's wine."
Till then I mimicked listening, wide-eyed
with piety, while underneath the table
I kicked my brother back for kicking me.
The bitter herbs and the unleavened bread
that my uncle said were meant to make me feel
the brick and mortar, and the hurrying
between the walls of water that wind held back —
to me meant only an eternity
of waiting while he prayed, before a meal.

But when that wine was poured, the door left open,
waiting seemed almost holy: a worshipper,
the candle flame bowed in the sudden draft.
And for a moment I thought I'd behold
Elijah's glad lips bend out of the dark
to brighten and drink up into His Light
the Red Sea in the glass
                            that never parted.
For soon my uncle closed the door when we
grew cold, and the flame straightened. "Where was Elijah?"
Nobody in the room had ever asked.

And now I think, knowing what I know,
if anyone had ever come to us,
he could have come only to keep watch
and not to drink; to look upon the glass,
seeing within the wine, as from across

the whole of night, the small flame still as God;
someone who would have known the numberless
doors that have been opened, to be closed;
the numberless who watched till they became
the shimmer in the wine he looked upon.

# Memoir

# ๙ The Penitent

from *Old-New Land*

THEODOR HERZL

And so they went through with the Seder ceremony — half ritual, half family festival. This most Jewish of all the festivals dates back farther in history than any other civilized usage in modern times. For hundreds and hundreds of years it has been observed without change, while the whole world changed. Nations disappeared from history, others rose. The world grew larger. Undreamed of continents emerged from the seas. Unimagined natural forces were harnessed for the pleasure and comfort of man. But this one people still remained unchanged, retaining its ancient customs, true to itself, rehearsing the woes of its forebears. Israel, a people of slavery and freedom, still prayed in ancient words to the Eternal its God.

One guest at the Seder table pronounced the Hebrew words of the Haggadah with the zeal of a penitent. He was finding himself again, and his throat was often so tight with emotion that he had to master his longing to cry out aloud. It was almost thirty years since he himself had asked the Four Questions. . . . Then had come "Enlightenment," the break with all that was Jewish, and the final logical leap into the void, when he had no further hold on life. At this Seder table he seemed to himself a prodigal son, returned to his own people.

The first part of the ceremony ended, dinner was served. Kingscourt called across the table. "Fritz! I'd no idea you were so perfect a Hebrew scholar."

"I confess I did not know it myself."

*Translated by Lotta Levensohn*

## ❧ from *A Leak in the Heart*

FAYE MOSKOWITZ

Passover? A piece of cake now, compared with the days when my grandfather marked the holiday's beginning by searching for crumbs of leavened bread with a candle and turkey feather duster. Today everything from chocolate-covered matzo to ersatz "bacon" can be purchased kosher for Passover. Years ago, the ritual search preceded eight days of abstinence from many foods we considered dietary mainstays.

During the middle of Passover, when we were permitted to go to school, most Jewish children I knew shunned the cafeteria and brown-bagged it with lunches that were virtually interchangeable: a crumbling piece of buttered matzo, two hardboiled eggs with yolks the tarnished green of old brass candlesticks, and a hunk of sponge cake. Breaking matzo together gave us a sense of community, but griping about our restricted diet truly bonded us.

By the time we were both approaching our teens, my cousin Sara, the rabbi's daughter, had begun to question the very foundations of the rituals she practiced so assiduously (and so ostentatiously, if I may say so). I had had my own crisis of faith a year or so earlier when the furtive consumption of a bacon, lettuce, and tomato sandwich at Woolworth's failed to bring forth the expected lightning bolt, so I was ready to share Sara's apostasy.

The spring Sara was thirteen and I twelve, my family came to Detroit for Passover, and I stayed at Sara's house. As usual, the Michigan weather double-crossed us that year. I remember Sara and I went walking in our new spring suits, fat white bobby sox, and the glaring brown-and-white saddle shoes we were under penalty of death not to scuff. Several inches of wet snow had fallen, perversely, the night before, and we hadn't been outdoors five minutes before our teeth were chattering. We didn't even discuss the possibility of covering our recently purchased splendor with last year's winter coats, and we headed toward the drugstore at Twelfth and Pingree, where I, at least, hoped the sight of some neighborhood boys might bring some heat to the situation.

Every couple of blocks, it seemed, we would run into some old woman or other who attended my uncle's synagogue and who, of course, knew Sara. That always happened when we walked together near her home. A two-bit trip to the bakery with her was like taking part in a royal progress, what with all the nodding and bowing. Believe me, Sara took advantage of it, too, holding her head high and acknowledging the stares as imperiously as any princess.

In those days, the Jewish groceries either closed down for the holidays or covered their regular stock and sold only food permitted for Passover. We looked in the shop windows for a while . . . not much to relieve the monotonous displays of matzo boxes stacked in pyramids. Sara skillfully swiped a couple of walnuts from a crate outside a store. I had that feeling I always got when near her: half anticipation, half apprehension; you never knew what she would do next. She was moaning, "Milky Ways, I'd give anything for a Milky Way!"

"Three more days," I said primly. "Three more days, and you can eat Milky Ways until they come out of your ears, and toast and butter, and ice cream and peanut butter sandwiches. . . ." I was getting carried away, but Sara wasn't listening to me.

By this time, we were almost at the drugstore. Sara stuck a fifty-cent piece in my hand and said, "You do it. They all know who I am around here." Like a sprinkling of brown sugar, the freckles stood out on her white skin. "Get nine of 'em," she said. I didn't know what she was talking about, and I must have looked like an idiot because she pushed me on the shoulder and said, "Nine Milky Ways, dummy, and hurry up!" I could feel the wet slush coming up through my saddle shoes, and my teeth were knocking together again. Yes, we had been having a theoretical discussion earlier about loss of faith and all that, but as arenas for testing belief, the anonymity of Woolworth's was one thing, and Twelfth Street another.

Up and down the sidewalks, an army of tightlipped women with black shopping bags marched, each a potential informer. "Sara," I said, "you're really crazy. I'm going back to the house."

"Go on, chicken," said Sara. "I'll do it myself."

So I walked up to the drugstore candy counter and asked for nine Milky Ways. For all the attention paid me by the yawning clerk, I might have been simply buying candy instead of committing a heretical act.

Sara and I carried the white paper bag around for a while, just savoring the latent explosive qualities of its contents. "Good afternoon, Mrs. Rabinowitz," Sara said politely to a woman in bifocals whose gray hair curled out from under an elaborate blond wig. "The old bag," Sara said. "If she had X-ray vision, her eyeballs would fall out on the sidewalk." At that unlikely picture, we burst into nervous laughter and leaned against the side of a building, gasping until our stomachs hurt.

The clock on the white-tiled wall of Katz's Kosher Butcher Shop read 3:45, and Sara said, "We'd better get rid of the evidence." I was still stupid enough to think that having made a symbolic gesture of defiance, Sara would be content to shove the bag of forbidden candy in the nearest trash can and go home. Instead, she pulled me into the dark vestibule of an apartment building over some stores facing Twelfth Street.

The hall reeked of gefilte fish and Roman Cleanser, and I felt sick even before Sara broke a Milky Way in two and said, "Here, we each get four wholes and a half." This was no time to observe the proper amenities of eating Milky Ways: slowly nibbling off the chocolate covering, pulling hunks of nougat with the fingers, and finally allowing the sticky caramel to dissolve on teeth and tongue. Half crouching in the dimly lit hall, we wolfed the bars, hardly taking time to chew, white-faced, hearts pounding.

After the third bar, I said, "Sara, I'm going to puke." Fish and bleach and the cloying sweet made the candy come back bitter in my throat. "I've gotta get some fresh air."

Sara stood barring the glass front door, chewing and gulping. "My gosh," she said. "Here comes Mrs. Litvin. I think she *lives* here."

I said, "Sara, I don't care. My *teeth* ache."

"*Chew*," she hissed at me.

Afterward, we threw the bag and candy wrappers down the apartment's incinerator and made it to the alley behind the building before we started throwing up. I felt the vomiting was punishment from God. If Sara did, she never said so.

## from *Debra, Golda, and Me*

LETTY COTTIN POGREBIN

Passover always reminds me of my mother. The eight-day holiday demanded attic-to-basement housecleaning to rid every surface of *chametz* (leaven products), and a complete change of dishes, and because she kept a (mostly) kosher kitehen, she had to pack away two sets of everything (meat and dairy), and unpack all their Passover equivalents right down to the can opener. I never heard her complain. Maybe the Passover makeover suited her optimistic nature, her love for fresh starts and rites of transformation. I remember how efficiently she unearthed her Passover recipe files or turned to the right section of her dog-eared copy of *Jewish Home Beautiful* to double-check the traditional recipes for gefilte fish, chopped liver, chicken soup with matzo balls, potato pudding, carrot tzimmes, macaroons—all of which she would make from scratch. There was no pressure cooker or electric mixer in her kitchen, no food processor or microwave. She used a hand-cranked meat grinder and a fat metal vegetable grater. She whipped with a fork, chopped in a wooden bowl, and beat with a wooden spoon. For years she even plucked her own chickens.

I have a sense memory of the aromas that wafted up to my bedroom just above the kitchen, but few recollections of helping my mother except when she was baking. My squeamish complaints about "yucky" raw liver and disgusting chicken feet must have made it preferable for her to let me stay upstairs.

To this day I can remember the look of our seder table: the damask cloth with dim pink shadows from red-wine spills of meals past; the ceremonial plate with separate compartments for the parsley, *haroset*, gnarled horseradish root, roasted shank bone, and charred hard-boiled egg; the cut-glass bowls for salt water; three matzot in their layered satin case; two pairs of candlesticks, chrome and brass; the silver goblet for the Prophet Elijah. But only in recent years have I let myself think about my mother's exhaustion. It shows on her face in our home movies of the last Passover of her life. Could she have been that exhausted every year?

On both seder nights, while she and the other women served the meal and cleared the dishes, my father reclined in an oversized chair at the head of the table, ennobled in his *kipah* (skullcap) and *kittel* (white ceremonial robe). Year after year, the Haggadah, the retelling of Israel's liberation from bondage, came to us in my father's authoritative bass voice, annotated by the symbols, songs, and rituals that he brought upstage like some great maestro conducting the solo parts of the seder symphony. It took me years to see that my father's virtuosity depended on my mother's labor and that the seders I remember with such heartwarming intensity were sanctified by her creation even more than his.

## ⁂ Passover

from *Miriam's Kitchen*

ELIZABETH EHRLICH

In the beginning there was Brooklyn, and it was Passover. We had journeyed east in our Plymouth from Detroit. We brought school books, and our spring coats. The call of our rich tradition had been heard—*Next year in New York!*—and heeded. We, the destined ones, would miss an extra week of school, right after Easter vacation.

We sat at my grandmother's dining room table, on stiff mahogany chairs upholstered in blood-red velvet. Candle flame flickered, chandelier glowed, crystal refracted, the dark of evening gently fell. Above the Belgian rug, my feet dangled in navy blue maryjanes. They weren't as fancy as patent leather, but you could wear them to school. A wineglass stood at every place, with an extra goblet for Elijah the prophet, who visits every Seder table. At the head of the table, my father, impressive in his high, boxy, black skullcap, resembling an Eastern Orthodox bishop, performed the Passover recounting, the Haggadah, in rapid, rusty, musical Hebrew.

We followed the English in our Haggadah pamphlets, the ones distributed gratis by Maxwell House. I, enrolled in Hebrew school, could sing the four questions in Hebrew. My cousins, Selina's children, in their miniature prep school blazers and gray slacks, read them in English, since they were being raised with no religion.

The four questions, posed by children at the Seder's start, never seemed entirely apt. *Why do we dip twice?* Why would you ask that before any dipping took place? *Why do we recline?* We never reclined. On my grandmother's slippery velvet chairs, the hard springs forming a dome in the seat center, reclining was problematic.

"Teach your children to remember," commanded God. And so my father would begin: "Once we were slaves in the land of Egypt," as parents had done for thousands of years. On to the pages of commentary, Talmudic scholars arguing interpretive points. "Rabban Gamliel used to say . . ."

"Let's go, Edward," spurred my grandmother. She had been cooking, cleaning, and changing dishes for days with my mother's help, and didn't want the roast chicken to dry up.

My father would charge through the Haggadah, reading ahead from right to left, letting his mind become a vessel of subconscious memory to recover the Hebrew studied until his thirteenth birthday, to embrace the tune, the cadence. He did recover it through force of mind. His voice enfolded us like smoke.

At points, he paused, performing the rituals as his father had, or as close as could be remembered. He was transformed in the Seder to teacher or priest, to Someone Who Knew, to the keeper of mysteries, serious things. I was transformed by the Seder, by candles and silver and ancient language and melody and the incantatory realization that this was my birthright, this belonged to me.

My father said when to raise glasses, and when to drink the four draughts of wine — or grape juice — draughts that a free person, celebrating redemption, can drink. He washed his hands ceremoniously, reciting the proper blessing. He pointed to a roasted lamb bone, which had been set on fire over the gas burner earlier that day, displayed as a symbol of the animal sacrifices practiced by early Hebrews.

Holding out his strong, freckled hands, my father broke matzo, the unleavened bread baked in speed by the escaping slaves, and we handed around the crisp pieces. During the eight days of Passover, or Pesach, one may not eat regular bread, or anything prepared with or touched by a leavening agent such as yeast or baking powder. We didn't miss it; the Seder's first matzo wipes bread-hunger from the mind.

Next came the dipping, once and twice. My father dipped parsley, a token of green spring and new beginnings, into the salt water that stands for Israelites' tears. Down the table the dripping sprigs were passed. Raw bits of horseradish root, to recall the bitterness of bondage, were dipped in haroses, a sweet, wet gravel of finely chopped apples, raisins, cinnamon, and wine. This haroses symbolized the mortar with which the slaves toiled under the cruel sun-god. "We built the pyramids!" I breathlessly discovered. From then on, history was personal.

Green-sprouted horseradish pieces were passed. Brave children, dying of hunger by then, tried the bitter herb, yelped, gulped water. Red-eyed, we fanned our open mouths. The physic worked. They taught their children to remember.

Finally, finally, the festive meal. Fruit salad in dishes of gold-rimmed glass. Invariably fruit, though I don't know why — for spring? There were grapefruits and oranges, chunks of pineapple and peeled apples marinated in lemon and orange juice, strawberries, bananas. I had watched this salad prepared. My father, sitting at the kitchen table with a paring knife, peeled and sectioned the citrus fruit. My mother hulled boxes of strawberries, berries selected each by each. The kitchen table grew juicy with brilliant color.

After the fruit, the hard-boiled egg, the pagan sign of life's renewal served whole to each person in a bowl of saltwater broth. Under the big spoon grasped in a small fist, the egg skittered dangerously. I supposed it was forbidden to cut the egg with a knife. I never asked. I crumbled matzo over the bowl and rose to the challenge of nailing the slippery egg.

Chicken soup with matzo balls, or kneydlekh, as we called them, and toasty soup nuts, bought in a blue-and-gray box in the store, kosher for Passover, to float in the shallow dishes.

Ahhh. Here we breathed deeply, wriggled expectantly in our seats. I wonder at our appetites, the quantities we ate as children. I think we ate it all.

Next issued gefilte fish. It came from the kitchen, on a thin china plate, a thick slab of it, homemade, with a slice of carrot and the detested jellied broth. It was served with knreyn, grated horseradish root, flavored with vinegar, sugar, and salt. Outside on the stoop that afternoon, my father had rubbed the pungent root on a hand grater balanced atop an enamel basin. His eyes streamed with the hot smell of it. My sister and brother and I ran up for a sniff, a hilarious scream, pretending to faint and die.

Roast chicken, huge quarters of spring pullets my mother had cleaned and plucked, had kashered — made kosher, had massaged, according to my grandmother's direction, with a paste of crushed garlic, paprika, pepper, salt, and sage, had roasted in glass baking pans. Skin side down, covered, skin side up, covered, then the foil off to crisp, roasted certainly for hours until the meat nearly fell off the bone, and velvety chunks of potatoes browned in the drippings.

I cannot picture a vegetable. Perhaps I did give up at some point, or was there none? No, this is all I remember, save for a slice of cucumber pickle and possibly a little more matzo, until the stewed prunes, the sponge cake, the coconut macaroons, the chocolate-covered orange peels, the tea with lemon and sugar, the last bit of matzo eaten as dessert, and the final songs.

After the meal, we opened the door for Elijah, and ran back to the table: a quiver ran through his cup of wine. My father looked innocent.

Once in a time gone by, Passover Seders lasted until midnight or even beyond. In the Old Country, we heard, children collapsed on heaps of coats in the corners, while parents and grandparents drank and made merry. My parents could even remember such times in their childhoods. They had grownups who lived through the winter looking forward to Pesach festivity and pomp.

Now Seders, mostly done for the children, are arranged to end at their bedtimes.

The Brooklyn Seders I remember, a bit past midcentury, bridged the eras of way back and now. We children were still awake but very tired, flushed with food and happiness, as we sang the many verses of "*Khad Gadya*," a song that traditionally ends the night. This song has been culled for meaning: Some say it stands for all of Jewish history. We sang it as a children's song, a medieval romp through weird and violent events unleashed by a father's purchase of a baby goat. In the end, God himself strikes down the Angel of Death.

It was the robust baritone of Uncle Charles, who was not Jewish, enthusiastically singing "*Khad Gadya!*" according to the Maxwell House phonetic transcription, and the counterpoint of my grandmother's droll laughter, that sealed and certified another Seder night for me.

In the kitchen next morning there was a lightness and cleanliness, a freshness, and Passover smells. New linen dishtowels hung on the rack. The kitchen table was spread with an ironed cloth. There would be eight days of matzo: matzo with whipped butter and salt, matzo sandwiches, matzo puddings, dumplings, farfel, sponge cakes, also egg dishes, and fruit salad, and stewed prunes. How many eggs would be purchased for Passover week? Eggs to boil whole, to mix into chopped liver, to make pancakes fluffy, to fry with onions. Five or six per person, per day? No one can do this anymore, but are we really more healthy for it?

My grandmother rendered chicken skin for the yellow fat, schmaltz. As we gathered round the fragrant stove like so many chubby fledglings, she gave us the cracklings, the *grivnes*, to eat.

She made a giant ginger-scented matzo-meal pancake, round in its iron skillet, half-fried, half-baked, dense, crisp-edged, and two inches high. This *fankukhn*, cut into wedges, lavished with sugar and cinnamon, was one kind of breakfast. She steamed matzos over hot boiling water, spread each limp matzo square with hot chicken fat, sprinkled it with coarse salt, and rolled it up, to be eaten with soft-boiled eggs. She poured boiling water over crumbled matzos and strained the pieces, scrambled them with egg, fried them in oil, and this was matzo *brei*. She poured sweet red wine into hot morning tea. There was a week of such breakfasts, a blissful week of spring.

During the days, we walked with my father and played in the neighborhood park, among spring puddles and sunbursts and chalk hopscotch boards. The only cloud in our sky was that vernal harbinger, the first sighting of the Ice Cream Man. Oh, we would badger my father for tempting wares we knew were not kosher for Pesach, or face an early crisis of consciousness. Sometimes we had to leave New York in an incomplete state, having partaken of no Good Humor bar.

The years rolled on, it seems so quickly now. One spring I remember teasing for an ice cream and being stunned when my father said, "O.K." The condition was it must be finished at the playground, before we strolled back within view of grandmother's house.

Was this, just maybe, what set our rites of spring so softly crumbling?

After this, my recollections blur. My father began to skip parts of the Haggadah, and to stumble on the Hebrew from time to time. My grandmother died. The family met in New York for Christmas then, not Pesach. Our small Detroit Seders drifted toward English, grew shorter. Teenagers tried for political relevance, dogmatic and sincere.

Gefilte fish came from a jar. We barely noticed when the green apple blossom dishes, our own Passover set, stayed packed up in the basement one time, then forever. When was the last bit of chicken skin crisped in the pan, the last grivn eaten?

My father still scoured the oven each spring. My mother made matzo balls. I don't blame my parents. One spring in college, I didn't go home for Passover, though spring break coincided with the full April moon. I wandered the empty campus, an exile from history, and I ate a burger in a bun. The tides were bearing my craft away from the high-church Seders I once loved, and I held the rudder.

At last the man I would marry brought me home to meet his parents and they chopped gefilte fish by hand.

. . . . . . . . . . . . . . . . . . . . . . . . . . . . . . .

And so, I began keeping Passover, and hosting an annual Seder. I get ready for Pesach, little by little, and do a little more each year. Some of it is spring cleaning: I dust and wipe and shake out the rugs, and in a good year, I get to the windows. Then I get rid of improper food, the crumbs and crusts and anything not kosher for Passover: the hametz. I line drawers and shelves with new paper, and fit them out with Passover dishes. I scour the sink and clean the oven. I cover the countertops and kitchen table. All for a span of eight days, and then I box up Pesach again for another year.

The preparations are insane. They get under your skin. One night in September, near on to the children's back-to-school, I dream Passover will begin in one hour, and I have done nothing. I have not cooked, cleaned, covered surfaces, shopped. Many guests are expected. As with a math exam for which one hasn't studied, I have failed at the geometry of switching dishes, lining shelves, at counting out place settings, estimating servings, timing errands. To a dazzling repertoire of anxiety dreams, add this.

At last, though, the new boxes and jars, kosher for Passover, are lined up in the cupboard. The last night, we search the house with our children, hunting crumbs hidden in corners by candlelight, sweeping the crumbs with a feather into a wooden spoon. I always forget at least one location and have to search too, for the misplaced hametz. We burn these crumbs the next day, saying a prayer that admits that no one is perfect, but that we did our best. I say it with feeling, and the holiday begins. The doing is part of it. It brings back all I saw and felt and knew. It is not the same without the doing.

I thought long about changing dishes. A year came when I took the leap. My parents were visiting; we leapt together. My dad commandeered the wheel and we drove to a distant housewares outlet. I chose dishes, enough for the big multiple-course Seder dinner. I bought pots and pans, cutting boards, paring knife, spatula, outfitting a phantom kitchen.

My mother showed me how to boil my silverware, kasher my glasses, make Pesach in fridge and sink, remembering this and that as we went along. We packed up the everyday things. And then, only then, we began to make the Seder.

Everyone cooked. We followed the Brooklyn menu, and we followed Miriam's menu. My mother made chicken soup and matzo balls, and Miriam brought her Passover egg noodles for the soup as well, delicate crepe threads of egg and potato starch. I attempted Miriam's rabinik, which means "grated thing," a mystery to my mother until she recognized her mother's potato pudding. We boiled eggs, for serving in salt water, for chasing around the bowl with your spoon. Miriam brought the gefilte fish.

We invited the family. My father's sister, Selina, arrived with a fankukhn, in a gift box, tied with gold ribbons. Forty years after perfecting soufflés, she had spent the day destroying fankukhn failures and had at last got it, "Sort of," she said.

We went through the rites, Jacob in his thick glasses leading, trying hard to read slow and allow for English. We drank wine and retold the story, as children giggled and showed off. It came time for the entrance of Elijah, whose full glass awaited at the table's heart. Children ran to the door, throwing it open under a starry sky.

"If you want wine, come in now!" a child yelled into the night.

It was our firmest apostate, Aunt Selina, who found herself shocked at the joke. "I was the oldest, I used to have to walk down a long dark hallway alone, to let in Elijah. I was scared," she mused. "Imagine them joking about it."

I remembered my grandmother's hallway, long and dark, remembered Elijah's wine in its tall goblet, shimmering and moving as if invisibly sipped, as my father, straight-faced, jostled the table leg with his knee. There was a glowing solemnity about Passover then. I don't know if it will return. Yet for my children, Passover is not a mausoleum, and I like this, too.

# Fiction

## 🦃 Home for Passover

### SHOLOM ALEICHEM

Two times a year, as punctually as a clock, in April and again in September, Fishel the *melamed* goes home from Balta to Hashtchavata to his wife and children, for Passover and for the New Year. Almost all his life it has been his destiny to be a guest in his own home, a most welcome guest it is true, but for a very short time, only over the holidays. And as soon as the holidays are over he packs his things and goes back to Balta, back to his teaching, back to the rod, to the *Gamorah* that he studies with the unwilling small boys of Balta, back to his exile among strangers and to his secret yearning for home.

However, when Fishel does come home, he is a king! Bath-Sheba, his wife, comes out to meet him, adjusts her kerchief, becomes red as fire, asks him quickly without looking him in the eye, "How are you, Fishel?" And he answers, "How are you?" And Froike, his boy, now almost thirteen, holds out his hand, and the father asks him, "Where are you now, Ephraim, in your studies?" And Reizel, his daughter, a bright-faced little girl with her hair in braids, runs up and kisses him.

"Papa, what did you bring me for the holidays?"

"Material for a dress, and for your mother a silk shawl. Here, give Mother the shawl."

And Fishel takes a new silk (or maybe half-silk) shawl out of his *tallis*-sack, and Bath-Sheba becomes redder than ever, pulls her kerchief low over her eyes, pretends to get busy around the house, bustles here and there and gets nothing done.

"Come, Ephraim, show me how far you've got in the *Gamorah*. I want to see how you're getting along."

And Froike shows his father what a good boy he has been, how well he has applied himself, the understanding he has of his work and how good his memory is. And Fishel listens to him, corrects him once or twice, and his soul expands with pride. He glows with happiness. What a fine boy Froike is! What a jewel!

"If you want to go to the Baths, here is a shirt ready for you," says Bath-Sheba, without looking him in the eye, and Fishel feels strangely happy, like a man who has escaped from prison into the bright, free world among his own people, his loved and faithful ones. And he pictures himself in the room thick with steam, lying on the top ledge together with a few of his cronies, all of them sweating, rubbing each other and beating each other with birch rods and calling for more, more . . .

"Harder! Rub harder! Can't you make it harder!"

And coming home from the bath, refreshed, invigorated, almost a new man, he dresses for the holiday. He puts on his best gabardine with the new cord, steals a glance at Bath-Sheba in her new dress with the new silk shawl, and finds her still a presentable woman, a good, generous, pious woman. . . . And then with Froike he goes to the synagogue. There greetings fly at him from all sides. "Well, well! Reb Fishel! How are you? How's the *melamed*?" "The *melamed* is still teaching." "What's happening in the world?" "What should happen? It's still the same old world." "What's doing in Balta?" "Balta is still Balta." Always, every six months, the same formula, exactly the same, word for word. And Nissel the cantor steps up to the lectern to start the evening services. He lets go with his good, strong voice that grows louder and stronger as he goes along. Fishel is pleased with the performance. He is also pleased with Froike's. The lad stands near him and prays, prays with feeling, and Fishel's soul expands with pride. He glows with happiness. A fine boy, Froike! A good Jewish boy!

"Good *yom-tev*! Good *yom-tev*!"

"Good *yom-tev* to you!"

They are home already and the *seder* is waiting. The wine in the glasses, the horseradish, the eggs, the *haroses*, and all the other ritual foods. His "throne" is ready — two stools with a large pillow spread over them. Any minute now Fishel will become the king, any minute he will seat himself on his royal throne in a white robe, and Bath-Sheba, his queen, with her new silk shawl will sit at his side. Ephraim, the prince, in his new cap and Princess Reizel with her braids will sit facing them.

Make way, fellow Israelites! Show your respect! Fishel the *melamed* has mounted his throne! Long live Fishel!

The wits of Hashtchavata, who are always up to some prank and love to make fun of the whole world (and especially of a humble teacher) once made up a story about Fishel. They said that one year, just before Passover, Fishel sent a telegram to Bath-Sheba reading like this: *Rabiata sobrani. Dengi vezu. Prigotov puli. Yedu tzarstvovat.* In ordinary language this is what it meant: "Classes dismissed. Purse full. Prepare *kneidlach*. I come to rule." This telegram, the story goes on, was immediately turned over to the authorities in Balta, Bath-Sheba was searched but nothing was found, and Fishel himself was brought home under police escort. But I can tell you on my word of honor that this is a falsehood and a lie. Fishel had never in his life sent a telegram to anyone. Bath-Sheba was never searched. And Fishel was never arrested. That is, he was arrested once, but not for sending a telegram. He was arrested because of a passport. And that not in Balta but in Yehupetz, and it was not before Passover but in the middle of summer. This is what happened.

Fishel had suddenly decided that he would like to teach in Yehupetz that year, and had gone there without a passport to look for work. He thought it was the same as Balta, where he needed no passport, but he was sadly mistaken. And before he was through with that experience he swore that not only he but even his children and grandchildren would never go to Yehupetz again to look for work . . .

And ever since that time he goes directly to Balta every season and in the spring he ends his classes a week or two before Passover and dashes off for home. What do you mean — dashes off? He goes as fast as he can — that is, assuming that the roads are clear and he can find a wagon to take him and he can cross the Bug either over the ice or by ferry. But what happens if the snows have melted and the mud is deep, there is no wagon to be gotten, the Bug has just opened and the ferry hasn't started yet because of the ice, and if you try to cross by boat you risk your very life — and Passover is right in front of your nose? What can you do? Take it the way a man does if he's on his way from Machnivka to Berdichev for the Sabbath, or from Sohatchov to Warsaw — it's late Friday afternoon, the wagon is going up a hill, it's getting dark fast, suddenly they're caught in a cloudburst, he's dead hungry — and just then the axle snaps! It's a real problem, I can assure you . . .

Well, Fishel the melamed knows what that problem is. As long as he has been a teacher and has taken the trip from Hashtchavata to Balta and from Balta to Hashtchavata, he has experienced every inconvenience that a journey can offer. He has known what it is to go more than halfway on foot, and to help push the wagon too. He has known what it is to lie together with a priest in a muddy ditch, with himself on bottom and the priest on top. He has known how it feels to run away from a pack of wolves that followed his wagon from Hashtchavata as far as Petschani — although later, it is true, he found out that it was not wolves but dogs. . . . But all these calamities were nothing compared with what he had to go through this year when he was on his way to spend the Passover with his family.

I was all the fault of the Bug. This one year it opened up a little later than usual, and became a torrent just at the time when Fishel was hurrying home—and he had reason to hurry! Because this year Passover started on Friday night—the beginning of Sabbath—and it was doubly important for him to be home on time.

Fishel reached the Bug—traveling in a rickety wagon with a peasant—Thursday night. According to his reckoning he should have come there Tuesday morning, because he had left Balta Sunday noon. If he had only gone with Yankel-Sheigetz, the Balta coachman, on his regular weekly trip—even if he had to sit at the rear with his back to the other passengers and his feet dangling—he would have been home a long time ago and would have forgotten all about the whole journey. But the devil possessed him to go into the marketplace to see if he could find a cheaper conveyance; and it is an old story that the less you pay for something, the more it costs. Jonah the Drunkard had warned him, "Take my advice, Uncle, let it cost you two *rubles* but you'll sit like a lord in Yankel's coach—right in the very back row! Remember, you're playing with fire. There is not much time to lose!" But it was just his luck that the devil had to drag an old peasant from Hashtchavata across his path.

"Hello, Rabbi! Going to Hashtchavata?"

"Good! Can you take me? How much will it cost?"

How much it would cost—that he found it necessary to ask; but whether or not he would get home in time for Passover—that didn't even occur to Fishel. After all, even if he went on foot and took only tiny steps like a shackled person, he should have been able to reach Hashtchavata in less than a week . . .

But they had hardly started out before Fishel was sorry that he had hired this wagon, even though he had all the room in the world to stretch out in. It became apparent very soon that at the rate at which they were creeping they would never be able to get anywhere in time. All day long they rode and they rode, and at the end of the day they had barely got started. And no matter how much he kept bothering the old peasant, no matter how many times he asked how far they still had to go, the man did not answer. He only shrugged his shoulders and said, "Who can tell?"

It was much later, toward evening, that Yankel-Sheigetz overtook them, with a shout and whistle and a crack of the whip—overtook them and passed them with his four prancing horses bedecked with tiny bells, and with his coach packed with passengers inside, on the driver's seat, and some hanging onto the rear. Seeing the teacher sitting alone in the wagon with the peasant, Yankel-Sheigetz cracked his whip in the air again and cursed them both, the driver and the passenger, as only he could curse, laughed at them and at the horse, and after he had passed them he turned back and pointed at one of the wheels:

"Hey *schlimazl!* Look! One of your wheels is turning!"

"Whoa!" the peasant yelled, and together the driver and passenger climbed down, looked at every wheel, at every spoke, crawled under the wagon, searched everywhere, and found nothing wrong.

Realizing that Yankel had played a trick on them, the peasant began to scratch the back of his neck, and at the same time he cursed Yankel and every other Jew on earth with fresh new curses that Fishel had never heard in all his life. He shouted louder and louder and with every word grew angrier and angrier.

"*Ah, shob tubi dobra ne bulo!*" he cried. "Bad luck to you, Jew! I hope you die! I hope you never arrive! Every one of you die! You and your horse and your wife and your daughter and your aunts and your uncles and your cousins and your second-cousins and—and—and all the rest of your cursed Jews!"

It was a long time before the peasant climbed into his wagon again and was ready to start. But even then he was still angry; he couldn't stop yelling. He continued to heap curses at the head of Yankel Sheigetz and all the Jews until, with God's help, they came to a village where they could spend the night.

The next morning Fishel got up very early, before dawn, said his morning prayers, read through the greater part of the Book of Psalms, had a *beigel* for breakfast, and was ready to go on. But Feodor was not ready. Feodor had found an old crony of his in the village and had spent the night with him, drinking and carousing. Then he slept the greater part of the day and was not ready to start till evening.

"Now, look here, Feodor," Fishel complained to him when they were in the wagon again, "the devil take you and your mother! After all, Feodor, I hired you to get me home for the holidays! I depended on you. I trusted you." And that wasn't all he said. He went on in the same vein, half pleading, half cursing, in a mixture of Russian and Hebrew, and when words failed him he used his hands. Feodor understood well enough what Fishel meant, but he did not answer a word, not a sound, as though he knew that Fishel was right. He was as quiet and coy as a little kitten until, on the fourth day, near Petschani, they met Yankel-Sheigetz on his way back from Hashtchavata with a shout and a crack of the whip and this good piece of news:

"You might just as well turn back to Balta! The Bug has opened up!"

When Fishel heard this his heart sank, but Feodor thought that Yankel was making fun of him again and began to curse once more with even greater vigor and originality than before. He cursed Yankel from head to foot, he cursed every limb and every bone of his body. And his mouth did not shut until Thursday evening, when they came to the Bug. They drove right up to Prokop Baraniuk, the ferryman, to find out when he would start running the ferry again.

And while Feodor and Prokop took a drink and talked things over, Fishel went off into a corner to say his evening prayers.

The sun was beginning to set. It cast its fiery rays over the steep hills on both sides of the river, in spots still covered with snow and in spots already green, cut through with rivulets and torrents that bounded down-hill and poured into the river itself with a roar where they met with the running waters from the melting ice. On the other side of the river, as if on a table, lay Hashtchavata, its church steeple gleaming in the sun like a lighted candle.

Standing there and saying his prayers with his face toward Hasht-chavata, Fishel covered his eyes with his hand and tried to drive from his mind the tempting thoughts that tormented him: Bath-Sheba with her new silk shawl, Froike with his *Gamorah*, Reizel with her braids, and the steaming bath. And fresh *matzo* with strongly seasoned fish and fresh horseradish that tore your nostrils apart, and Passover borsht that tasted like something in Paradise, and other good things that man's evil spirit can summon . . . And no matter how much Fishel drove these thoughts from his mind they kept coming back like summer flies, like mosquitoes, and they did not let him pray as a man should.

And when he had finished his prayers Fishel went back to Prokop and got into a discussion with him about the ferry and the approaching hol-iday, explaining to him half in Russian, half in Hebrew, and the rest with his hands, how important a holiday Passover was to the Jews, and what it meant when Passover started on Friday evening! And he made it clear to him that if he did not cross the Bug by that time tomorrow — all was lost: in addition to the fact that at home everybody was waiting for him — his wife and children (and here Fishel gave a heart-rending sigh) — if he did not cross the river before sunset, then for eight whole days he would not be able to eat or drink a thing. He might as well throw himself into the river right now! (At this point Fishel turned his face aside so that no one could see that there were tears in his eyes.)

Prokop Baraniuk understood the plight that poor Fishel was in, and he answered that he knew that the next day was a holiday; he even knew what the holiday was called, and he knew that it was a holiday when people drank wine and brandy. He knew of another Jewish holiday when people drank brandy too, and there was a third when they drank still more, in fact they were supposed to become drunk, but what they called that day he had forgotten . . .

"Good, that's very good!" Fishel interrupted with tears in his voice. "But what are we going to do now? What if tomorrow—God spare the thought . . ." Beyond that poor Fishel could not say another word.

For this Prokop had no answer. All he did was to point to the river with his hand, as though to say, "Well—see for yourself . . ."

And Fishel lifted his eyes and beheld what his eyes had never before seen in all his life, and he heard what his ears had never heard. For it can truthfully be said that never before had Fishel actually seen what the out-of-doors was like. Whatever he had seen before had been seen at a glance while he was on his way somewhere, a glimpse snatched while hurrying from *cheder* to the synagogue or from synagogue to *cheder*. And now the sight of the majestic blue Bug between its two steep banks, the rush of the spring freshets tumbling down the hills, the roar of the river itself, the dazzling splendor of the setting sun, the flaming church steeple, the fresh, exhilarating odor of the spring earth and the air, and above all the simple fact of being so close to home and not being able to get there— all these things together worked on Fishel strangely. They picked him up and lifted him as though on wings and carried him off into a new world, a world of fantasy, and he imagined that to cross the Bug was the simplest thing in the world—like taking a pinch of snuff—if only the Eternal One cared to perform a tiny miracle and rescue him from his plight.

These thoughts and others like them sped through Fishel's head and carried him aloft and bore him so far from the river bank that before he was aware of it, night had fallen, the stars were out, a cool wind had sprung up and had stolen in under his gabardine and ruffled his undershirt. And Fishel went on thinking of things he had never thought of before —of time and eternity, of the unlimited expanse of space, of the vastness of the universe, of the creation of heaven and earth itself . . .

It was a troubled night that Fishel the *malamed* spent in the hut of Prokop the ferryman. But even that night finally came to an end and the new day dawned with a smile of warmth and friendliness. It was a rare and balmy morning. The last patches of snow became soft, like *kasha*, and the *kasha* turned to water, and the water poured into the Bug from all directions . . . Only here and there could be seen huge blocks of ice that looked like strange animals, like polar bears that hurried and chased each other, as if they were afraid that they would be too late in arriving where they were going . . .

And once again Fishel the *malamed* finished his prayers, ate the last crust of bread that was left in his sack, and went out to take a look at the river and to see what could be done about getting across it. But when he heard from Prokop that they would be lucky if the ferry could start Sunday afternoon, he became terrified. He clutched his head with both hands and shook all over. He fumed at Prokop, and scolded him in his own mixture of Russian and Hebrew. Why had Prokop given him hope the night before, why had he said that they might be able to get across today? To this Prokop answered coldly that he had not said a word about crossing by ferry, he had only said that they might be able to get across, and this they could still do. He could take him over any way he wanted to — in a rowboat or on a raft, and it would cost him another half *ruble* — not a *kopek* more.

"Have it your own way" sobbed Fishel. "Let it be a rowboat. Let it be a raft. Only don't make me spend the holiday here on the bank!"

That was Fishel's answer. And at the moment he would have been willing to pay two *rubles*, or even dive in and swim across — if he could only swim. He was willing to risk his life for the holy Passover. And he went after Prokop heatedly, urged him to get out the boat at once and take him across the Bug to Hashtchavata, where Bath-Sheba, Froike and Reizel were waiting for him. They might even be standing on the other side now, there on the hilltop, calling to him, beckoning, waving to him . . . But he could not see them or hear their voices, for the river was wide, so fearfully wide, wider than it had ever been before.

The sun was more than halfway across the clear, deep-blue sky before Prokop called Fishel and told him to jump into the boat. And when Fishel heard these words his arms and legs went limp. He did not know what to do. In all his life he had never been in a boat like that. Since he was born he had never been in a boat of any kind. And looking at the boat he thought that any minute it would tip to one side — and Fishel would be a martyr!

"Jump in and Let's go!" Prokop called to him again, and reaching up he snatched the pack from Fishel's hand.

Fishel the *melamed* carefully pulled the skirt of his gabardine high up around him and began to turn this way and that. Should he jump — or shouldn't he? On the one hand — Sabbath and Passover in one, Bath-Sheba, Froike, Reizel, the scalding bath, the *seder* and all its ceremonial, the royal throne. On the other hand — the terrible risk, almost certain death. You might call it suicide. Because after all, if the boat tipped only once, Fishel was no more. His children were orphans. And he stood with his coat pulled up so long that Prokop lost his patience and began to shout at him. He warned him that if Fishel did not jump in at once he would spit at him and go across by himself to Hashtchavata. Hearing the beloved word Hash-tcha-va-ta, Fishel remembered his dear and true ones again, summoned up all his courage — and fell into the boat. I say "fell into" because, with his first step the boat tipped ever so slightly, and Fishel, thinking he would fall, drew suddenly back, and this time he really did fall, right on his face . . . Several minutes passed before he came to. His face felt clammy, his arms and legs trembled, and his heart pounded like an alarm clock: tick-tock, tick-tock, tick-tock!

As though he were sitting on a stool in his own home, Prokop sat perched in the prow of the boat and coolly pulled at his oars. The boat slid through the sparkling waters, and Fishel's head whirled. He could barely sit upright. No, he didn't even try to sit. He was hanging on, clutching the boat with both hands. Any second, he felt, he would make the wrong move, any second now he would lose his grip, fall back or tumble forward into the deep — and that would be the end of Fishel! And at this thought the words of Moses' song in *Exodus* came back to him: "They sank as lead in the mighty waters." His hair stood straight up. He would not even be buried in consecrated ground! And he made a vow . . .

But what could Fishel promise? Charity? He had nothing to give. He was such a poor, poor man. So he vowed that if the Lord brought him back home in safety he would spend the rest of his nights studying the Holy Writ. By the end of the year he would go, page by page, through the entire Six Orders of the *Talmud*. If only he came through alive . . .

Fishel would have liked to know if it was still far to the other shore, but it was just his luck to have sat down with his face to Prokop and his back to Hashtchavata. And to ask Prokop he was afraid. He was afraid even to open his mouth. He was so sure that if he so much as moved his jaws the boat would tip again, and if it did, where would Fishel be then? And to make it worse, Prokop became suddenly talkative. He said that the worst possible time to cross the river was during the spring floods. You couldn't even go in a straight direction. You had to use your head, turn this way and that. Sometimes you even had to go back a little and then go forward again.

"There goes one as big as an iceberg!" Prokop warned. "It's coming straight at us!" And he swung the boat back just in time to let a huge mass of ice go past with a strange roar. And then Fishel began to understand what kind of trip this was going to be!

"Ho! Look at that!" Prokop shouted again, and pointed upstream.

Fishel lifted his eyes slowly, afraid to move too fast, and looked — looked and saw nothing. All he could see anywhere was water — water and more water.

"There comes another! We'll have to get past — it's too late to back up!"

And this time Prokop worked like mad. He hurled the boat forward through the foaming waves, and Fishel became cold with fear. He wanted to say something, but was afraid. And once more Prokop spoke up:

"If we don't make it in time, it's just too bad."

"What do you mean — too bad?"

"What do you think it means? We're lost — that's what."

"Lost?"

"Sure! Lost."

"What do you mean — lost?"

"You know what I mean. Rubbed out."

"Rubbed out?"

"Rubbed out."

Fishel did not understand exactly what these words meant. He did not even like the sound — lost — rubbed out. He had a feeling that it had to do with eternity, with that endless existence on a distant shore. And a cold sweat broke out all over his body, and once again the verse came to him, "They sank as lead in the mighty waters."

To calm him down Prokop started to tell a story that had happened a year before at this same time. The ice of the Bug had torn loose and the ferry could not be used. And just his luck one day an important-looking man drove up and wanted to go across. He turned out to be a tax officer from Ouman, and he was ready to pay no less than a *ruble* for the trip. Halfway across two huge chunks of ice bore down upon them. There was only one thing for Prokop to do and he did it: he slid in between the two chunks, cut right through between them. Only in the excitement he must have rocked the boat a trifle too much, because they both went overboard into the icy water. It was lucky that he could swim. The tax collector apparently couldn't, and they never found him again Too bad . . . A *ruble* lost like that . . . He should have collected in advance . . .

Prokop finished the story and sighed deeply, and Fishel felt an icy chill go through him and his mouth went dry. He could not say a word. He could not make a sound, not even a squeak.

When they were halfway over, right in the middle of the current, Prokop paused and looked upstream. Satisfied with what he saw, he put the oars down, dug a hand deep into his pocket and pulled out a bottle from which he proceeded to take a long, long pull. Then he took out a few black cloves and while he was chewing them he apologized to Fishel for his drinking. He did not care for the whiskey itself, he said, but he had to take it, at least a few drops, or he got sick every time he tried to cross the river. He wiped his mouth, picked up his oars, glanced again upstream, and exclaimed:

"Now we're in for it!"

In for what? Where? Fishel did not know and he was afraid to ask, but instinctively he felt that if Prokop had been more specific he would have added something about death or drowning. That it was serious was apparent from the way Prokop was acting. He was bent double and was thrashing like mad. Without even looking at Fishel he ordered:

"Quick, uncle! Lie down!"

Fishel did not have to be told twice. He saw close by a towering block of ice bearing down upon them. Shutting his eyes, he threw himself face down on the bottom of the boat and trembling all over began, in a hoarse whisper, to recite *Shma Yisroel*. He saw himself already sinking through the waters. He saw the wide-open mouth of a gigantic fish; he pictured himself being swallowed like the prophet Jonah when he was escaping to Tarshish. And he remembered Jonah's prayer, and quietly, in tears, he repeated the words: "The waters compassed me about, even to the soul; the deep was round about me. The weeds were wrapped about my head."

Thus sang Fishel the *melamed* and he wept, wept bitterly, at the thought of Bath-Sheba, who was as good as a widow already, and the children, who were as good as orphans. And all this time Prokop was working with all his might, and as he worked he sang this song:

> "Oh, you waterfowl!
> You black-winged waterfowl—
> You black-winged bird!"

And Prokop was as cool and cheerful as if he were on dry land, sitting in his own cottage. And Fishel's "encompassed me about" and Prokop's "waterfowl," and Fishel's "the weeds were wrapped" and Prokop's "black-winged bird" merged into one, and on the surface of the Bug was heard a strange singing, a duet such as had never been heard on its broad surface before, not ever since the river had been known as Bug . . .

"Why is he so afraid of death, little man?" Prokop Baraniuk sat wondering, after he had got away from the icefloe and pulled his bottle out of his pocket again for another drink. "Look at him, a little fellow like that — poor, in tatters . . . I wouldn't trade this old boat for him. And he's afraid to die!"

And Prokop dug his boot into Fishel's side, and Fishel trembled. Prokop began to laugh, but Fishel did not hear. He was still praying, he was saying *Kaddish* for his own soul as if he were dead . . .

But if he were dead would he be hearing what Prokop was saying now?

"Get up, Uncle. We're there already. In Hashtchavata."

Fishel lifted his head up slowly, cautiously, looked around on all sides with his red, swollen eyes.

"Hash-tcha-va-ta?"

"Hashtchavata! And now you can give me that half-*ruble*!"

And Fishel crawled out of the boat and saw that he was really home at last. He didn't know what to do first. Run home to his wife and children? Dance and sing on the bank? Or should he praise and thank the Lord who had preserved him from such a tragic end? He paid the boatman his half-*ruble*, picked up his pack, and started to run as fast as he could. But after a few steps he stopped, turned back to the ferryman:

"Listen, Prokop, my good friend! Come over tomorrow for a glass of Passover brandy and some holiday fish. Remember the name — Fishel the *melamed*! You hear? Don't forget now!"

"Why should I forget? Do you think I'm a fool?"

And he licked his lips at the thought of the Passover brandy and the strongly seasoned Jewish fish.

"That's wonderful, Uncle! That's wonderful!"

When Fishel the *melamed* came into the house, Bath-Sheba, red as fire, with her kerchief low over her eyes, asked shyly, "How are you?" And he answered, "How are *you*?" And she asked, "Why are you so late?" And he answered, "We can thank God. It was a miracle." And not another word, because it was so late.

He did not even have time to ask Froike how he was getting along in the *Talmud*, or give Reizel the gift he had brought her, or Bath-Sheba the new silk shawl. Those things would have to wait. All he could think of now was the bath. And he just barely made it.

And when he came home from the bath he did not say anything either. Again he put it off till later. All he said was, "A miracle from heaven. We can thank the Lord. He takes care of us . . ."

And taking Froike by the hand, he hurried off to the synagogue.

*Translated by Julius and Frances Butwin*

# The Four Questions

ALLEGRA GOODMAN

Ed is sitting in his mother-in-law Estelle's gleaming kitchen. "Is it coming in on time?" Estelle asks him. He is calling to check on Yehudit's flight from San Francisco.

"It's still ringing," Ed says. He sits on one of the swivel chairs and twists the telephone cord through his fingers. One wall of the kitchen is papered in a yellow-and-brown daisy pattern, the daisies as big as Ed's hand. The window shade has the same pattern on it. Ed's in-laws live in a 1954 ranch house with all the original period details. Nearly every year since their wedding, he and Sarah have come out to Long Island for Passover, and the house has stayed the same. The front bathroom is papered, even on the ceiling, in brown with white and yellow flowers, and there is a double shower curtain over the tub, the outer curtain held back with brass chains. The front bedroom, Sarah's old room, has a blue carpet, organdy curtains, and white furniture, including a kidney-shaped vanity table.

There is a creaky trundle bed to wheel out from under Sarah's bed, and Ed always sleeps there, a step below Sarah.

In the old days, Sarah and Ed would fly up from Washington with the children, but now the kids come in on their own. Miriam and Ben take the shuttle down from Boston, Avi is driving in from Wesleyan, and Yehudit, the youngest, is flying in from Stanford. She usually can't come at all, but this year the holiday coincides with her spring break. Ed is going to pick her up at Kennedy tonight. "It's coming in on time," Ed tells Estelle.

"Good," she says, and she takes away his empty glass. Automatically, instinctively, Estelle puts things away. She folds up the newspaper before Ed gets to the business section. She'll clear the table while the slower eaters are contemplating seconds. And, when Ed and Sarah come to visit and sleep in the room Sarah and her sister used to share, Ed will come in and find that his things have inexorably been straightened. On the white-and-gold dresser, Ed's tangle of coins, keys, watch, and comb is untangled. The shirt and socks on the bed have been washed and folded. It's the kind of service you might expect in a fine hotel. In West Hempstead it makes Ed uneasy. His mother-in-law is in constant motion — sponging, sweeping, snapping open and shut the refrigerator door. Flicking off lights after him as he leaves the room. Now she is checking the oven. "This is a beautiful bird. Sarah," she calls into the den. "I want you to tell Miriam when she gets here that this turkey is kosher. Is she going to eat it?"

"I don't know," Sarah says. Her daughter the medical student (Harvard Medical School) has been getting more observant every year. In college she started bringing paper plates and plastic utensils to her grandparents' house because Estelle and Sol don't keep kosher. Then she began eating off paper plates even at home in Washington. Although Ed and Sarah have a kosher kitchen, they wash their milk and meat dishes together in the dishwasher.

"I never would have predicted it," Estelle says. "She used to eat everything on her plate. Yehudit was always finicky. I could have predicted she would be a vegetarian. But Miriam used to come and have more of everything. She used to love my turkey."

"It's not that, Mommy," Sarah says.

"I know. It's this orthodoxy of hers. I have no idea where she gets it from. From Jonathan, I guess." Jonathan is Miriam's fiancé.

"No," Ed says, "she started in with it before she even met Jon."

"It wasn't from anyone in this family. Are they still talking about having that Orthodox rabbi marry them?"

"Well—" Sarah begins.

"We met with him," Ed says.

"What was his name, Lowenthal?"

"Lewitsky," Ed says.

"Black coat and hat?"

"No, no, he's a young guy—"

"That doesn't mean anything," Estelle says.

"He was very nice, actually," Sarah says. "The problem is that he won't perform a ceremony at Congregation S.T."

"Why not? It's not Orthodox enough for him?"

"Well, it's a Conservative synagogue. Of course, our rabbi wouldn't let him use S.T. anyway. Rabbi Landis performs all the ceremonies there. They don't want the sanctuary to be treated like a hall to be rented out. Miriam is talking about getting married outside."

"Outside!" Estelle says. "In June! In Washington, D.C.? When I think of your poor mother, Ed, in that heat!" Estelle is eleven years younger than Ed's mother, and always solicitous about Rose's health. "What are they thinking of? Where could they possibly get married outside?"

"I don't know," Ed says. "Dumbarton Oaks. The Rose Garden. They're a couple of silly kids."

"This is not a barbecue," Estelle says.

"What can we do?" Sarah asks. "If they insist on this rabbi."

"And it's March already," Estelle says grimly. "Here, Ed" — she takes a pink bakery box from the refrigerator — "you'd better finish these eclairs before she gets here."

"I'd better not." Ed is trying to watch his weight.

"It's a long time till dinner," Estelle warns as she puts the box back.

"That's okay. I'll live off the fat of the land," says Ed, patting his stomach.

"I got her sealed matzos, sealed macaroons, vacuum-packed gefilte fish." Estelle displays the packages on the scalloped wood shelves of her pantry.

"Don't worry. Whatever else happens, the boys are going to be ravenous. They're going to eat," Sarah assures her mother. They bring the tablecloth out to the dining room. "Remember Avi's friend Noam?"

"The gum chewer. He sat at this table and ate four pieces of cake!"

"And now Noam is an actuary," says Sarah.

"And Avi is bringing a girl to dinner."

"She's a lovely girl," Sarah says.

"Beautiful," Estelle agrees with a worried look.

In the kitchen Ed is thinking he might have an eclair after all. Estelle always has superb pastry in the house. Sol had started out as a baker, and still has a few friends in the business. "Are these from Leonard's?" Ed asks when Sol comes in.

"Leonard's was bought out," Sol says, easing himself into a chair. "These are from Magic Oven. How is the teaching?"

"Well, I have a heavy load. Two of my colleagues went on sabbatical this year —"

"Left you shorthanded."

"Yeah," Ed says. "I've been teaching seven hours a week."

"That's all?" Sol is surprised.

"I mean, on top of my research."

"It doesn't sound that bad."

Ed starts to answer. Instead, he goes to the refrigerator and gets out the eclairs.

"Leonard's were better," Sol muses. "He used a better custard."

"But these are pretty good. What was that? Was that the kids?" Ed runs out to meet the cab in the driveway, pastry in hand. He pays the driver as his two oldest tumble out of the cab with their luggage — Ben's backpack and duffel, Miriam's canvas tote and the suitcase she has inherited, bright pink, patched with silver metallic tape, dating from Ed and Sarah's honeymoon in Paris.

"Daddy!" Miriam says. "What are you eating?"

Ed looks at his eclair. Technically all this sort of thing should be out of the house by now — all bread, cake, pastry, candy, soda, ice cream — anything even sweetened with corn syrup. And, of course, Miriam takes the technicalities seriously. He knows she must have stayed up late last night in her tiny apartment in Cambridge, vacuuming the crevices in the couch, packing away her toaster oven. He finishes off the eclair under her disapproving eyes. He doesn't need the calories, either, she is thinking. She has become very puritanical, his daughter, and it baffles him. They had raised the children in a liberal, rational, joyous way — raised them to enjoy the Jewish tradition, and Ed can't understand why Miriam would choose austerity and obscure ritualism. She is only twenty-three — even if she is getting married in June. How can a young girl be attracted to this kind of legalism? It disturbs him. On the other hand, he knows she is right about his weight and blood pressure. He hadn't really been hungry. He'll take it easy on dinner.

Meanwhile, Ben carries in the bags and dumps them in the den. "Hi, Grandma! Hi, Grandpa! Hi, Mom!" He grabs the TV remote and starts flipping channels. No one is worried about Ben becoming too intense. He is a senior at Brandeis, six feet tall with overgrown ash-brown hair. He has no thoughts about the future. No ideas about life after graduation. No plan. He is studying psychology in a distracted sort of way. When he flops down on the couch he looks like a big, amiable golden retriever.

"Get me the extra chairs from the basement, dear," Estelle tells him. "We've been waiting for you to get here. Then, Sarah, you can get the wineglasses. You can reach up there." Estelle is in her element. Her charm bracelet jingles as she talks. She directs Ben to go down under the Ping-Pong table without knocking over the boxes stacked there; she points Sarah to the cabinet above the refrigerator. Estelle is smaller than Sarah — five feet two and a quarter — and her features are sharper. She had been a brunette when she was younger, but now her hair is auburn. Her eyes are lighter brown as well, and her skin dotted with sun spots from the winters in Florida. "Oh —" she sighs suddenly as Miriam brings a box of paper plates from the kitchen. "Why do you have to —?"

"Because these dishes aren't Pesach dishes."

Estelle looks at the table, set with her white-and-gold Noritake china. "This is the good china," she says. "These are the Pesach dishes."

"But you use them for the other holidays, too," Miriam tells her.

"They've had bread on them and cake and pumpkin pie and all kinds of stuff."

"Ooo, you are sooo stubborn!" Estelle puts her hands on her tall granddaughter's shoulders and gives her a shake. The height difference makes it look as though she is pleading with her as she looks up into Miriam's face. Then the oven timer goes off and she rushes into the kitchen. Sarah is washing lettuce at the sink. "I'll do the salads last," Estelle tells her. "After Ed goes to the airport." Miriam is still on her mind. What kind of seder will Miriam have next year after she is married? Estelle has met Miriam's fiancé, who is just as observant as she is. "Did you see?" she asks Sarah. "I left you my list, for Miriam's wedding."

"What list?"

"On the table. Here." Estelle gives Sarah the typed list. "These are the names and addresses you asked for — the people I need to invite."

Sarah looks at the list. She turns the page and scans the names, doing some calculations in her head. "Mommy!" she says. "There are forty-two people on this list!"

"Not all of them will be able to come, of course," Estelle reassures her.

"We're having one hundred people at this wedding, remember? Including Ed's family, and the kids' friends —"

"Well, this is our family. These are your cousins, Sarah."

Sarah looks again at the list. "When was the last time I saw these people?" she asks. "Miriam wouldn't even recognize some of them. And what's this? The Seligs? The Magids? Robert and Trudy Rothman? These aren't cousins."

"Sarah! Robert and Trudy are my dearest friends. We've known the Seligs and the Magids for thirty years."

"This is a small family wedding," Sarah tells her mother. "I'm sure they'll understand —"

Estelle knows that they wouldn't understand.

"I think we have to cut down this list," Sarah says.

Estelle doesn't get a chance to reply. Avi has arrived, and he's standing in the living room with Ed, Miriam, and Ben. She stands next to him: Amy, his friend from Wesleyan. Estelle still holds back from calling her his girlfriend. Nevertheless, there she is. She has gorgeous strawberry-blond hair, and she has brought Estelle flowers — mauve and rose tulips with fancy curling petals. No one else brought Estelle flowers.

"They're beautiful. Look, Sol, aren't they beautiful?" Estelle says. "Avi, you can take your bag to the den. The boys are sleeping in the den; the girls are sleeping in the sun room."

"I don't want to sleep in the den," Avi says.

"Why not?" asks Estelle.

"Because he snores." Avi points at his brother. "Seriously, he's so loud. I'd rather sleep in the basement."

Everyone looks at him. It's a finished basement and it's got carpeting, but it is cold down there.

"You've shared a room with Ben for years," Sarah says.

"You'll freeze down there," Estelle tells him.

"I have a down sleeping bag."

"You never complained at home," Sarah says.

"Oh, give me a break," Ben mutters under his breath. "You aren't going to have wild sex in a sleeping bag in the basement."

"What?" Ed asks. "Did you say something, Ben?"

"No," Ben says, and ambles back into the den.

"I don't want you in the basement," Estelle tells her grandson.

"Can I help you in the kitchen, Mrs. Kirshenbaum?" asks Amy.

Estelle and Amy make the chopped liver. The boys are watching TV in the den, and Ed and Sarah are lying down in the back. Miriam is on the phone with Jon.

"Did you want me to chop the onions, too?" Amy asks Estelle.

"Oh no. Just put them there and I'll take out the liver, and then we attach the grinder—" She snaps the grinder onto the Kitchen Aid and starts feeding in the broiled liver. "And then you add the onions and the eggs." Estelle pushes in the hard-boiled eggs. "And the schmaltz." She is explaining to Amy all about chopped liver, but her mind is full of questions. How serious is it with Avi? What do Amy's parents think? They are Methodist, Estelle knows that. And Amy's uncle is a Methodist minister! They can't approve of all this. But, then, of course, how much do they know about it? Avi barely talks about Amy. Estelle and Sol have only met her once before, when they came up for Avi's jazz band concert. And then, suddenly, Avi said he wanted to bring her with him to the seder. But he's never really dated anyone before, and kids shy away from anything serious at this age. Avi's cousin Jeffrey had maybe five different girlfriends in college, and he's still unmarried.

Amy's family goes to church every Sunday. They're quite religious. Amy had explained that to Estelle on the phone when she called up about the book. She wanted Estelle to recommend a book for her to read about

Passover. Estelle didn't know what to say. She had never dreamed something like this would happen. If only Amy weren't Methodist. She is everything Estelle could ever want. An absolute doll. The tulips stand in the big barrel-cut crystal vase on the counter. The most beautiful colors.

By the time Ed goes off to the airport, everything is ready except the salad. They dress for dinner while he is gone.

"Do you have a decent shirt?" Sarah asks Ben, who is still watching television. "Or is that as good as it gets?"

"I didn't have a chance to do my laundry before I got here, so I have hardly any clothes," Ben explains.

"Ben!" Estelle looks at him in his red-and-green-plaid hunting shirt. Avi is wearing a nice starched Oxford.

"Maybe he could borrow one of Grandpa's," Miriam suggests.

"He's broader in the shoulders than I am," says Sol. "Come on, Ben, let's see if we can stuff you into something."

They wait for Ed and Yehudit in the living room, almost as if they were expecting guests. Ben sits stiffly on the couch in his small, stiff shirt. He stares at the silver coffee service carefully wrapped in clear plastic. He cracks his knuckles, and then he twists his neck to crack his neck joints. Everyone screams at him. Then, finally, they hear the car in the driveway.

"You're sick as a dog!" Sarah says when Yehudit gets inside.

Yehudit blows her nose and looks at them with feverish, jet-lagged eyes. "Yeah, I think I have mono," she says.

"Oh, my God," says Estelle. "She has to get into bed. That cot in the sun room isn't very comfortable."

"How about a hot drink?" suggests Sarah.

"I'll get her some soup," Estelle says.

"Does it have a vegetable base?" Yehudit asks.

"What she needs is a decongestant," says Ed.

They bundle her up in the La-Z-Boy chair in the den and tuck her in with an afghan and a mug of hot chocolate. "That's not kosher for Pesach," says Miriam, worried.

"Cool it," Ed says. Then they sit down at the seder table.

Ed always leads the seder. Sol and Estelle love the way he does it because he is so knowledgeable. Ed's area of expertise is the Middle East, so he ties Passover to the present day. And he is eloquent. They are very proud of their son-in-law.

"This is our festival of freedom," Ed says, "commemorating our liberation from slavery." He picks up a piece of matzo and reads from his

New Revised Haggadah: "'This is the bread which our fathers and mothers ate in Mitzrayim when they were slaves.'" He adds from the translator's note: "'We use the Hebrew word Mitzrayim to denote the ancient land of Egypt—'"

"As opposed to modern-day Mitzrayim," Miriam says dryly.

"'To differentiate it from modern Egypt,'" Ed reads. Then he puts down the matzo and extemporizes. "We eat this matzo so we will never forget what slavery is, and so that we continue to empathize with afflicted peoples throughout the world: those torn apart by civil wars, those starving or homeless, those crippled by poverty and disease. We think of the people oppressed for their religious or political beliefs. In particular, we meditate on the people in our own country who have not yet achieved full freedom; those discriminated against because of their race, gender, or sexual preference. We think of the subtle forms of slavery as well as the obvious ones—the gray areas that are now coming to light: sexual harassment, verbal abuse—" He can't help noticing Miriam as he says this. It's obvious that she is ignoring him. She is sitting there chanting to herself out of her Orthodox Birnbaum Haggadah, and it offends him. "Finally, we turn to the world's hot spot—the Middle East," Ed says. "We think of war-torn Israel and pray for compromises. We consider the Palestinians, who have no land to call their own, and we call for moderation and perspective. As we sit around the seder table, we look to the past to give us insight into the present."

"Beautiful," murmurs Estelle. But Ed looks down unhappily to where the kids are sitting. Ben has his feet up on Yehudit's empty chair, and Avi is playing with Amy's hair. Miriam is still poring over her Haggadah.

"It's time for the four questions," he says sharply. "The youngest child will chant the four questions," he adds for Amy's benefit.

Sarah checks on Yehudit in the den. "She's asleep. Avi will have to do it."

"Amy is two months younger than I am," Avi says.

"Why don't we all say it together?" Estelle suggests. "She shouldn't have to read it all alone."

"I don't mind," Amy says. She reads: "'Why is this night different from all other nights? On other nights we eat leavened bread; why on this night do we eat matzo? On other nights we eat all kinds of herbs; why on this night do we eat bitter herbs? On other nights we do not dip even once; why on this night do we dip twice? On other nights we eat either sitting up or reclining; why on this night do we all recline?'"

"Now, Avi, read it in Hebrew," Ed says, determined that Avi should take part — feeling, as well, that the questions sound strange in English. Anthropological.

"What was that part about dipping twice?" Amy asks when Avi is done.

"That's when you dip the parsley into the salt water," Ben tells her.

"It doesn't have to be parsley," Sarah says. "Just greens."

"We're not up to that yet," Ed tells them. "Now I'm going to answer the questions." He reads: "'We do these things to commemorate our slavery in Mitzrayim. For if God had not brought us out of slavery, we and all future generations would still be enslaved. We eat matzo because our ancestors did not have time to let their bread rise when they left E— Mitzrayim. We eat bitter herbs to remind us of the bitterness of slavery. We dip greens in salt water to remind us of our tears, and we recline at the table because we are free men and women.' Okay." Ed flips a few pages. "The second theme of Passover is about transmitting tradition to future generations. And we have here in the Haggadah examples of four kinds of children — each with his or her own needs and problems. What we have here is instructions on how to tailor the message of Passover to each one. So we read about four hypothetical cases. Traditionally, they were described as four sons: the wise son, the wicked son, the simple son, and the one who does not know how to ask. We refer to these children in modern terms as: committed, uncommitted, unaffiliated, and assimilated. Let's go around the table now. Estelle, would you like to read about the committed child?"

"'What does the committed child say?'" Estelle reads. "'What are the practices of Passover which God has commanded us? Tell him or her precisely what the practices are.'"

"'What does the uncommitted child say?'" Sol continues. "'What use to you are the practices of Passover? To you, and not to himself. The child excludes him- or herself from the community. Answer him/her: This is on account of what God did for me when I went out of Mitzrayim. For me, and not for us. This child can only appreciate personal gain.'"

"'What does the unaffiliated child say?'" asks Sarah. "'What is all this about? Answer him or her simply: We were slaves and now we are free.'"

"'But for the assimilated child,'" Ben reads, "'it is up to us to open the discussion.'"

"We can meditate for a minute," Ed says, "on a fifth child who died in the Holocaust." They sit silently and look at their plates.

"It's interesting," says Miriam, "that so many things come in fours on Passover. There are four questions, four sons; you drink four cups of wine—"

"It's probably just coincidence," Ben says.

"Thanks," Miriam tells him. "I feel much better. So much for discussion at the seder." She glares at her brother. Couldn't he even shave before he came to the table? She pushes his feet off the chair. "Can't you sit normally?" she hisses at him.

"Don't be such a pain in the butt," Ben mutters.

Ed speeds on, plowing through the Haggadah. " 'The ten plagues that befell the Egyptians: Blood, frogs, vermin, wild beasts, murrain, boils, hail, locusts, darkness, death of the firstborn.' " He looks up from his book and says, "We think of the suffering of the Egyptians as they faced these calamities. We are grateful for our deliverance, but we remember that the oppressor was also oppressed." He pauses there, struck by his own phrase. It's very good. "We cannot celebrate at the expense of others, nor can we say that we are truly free until the other oppressed peoples of the world are also free. We make common cause with all peoples and all minorities. Our struggle is their struggle, and their struggle is our struggle. We turn now to the blessing over the wine and the matzo. Then"—he nods to Estelle—"we'll be ready to eat."

"Daddy," Miriam says.

"Yes."

"This is ridiculous. This seder is getting shorter every year."

"We're doing it the same way we always do it," Ed tells her.

"No, you're not. It's getting shorter and shorter. It was short enough to begin with! You always skip the most important parts."

"Miriam!" Sarah hushes her.

"Why do we have to spend the whole time talking about minorities?" she asks. "Why are you always talking about civil rights?"

"Because that's what Passover is about," Sol tells her.

"Oh, okay, fine," Miriam says.

"Time for the gefilte fish," Estelle announces. Amy gets up to help her, and the two of them bring in the salad plates. Each person has a piece of fish on a bed of lettuce with two cherry tomatoes and a dab of magenta horseradish sauce.

Sarah stands up, debating whether to wake Yehudit for dinner. She ends up walking over to Miriam and sitting next to her for a minute. "Miriam," she whispers, "I think you could try a little harder—"

"To do what?" Miriam asks.

"To be pleasant!" Sarah says. "You've been snapping at everyone all evening. There's no reason for that. There's no reason for you to talk that way to Daddy."

Miriam looks down at her book and continues reading to herself in Hebrew.

"Miriam?"

"What? I'm reading all the stuff Daddy skipped."

"Did you hear what I said? You're upsetting your father."

"It doesn't say a single word about minorities in here," Miriam says stubbornly.

"He's talking about the modern context—"

Miriam looks up at Sarah. "What about the original context?" she asks. "As in the Jewish people? As in God?"

Yehudit toddles in from the den with the afghan trailing behind her. "Can I have some plain salad?" she asks.

"This fish is wonderful," Sol says.

"Outstanding," Ed agrees.

"More," says Ben, with his mouth full.

"Ben! Gross! Can't you eat like a human being?" Avi asks him.

"It's Manishevitz Gold Label," Estelle says. "Yehudit, how did you catch this? Did they say it was definitely mono?"

"No—I don't know what it is," Yehudit says. "I started getting sick on the weekend when we went to sing at the Jewish Community Center for the seniors."

"It's nice that you do that," Estelle says. "Very nice. They're always so appreciative."

"Yeah, I guess so. There was this old guy there and he asked me, 'Do you know "Oyfn Pripitchik"?' I said, 'Yes, we do,' and he said, 'Then please, can I ask you, don't sing "Oyfn Pripitchik." They always come here and sing it for us, and it's so depressing.' Then, when we left, this little old lady beckoned to me and she said, 'What's your name?' I told her, and she said, 'You're very plain, dear, but you're very nice.'"

"That's terrible!" Estelle says. "Did she really say that?"

"Yup."

"It's not true!" Estelle says. "You should hear what everyone says about my granddaughters when they see your pictures. Wait till they see you— maid of honor at the wedding! What color did you pick for the wedding?" she asks Miriam.

"What?" Miriam asks, looking up from her Haggadah.

Ed is looking at Miriam and feeling that she is trying to undermine his whole seder. What is she doing accusing him of shortening the service every year? He does it the same way every year. She is the one who has changed — becoming more and more critical. More literal-minded. Who is she to criticize the way he leads the service? What does she think she is doing? He can remember seders when she couldn't stay awake until dinner. He remembers when she couldn't even sit up. When he could hold her head in the palm of his hand.

"I think peach is a hard color," Estelle is saying. "It's a hard color to find. You know, a pink is one thing. A pink looks lovely on just about everyone. Peach is a hard color to wear. When Mommy and Daddy got married, we had a terrible time with the color because the temple was maroon. There was a terrible maroon carpet in the sanctuary, and the social hall was maroon as well. There was maroon flocked wallpaper. Remember, honey?" she asks Sol. He nods. "Now it's a rust color. Why it's rust, I don't know. But we ended up having the maids in pink because that was about all we could do. And in the pictures it looked beautiful."

"It photographed very well," Sol says.

"I'll have to show you the pictures," Estelle tells Miriam. "The whole family was there and such dear, dear friends. God willing, they'll be at your wedding, too."

"No, I don't think so," says Ed. "We're just having the immediate family. We're only having one hundred people."

Estelle smiles. "I don't think you can keep a wedding to one hundred people."

"Why not?" Ed asks.

Sarah clears the fish plates nervously. She hates it when Ed takes this tone of voice with her parents.

"Well, I mean, not without excluding," Estelle says. "And at a wedding you don't want to exclude     "

"I don't think it's incumbent on us to invite everyone we know to Miriam's wedding," Ed says crisply. Sarah puts her hand on his shoulder. "It's not even necessary to invite everyone you know."

Estelle raises her eyebrows, and Sarah hopes silently that her mother will not whip out the invitation list she's written up. The list with forty-two names that, mercifully, Ed has not yet seen.

"I'm not inviting everyone I know," Estelle says.

"Grandma," Miriam says, looking up. "Are you inviting people to my wedding?"

"Of course not," says Estelle. "But I've told my cousins about it and my dear friends. You know, some of them were at your parents' wedding. The Magids. The Rothmans."

"Whoa, whoa, wait a second," says Ed. "We aren't going to revive the guest list from our wedding thirty years ago. I think we need to define our terms here and straighten out what we mean by immediate family."

"I'll define for you," Estelle says, "what I mean by the family. These are the people who knew us when we lived above the bakery. It wasn't just at your wedding. They were at our wedding before the war. We grew up with them. We've got them in the home movies, and you can see them all forty-five years ago—fifty years ago! You can go in the den and watch —we've got all the movies on videotape now. You can see them at Sarah's first birthday party. We lived within blocks; and when we moved out to the Island and left the bakery, they moved too. I still talk to Trudy Rothman every day. Who has friends like that? We used to walk over. Years ago in the basement we hired a dancing teacher, and we used to take dancing lessons together. Fox trot, cha-cha, tango. We went to temple with them. We celebrated such times! I think you don't see the bonds, because you kids are scattered. We left Bensonhurst together and we came out to the Island together. We've lived here since fifty-four in this house. We saw this house go up, and their houses were going up, too. We went through it together, coming into the wide-open spaces, having a garden, trees, and parks. We see them all the time. In the winters we meet them down in Florida; we go to their grandchildren's weddings—"

"But I'm paying for this wedding," Ed says.

At that Estelle leaves the table and goes into the kitchen. Sarah glares at Ed.

"Dad," Avi groans. "Now look what you did." He whispers to Amy, "I warned you my family is weird."

"I'm really hungry," Ben says. "Can we have the turkey, Grandma? Seriously, all I've had to eat today was a Snickers bar."

In silence Estelle returns from the kitchen carrying the turkey. In silence she hands it to Sol to carve up. She passes the platter around the table. Only slowly does the conversation sputter to life. Estelle talks along with the rest, but she doesn't speak to Ed. She won't even look at him.

Ed lies on his back in the trundle bed next to Sarah. She is lying on the other bed staring at the ceiling. Every time either of them moves an inch, the bed creaks. Ed has never heard such loud creaking; the beds seem to moan and cry out in the night.

"The point? The point is this," Sarah tells him, "it was neither the time nor the place to go over the guest list."

"Your mother was the one who brought it up!" Ed exclaims.

"And you were the one who started in on her."

"Sarah, what was I supposed to say — Thank you for completely disregarding what we explicitly told you. Yes, you can invite everyone you know to your granddaughter's wedding. I'm not going to get steamrollered into this — that's what she was trying to do, manipulate this seder into an opportunity to get exactly who she wants, how many she wants, with no discussion whatsoever."

"The discussion does not have to dominate this holiday," Sarah says.

"You let these things go and she'll get out of control. She'll go from giving us a few addresses to inviting twenty, thirty people. Fifty people."

"She's not going to do that."

"She knows hundreds of people. How many people were at our wedding? Two hundred? Three hundred?"

"Oh, stop. We're mailing all the invitations ourselves from D.C."

"Fine."

"So don't be pigheaded about it," Sarah says.

"Pigheaded? Is that what you said?"

"Yes."

"That's not fair. You don't want these people at the wedding any more than I do —"

"Ed, there are ways to explain that, there are tactful ways. You have absolutely no concept —"

"I am tactful. I am a very tactful person. But there are times when I'm provoked."

"What you said about paying for the wedding was completely uncalled for."

"But it was true!" Ed cries out, and his bed moans under him as if it feels the weight of his aggravation.

"Sh," Sarah hisses.

"I don't know what you want from me."

"I want you to apologize to my mother and try to salvage this holiday for the rest of us," she says tersely.

"I'm not going to apologize to that woman," Ed mutters. Sarah doesn't answer him. "What?" he asks into the night. His voice sounds to his ears not just defensive but wronged, deserving of sympathy. "Sarah?"

"I have nothing more to say to you," she says.

"Sarah, she is being completely unreasonable."

"Oh, stop it."

"I'm not going to grovel in front of someone intent on sabotaging this wedding."

Sarah doesn't answer.

The next day Ed wakes up with a sharp pain in his left shoulder. It is five-nineteen in the morning, and everyone else is sleeping — except Estelle. He can hear her moving around in the house adjusting things, flipping light switches, twitching lamp shades, tweaking pillows. He lies in bed and doesn't know which is worse, his shoulder or those fussy little noises. They grate on him like the rattling of cellophane paper. When at last he struggles out of the sagging trundle bed, he runs to the shower and blasts hot water on his head. He takes an inordinately long shower. He is probably using up all the hot water. He imagines Estelle pacing around outside wondering how in the world anyone can stand in the shower an hour, an hour and fifteen minutes. She is worried about wasting water, frustrated that the door is locked, and she cannot get in to straighten the toothbrushes. The fantasy warms him. It soothes his muscles. But minutes after he gets out, it wears off.

By the time the children are up, it has become a muggy, sodden spring day. Yehudit sleeps off her cold medicine, Ben watches television in the den with Sol, and Miriam shuts herself up in her room in disgust because watching TV violates the holiday. Avi goes out with Amy for a walk. They leave right after lunch and are gone for hours. Where could they be for three hours in West Hempstead? Are they stopping at every duck pond? Browsing in every strip mall? It's a long, empty day. The one good thing is that Sarah isn't angry at him anymore. She massages his stiff shoulder. "These beds have to go," she says. "They're thirty years old."

"It would probably be more comfortable to lie on the floor," Ed says. He watches Estelle as she darts in and out of the kitchen setting the table for the second seder. "You notice she still isn't speaking to me."

"Well," Sarah says, "what do you expect?" But she says it sympathetically. "We have to call your mother," she reminds him.

"Yeah, I suppose so." Ed heaves a sigh. "Get the kids. Make them talk to her."

"Hey, Grandma," says Ben when they get him on the phone. "What's up? Oh yeah? It's dull here, too. No, we aren't doing anything. Just sitting around. No, Avi's got his girlfriend here, so they went out. Yeah, Amy. I don't know. Don't ask me. Miriam's here, too. Yup. What? Everybody's like dealing with who's going to come to her wedding. Who, Grandma E? Oh, she's fine. I think she's kind of pissed at Dad, though."

Ed takes the phone out of Ben's hands.

"Kind of what?" Rose is asking.

"Hello, Ma?" Ed carries the cordless phone into the bedroom and sits at the vanity table. As he talks, he can see himself from three angles in the triptych mirror, each one worse than the next. He sees the dome of his forehead with just a few strands of hair, his eyes tired, a little bloodshot even, the pink of his ears soft and fleshy. He looks terrible.

"Ed," his mother says, "Sarah told me you are excluding Estelle's family from the wedding."

"Family? What family? These are Estelle's friends."

"And what about Henny and Pauline? Should I disinvite them, too?"

"Ma! You invited your neighbors?"

"Of course! To my own granddaughter's wedding? Of course I did."

"Ma," Ed snaps. "As far as I'm concerned, the only invitations to this wedding are going to be the ones printed up and issued by me, from my house. This is Miriam's wedding. For her. Not for you, not for Estelle. Not for anyone but the kids."

"You are wrong," Rose says simply. Throughout the day these words ring in Ed's ears. It is he who feels wronged. It's not as if his mother or Sarah's mother were contributing to the wedding in any way. They just make their demands. They aren't doing anything.

Miriam is sitting in the kitchen spreading whipped butter on a piece of matzo. Ed sits down next to her. "Where's Grandma?" he asks.

"She went out to get milk," says Miriam, and then she bursts out, "Daddy, I don't want all those people at the wedding."

"I know, sweetie." It's wonderful to hear Miriam appeal to him, to be able to sympathize with her as if she weren't almost a doctor with severe theological opinions.

"I don't even know them," Miriam says.

"We don't have to invite anyone you don't want to invite," Ed says firmly.

"But I don't want Grandma all mad at me at the wedding." Her voice wavers. "I don't know what to do."

"You don't have to do anything," Ed says. "You just relax."

"I think maybe we should just invite them," Miriam says in a small voice.

"Oy," says Ed.

"Or some of them," she says.

Someone rattles the back door, and they both jump. It's just Sarah. "Let me give you some advice," she says. "Invite these people, invite your mother's people, and let that be an end to it. We don't need this kind of tsuris."

"No!" Ed says.

"I think she's right," says Miriam.

He looks at her. "Would that make you feel better?" She nods, and he gets to give her a hug. "I don't get to hug my Miriam anymore," he tells Sarah.

"I know," she says. "That's Grandma's car. I'm going to tell her she can have the Magids."

"But you make it clear to her," Ed starts.

"Ed," she says, "I'm not making *anything* clear to her."

At the second seder, Estelle looks at everyone benignly from where she stands between the kitchen and the dining room. Sol makes jokes about weddings, and Avi gets carried away by the good feeling, puts his arm around Methodist Amy, and says, "Mom and Dad, I promise when I get married I'll elope." No one laughs at this.

When it's time for the four questions, Ed reads them himself. " 'Why is this night different from all other nights? On other nights we eat leavened bread. Why on this night do we eat matzo?' Ben, could you put your feet on the floor?" When Ed is done with the four questions, he says, "So, essentially, each generation has an obligation to explain our exodus to the next generation—whether they like it or not."

That night in the moaning trundle bed, Ed thinks about the question Miriam raised at the first Seder. Why are there four of everything on Passover? Four children. Four questions. Four cups of wine. Lying there with his eyes closed, Ed sees these foursomes dancing in the air. He sees them as in the naive illustrations of his 1960s Haggadah. Four gold cups, the words of the four questions outlined in teal blue, four children's faces. The faces of his own children, not as they are now but as they were nine, ten years ago. And then, as he falls asleep, a vivid dream flashes before him. Not the children, but Sarah's parents, along with the Rothmans, the Seligs, the Magids, and all their friends, perhaps one thousand of them walking en masse like marathoners over the Verrazano Bridge. They are carrying suitcases and ironing boards, bridge tables, tennis rackets, and lawn chairs. They are driving their poodles before them as they march together. It is a procession both majestic and frightening. At Estelle's feet, at the feet of her one thousand friends, the steel bridge trembles. Its long cables sway above the water. And as Ed watches, he feels the trembling, the pounding footsteps. It's like an earthquake rattling, pounding, vibrating through his whole body. He wants to turn away; he wants to dismiss it, but still he feels it, unmistakable, not to be denied. The thundering of history.

# Biographic Notes

**Agosín, Marjorie** (b. 1955)

Born in Maryland, but raised in Chile, Agosín returned with her family to the United States in 1969. A poet, editor, and essayist, her recent books include *A Cross and a Star: Memoirs of a Jewish Girl in Chile*; *The Alphabet in My Hands: A Writing Life*; and the poetry collections *Dear Anne Frank*, *An Absence of Shadows*, and *The Angel of Memory*. She is professor of Spanish at Wellesley College in Massachusetts.

**Aleichem, Sholom** (1859–1916)

Born Sholom Rabinovitz in the Ukraine, near Kiev, Aleichem adopted his pseudonym (which is the traditional Yiddish greeting, meaning "Peace be with you"), to be closer to the masses. He began writing in Hebrew, but later turned to Yiddish. His more than forty volumes of novels, stories, and plays include *Teyve the Dairyman*; *Motl Peysi, the Cantor's Son*; *Old Country Tales*; *Some Laughter, Some Tears*; and *Menakhem Mendl*. He died in New York after moving there with his family in 1914.

**Amichai, Yehuda** (1924–2000)

Born in Germany, Amichai emigrated to Palestine in 1935. In addition to many volumes of poetry, Amichai published short stories, plays, novels, and children's books. His works include *A Life of Poetry: 1948–1994*; *Exile at Home*; and *Not of This Time, Not of This Place*.

**Asch, Sholom** (1880–1957)

Asch was born in Poland, came to the United States in 1914, and later lived in Poland, Germany, and Israel. He first published in Hebrew, but soon turned to Yiddish. His more than forty volumes of fiction and nonfiction include *A Passage in the Night*, *East River*, *The Burning Bush*, and *The Prophet*.

**Becker, Robin** (b. 1951)

Becker is the author of five poetry collections, including *All-American Girl*, *Giacometti's Dog*, and *The Horse Fair*. Her poems and essays have appeared in *American Poetry Review*, *Ploughshares*, and *Gettysburg Review*, among others. She is professor of English and women's studies at Pennsylvania State University.

**Ben Labrat, Dunash Ha-Levi** (c. 920–990)

Born in Morocco, Ben Labrat lived in Fez, Baghdad, and Cordoba, where he died. Popular in Spain's Jewish communities during the tenth century, he was the first to adapt Arabic meter to Hebrew poetry. Only a few of his poems are in existence today.

**Bialik, Hayyim Nahman** (1873–1934)

Born in Russia, Bialik migrated to Palestine in 1924, where he lived until his death. Although he began writing in Yiddish, he early turned to Hebrew as his medium of expression and is generally considered to be one of the most renowned modern Hebrew writers. Among his works in English are *Random Harvest: The Novellas of Hayyim Nahman Bialik; Songs from Bialik: Selected Poems;* and *Aftergrowth and Other Stories.*

**Bloch, Chana** (b. 1940)

Known as both a translator (from the Hebrew) and poet, Bloch was born in New York City and teaches at Mills College in California. She is the author of several volumes of poetry, including *The Secrets of the Tribe, The Past Keeps Changing,* and *Mrs. Dumpty.*

**Brin, Ruth Firestone** (b. 1921)

A native of St. Paul, Minnesota, Brin is the author of several collections of poetry, children books, and a memoir. Among her titles are *Butterflies Are Beautiful; Harvest: Collected Poems and Prayers;* and *Bittersweet Berries: Growing Up Jewish in Minnesota.*

**Chagall, Bella** (1895–1944)

Chagall was born and raised in Vitsebsk, Belarus. Her memoir of *shtetl* life, written in Yiddish and published in English first as *Burning Lights* and later as *First Encounters,* was illustrated by her husband, artist Marc Chagall.

**Chess, Richard** (b. 1953)

Richard Chess is the author of two books of poetry, *Chair in the Desert* and *Tekiah.* His poems have been published in *Prairie Schooner, Anthology of Contemporary Jewish American Writing,* and *Telling and Remembering: A Century of American Jewish Poetry.* He is director of the Center for Jewish Studies at the University of North Carolina in Asheville.

**Ehrlich, Elizabeth** (b. 1954)

A former *Business Week* writer, Ehrlich published her memoir *Miriam's Kitchen* in 1997. Her biography of the female journalist Nelly Bly (*Nelly Bly*) appeared in 1989.

**Englander, Nathan** (b. 1970)

Although he currently resides in Jerusalem, Englander was born and raised in New York City and is a graduate of the Iowa Writer's Workshop. His fiction has been published in *The New Yorker* and *Story* magazine, among others. His collection *For the Relief of Unbearable Urges* appeared in 1999.

**Falk, Marcia** (b. 1946)

Born in New York City, Falk is a poet and translator of Hebrew and Yiddish verse. Her works include *Love Lyrics from the Bible; The Book of Blessings: New Jewish*

*Prayers for Daily Life, the Sabbath, and the New Moon Festival;* and *With Teeth in the Earth: Selected Poems of Malka Heifetz Tussman.*

**Feld, Merle** (b. 1947)

Feld's poems and essays have appeared in such journals as *Response, Tikkun,* and *The Reconstructionist,* as well as in the anthologies *Sarah's Daughters Sing* and *Reading Ruth.* Her memoir *A Spiritual Life* was published in 1999.

**Goldemberg, Isaac** (b. 1945)

Goldemberg was born in Peru and emigrated to the United States in 1964 by way of Israel. His two novels were published in translation as *The Fragmented Life of Don Jacobo Lerner* and *Play by Play.* A collection of poems, *Hombre de paso/ Just Passing Through,* appeared in 1981.

**Goldstein, Rebecca** (b. 1950)

Goldstein was born in New York City and received a Ph.D. in philosophy from Princeton University. Her books include *The Mind-Body Problem, The Dark Sister, Mazel, Strange Attractors,* and *Properties of Light.* She has received several prizes, including the Whiting Writers' Award, The National Jewish Book Award (for *Mazel* in 1995), and a MacArthur Foundation Fellowship.

**Goodman, Allegra** (b. 1967)

Born in Brooklyn, New York, and raised in Honolulu, Hawaii, Goodman began publishing short stories at an early age in such journals and magazines as *The New Yorker* and *Commentary.* Her books include *Total Immersion, The Family Markowitz, Kaaterskill Falls,* and *Paradise Park.*

**Grade, Chaim** (1910–1982)

Grade was born in Vilna, Poland, and emigrated to the United States in 1948 after spending several years in Paris. Among his works published in English are *My Mother's Sabbath Days: A Memoir; The Agunah; Songs and Poems; Rabbis and Wives;* and *The Sacred and the Profane: Three Novellas.*

**Halevi, Yehuda** (1086–1142)

A Hebrew poet and philosopher, Halevi was born and raised in Toledo, Spain, where he was trained as a physician. He probably died in Egypt, although legend has it he perished while making a pilgrimage to Jerusalem. Among his writings available in English are *Ninety-Two Poems and Hymns; Selected Poems;* and *The Kuzari: In Defense of the Despised Faith.*

**Herman, Michelle** (b. 1955)

Born in Brooklyn, New York, Herman received her MFA from the University of Iowa. She is editor of *The Journal* and director of the Creative Writing Program at Ohio State University. She is the author of *Missing* and *A New and Glorious Life: Novellas.*

**Herzl, Theodor** (1860–1904)

Founder of the World Zionist Organization, Herzl was born in Budapest, Hungary, and died in Vienna, Austria. After studying law, he made a name for himself as journalist, literary editor, and playwright. Among his works available in translation are *Old-New Land*, *The Jewish State*, and *Complete Diaries*.

**Hollander, John** (b. 1929)

A native of New York City, Hollander is the author of more than twenty volumes of poetry, including *Tesserae and Other Poems*, *The Night Mirror*, *Harp Lake*, *Powers of Thirteen*, *Spectral Emanations*, *Figurehead and Other Poems*, and *A Crackling of Thorns*. He is Sterling Professor of English at Yale University.

**Ibn Gabirol, Solomon** (c. 1021–1058)

Ibn Gabirol was born in Malaga, Spain. Of his more than twenty reputed books of philosophy and ethics, only two have survived. He is best known for his poetry, much of which has been translated into English. *Selected Religious Poems of Solomon Ibn Gabirol* originally appeared in 1923. *Selected Poems of Solomon Ibn Gabirol* was published by Princeton University Press in 2001.

**Kazin, Alfred** (1915–1998)

A renowned editor, essayist, and critic, Kazin was born in Brooklyn, New York. Among his many works of literary criticism are *On Native Grounds*, *Contemporaries*, *A Bright Book of Life*, *An American Procession*, *A Writer's America*, and *God and the American Writer*. He is the author of the memoirs: *A Walker in the City*, *Starting Out in the Thirties*, and *New York Jew*.

**Klein, Abraham M.** (1909–1972)

Abraham Moses Klein was born in the Ukraine and emigrated to Montreal with his family in 1910. One of Canada's most celebrated Jewish writers, he edited the *Canadian Jewish Chronicle* from 1939 to 1955 and won the Governor General's Award for *The Rocking Chair and Other Poems* in 1949. His books include *Hath Not a Jew . . .* , *The Hitleriad*, and *The Second Scroll*. His collected stories (*A. M. Klein: Short Stories*) were published posthumously in 1983.

**Klepfisz, Irena** (b. 1941)

Klepfisz was born in Warsaw, Poland, during the Nazi occupation. With her mother, she managed to escape to Sweden and eventually emigrated to the United States in 1955. A poet, essayist, and translator, her books include *Keeper of Accounts; Different Enclosures;* and *A Few Words in the Mother Tongue: Poems Selected and New, 1971–1990*.

**Kumin, Maxine** (b. 1925)

Kumin is the author of twelve collections of poetry, a memoir, several volumes of fiction and essays, and more than twenty books for children. She received the Pulitzer Prize in 1973 for *Up Country: Poems of New England*. Her most recent volume of poetry, *The Long Marriage*, was published in 2001.

**Lazarus, Emma** (1848–1887)

Born in New York City, Lazarus is most remembered for her 1883 sonnet "The New Colossus," which is inscribed on the base of the Statue of Liberty. *The Poems of Emma Lazarus in Two Volumes* was published in 1888. *Emma Lazarus: Selections from Her Poetry and Prose* appeared in 1967.

**Levin, Meyer** (1905–1981)

Born and raised in Chicago, Levin is the author of sixteen novels and two memoirs, as well as numerous short stories, essays, and plays. Among his best-known works are the novels *Compulsion*, *The Old Bunch*, and *Citizens*; and his autobiography, *In Search*.

**Leyeles, A.** (1889–1966)

Leyeles was born Aaron Glantz in Poland and came to the United States in 1909 after several years of study in London. One of the leading Yiddish-language authors in America, Leyeles was well known as a poet, journalist, dramatist, and translator. Among his many volumes of poetry are *A Jew in the Sea* and *At the Foot of the Mountain*.

**Linik, Abraham**

Linik is a retired school principal whose poems have been published in *Piedmont*, *The Poet's Page*, *Midstream*, *Connecticut River Review*, *Black Buzzard Review*, *Skylark*, and *The 1997 Yearbook of American Poetry*.

**Luria, Isaac** (1534–1572)

Luria was a Kabbalist and a mystic who was born in Jerusalem, lived and studied in Egypt, and eventually settled in Safed, Palestine. Luria's writing has survived through the numerous works of his chief disciple, Hayim Vital (1562–1620). Very little of Luria's material is available in English. A sample of his poetry appears in *Festivals of the New Year: A Modern Interpretation and Guide* by Theodor Gaster.

**Meir, Golda** (1898–1978)

Born in Kiev, Russia, Meir came to the United States with her family in 1906 and settled in Milwaukee, Wisconsin. In 1921 she emigrated to Palestine, eventually becoming active in politics. In 1969 she was elected the fourth Prime Minister of Israel. Her writings include *This Is Our Strength*, *A Land of Our Own*, and her autobiography *My Life*.

**Minco, Marga** (b. 1920)

Minco was born in Breda, Holland. She writes often of the Holocaust, which she alone of her family escaped. She is the author of several volumes of fiction, including *An Empty House*, *The Glass Bridge*, *The Fall*, and *The Other Side*; as well as a memoir, *Bitter Herbs: A Little Chronicle*.

**Mirvis, Tova**

Mirvis lives in New York City, but was born in Memphis, Tennessee, the setting of *The Ladies' Auxiliary*, her debut novel published in 1999.

**Moise, Penina** (1797–1880)

Born in Charleston, South Carolina, Moise directed a Jewish school for girls and published poetry prolifically. Much of her later work is in the form of hymns and prayers, the best-known of which is *Hymns Written for the Use of Hebrew Congregations*. Her earlier collection, *Fancy's Sketchbook* (1883), is believed to be the first collection of poems by a Jewish American.

**Molodowsky, Kadia** (1894–1975)

Born in Lithuania, Molodowsky emigrated to New York in 1935. She published six books of poetry in Yiddish, a well as several volumes of fiction, plays, and essays. The first comprehensive collection of her poetry in English, *Selected Poems of Kadya Molodowsky*, was published posthumously in 1999.

**Moskowitz, Faye** (b. 1930)

A native of Detroit, Michigan, Moskowitz is the author of a collection of short stories, *Whoever Finds This: I Love You*; and two memoirs, *And the Bridge is Love* and *A Leak in the Heart*. She is chair and professor of English at George Washington University.

**Nemerov, Howard** (1920–1991)

In addition to more than fifteen volumes of poetry, Nemerov, a native of New York City, is the author of a wide range of fiction, memoir, and criticism. His *Collected Poems* (1977) won both the Pulitzer Prize and the National Book Award. From 1988 to 1990 he served as the Poet Laureate of the United States.

**Opatoshu, Joseph** (1887–1954)

Opatoshu was born in Poland and came to the United States in 1910, where his fiction became widely known to Yiddish readers. Works that have appeared in English include *In Polish Woods* and *A Day in Regensburg*.

**Ostriker, Alicia Suskin** (b. 1937)

In addition to several respected critical studies, Ostriker is the author of ten volumes of poetry, including *The Crack in Everything* and *The Little Space*, both of which were National Book Award finalists. Her collection, *The Volcano Sequence*, appeared in 2002. She is professor of English at Rutgers University.

**Ozick, Cynthia** (b. 1928)

Ozick was born in New York City and is a translator, novelist, short story writer, critic, and essayist. She is the author of the novels *Trust*, *The Cannibal Galaxy*, and *The Messiah of Stockholm*. Among her collections of short stories and novellas are *The Pagan Rabbi and Other Stories*; *Bloodshed and Three Novellas*; *Levitation: Five Fictions*; *The Shawl*; and *The Puttermesser Papers*.

**Paley, Grace** (b. 1922)

The daughter of Russian immigrants, Paley was born in the Bronx, New York. She has published short fiction and poetry, as well as essays and memoirs. Her fiction collections include *The Little Disturbances of Man*, *Enormous Changes at the Last Minute*, and *Later the Same Day*. Among her poetry volumes are *Leaning Forward* and *Begin Again*. She is also the author of two books of personal essays: *Long Walks and Intimate Talks* and *Just as I Thought*.

**Pastan, Linda** (b. 1932)

Pastan is the author of eleven volumes of poetry, including *Carnival Evening: New and Selected Poems 1968–1988*; *Aspects of Eve*; *The Imperfect Paradise*; *Even as We Sleep*; *PM/AM*; and *An Early Afterlife*. *The Last Uncle* was published in 2002. She was born in the Bronx, New York, and is the long-time Poet Laureate of Maryland.

**Peretz, Isaac Loeb** (1852–1915)

Peretz was born in Poland and was a major influence on later Jewish writers. He started as a Hebrew poet and writer, but later turned to Yiddish. His works in English include *At Night in the Old Marketplace*, *My Memoirs*, *The Book of Fire*, and *Selected Poems*.

**Piercy, Marge** (b. 1936)

Piercy is the author of more than twenty volumes of poetry, fiction, and nonfiction. Her collections of poetry include *Mars and Her Children*, *The Art of Blessing the Day*, and *Available Light*. Among her novels are *Woman on the Edge of Time*; *The Longings of Women*; *He, She, and It*; and *City of Darkness, City of Light*. Her memoir *Sleeping With Cats* was published in 2001.

**Pinsky, Robert** (b. 1940)

A poet, essayist, critic, and translator, Pinsky served as Poet Laureate of the United States from 1997 to 2000. His poetry collections include *The Figured Wheel: New and Collected Poems 1966–1996*; *The Want Bone*; and *Jersey Rain*. He is the editor of the weekly on-line journal *Slate*.

**Pogrebin, Letty Cottin** (b. 1939)

Born in New York City and one of the founding editors of *Ms. Magazine*, Pogrebin is the author of several works of nonfiction, including *Debra, Golda, and Me: Being Female and Jewish in America* and *Getting Over Getting Older: An Intimate Journey*.

**Potok, Chaim** (1929–2002)

Potok was born in the Bronx, New York, and educated at Yeshiva University and the Jewish Theological Seminary of America. An ordained rabbi, he also earned a Ph.D. degree from the University of Pennsylvania. Among his many novels are *The Chosen*, *The Promise*, *My Name Is Asher Lev*, *The Gift of Asher Lev*, and *Old Men at Midnight*.

**Raskin, Philip M.** (1878–1944)

Born in Sklov, Russia, Raskin emigrated to London in 1897 and to New York in 1916. A poet who wrote in both English and Hebrew, he also edited the first collection of Jewish poetry in English, *Anthology of Modern Jewish Poetry*, in 1927. His own volumes include *Lanterns in The Wind* and *Songs of a Wanderer*.

**Reisen, Abraham** (1876–1953)

Reisen was born in Russia and came to New York City in 1908. A prolific chronicler of immigrant life, Reisen was a frequent contributor to the American Yiddish press. The first and only collection of his sketches and short stories in English did not appear until 1992, published under the title *The Heart-Stirring Sermon and Other Stories*.

**Reznikoff, Charles** (1894–1976)

The son of Russian immigrants, Reznikoff was born in Brooklyn, New York. Although he graduated from New York University's Law School, he soon turned to writing, editing, and translating. A comprehensive two-volume collection of his poetry (*Poems 1918–1975: The Complete Poems of Charles Reznikoff*) was published in 1976–77.

**Rich, Adrienne** (b. 1929)

Rich is the author of more than fifteen volumes of poetry and several collections of essays. In 1974 she received the National Book Award for *Diving into the Wreck*. Her work includes *Arts of the Possible: Essays and Conversations* and *Fox: Poems 1998–2000*.

**Roiphe, Anne** (b. 1935)

Born in New York City, Roiphe is the author of more than a dozen volumes of fiction, nonfiction, and drama. Among her works are *1185 Park Avenue: A Memoir*; *Lovingkindness*; *For Rabbit, With Love and Squalor*; *Generation Without Memory: A Jewish Journey in Christian America*; and *A Season For Healing: Reflections on the Holocaust*.

**Rosen, Norma** (b. 1926)

Rosen is the author of several novels, including *Joy to Levine!*; *Touching Evil*; *John and Anzia: An American Romance*; a collection of short stories, *Green*; and the nonfiction volumes *Accidents of Influence: Writing as a Woman and a Jew in America* and *Biblical Women Unbound: Counter Tales*.

**Rukeyser, Muriel** (1913–1980)

Born in New York City, Rukeyser is the author of sixteen collections of poetry, as well as dozens of volumes of fiction, nonfiction, criticism, and children's books. Among her works are *The Life of Poetry*; *Theory of Flight*; *Early Poems, 1935–1955*; *The Speed of Darkness*; and *The Collected Poems*.

**Sampter, Jessie Ethel** (1883–1938)

Sampter, an avid Zionist, was born in New York City. Among her many works are books advocating the Zionist cause (*A Course in Zionism* and *The Coming of Peace*), poetry for children and adults (*Brand Plucked from Fire*), and a volume of personal essays (*The Emek or the Valley of the Children*).

**Shapiro, Alan** (b. 1952)

Shapiro is the author of seven books of poetry, a memoir, and several volumes of critical essays. His works include *The Dead, Alive and Busy, Vigil*, and the 2002 collection *Song and Dance*. He was born in Boston, Massachusetts, and is professor of English and creative writing at the University of North Carolina.

**Shapiro, Harvey** (b. 1924)

The author of almost a dozen volumes of poetry, Shapiro has served as an editor for *The New York Times* and *The New Yorker*. His work includes *National Cold Storage Company, A Day's Portion*, and *How Charlie Shavers Died and Other Poems*.

**Singer, Isaac Bashevis** (1904–1991)

The 1978 Nobel Prize winner for literature, Singer was born in Poland, the son and grandson of rabbis. He came to the United States in 1935 and began publishing in the Yiddish press. His work spans more than six decades and comprises dozens of volumes of fiction, stories for children, and memoir. Among his many works are: *The Family Moskat; A Friend of Kafka; The Magician of Lublin; Gimpel the Fool; Short Friday and Other Stories; Enemies: A Love Story;* and *A Day of Pleasure: Stories of a Boy Growing Up in Warsaw*.

**Singer, Israel Joseph** (1893–1944)

Older brother of the more renowned Isaac Bashevis, Singer achieved considerable recognition as an author in his own right. Born in Poland, he emigrated to New York at age forty, two years before his younger brother. His best known novels are *Yoshe Kalb, The Family Carnovsky*, and *The Brothers Ashkenazi*.

**Sklarew, Myra** (b. 1934)

Sklarew is the author of seven volumes of poetry, including *From the Backyard of the Diaspora; The Science of Goodbyes; Lithuania: New and Selected Poems;* and *The Witness Tree*. She is professor of English and creative writing at The American University in Washington, D.C.

**Stavans, Ilan** (b. 1961)

Stavans was born in Mexico and moved to New York City in 1985. A professor of Spanish at Amherst College, he is a prolific author, translator, and editor who writes in both Spanish and English. Among his many works in English are *The One-Handed Pianist and Other Stories; The Inveterate Dreamer: Essays and Conversations on Jewish Culture;* and *On Borrowed Words: A Memoir of Language*.

**Stern, Gerald** (b. 1925)

Stern is the author of *This Time: New and Selected Poems*, which won the National Book Award in 1999. Other poetry collections include *Last Blue, The Naming of Beasts, Lucky Life, Paradise Poems, Lovesick*, and *Odd Mercy*. His most recent volume, *59 American Sonnets*, was published in 2002.

**Stern, Menahem** (b. 1914)

Stern's collection of poetry, *100 Poems Plus*, was published in 1992.

**Tchernichovsky, Saul** (1875–1943)

Born in Russia, Tchernichovsky studied medicine in Germany and Switzerland and practiced in Odessa, Russia, before emigrating to Palestine in 1931. He translated Homer and Plato into Hebrew and authored more than twenty books, including fiction, poetry, and stories for children. His *Selected Poems* was published in English in 1944.

**Wiesel, Elie** (b. 1928)

Born in Siget, Transylvania, and deported to Auschwitz with his family by the Nazis in 1944, Wiesel survived the Holocaust to become one of its foremost chroniclers. After the war he went to Paris before settling in New York City. Writing first in Yiddish, then in French and English, Wiesel is the author of more than three dozen works of fiction, memoirs, essays, and plays. His books include *Night, Dawn, The Gates of the Forest, Beggar in Jerusalem, All Rivers Run to the Sea,* and *And the Sea Is Never Full.* Wiesel was awarded the Nobel Prize for Peace in 1986.

**Wilner, Eleanor** (b. 1937)

Wilner is the author of five collections of poetry, including *Otherwise, Sarah's Choice, Shekina,* and *Reversing the Spell.* She was born in Cleveland, Ohio, and received her Ph.D. degree from Johns Hopkins University.

**Zangwill, Israel** (1864–1926)

Zangwill was born in London and achieved fame through his novels and memoirs of Jewish life. Among his fictional works are *Children of the Ghetto, Ghetto Tragedies,* and *The King of Schnorrers.* An avid Zionist, his political writings include *The East African Question: Zionism and England's Offer.*

# Acknowledgments

I would like to express my appreciation to the Publication Council of the University of South Florida for its generous support of this project. I am most grateful to Marilyn Hobbs from the University of South Florida for her invaluable assistance in assembling the manuscript, and to my colleagues Susan Balee and Rabbi Lewis Warshauer for their perceptive reading of the manuscript. I would also like to thank my editor, Phyllis Deutsch, at the University Press of New England for her advocacy and belief in the worthiness of this volume. I am especially indebted to Jennifer Thomas at University Press of New England, not only for her efficient efforts in seeing this project to completion, but also for her wise counsel and encouragement throughout. As always, my gratitude to my wife and ideal reader, Jean Moore.

Motif appearing on the part pages and elsewhere in the book: Papercut by Yosef Wisnitzer (1899–1942), Tel Aviv.

Grateful acknowledgement is made for the use of the following previously published materials.

Marjorie Agosín: "Kol Nidre," "Rosh Hashannah," and "Yom Kippur" from *The Alphabet in My Hands*. Copyright © 2000 by Marjorie Agosín. Reprinted by permission of Rutgers University Press.

Sholom Aleichem: "Home for Passover" and "A Yom Kippur Scandal" from *The Old Country* by Sholom Aleichem. Copyright © 1946, 1974 by Crown Publishers, Inc. Reprinted by permission of Crown Publishers, a division of Random House, Inc.

Yehuda Amichai: "The Eve of Rosh Hashanah" from *The Selected Poetry of Yehuda Amichai*, translated and edited by Chana Bloch and Stephen Mitchell. Copyright © 1996 The Regents of the University of California. Reprinted by permission of the University of California Press. "On the Day of Atonement" from *Voices Within the Ark: Modern Jewish Poets* (N.Y.: HarperCollins). Translation © Shirley Kaufman. Reprinted by permission of Shirley Kaufman and Hanna Amichai.

Sholem Asch: Excerpt from Sholom Asch's "The Weekday Mother and the Sabbath Mother," from *Salvation*. Reprinted by permission of the Sholem Asch Literary Estate.

Robin Becker: "Yom Kippur, Taos, New Mexico" from *All-American Girl*, by Robin Becker, © 1996. Reprinted by permission of the University of Pittsburgh Press.

Dunash Ha-Levi Ben Labrat: "A Song for the Sabbath" by Dunash Ha-Levi Ben Labrat from *The Jewish Poets of Spain: 900–1250*, edited by David Goldstein, published by Penguin. Reprinted by permission of David Higham Associates.

Hayim Naham Bialik: "My Mother, May Her Memory Be Blessed" from *Songs From Bialik: Selected Poems of Hayim Naham Bialik*, translated by Atar Hadari, with an introduction by Dan Miron (Syracuse University Press, Syracuse, N.Y., 1999). Reprinted by permission of Syracuse University Press.

Chana Bloch: "The Converts" from *The Secrets of the Tribe* (New York: Sheep Meadow Press, 1981). Reprinted by permission of the author.

Ruth F. Brin: "Ceremony of Spring" and "Hannukah" by Ruth F. Brin from *Harvest: Collected Poems and Prayers*, 2nd edition 1999 (Duluth, Minn.: Holy Cow! Press). Reprinted by permission of the author and Holy Cow! Press.

Bella Chagall: excerpt from *Burning Lights* (N.Y.: Random House).

Richard Chess: "Bless Us with Peace, Angels of Peace" and "The Eve of Rosh Hashanah, 500 Years After the Inquisition" by Richard Chess is from *Tekiah*. Copyright © The University of Georgia Press. Reprinted by permission of the University of Georgia Press.

Elizabeth Ehrlich: "Passover" and "Sabbath" from *Miriam's Kitchen* by Elizabeth Ehrlich, copyright © 1997 by Elizabeth Ehrlich. Used by permission of Viking Penguin, a division of Penguin Putnam Inc.

Nathan Englander: "Reb Kringle" from *For the Relief of Unbearable Urges* by Nathan Englander. Copyright © 1999 by Nathan Englander. Reprinted by permission of Alfred A. Knopf, a Division of Random House Inc.

Marcia Falk: "Will" and "Open Gate," copyright 1996 by Marcia Lee Falk. Excerpted from *The Book of Blessings: New Jewish Prayers for Daily Life, the Sabbath and the New*

Moon Festival by Marcia Falk (HarperCollins, 1996; paperback edition, Beacon Press, 1999). Used by permission.

Merle Feld: "Broken Matzoh" reprinted from A Spiritual Life: A Jewish Feminist Journey by Merle Feld, by permission of the State University of New York Press © 1999, State University of New York. All rights reserved.

Isaac Goldemberg: "Haggadah" and "Yom Kippur" from Just Passing Through (Point of Contact, 1981). Copyright © Translation David Unger.

Rebecca Goldstein: "Gifts of the Last Night." Reprinted by permission of the author.

Allegra Goodman: "The Four Questions" from The Family Markowitz by Allegra Goodman. Copyright © 1996 by Allegra Goodman. Reprinted by permission of Farrar, Straus and Giroux, LLC.

Chaim Grade: Excerpts from My Mother's Sabbath Days by Chaim Grade. Copyright © 1986 by the Estate of Chaim Grade. Reprinted by permission of Alfred A. Knopf, a Division of Random House Inc.

Yehuda Halevi: "Festival of Lights" and "Hear" reprinted by permission from Ninety-Two Poems and Hymns of Yehuda Halevi by Franz Rosenzweig, the State University of New York Press © 2000, State University of New York. All rights reserved.

Michelle Herman: From Missing, copyright © 1990 by Michelle Herman. Reprinted by permission of the Ohio State University Press.

Theodore Herzl: "The Menorah" by Theodor Herzl from Gates to the City: A Treasury of Modern Jewish Tales (Avon, 1983); and "The Penitent," an excerpt from Old-New Land (Princeton, N.J.: Markus Wiener, 1997). Reprinted by permission of Herzl Press.

John Hollander: "At the New Year" from Selected Poetry by John Hollander. Copyright © 1993 by John Hollander. Reprinted by permission of Alfred A. Knopf, a Division of Random House Inc.

Solomon Ibn Gabirol: Solomon Ibn Gabirol, "For New Year's Day," from Selected Religious Poems of Solomon Ibn Gabirol (Philadelphia: Jewish Publication Society of America, 1952). Reprinted by permission of the Jewish Publication Society of America.

Alfred Kazan: Excerpt from "The Kitchen" in *A Walker in the City*, copyright 1951 and renewed 1979 by Alfred Kazin. Reprinted by permission of Harcourt, Inc.

A. M. Klein: "Festival," "Five Characters," and "These Candle Lights" by A. M. Klein, *Complete Poems*, 2 vol., ed. Zailig Pollack (University of Toronto Press 1990). Reprinted with permission of the publisher.

Irena Klepfisz: "*Der mames shabbosim*/My Mother's Sabbath Days" from *A Few Words in the Mother Tongue: Poems Selected and New 1971–1990* (Eighth Mountain Press, 1990). Reprinted by permission of the poet.

Maxine Kumin: "Haman's Ears" by Maxine Kumin. Originally published in *The Privilege*. Copyright © 1965 by Maxine Kumin. Reprinted by permission of the author.

Meyer Levin: "The Prophecy of the New Year" from *Classic Hasidic Tales*, by Meyer Levin. All rights reserved. Reprinted by permission of Citadel Press/Kensington Publishing Corp.

A. Leyeles: A. Leyeles' "Sabbath Hours" from *American Yiddish Poetry: A Bilingual Edition* (Berkeley: University of California Press, 1986), edited and translated by Benjamin Harshav and Barbara Harshav. Copyright © 1986 The Regents of the University of California. Reprinted by permission of University of California Press.

Abraham Linik: "Esther" first appeared in *Midstream* Feb/Mar (1998). Reprinted with permission of the editor.

Golda Meir: "The Yom Kippur War," from *My Life* by Gold Meir, copyright © 1975 by Golda Meir. Used by permission of Putnam Berkley, a division of Penguin Putnam Inc.

Marga Minco: "Sabbath" from *Bitter Herbs* by Marga Minco. Penguin Putnam, 1991.

Tova Mirvis: From *The Ladies Auxiliary* by Tova Mirvis. Copyright © 1999 by Tova Mirvis. Used by permission of W. W. Norton & Company, Inc.

Kadia Molowdowsky: "Song of the Sabbath" by Kadia Molodowsky, from *A Treasury of Yiddish Poetry*, edited by Irving Howe and Eliezer Greenberg, © 1969 by Irving Howe and Eliezer Greenberg. Reprinted by permission of Henry Holt and Company, LLC.

Faye Moskowitz: From *A Leak in the Heart* by Faye Moskowitz. Reprinted by permission of David R. Godine, Publisher, Inc. Copyright© 1985 by Faye Moskowitz.

Howard Nemerov: "Pharaoh's Meditation on the Exodus," from "Moses," in *Windows and Mirrors*. University of Chicago Press, 1958. Reprinted by permission of Margaret Nemerov.

Joseph Opatashu: "A Bratslaver Hassid" from *A Day in Regensburg*. (Philadelphia: Jewish Publication Society of America, 1969). Reprinted by permission of the Jewish Publication Society of America.

Alicia Suskin Ostriker: The excerpt from "A Meditation in Seven Days" is from *Green Age*, by Alicia Suskin Ostriker, © 1989. Reprinted by permission of the University of Pittsburg Press.

Cynthia Ozick: "Yom Kippur, 5726" by Cynthia Ozick. Reprinted by permission of the author.

Grace Paley: "The Five Day Week" by Grace Paley from *Grace Paley: New and Collected Poems* (Gardiner, Maine: Tilbury House, 1992) Copyright © 1992 by Grace Paley. Reprinted by permission of the poet.

Linda Pastan: "Passover." Copyright © 1971 by Linda Pastan, from *PM/AM: New and Selected Poems* by Linda Pastan. Used by permission of W. W. Norton & Company, Inc.

I. L. Peretz: "Yom Kippur in Hell" from the *I.L. Peretz Reader*, edited by Ruth R. Wisse (N.Y.: Schocken Books, 1990.) Used by permission of Ruth R. Wisse.

Marge Piercy: "Maggid" from *Available Light* by Marge Piercy. Copyright © 1988 by Middlemarsh, Inc. Reprinted by permission of Alfred A. Knopf, a Division of Random House Inc. "Shabbat Moment" from *Mars and Her Children* by Marge Piercy. Copyright © 1992 by Middlemarch, Inc. Reprinted by permission of Alfred A. Knopf, a Division of Random House Inc. "Tashlich" from *My Mother's Body* by Marge Piercy. Copyright © 1985 by Marge Piercy. Reprinted by permission of Alfred A. Knopf, a Division of Random House Inc.

Robert Pinsky: "Avenue" from *The Figured Wheel: New and Collected Poems 1966–1996* by Robert Pinsky. Copyright © 1996 by Robert Pinsky. Reprinted by permission of Farrar, Straus and Giroux, LLC.

Letty Cottin Pogrebin: From *Deborah, Golda and Me* by Letty Cottin Pogrebin. Copyright © 1991 by Letty Cottin Pogrebin. Reprinted by permission of Crown Publishers, a division of Random House, Inc.

Chaim Potok: "Miracles for a Broken Planet" by Chaim Potok first appeared in *McCall's*, vol. 100, no. 3 (December 1972).

Philip Raskin: "Hanukah Lights" from *Collected Poems of Philip M. Raskin*. (New York: Bloch Publishing, 1951). Reprinted by permission, Bloch Publishing Co. Inc. "Satan and Haman" from *Songs of the Wanderer*. (Philadelphia: Jewish Publication Society of America, 1917). Reprinted by permission of the Jewish Publication Society of America.

Abraham Reisen: "The Poor Community" by Abraham Reisen, transl. Charles Angoff, from *A Treasury of Yiddish Stories* by Irving Howe and Eliezer Greenberg, copyright 1953, 1954, 1989 by Viking Penguin, renewed © 1981, 1982 by Irving Howe and Eva Greenberg. Used by permission of Viking Penguin, a division of Penguin Putnam Inc.

Charles Reznikoff: "Hannukah" from "Meditations on the Fall and Winter Holidays." Copyright © 1977 by Marie Syrkin Reznikoff. Reprinted from *Poems 1918–1975: The Complete Poems of Charles Reznikoff* with the permission of Black Sparrow Press.

Adrienne Rich: "At the Jewish New Year," from *Collected Early Poems: 1950–1970* by Adrienne Rich. Copyright © 1993 by Adrienne Rich. Copyright © 1967, 1963, 1962, 1961, 1960, 1959, 1958, 1957, 1956, 1955, 1954, 1953, 1952, 1951 by Adrienne Rich. Copyright © 1984, 1975, 1971, 1969, 1966 by W. W. Norton & Company, Inc. Used by permission of the author and W. W. Norton & Company, Inc.

Anne Roiphe: "Taking Down the Chirstmas Tree." Reprinted by permission of Anne Roiphe.

Norma Rosen: "A Generation Reclaims Hanukkah" was originally published in the *New York Times*; it was later published in Norma Rosen's collection of essays, *Accidents of Influence: Writing as a Woman and a Jew in America* (State University of New York Press). Reprinted by permission of the Watkins/Loomis Agency.

Muriel Rukeyser: "The Way Out" from *The Speed of Darkness*. Reprinted by permission of International Creative Mangement, Inc. Copyright © Muriel Rukeyser.

Alan Shapiro: "A Christmas Story" from *Happy Hour* (University of Chicago Press, 1987). "On the Eve of the Warsaw Uprising" from *The Courtesy* (University of Chicago Press, 1983).

Harvey Shapiro: "For Paul Celan and Primo Levy" reprinted from *A Day's Portion* © 1994 by Harvey Shapiro, by permission of Hanging Loose Press.

Isaac Bachevis Singer: "Hannukah in the Poorhouse" from *Stories for Children* by Isaac Bashevis Singer, copyright © 1984 by Isaac Bashevis Singer; "The Purim Gift" from *In My Father's Court* by Isaac Bachevis Singer, copyright © 1966 by Isaac Bachevis Singer and copyright renewed 1994 by Alma Singer; "Short Friday" from *Short Friday* by Issac Bachevis Singer, copyright © 1964 by Isaac Bachevis Singer and copyright renewed © 1992 by Alma Singer. Reprinted by permission of Farrar, Straus and Giroux, LLC.

Myra Sklarew: "A Three Course Meal for the New Year" from *The Science of Goodbyes*, 1982. Reprinted by permission of Myra Sklarew.

Ilan Stavans: "Hanukkah: A Brief Reminiscence," by Ilan Stavans. First published in *las Chrismas* (Knopf, 1998), edited by Joie Davidson and Esmeralda Santiago. Reprinted from *The Inveterate Dreamer: Essays and Conversations on Jewish Culture* by Ilan Stavans by permission of the University of Nebraska Press. © 2001 by Ilan Stavans.

Gerald Stern: "Tashlikh" from *Lovesick: Poems* by Gerald Stern. Copyright © 1987 by Gerald Stern. Reprinted by permission of HaperCollins Publishers, Inc.

Menachem Stern: "Purim in Winter" appeared in *Midstream*, vol. 41-3, 1995. Reprinted by permission of the publisher.

Excerpts from Esther are from the *Tanakh: A New Translation of the Holy Scriptures According to the Traditional Hebrew Text*. Copyright © 1985 by the Jewish Publication Society. Used by permission of the Jewish Publication Society.

Elie Wiesel: "On the eve of Rosh Hashanah . . ." excerpt from *Night* by Elie Wiesel. Reprinted by permission of Farrar, Straus and Giroux, LLC. "Yom Kippur: The Day Without Forgiveness" from *Legends of Our Time*, by Elie Wiesel. Copyright © 1968 by Elie Wiesel. Reprinted by permission of Georges Borchardt, Inc., for the author.

Elinor Wilner: "Miriam's Song" by Eleanor Wilner, from *Sarah's Choice* (University of Chicago Press, 1989). Reprinted by permission of the author.